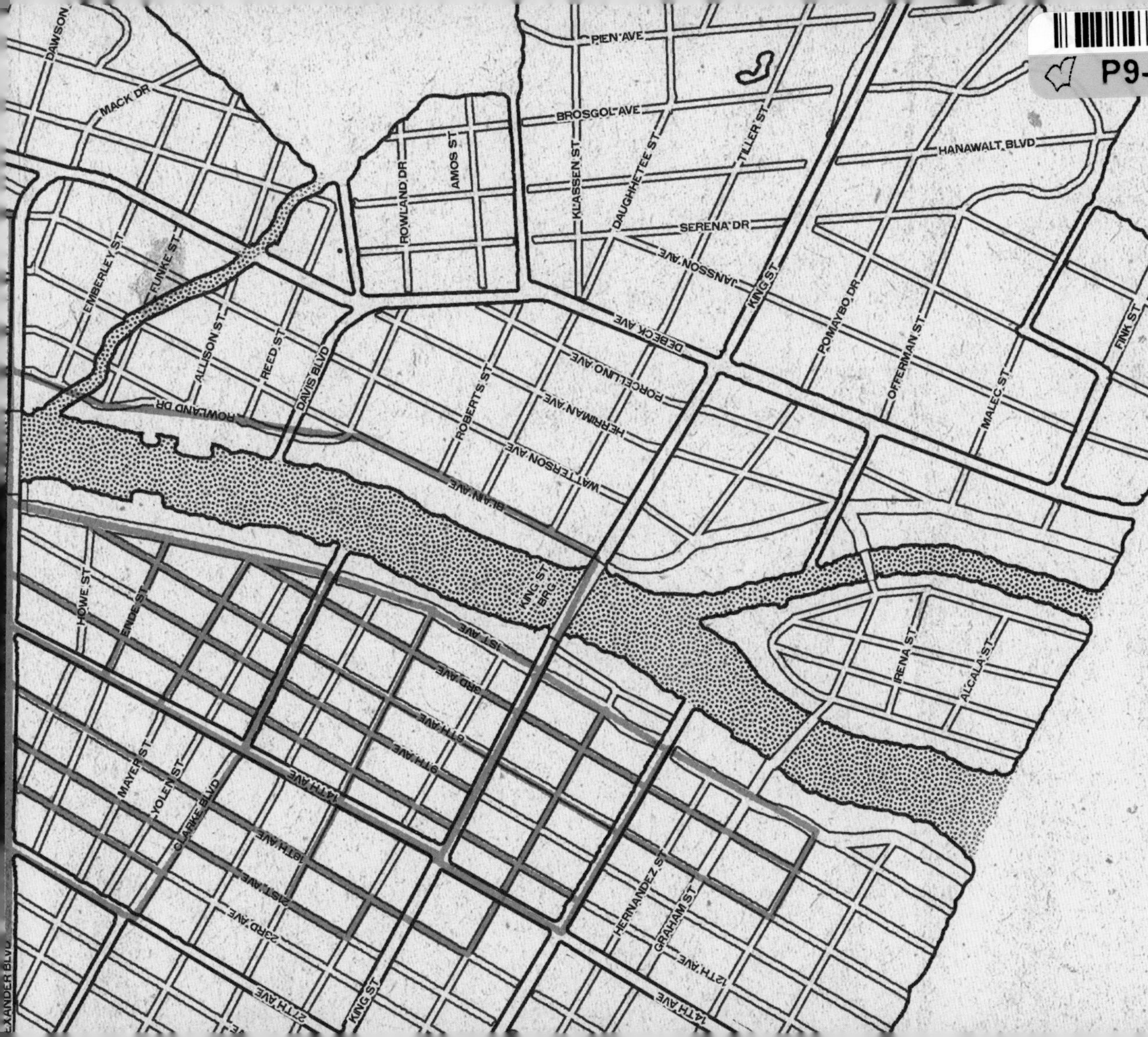
DAWSON
MACK DR
PIEN AVE
BROSGOL AVE
HANAWALT BLVD
ROWLAND DR
AMOS ST
KLASSEN ST
DAUGHHETEE ST
TILLER ST
SERENA DR
JANSSON AVE
KING ST
POMAYBO DR
DEBECK AVE
OFFERMAN ST
FINK ST
MALEC ST
PORCELLINO AVE
HERRIMAN AVE
WATTERSON AVE
BLAIN AVE
ROBERTS ST
DAVIS BLVD
REED ST
ALLISON ST
EMBERLEY ST
FUNKE ST
ROWLAND DR
KING ST BRG
1ST AVE
3RD AVE
5TH AVE
9TH AVE
14TH AVE
18TH AVE
21ST AVE
23RD AVE
27TH AVE
HOWE ST
ENDE ST
MAYER ST
YOLEN ST
CLARKE BLVD
IRENA ST
ALCALA ST
HERNANDEZ ST
GRAHAM ST
12TH AVE
14TH AVE
KING ST

THE CREEPY CASE FILES OF

MARGO MALOO

THE TANGLED WEB

DREW WEING

First Second

NEW YORK

Published by First Second
First Second is an imprint of Roaring Brook Press,
a division of Holtzbrinck Publishing Holdings Limited Partnership
120 Broadway, New York, NY 10271
firstsecondbooks.com
mackids.com

Library of Congress Cataloging-in-Publication Data is available.

Our books may be purchased in bulk for promotional, educational, or business use.
Please contact your local bookseller or the Macmillan Corporate and Premium Sales Department
at (800) 221-7945 ext. 5442 or by email at MacmillanSpecialMarkets@macmillan.com.

First edition, 2021
Edited by Robyn Chapman
Cover design and interior book design by Drew Weing and Molly Johanson
Color assistance by Eleanor Davis and Sophia Foster-Dimino

Drawn with a Zebra .05mm mechanical pencil and a variety of Mitsubishi HB pencils. Inked with a Platinum Carbon
fountain pen, a Kuretake No. 8 Fountain Brush Pen, and Platinum Carbon Ink Cartridges, with white Uni Posca Paint
Markers for corrections. Drawn on Strathmore 400 Series smooth bristol. Colored with Photoshop, partly on an elderly
Cintiq monitor, partly on a new iPad Pro with an Apple pencil.

Printed in China by Toppan Leefung Printing Ltd., Dongguan City, Guangdong Province

ISBN 978-1-250-20683-1
10 9 8 7 6 5 4 3 2 1

Don't miss your next favorite book from First Second!
For the latest updates go to firstsecondnewsletter.com and sign up for our enewsletter.

FOR LORI AND DANNY, WHO JUST MISSED EACH OTHER.

Expedition File Edit View History Bookmarks Window (0:34) Tue 11:26 AM

SMOKE – Grown-ups stay out!!!

http://www.margomaloo.com

SMOKE

If you are a grown-up, stop reading now!!!

Greetings, new SMOKE members!

July 29 at 9:37 pm

If you're reading this, you've made it through our ULTRA security protocols and now have access to this TOP SECRET website. Protect your password with your life! You're one of the few kids who know something no grown-up knows: Echo City is full of MONSTERS! Welcome to...the Secret Monster Organization for Kids Everywhere (SMOKE)! I'm your humble co-founder and journalist, Charles Thompson.

SMOKE co-founders, Charles and Kevin, at our secret HQ

Like me, you had some sort of MONSTER problem. A banshee in your treehouse? A ghoul in the toolshed? Like me, you called on the services of Margo Maloo, monster mediator, to help solve your supernatural situation! And, like me, you discovered the monsters weren't so bad! And that's where we need your HELP.

When I first moved to Echo City, I was HORRIFIED to learn that there was a huge troll living in our basement. My new friend Kevin told me to call Margo Maloo. At first I was SHOCKED that Margo was going to leave the troll down in the basement, but I came to learn that Marcus was a gentleman (and a fine Battlebeanz player). I assisted Margo in other cases and it took me into MANY dark corners of Echo City.

We rescued a crew of teens from a ghost in an old newspaper office, and tracked an ogre's baby across the city only to find her being fed CANDY by some kid zoologists. A pair of twins thought they were being pranked by a poltergeist, only to find a little lost imp stranded in their attic. (Margo's STILL trying to track down the imp's parents! Let us know if you have any leads.) And we helped out a group of young vampires whose

Search

Meta

» Log out

Recent Posts

» Greetings, new SMOKE members!
» How to barter with a troll
» Ghosts: Are they really dead people?
» 50 funniest imp pranks
» What's living in the corner mailbox?
» Is it a good idea to make a bet with an ogre?
» Vampires: Do they vant to suck your blood?
» 10 grossest monster foods (for humans)
» Testing testing

Categories

» Ant People
» Apparitions
» Banshees

Expedition File Edit View History Bookmarks Window (0:33) Tue 11:27 A

SMOKE – Grown-ups stay out!!!

http://www.margomaloo.com

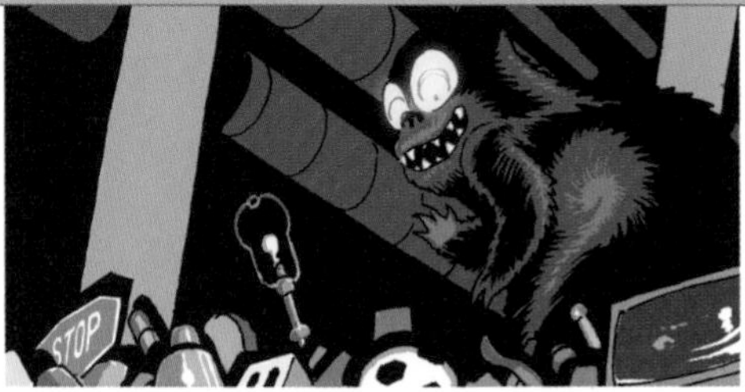

Marcus the troll and his horde, in an undisclosed location

by some kid zoologists. A pair of twins thought they were being pranked by a poltergeist, only to find a little lost imp stranded in their attic. (Margo's STILL trying to track down the imp's parents! Let us know if you have any leads.) And we helped out a group of young vampires whose mall home was being invaded by a pack of rowdy teens—the SAME ones from the newspaper ghost case!

After I proved myself, Margo took me into her trust, and I visited her office and met her unusual uncle. We realized kids need INFORMATION to stop the misunderstandings that kids and monsters get into. My friend Kevin and I had a brilliant idea. Margo can't cover a whole city by herself. What we needed was a SECRET ORGANIZATION—to get information to kids, so they could learn what to avoid about monsters. And so we founded SMOKE!

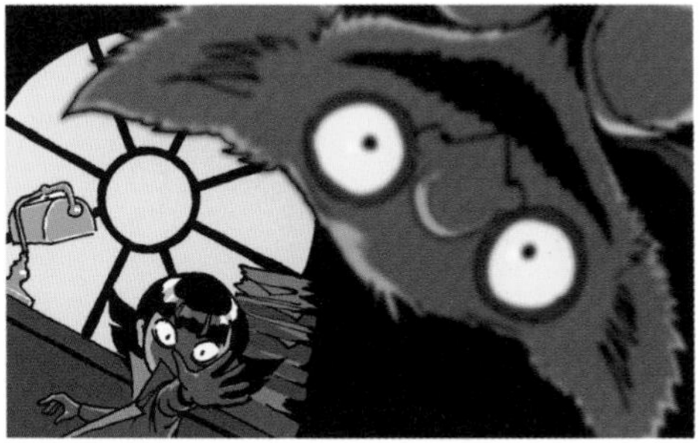

Margo and Fyo the imp

That's why you've been invited to join SMOKE. We're planning our first meeting in our secret headquarters soon, and we want you there. But there are two rules you have to follow:

Rule #1: Never tell any grown-up about monsters!
Rule #2: Don't mess with monsters unless they mess with you!

Got that? If so, get ready to enter an amazing world of monstrous knowledge...

Posted in Uncategorized | Edit | 1 Comment

Kevin R says:
July 30 at 8:17 am
TLDR but looks great!!! Can't wait for the big meeting!

Categories

» Ant People
» Apparitions
» Banshees
» Basilisks
» Bird People
» Blobs
» Bogles
» Bugbears
» Bunyips
» Catoblepas
» Chupacabras
» Devils
» Dragons
» Ghosts
» Ghouls
» Goblins
» Gremlins
» Griffins
» Grootslangs
» Hags
» Harpies
» Hydras
» Imps
» Kappa
» Kelpies
» Kobolds
» Krakens
» Lizard People
» Manticores
» Mer People
» Mummies
» Nagas
» Ogres

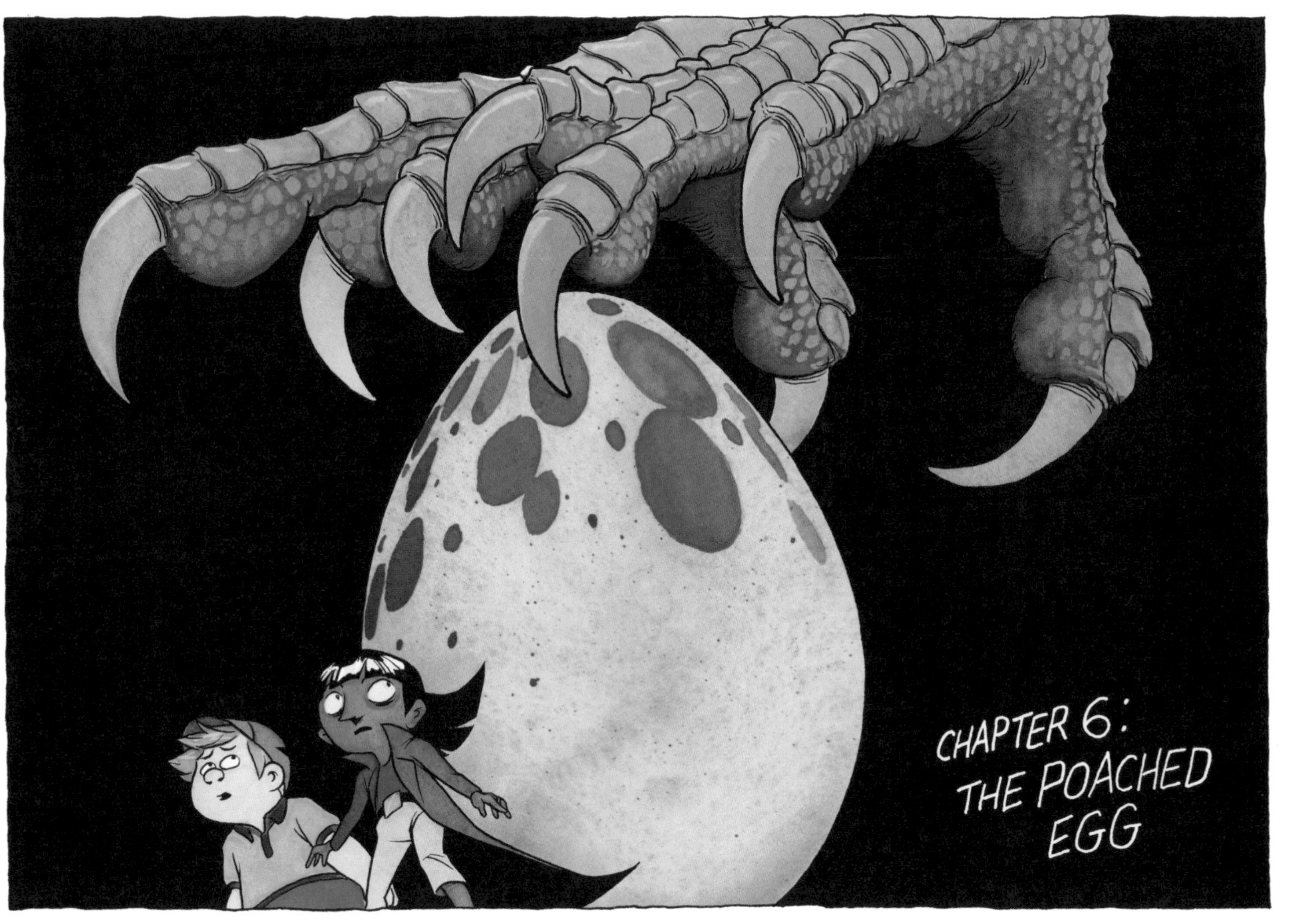
CHAPTER 6:
THE POACHED
EGG

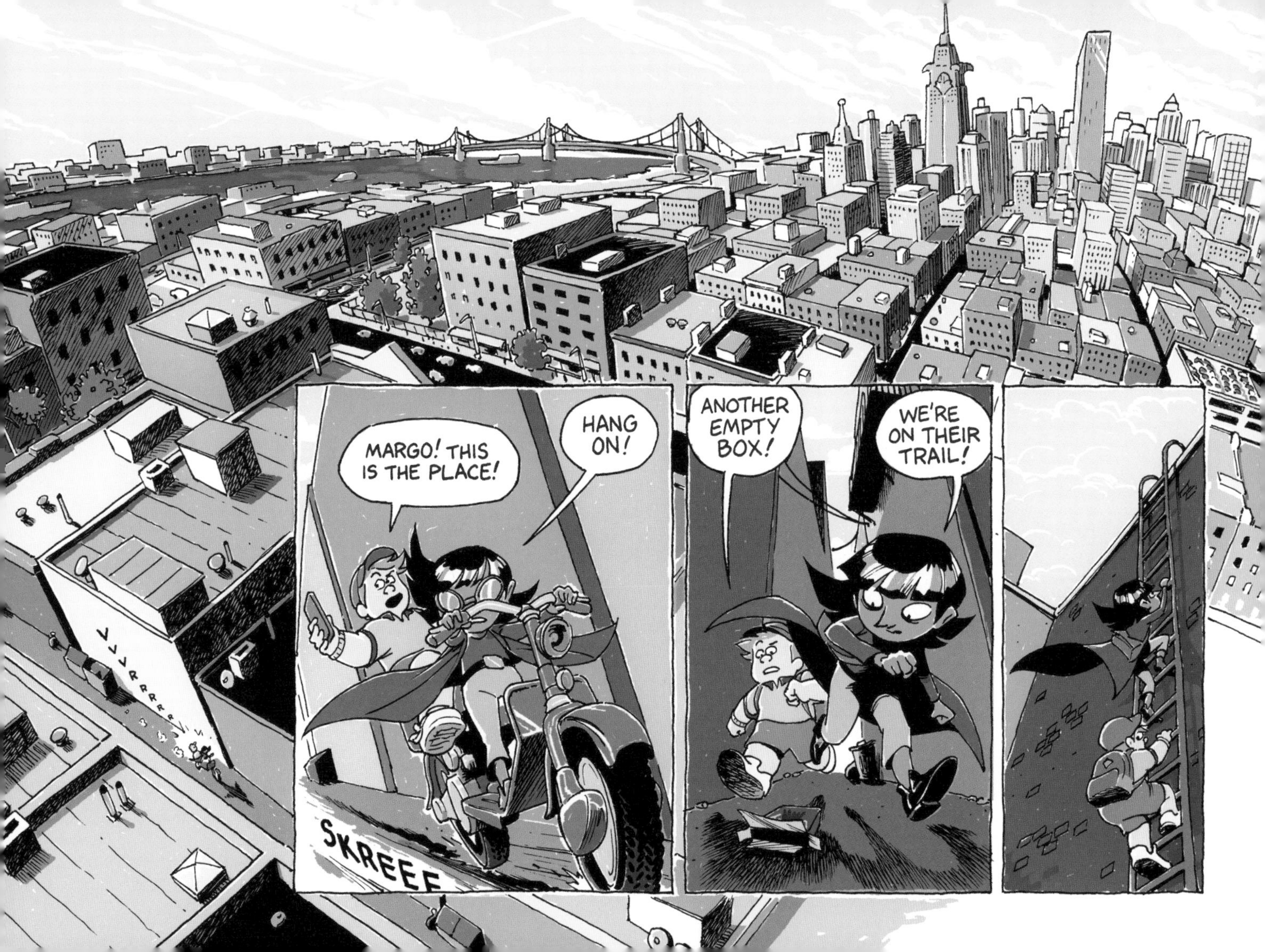
VVVRRRRRRVV
MARGO! THIS IS THE PLACE!
HANG ON!
SKREEEE
ANOTHER EMPTY BOX!
WE'RE ON THEIR TRAIL!

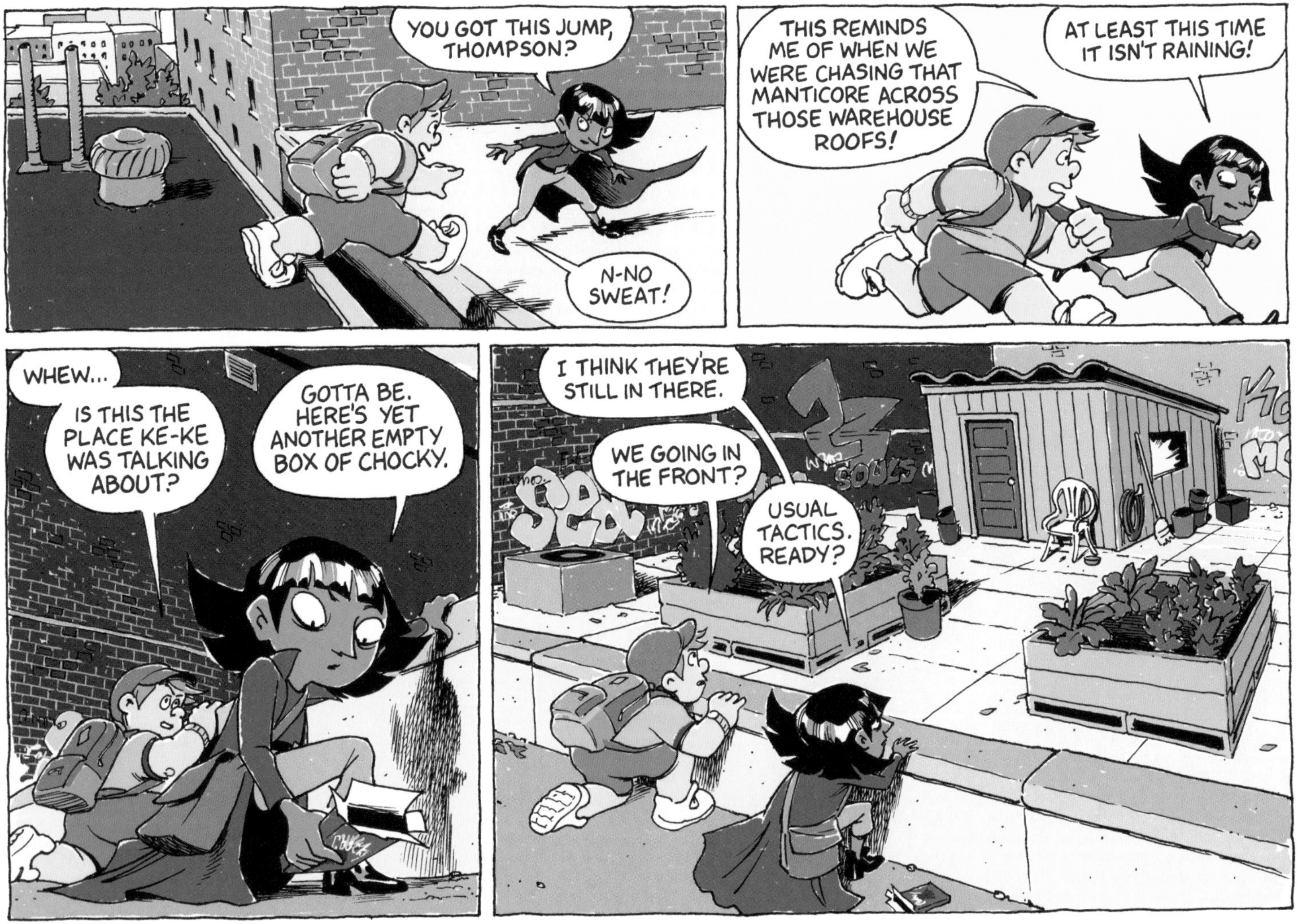
YOU GOT THIS JUMP, THOMPSON?
N-NO SWEAT!
THIS REMINDS ME OF WHEN WE WERE CHASING THAT MANTICORE ACROSS THOSE WAREHOUSE ROOFS!
AT LEAST THIS TIME IT ISN'T RAINING!
WHEW...
IS THIS THE PLACE KE-KE WAS TALKING ABOUT?
GOTTA BE. HERE'S YET ANOTHER EMPTY BOX OF CHOCKY.
I THINK THEY'RE STILL IN THERE.
WE GOING IN THE FRONT?
USUAL TACTICS. READY?

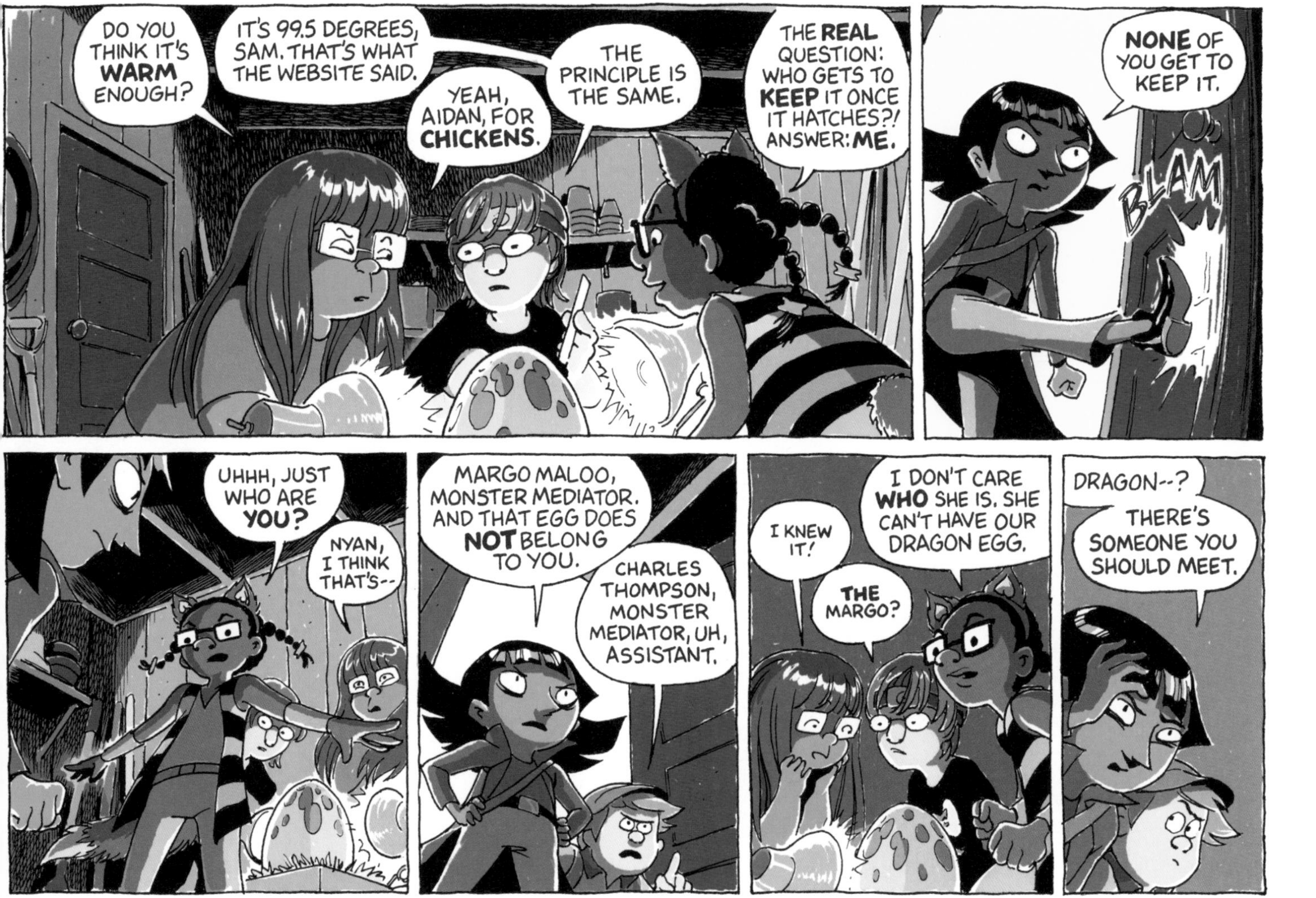
DO YOU THINK IT'S **WARM** ENOUGH?
IT'S 99.5 DEGREES, SAM. THAT'S WHAT THE WEBSITE SAID.
YEAH, AIDAN, FOR **CHICKENS**.
THE PRINCIPLE IS THE SAME.
THE **REAL** QUESTION: WHO GETS TO **KEEP** IT ONCE IT HATCHES?! ANSWER: **ME.**
NONE OF YOU GET TO KEEP IT.
BLAM
UHHH, JUST WHO ARE **YOU?**
NYAN, I THINK THAT'S--
MARGO MALOO, MONSTER MEDIATOR. AND THAT EGG DOES **NOT** BELONG TO YOU.
CHARLES THOMPSON, MONSTER MEDIATOR, UH, ASSISTANT.
I KNEW IT!
THE MARGO?
I DON'T CARE **WHO** SHE IS. SHE CAN'T HAVE OUR DRAGON EGG.
DRAGON--?
THERE'S SOMEONE YOU SHOULD MEET.

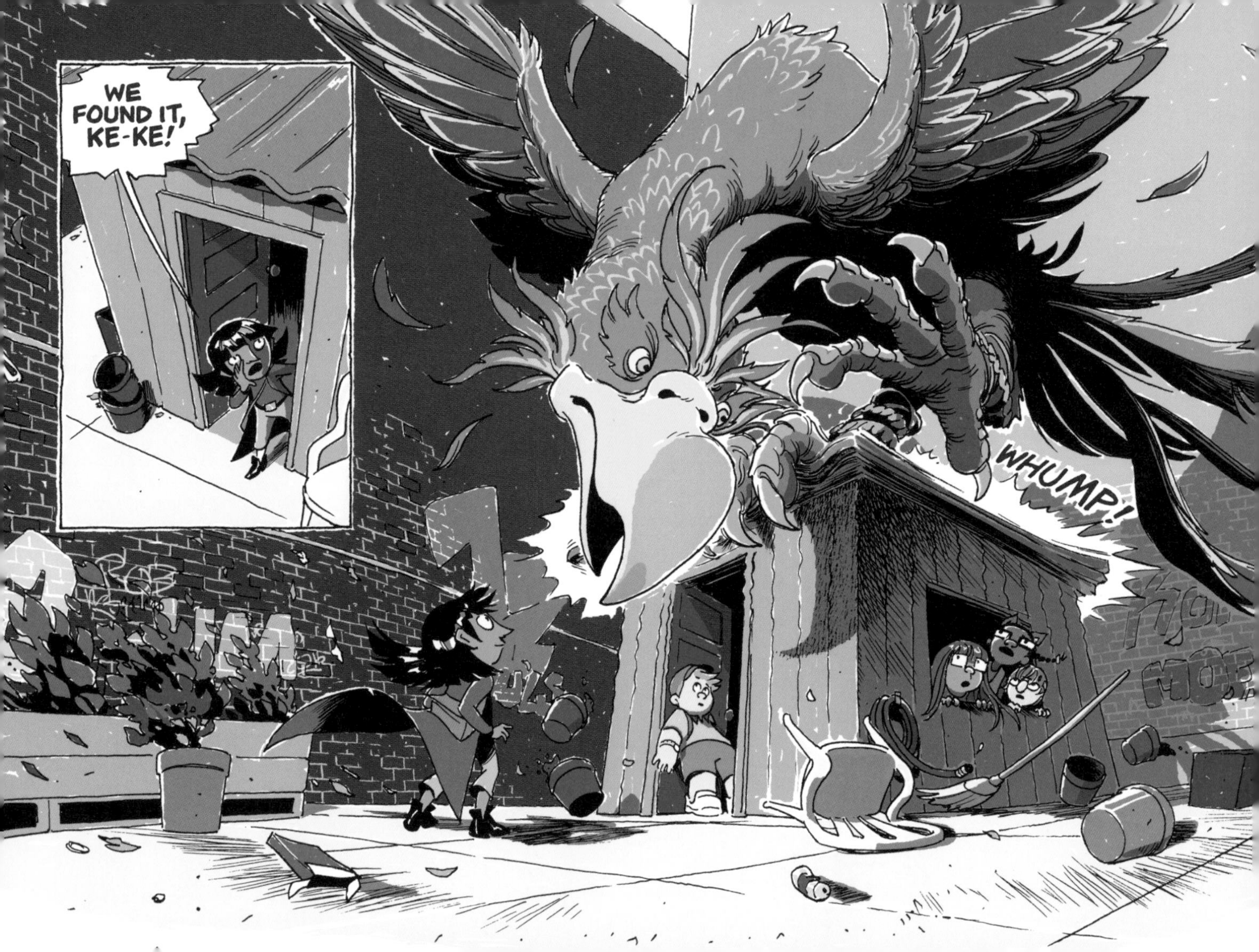
WE FOUND IT, KE-KE!
WHUMP!

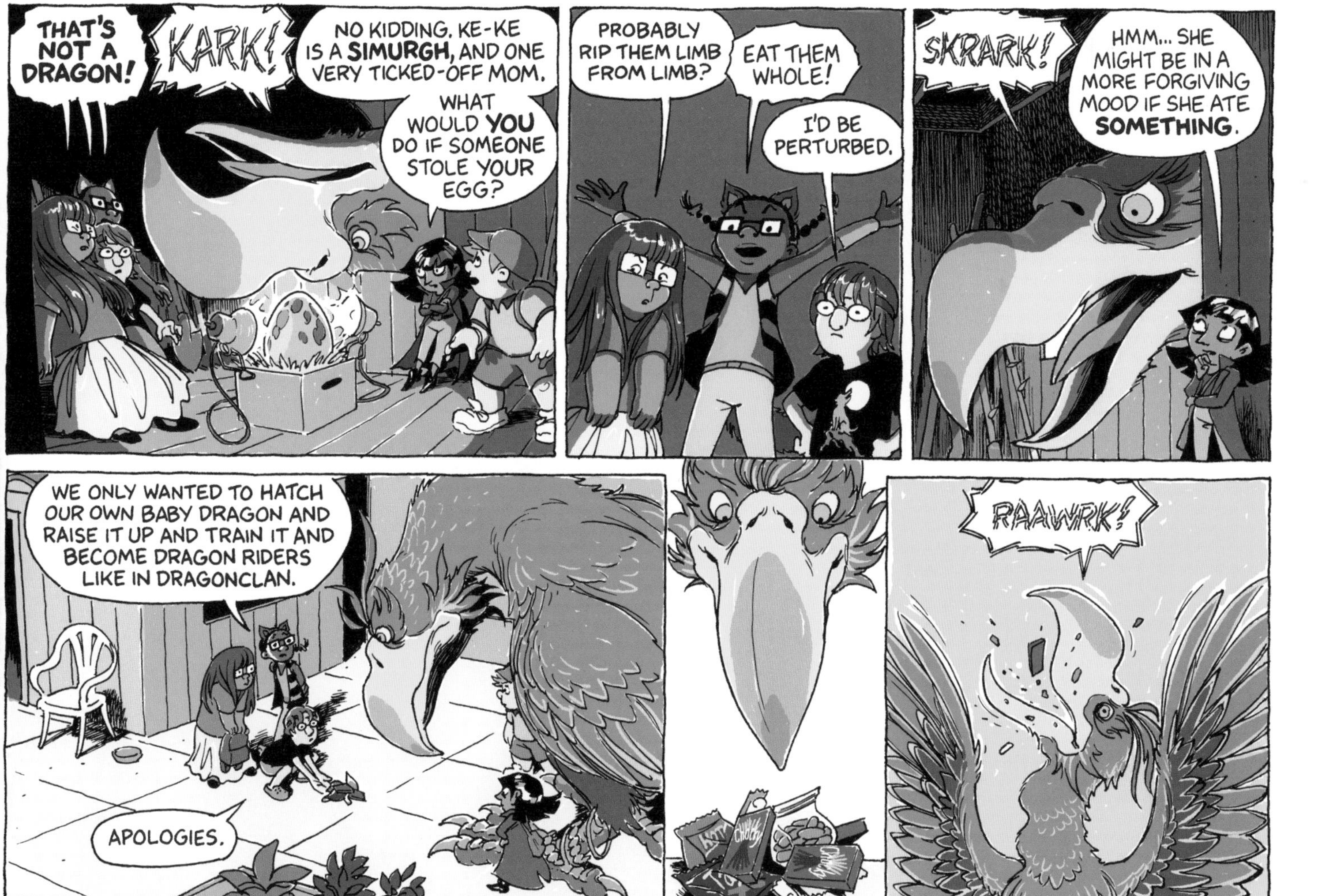
THAT'S NOT A DRAGON!
KARK!
NO KIDDING. KE-KE IS A SIMURGH, AND ONE VERY TICKED-OFF MOM.
WHAT WOULD YOU DO IF SOMEONE STOLE YOUR EGG?
PROBABLY RIP THEM LIMB FROM LIMB?
EAT THEM WHOLE!
I'D BE PERTURBED.
SKRARK!
HMM... SHE MIGHT BE IN A MORE FORGIVING MOOD IF SHE ATE SOMETHING.
WE ONLY WANTED TO HATCH OUR OWN BABY DRAGON AND RAISE IT UP AND TRAIN IT AND BECOME DRAGON RIDERS LIKE IN DRAGONCLAN.
APOLOGIES.
RAAWRK!

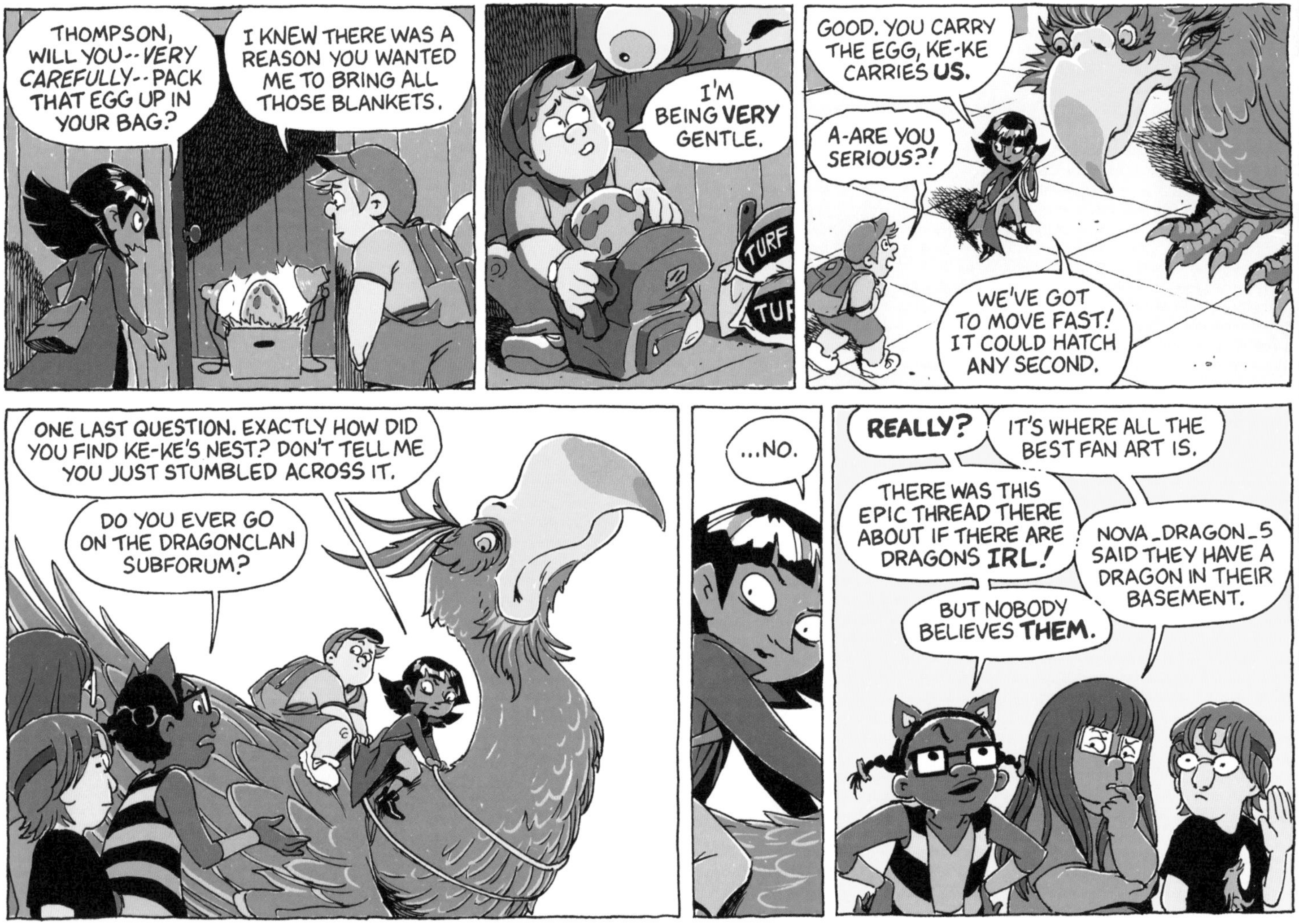
THOMPSON, WILL YOU--VERY CAREFULLY--PACK THAT EGG UP IN YOUR BAG?
I KNEW THERE WAS A REASON YOU WANTED ME TO BRING ALL THOSE BLANKETS.
I'M BEING VERY GENTLE.
TURF
TUR
GOOD. YOU CARRY THE EGG, KE-KE CARRIES US.
A-ARE YOU SERIOUS?!
WE'VE GOT TO MOVE FAST! IT COULD HATCH ANY SECOND.
ONE LAST QUESTION. EXACTLY HOW DID YOU FIND KE-KE'S NEST? DON'T TELL ME YOU JUST STUMBLED ACROSS IT.
DO YOU EVER GO ON THE DRAGONCLAN SUBFORUM?
...NO.
REALLY?
IT'S WHERE ALL THE BEST FAN ART IS.
THERE WAS THIS EPIC THREAD THERE ABOUT IF THERE ARE DRAGONS IRL!
BUT NOBODY BELIEVES THEM.
NOVA_DRAGON_5 SAID THEY HAVE A DRAGON IN THEIR BASEMENT.

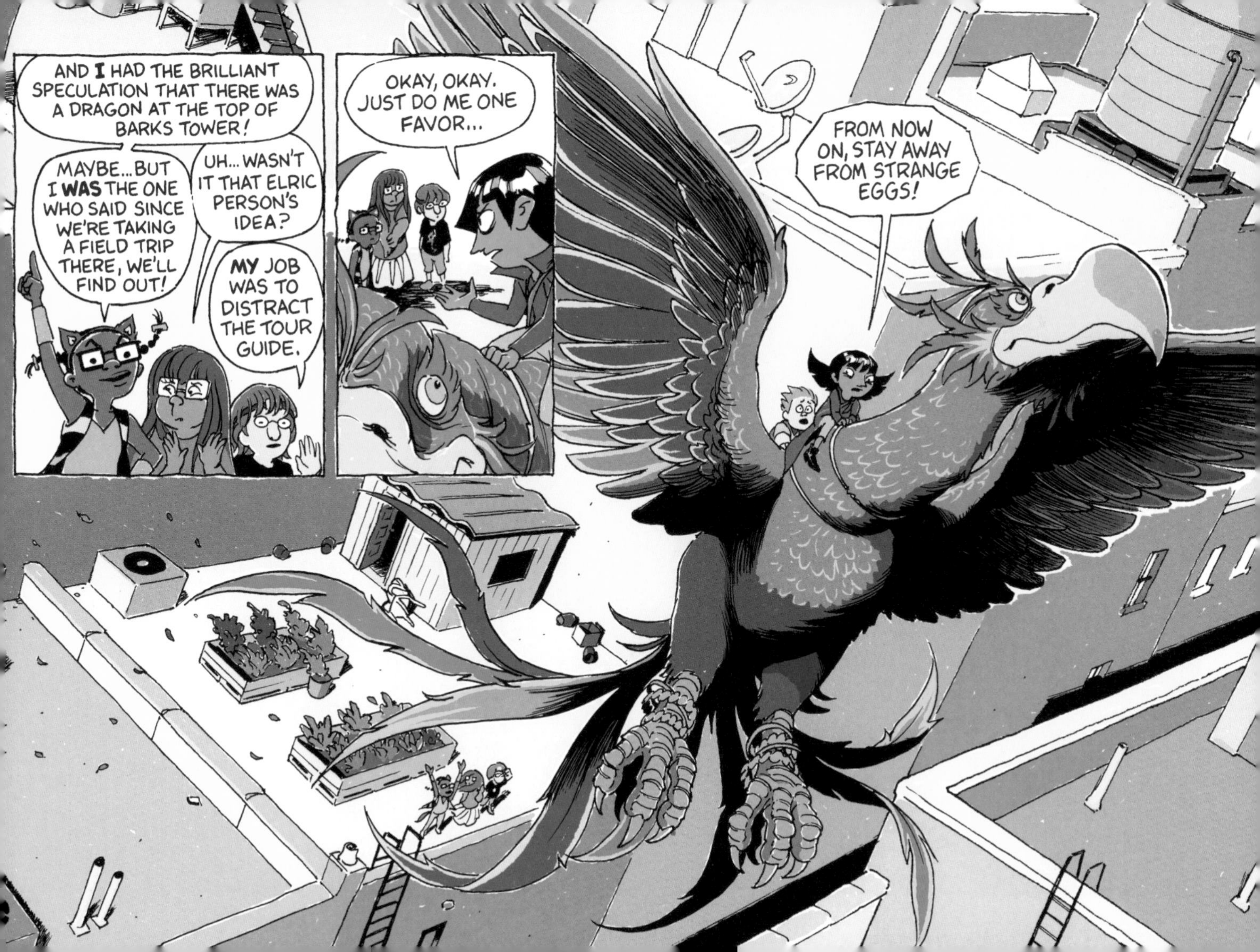
AND I HAD THE BRILLIANT SPECULATION THAT THERE WAS A DRAGON AT THE TOP OF BARKS TOWER!
MAYBE...BUT I WAS THE ONE WHO SAID SINCE WE'RE TAKING A FIELD TRIP THERE, WE'LL FIND OUT!
UH...WASN'T IT THAT ELRIC PERSON'S IDEA?
MY JOB WAS TO DISTRACT THE TOUR GUIDE.
OKAY, OKAY. JUST DO ME ONE FAVOR...
FROM NOW ON, STAY AWAY FROM STRANGE EGGS!

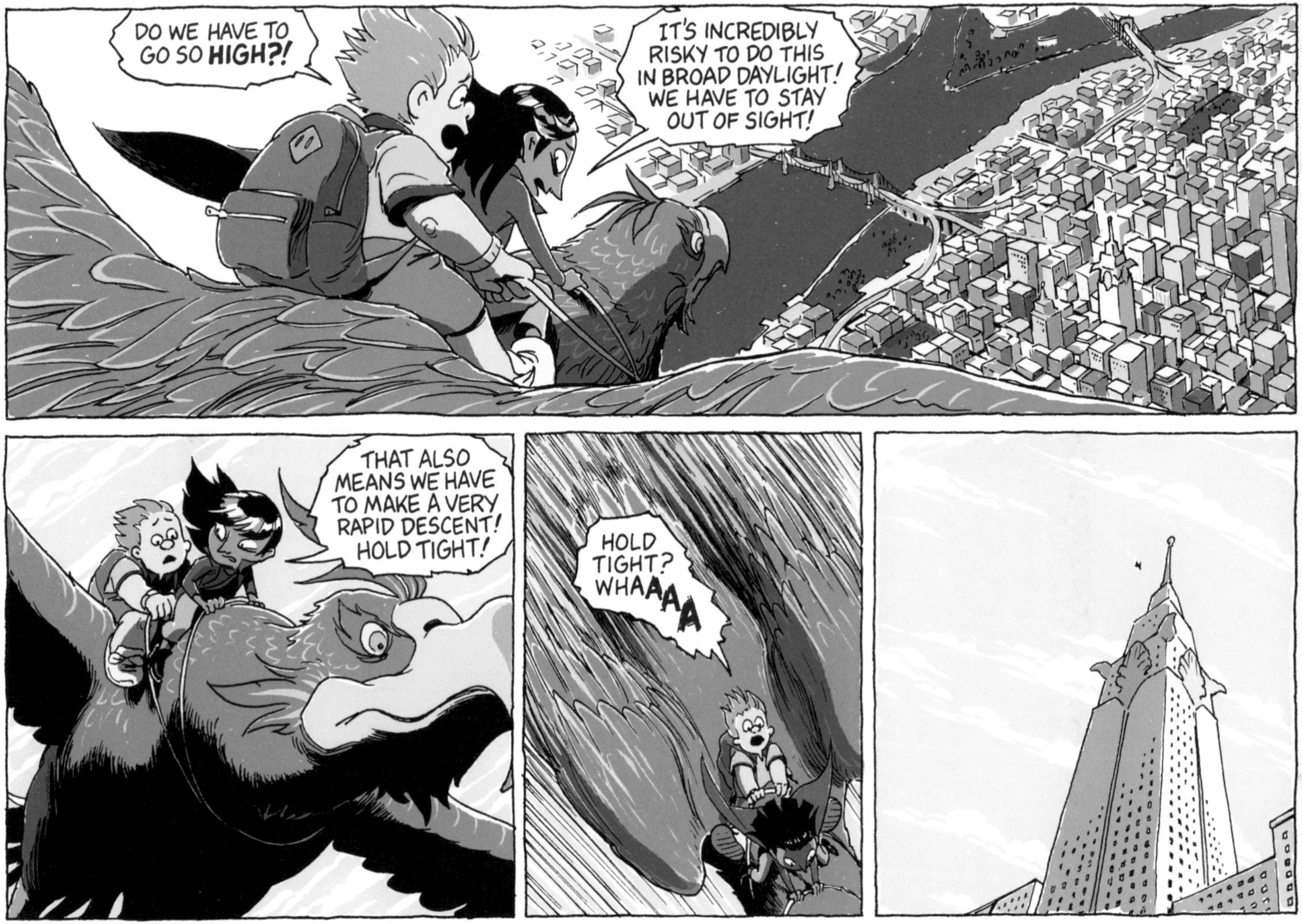
DO WE HAVE TO GO SO HIGH?!
IT'S INCREDIBLY RISKY TO DO THIS IN BROAD DAYLIGHT! WE HAVE TO STAY OUT OF SIGHT!
THAT ALSO MEANS WE HAVE TO MAKE A VERY RAPID DESCENT! HOLD TIGHT!
HOLD TIGHT? WHAAAA

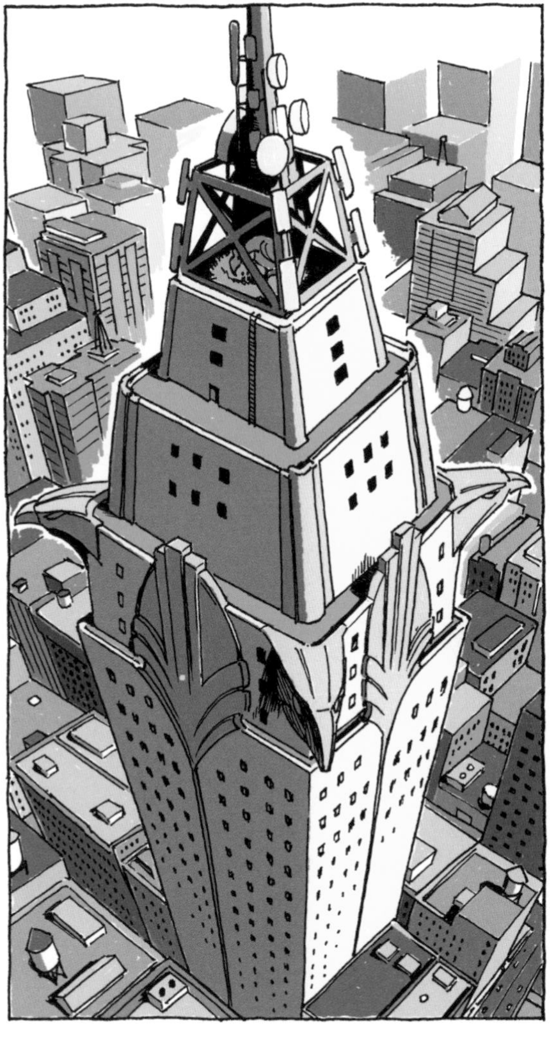

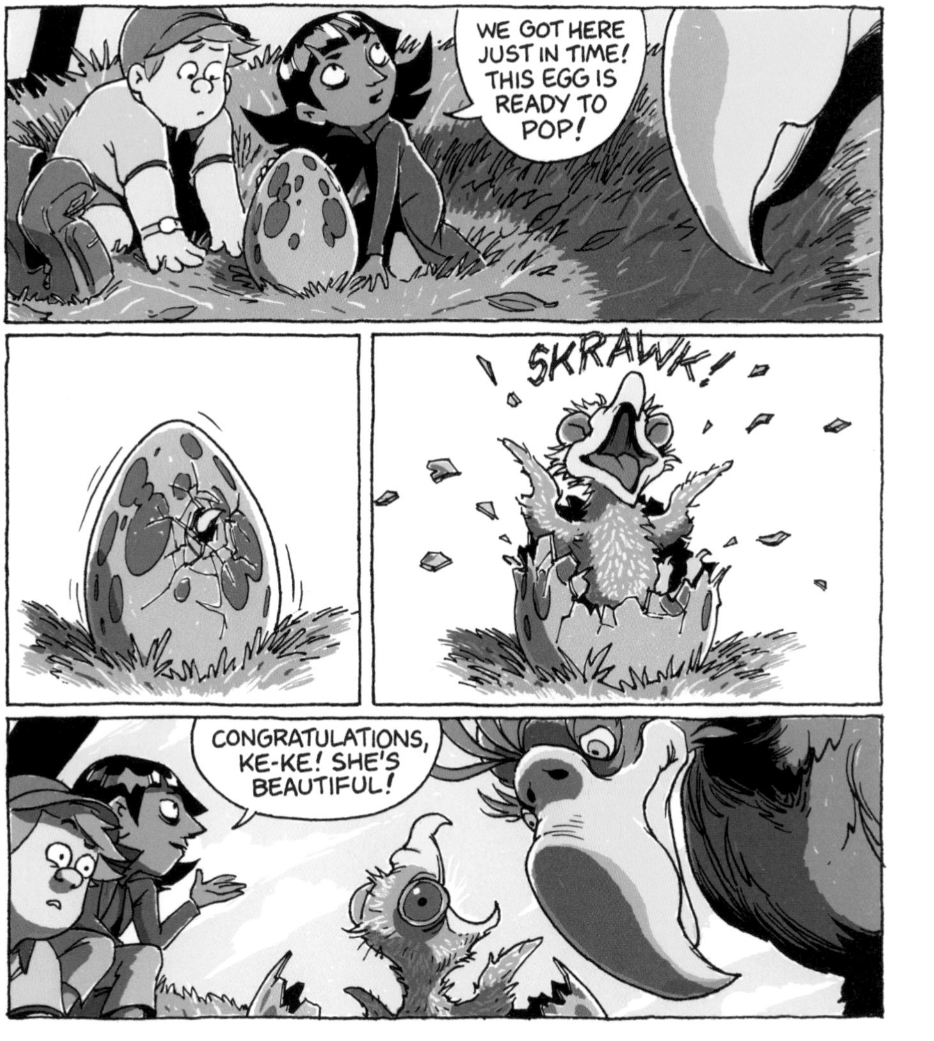
WE GOT HERE JUST IN TIME! THIS EGG IS READY TO POP!
SKRAWK!
CONGRATULATIONS, KE-KE! SHE'S BEAUTIFUL!

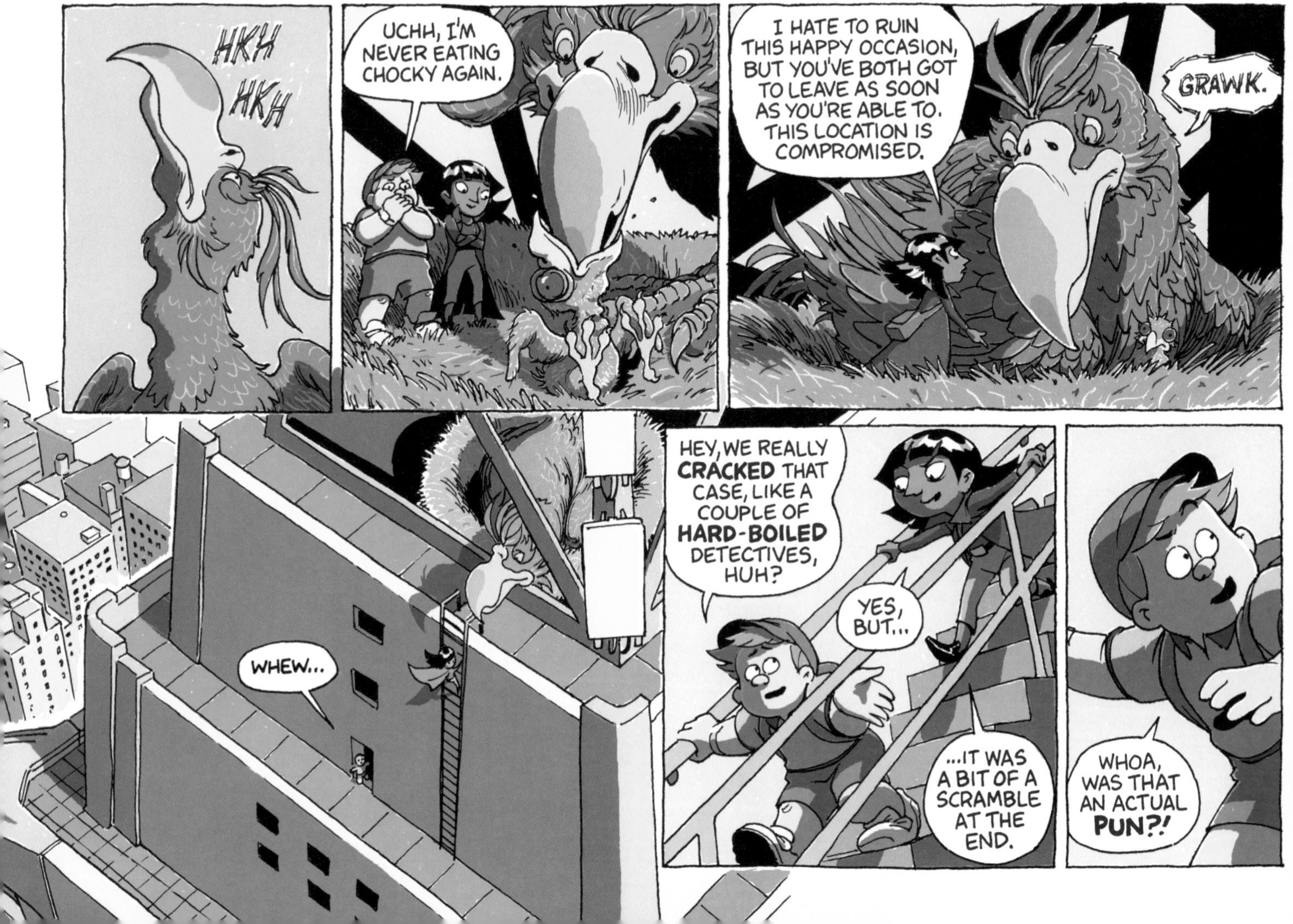
HKH
HKH
UCHH, I'M NEVER EATING CHOCKY AGAIN.
I HATE TO RUIN THIS HAPPY OCCASION, BUT YOU'VE BOTH GOT TO LEAVE AS SOON AS YOU'RE ABLE TO. THIS LOCATION IS COMPROMISED.
GRAWK.
WHEW...
HEY, WE REALLY CRACKED THAT CASE, LIKE A COUPLE OF HARD-BOILED DETECTIVES, HUH?
YES, BUT...
...IT WAS A BIT OF A SCRAMBLE AT THE END.
WHOA, WAS THAT AN ACTUAL PUN?!

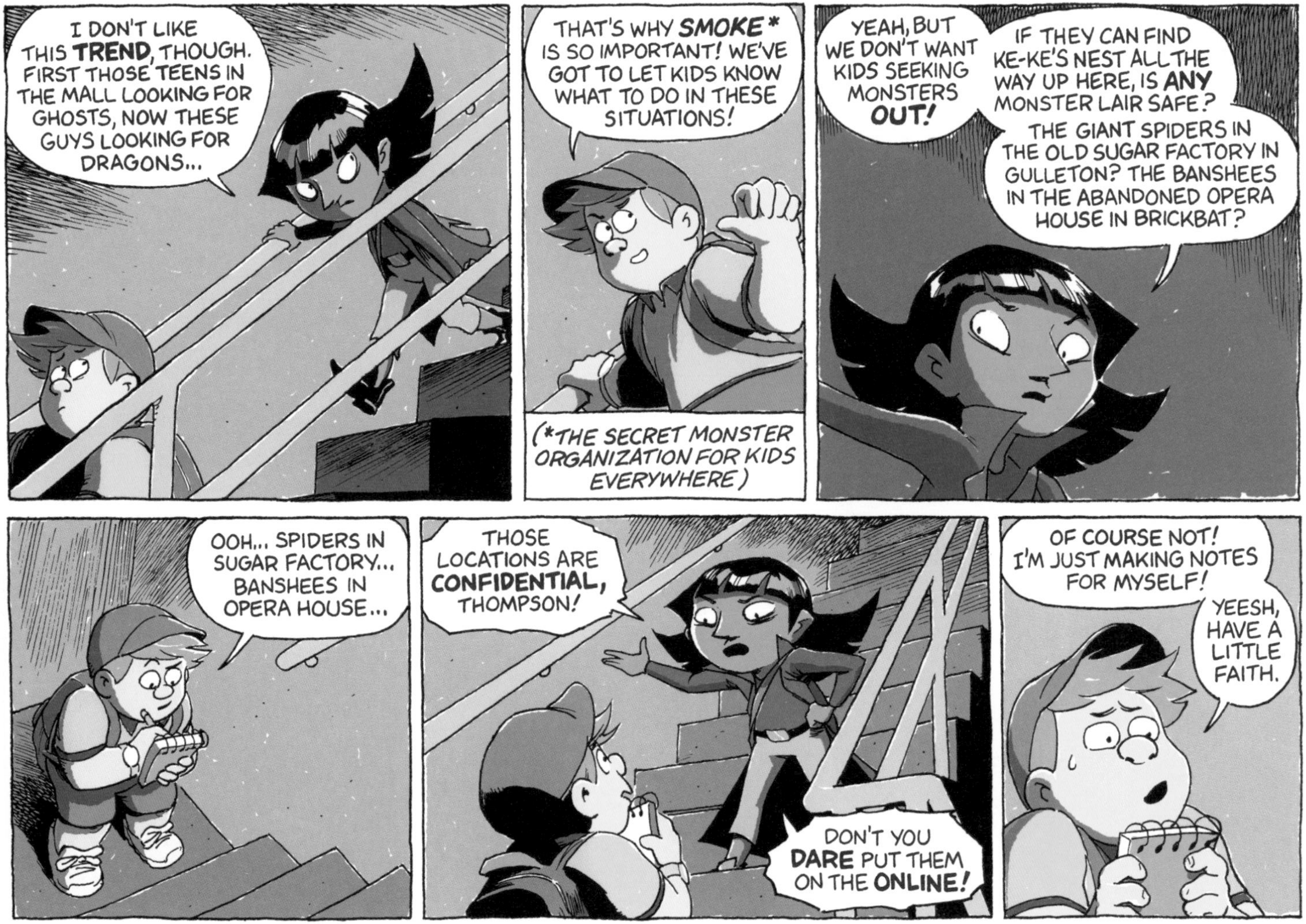

I DON'T LIKE THIS TREND, THOUGH. FIRST THOSE TEENS IN THE MALL LOOKING FOR GHOSTS, NOW THESE GUYS LOOKING FOR DRAGONS...
THAT'S WHY SMOKE* IS SO IMPORTANT! WE'VE GOT TO LET KIDS KNOW WHAT TO DO IN THESE SITUATIONS!
(*THE SECRET MONSTER ORGANIZATION FOR KIDS EVERYWHERE)
YEAH, BUT WE DON'T WANT KIDS SEEKING MONSTERS OUT!
IF THEY CAN FIND KE-KE'S NEST ALL THE WAY UP HERE, IS ANY MONSTER LAIR SAFE?
THE GIANT SPIDERS IN THE OLD SUGAR FACTORY IN GULLETON? THE BANSHEES IN THE ABANDONED OPERA HOUSE IN BRICKBAT?
OOH... SPIDERS IN SUGAR FACTORY... BANSHEES IN OPERA HOUSE...
THOSE LOCATIONS ARE CONFIDENTIAL, THOMPSON!
DON'T YOU DARE PUT THEM ON THE ONLINE!
OF COURSE NOT! I'M JUST MAKING NOTES FOR MYSELF!
YEESH, HAVE A LITTLE FAITH.

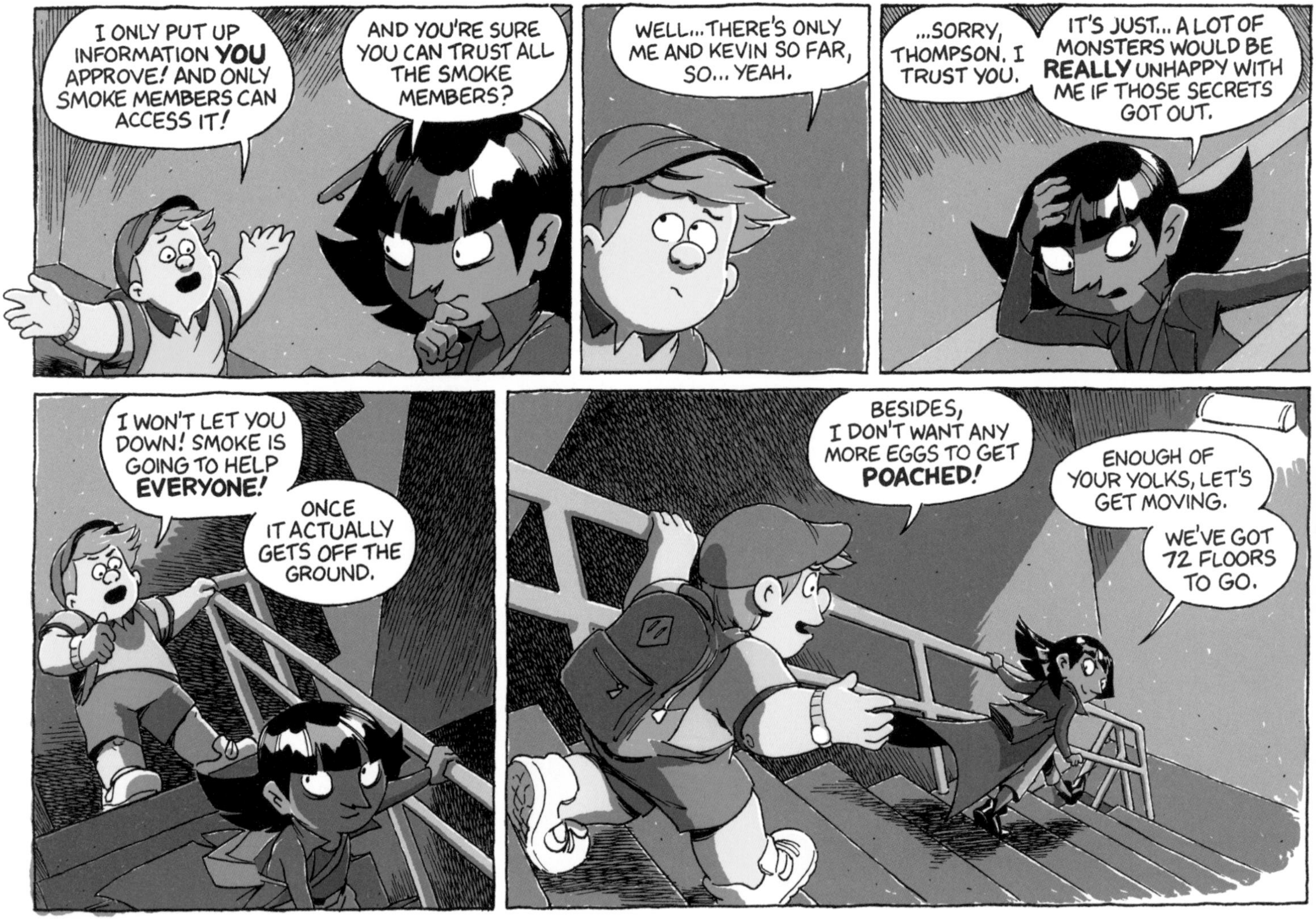
I ONLY PUT UP INFORMATION **YOU** APPROVE! AND ONLY SMOKE MEMBERS CAN ACCESS IT!
AND YOU'RE SURE YOU CAN TRUST ALL THE SMOKE MEMBERS?
WELL... THERE'S ONLY ME AND KEVIN SO FAR, SO... YEAH.
...SORRY, THOMPSON. I TRUST YOU.
IT'S JUST... A LOT OF MONSTERS WOULD BE **REALLY** UNHAPPY WITH ME IF THOSE SECRETS GOT OUT.
I WON'T LET YOU DOWN! SMOKE IS GOING TO HELP **EVERYONE!**
ONCE IT ACTUALLY GETS OFF THE GROUND.
BESIDES, I DON'T WANT ANY MORE EGGS TO GET **POACHED!**
ENOUGH OF YOUR YOLKS, LET'S GET MOVING.
WE'VE GOT 72 FLOORS TO GO.

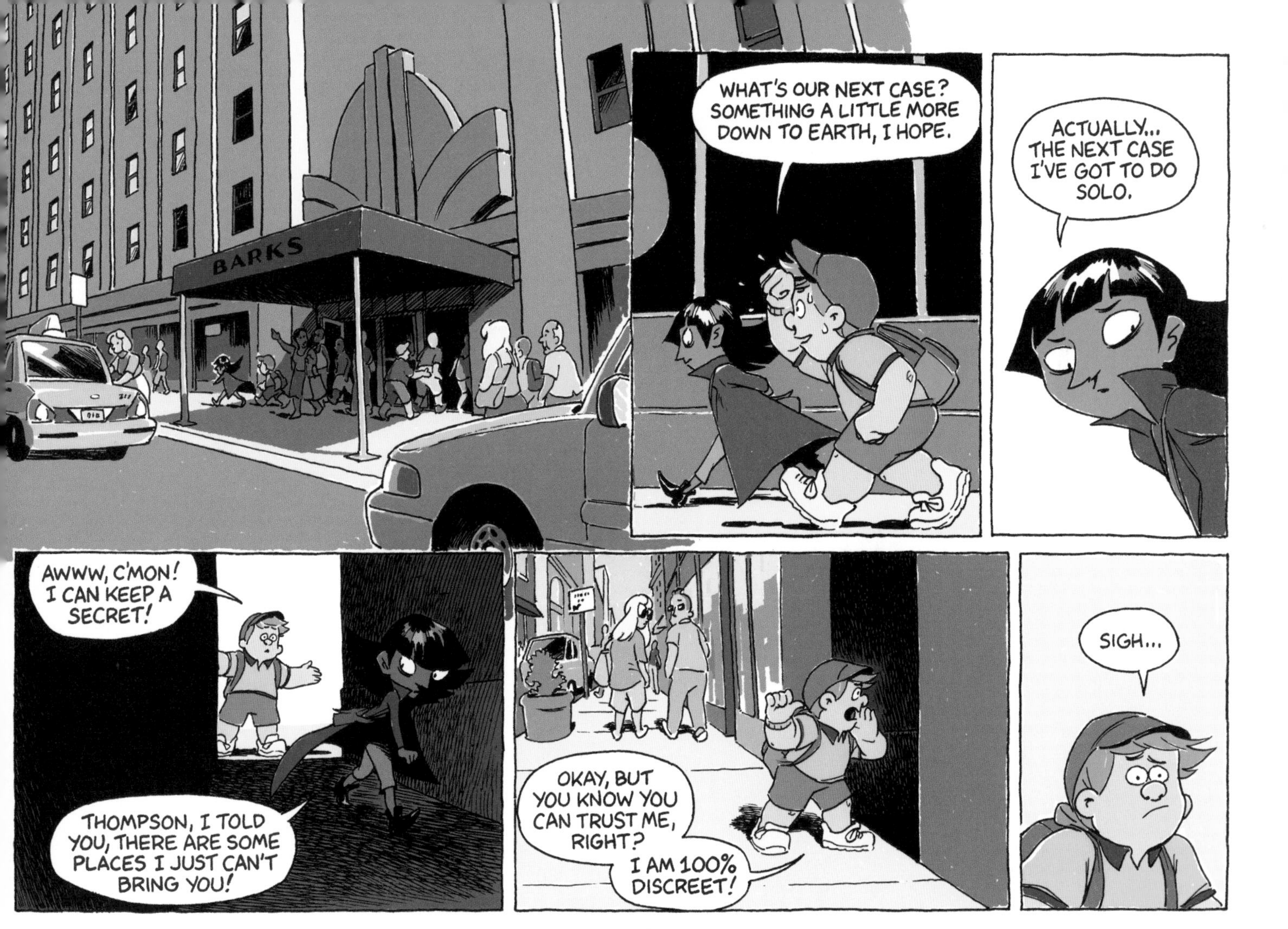
BARKS
WHAT'S OUR NEXT CASE? SOMETHING A LITTLE MORE DOWN TO EARTH, I HOPE.
ACTUALLY... THE NEXT CASE I'VE GOT TO DO SOLO.
AWWW, C'MON! I CAN KEEP A SECRET!
THOMPSON, I TOLD YOU, THERE ARE SOME PLACES I JUST CAN'T BRING YOU!
OKAY, BUT YOU KNOW YOU CAN TRUST ME, RIGHT?
I AM 100% DISCREET!
SIGH...

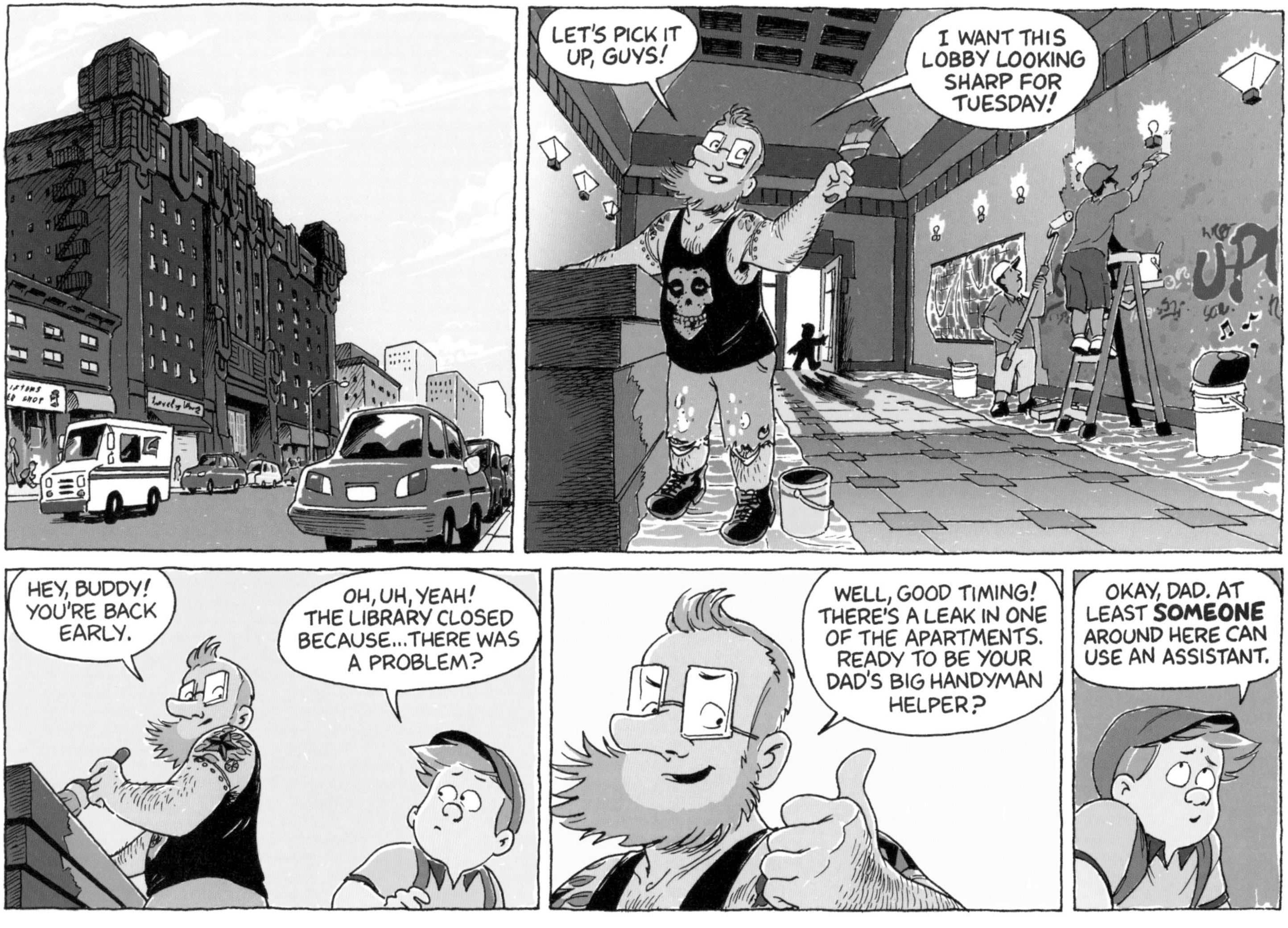
LET'S PICK IT UP, GUYS!
I WANT THIS LOBBY LOOKING SHARP FOR TUESDAY!
HEY, BUDDY! YOU'RE BACK EARLY.
OH, UH, YEAH! THE LIBRARY CLOSED BECAUSE...THERE WAS A PROBLEM?
WELL, GOOD TIMING! THERE'S A LEAK IN ONE OF THE APARTMENTS. READY TO BE YOUR DAD'S BIG HANDYMAN HELPER?
OKAY, DAD. AT LEAST **SOMEONE** AROUND HERE CAN USE AN ASSISTANT.

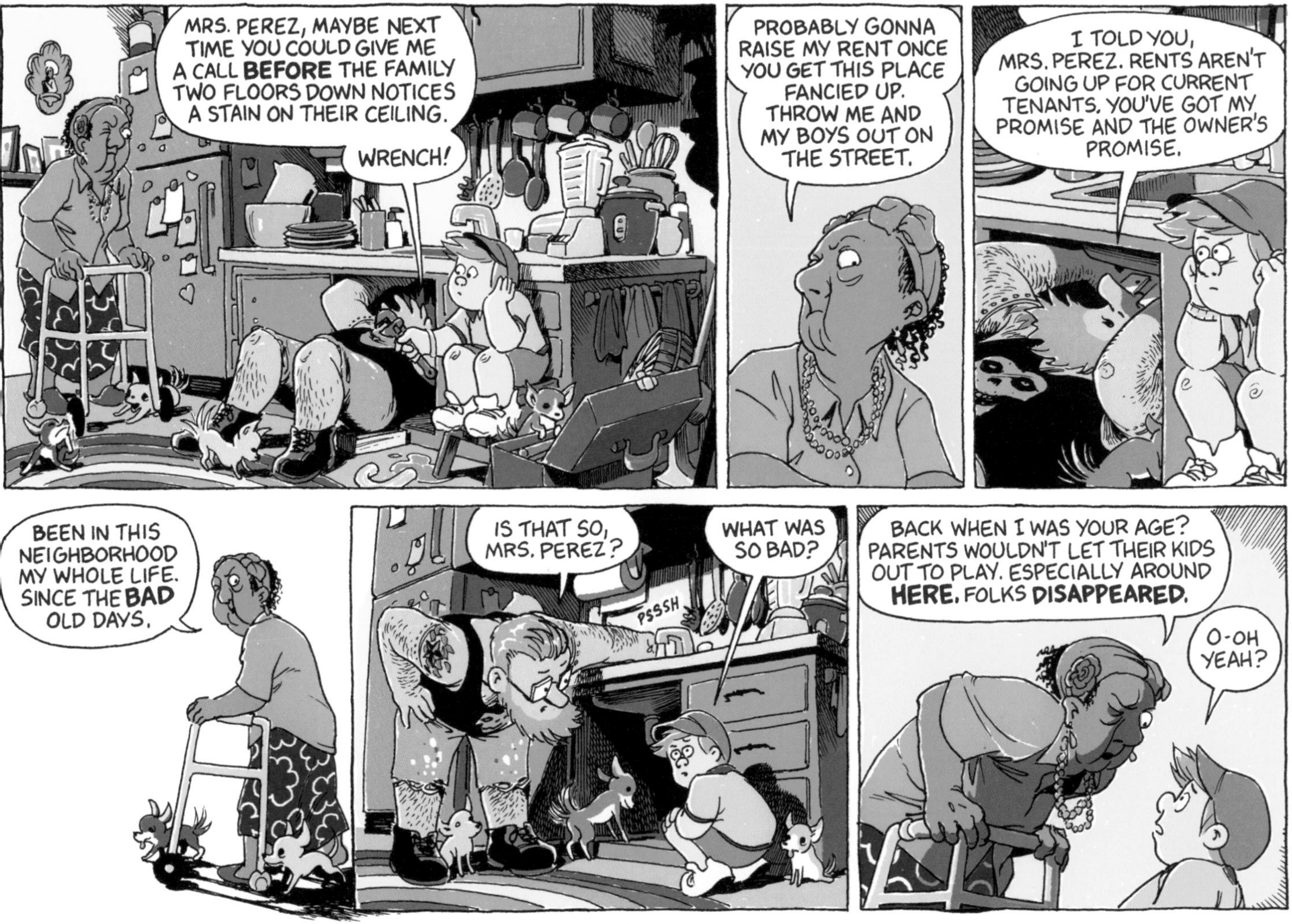
MRS. PEREZ, MAYBE NEXT TIME YOU COULD GIVE ME A CALL BEFORE THE FAMILY TWO FLOORS DOWN NOTICES A STAIN ON THEIR CEILING.
WRENCH!
PROBABLY GONNA RAISE MY RENT ONCE YOU GET THIS PLACE FANCIED UP. THROW ME AND MY BOYS OUT ON THE STREET.
I TOLD YOU, MRS. PEREZ. RENTS AREN'T GOING UP FOR CURRENT TENANTS. YOU'VE GOT MY PROMISE AND THE OWNER'S PROMISE.
BEEN IN THIS NEIGHBORHOOD MY WHOLE LIFE. SINCE THE BAD OLD DAYS.
IS THAT SO, MRS. PEREZ?
WHAT WAS SO BAD?
PSSSH
BACK WHEN I WAS YOUR AGE? PARENTS WOULDN'T LET THEIR KIDS OUT TO PLAY. ESPECIALLY AROUND HERE. FOLKS DISAPPEARED.
O-OH YEAH?

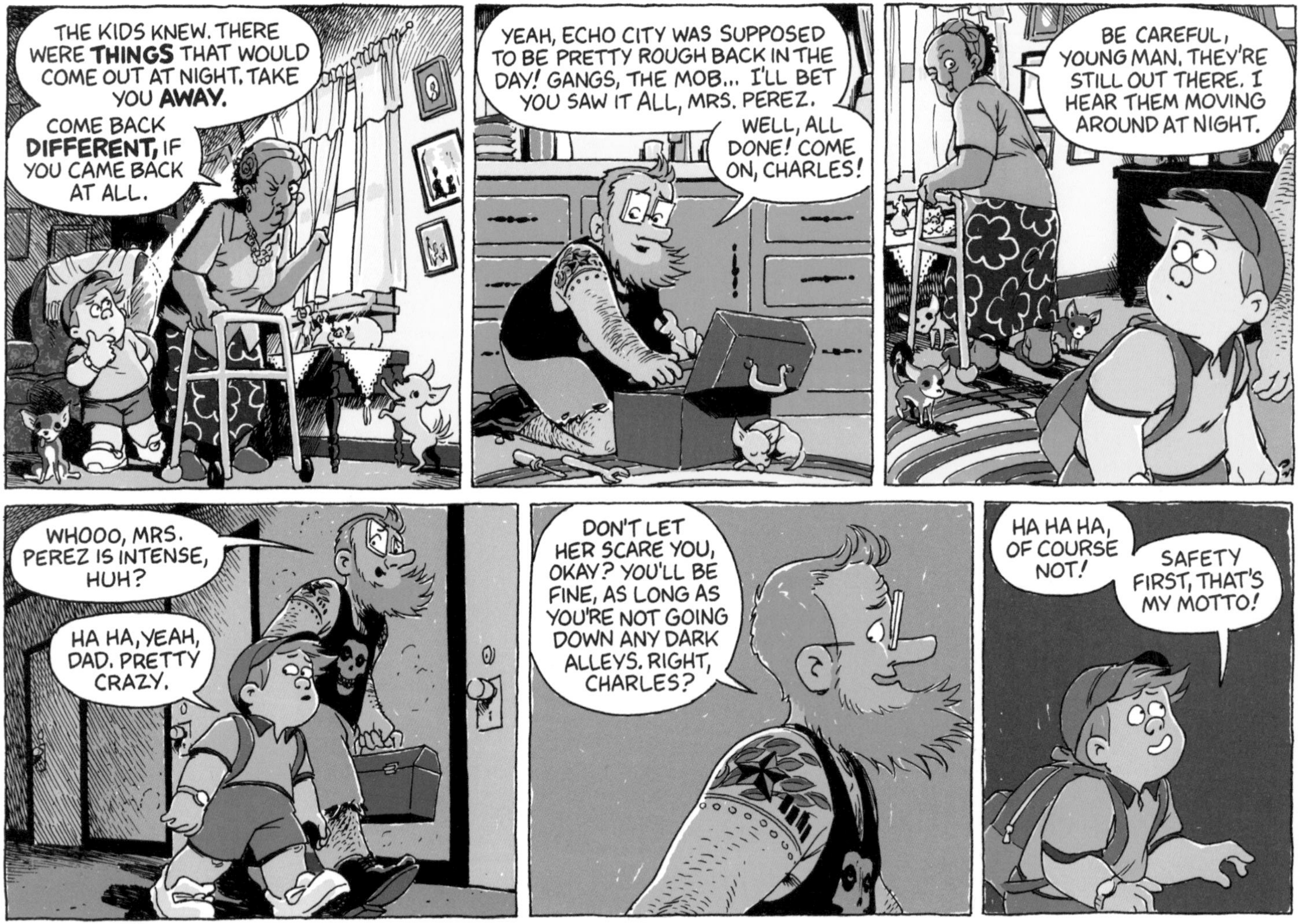

THE KIDS KNEW. THERE WERE **THINGS** THAT WOULD COME OUT AT NIGHT. TAKE YOU **AWAY.**
COME BACK **DIFFERENT,** IF YOU CAME BACK AT ALL.
YEAH, ECHO CITY WAS SUPPOSED TO BE PRETTY ROUGH BACK IN THE DAY! GANGS, THE MOB... I'LL BET YOU SAW IT ALL, MRS. PEREZ.
WELL, ALL DONE! COME ON, CHARLES!
BE CAREFUL, YOUNG MAN. THEY'RE STILL OUT THERE. I HEAR THEM MOVING AROUND AT NIGHT.
WHOOO, MRS. PEREZ IS INTENSE, HUH?
HA HA, YEAH, DAD. PRETTY CRAZY.
DON'T LET HER SCARE YOU, OKAY? YOU'LL BE FINE, AS LONG AS YOU'RE NOT GOING DOWN ANY DARK ALLEYS. RIGHT, CHARLES?
HA HA HA, OF COURSE NOT!
SAFETY FIRST, THAT'S MY MOTTO!

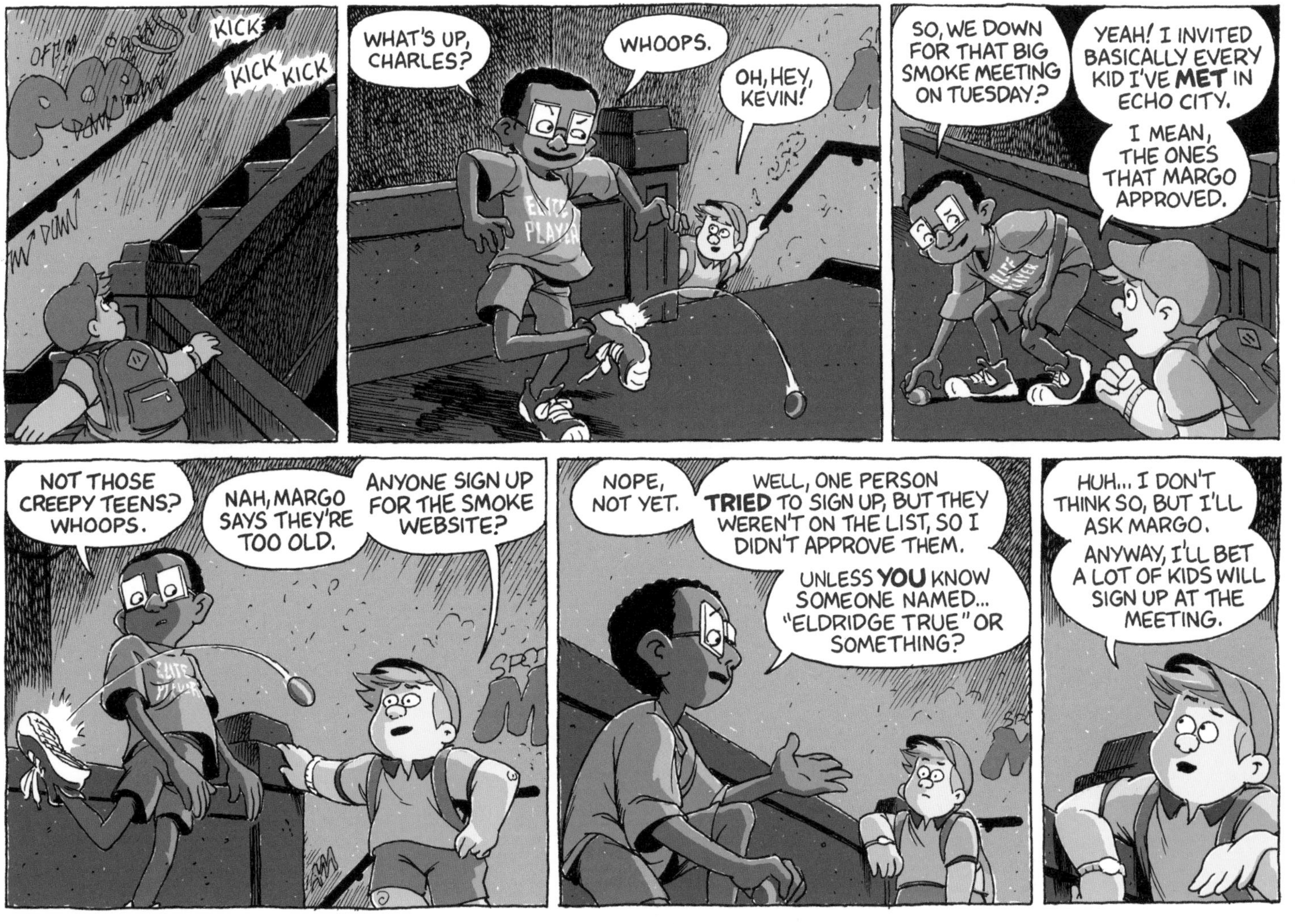

KICK
KICK KICK
WHAT'S UP, CHARLES?
WHOOPS.
OH, HEY, KEVIN!
SO, WE DOWN FOR THAT BIG SMOKE MEETING ON TUESDAY?
YEAH! I INVITED BASICALLY EVERY KID I'VE **MET** IN ECHO CITY.
I MEAN, THE ONES THAT MARGO APPROVED.
NOT THOSE CREEPY TEENS? WHOOPS.
NAH, MARGO SAYS THEY'RE TOO OLD.
ANYONE SIGN UP FOR THE SMOKE WEBSITE?
NOPE, NOT YET.
WELL, ONE PERSON **TRIED** TO SIGN UP, BUT THEY WEREN'T ON THE LIST, SO I DIDN'T APPROVE THEM.
UNLESS **YOU** KNOW SOMEONE NAMED... "ELDRIDGE TRUE" OR SOMETHING?
HUH... I DON'T THINK SO, BUT I'LL ASK MARGO.
ANYWAY, I'LL BET A LOT OF KIDS WILL SIGN UP AT THE MEETING.

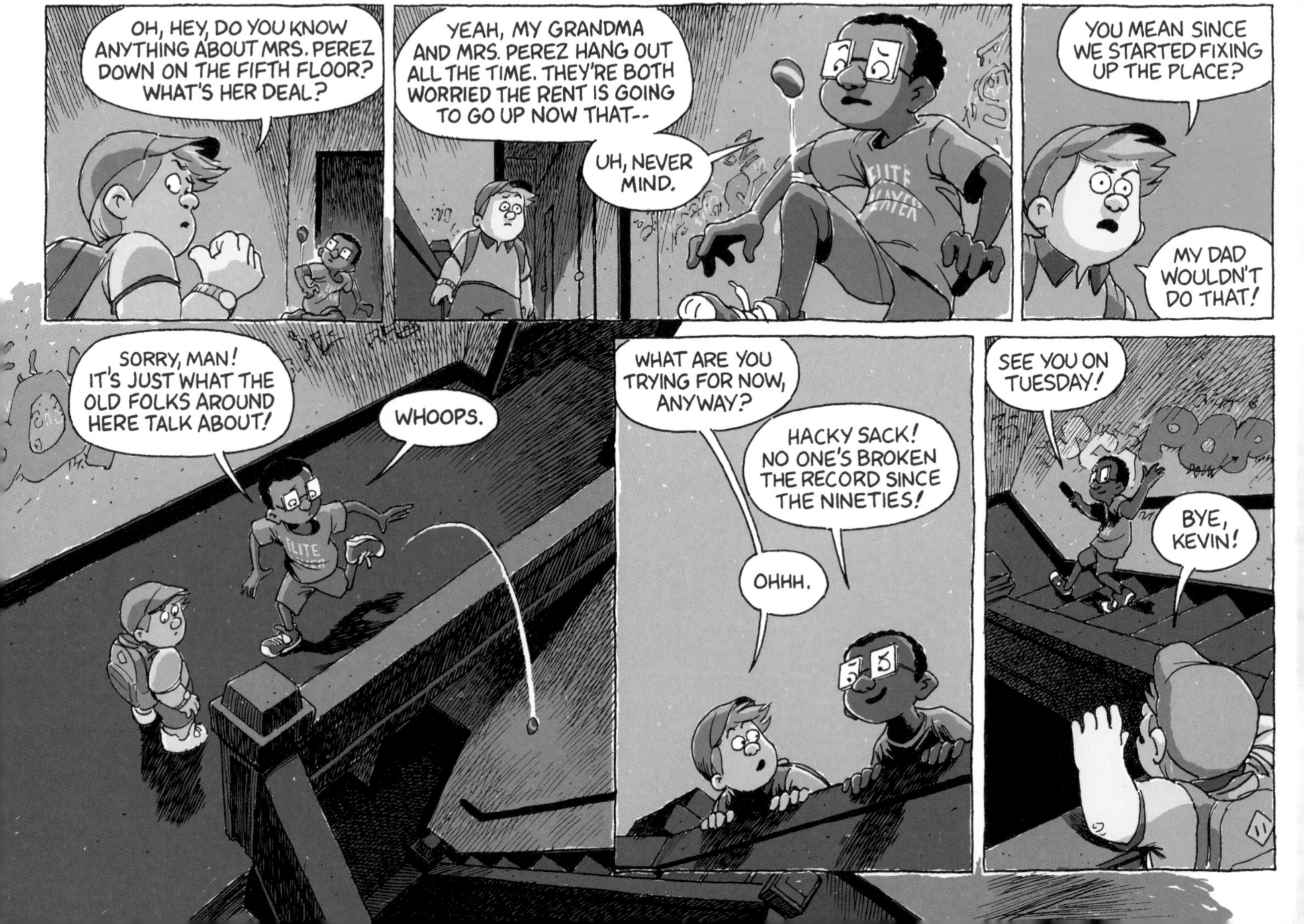
OH, HEY, DO YOU KNOW ANYTHING ABOUT MRS. PEREZ DOWN ON THE FIFTH FLOOR? WHAT'S HER DEAL?
YEAH, MY GRANDMA AND MRS. PEREZ HANG OUT ALL THE TIME. THEY'RE BOTH WORRIED THE RENT IS GOING TO GO UP NOW THAT--
UH, NEVER MIND.
YOU MEAN SINCE WE STARTED FIXING UP THE PLACE?
MY DAD WOULDN'T DO THAT!
SORRY, MAN! IT'S JUST WHAT THE OLD FOLKS AROUND HERE TALK ABOUT!
WHOOPS.
WHAT ARE YOU TRYING FOR NOW, ANYWAY?
HACKY SACK! NO ONE'S BROKEN THE RECORD SINCE THE NINETIES!
OHHH.
SEE YOU ON TUESDAY!
BYE, KEVIN!

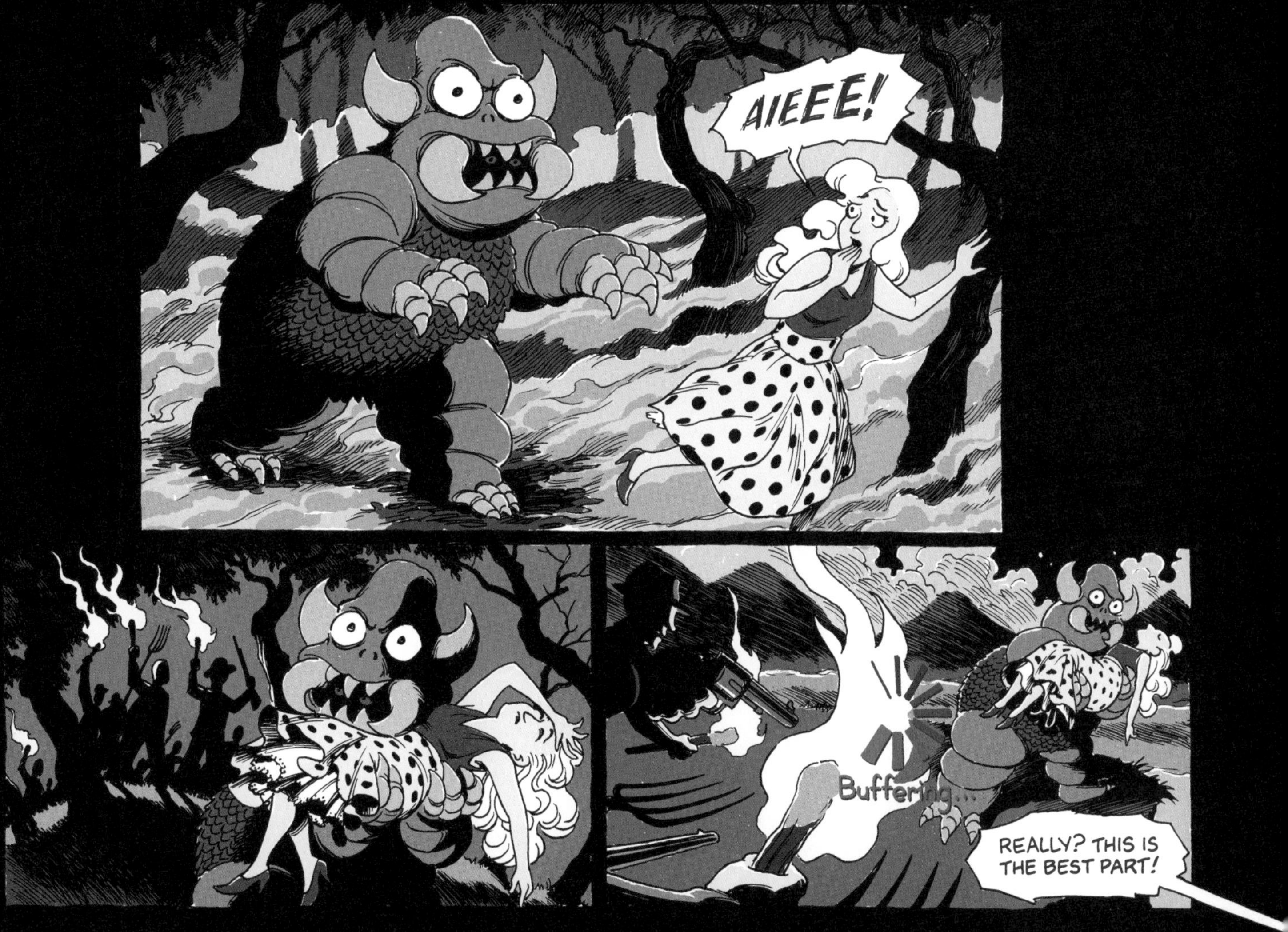
AIEEE!
Buffering...
REALLY? THIS IS THE BEST PART!

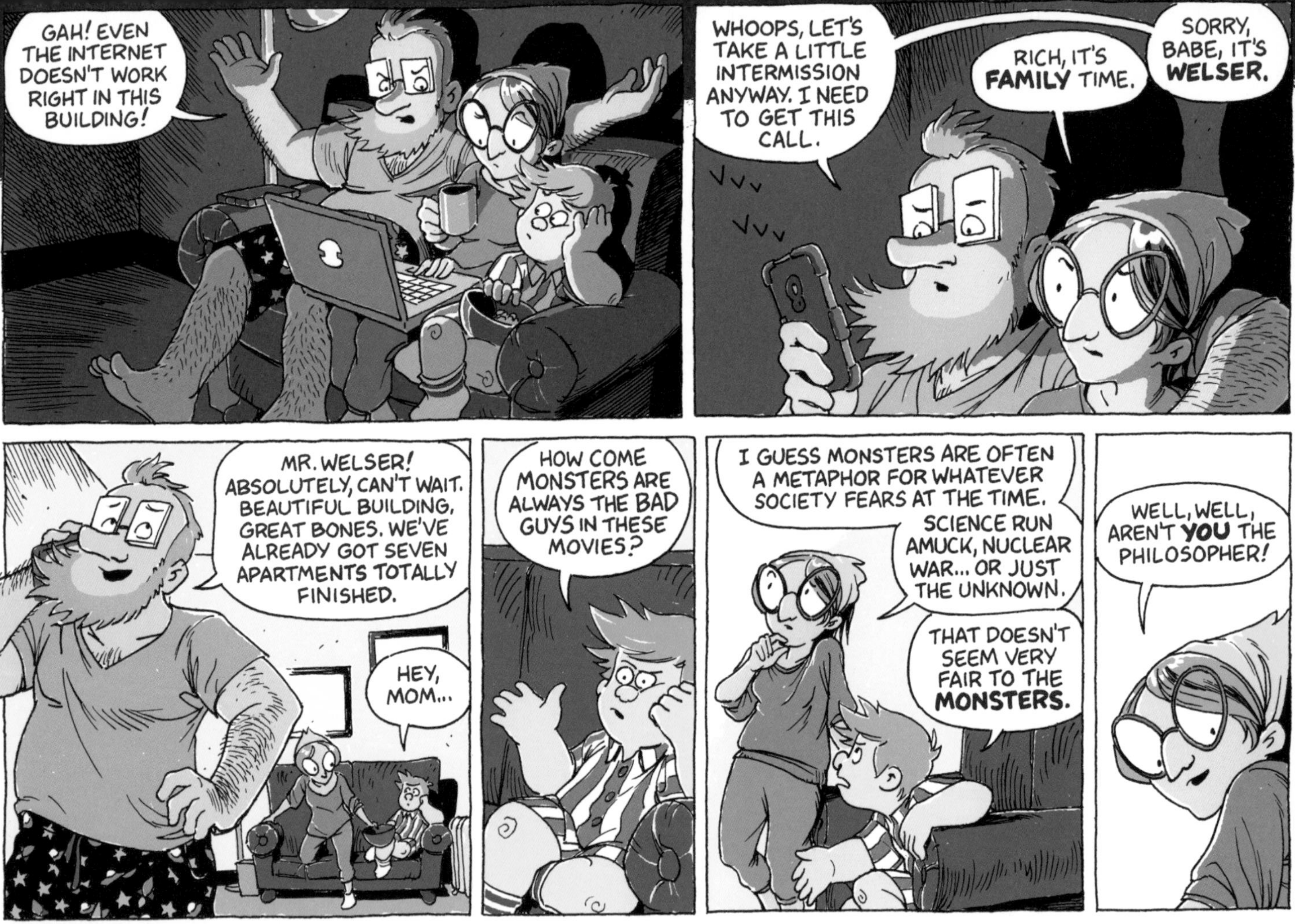

GAH! EVEN THE INTERNET DOESN'T WORK RIGHT IN THIS BUILDING!
WHOOPS, LET'S TAKE A LITTLE INTERMISSION ANYWAY. I NEED TO GET THIS CALL.
RICH, IT'S **FAMILY** TIME.
SORRY, BABE, IT'S **WELSER.**
MR. WELSER! ABSOLUTELY, CAN'T WAIT. BEAUTIFUL BUILDING, GREAT BONES. WE'VE ALREADY GOT SEVEN APARTMENTS TOTALLY FINISHED.
HEY, MOM...
HOW COME MONSTERS ARE ALWAYS THE BAD GUYS IN THESE MOVIES?
I GUESS MONSTERS ARE OFTEN A METAPHOR FOR WHATEVER SOCIETY FEARS AT THE TIME.
SCIENCE RUN AMUCK, NUCLEAR WAR... OR JUST THE UNKNOWN.
THAT DOESN'T SEEM VERY FAIR TO THE **MONSTERS.**
WELL, WELL, AREN'T **YOU** THE PHILOSOPHER!

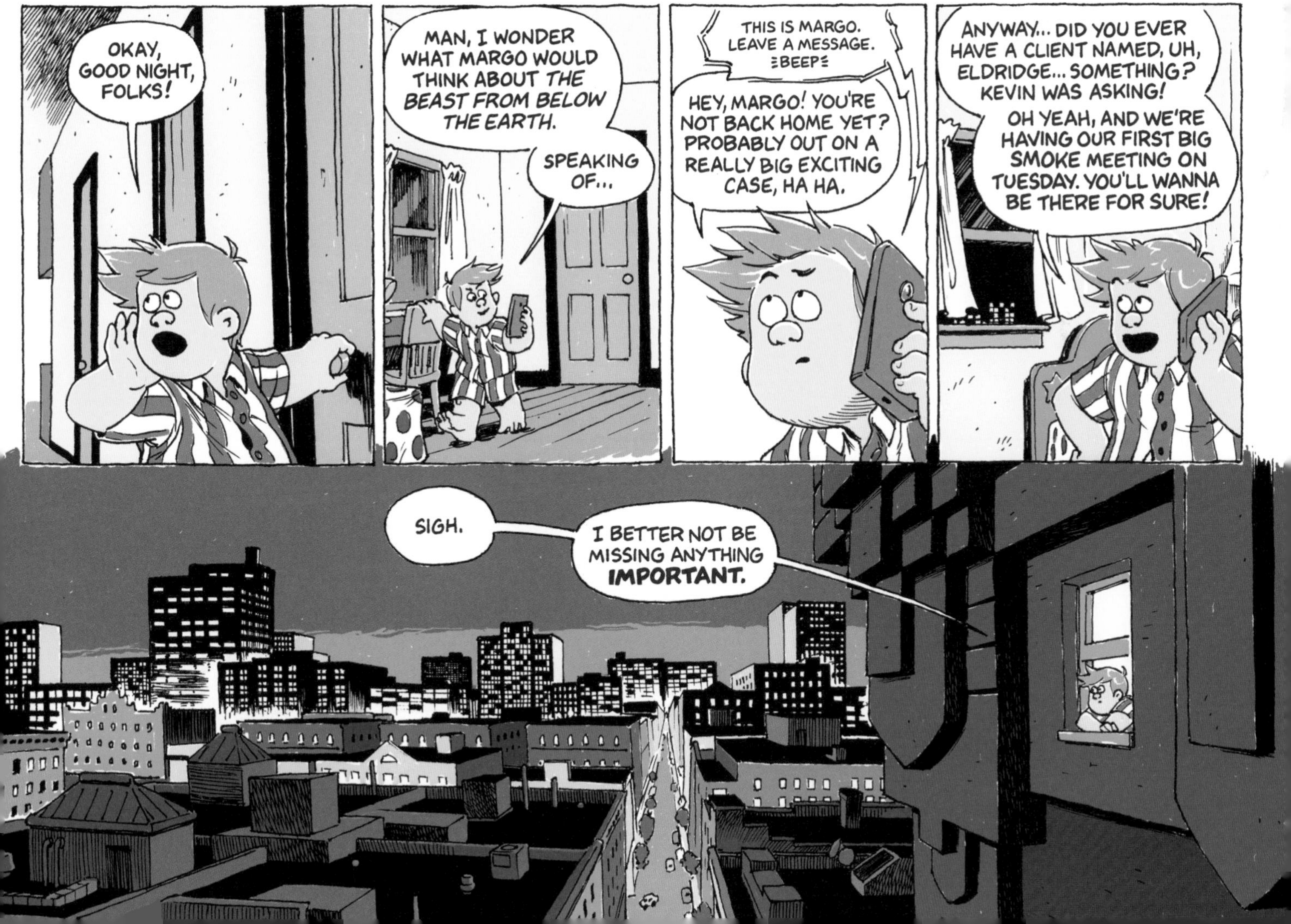
OKAY, GOOD NIGHT, FOLKS!
MAN, I WONDER WHAT MARGO WOULD THINK ABOUT THE BEAST FROM BELOW THE EARTH.
SPEAKING OF...
THIS IS MARGO. LEAVE A MESSAGE. BEEP
HEY, MARGO! YOU'RE NOT BACK HOME YET? PROBABLY OUT ON A REALLY BIG EXCITING CASE, HA HA.
ANYWAY... DID YOU EVER HAVE A CLIENT NAMED, UH, ELDRIDGE... SOMETHING? KEVIN WAS ASKING!
OH YEAH, AND WE'RE HAVING OUR FIRST BIG SMOKE MEETING ON TUESDAY. YOU'LL WANNA BE THERE FOR SURE!
SIGH.
I BETTER NOT BE MISSING ANYTHING IMPORTANT.

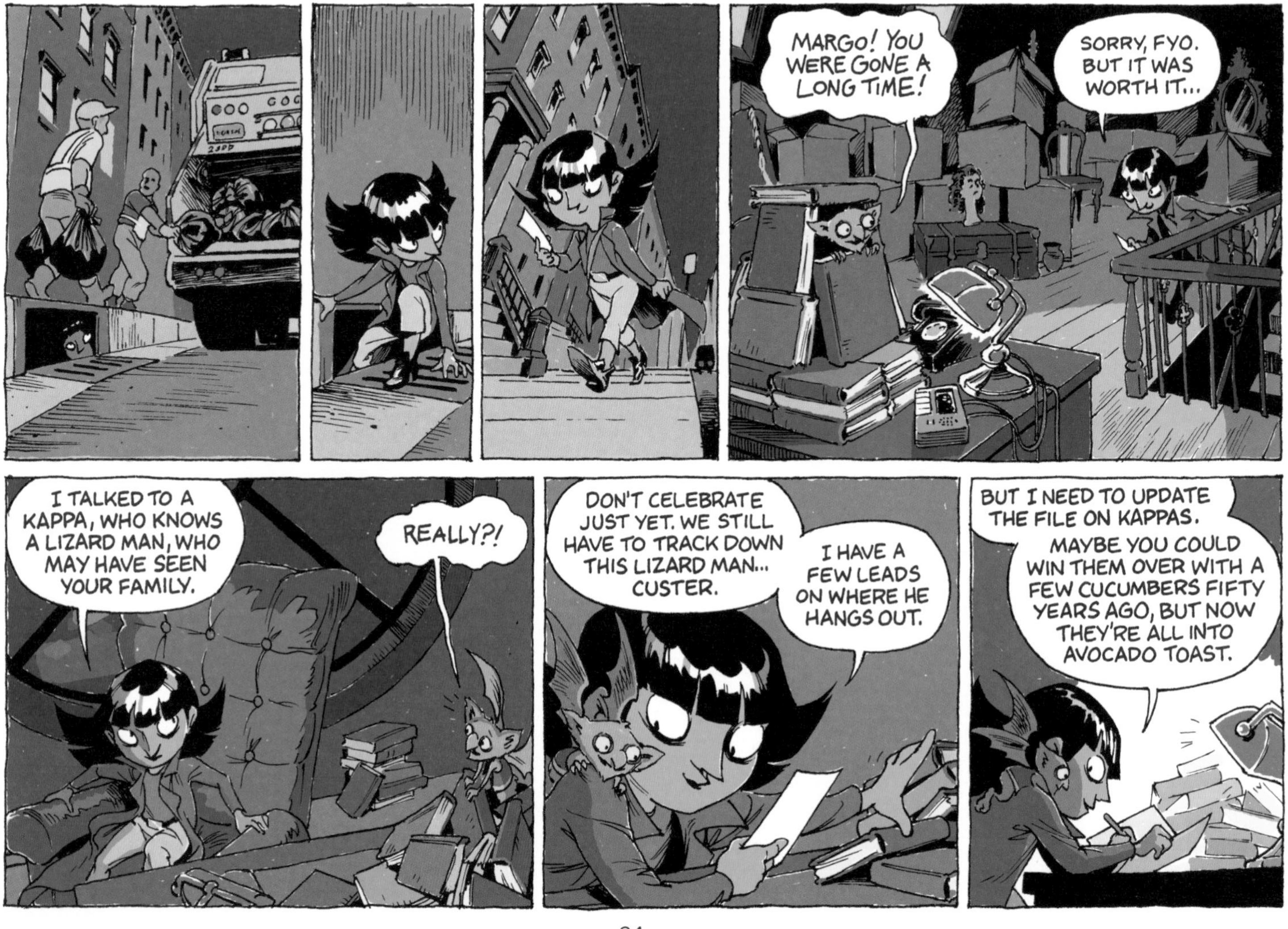
MARGO! YOU WERE GONE A LONG TIME!
SORRY, FYO. BUT IT WAS WORTH IT...
I TALKED TO A KAPPA, WHO KNOWS A LIZARD MAN, WHO MAY HAVE SEEN YOUR FAMILY.
REALLY?!
DON'T CELEBRATE JUST YET. WE STILL HAVE TO TRACK DOWN THIS LIZARD MAN... CUSTER.
I HAVE A FEW LEADS ON WHERE HE HANGS OUT.
BUT I NEED TO UPDATE THE FILE ON KAPPAS.
MAYBE YOU COULD WIN THEM OVER WITH A FEW CUCUMBERS FIFTY YEARS AGO, BUT NOW THEY'RE ALL INTO AVOCADO TOAST.

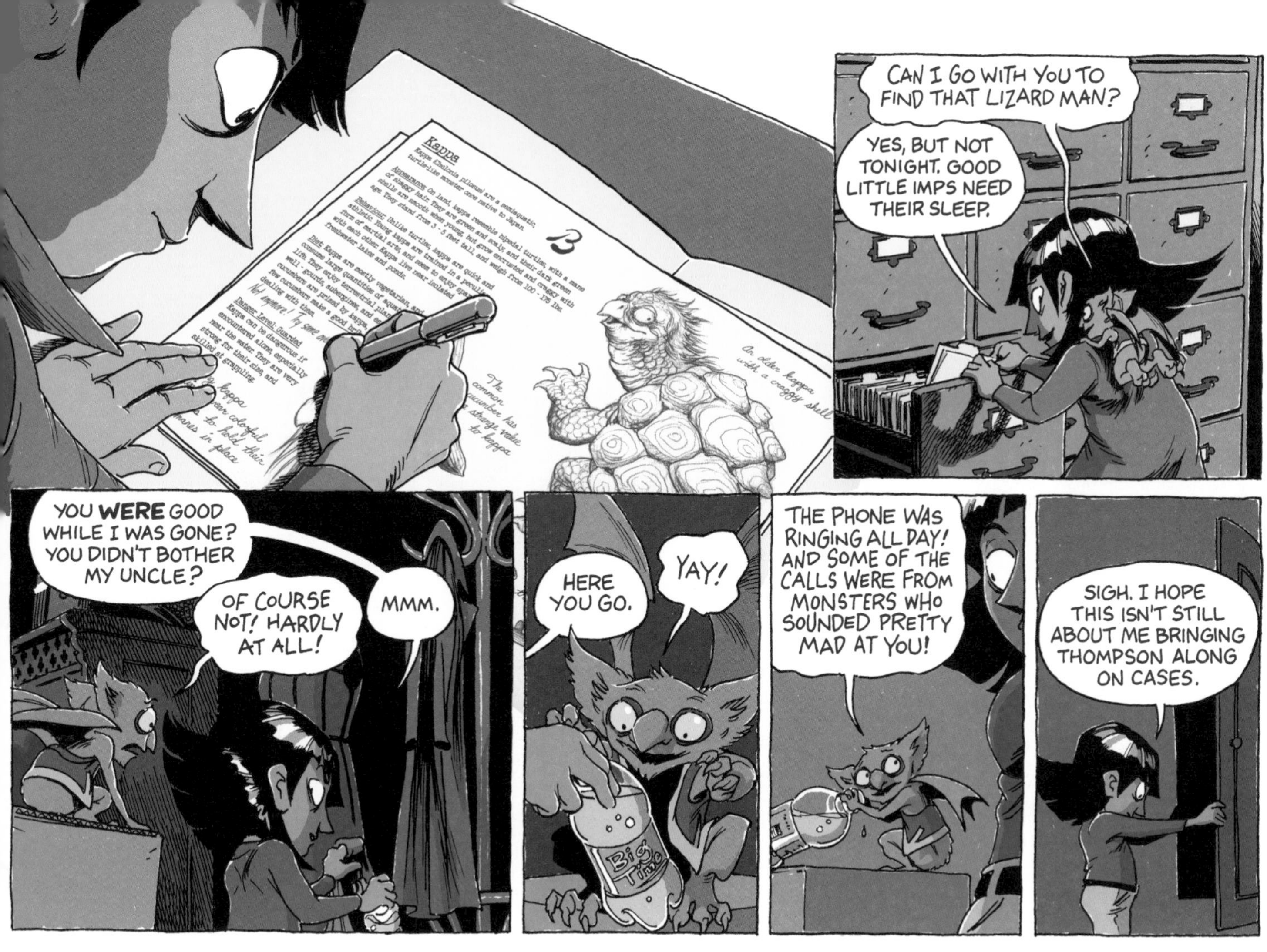
CAN I GO WITH YOU TO FIND THAT LIZARD MAN?
YES, BUT NOT TONIGHT. GOOD LITTLE IMPS NEED THEIR SLEEP.
YOU WERE GOOD WHILE I WAS GONE? YOU DIDN'T BOTHER MY UNCLE?
OF COURSE NOT! HARDLY AT ALL!
MMM.
HERE YOU GO.
YAY!
BIG TIME
THE PHONE WAS RINGING ALL DAY! AND SOME OF THE CALLS WERE FROM MONSTERS WHO SOUNDED PRETTY MAD AT YOU!
SIGH. I HOPE THIS ISN'T STILL ABOUT ME BRINGING THOMPSON ALONG ON CASES.

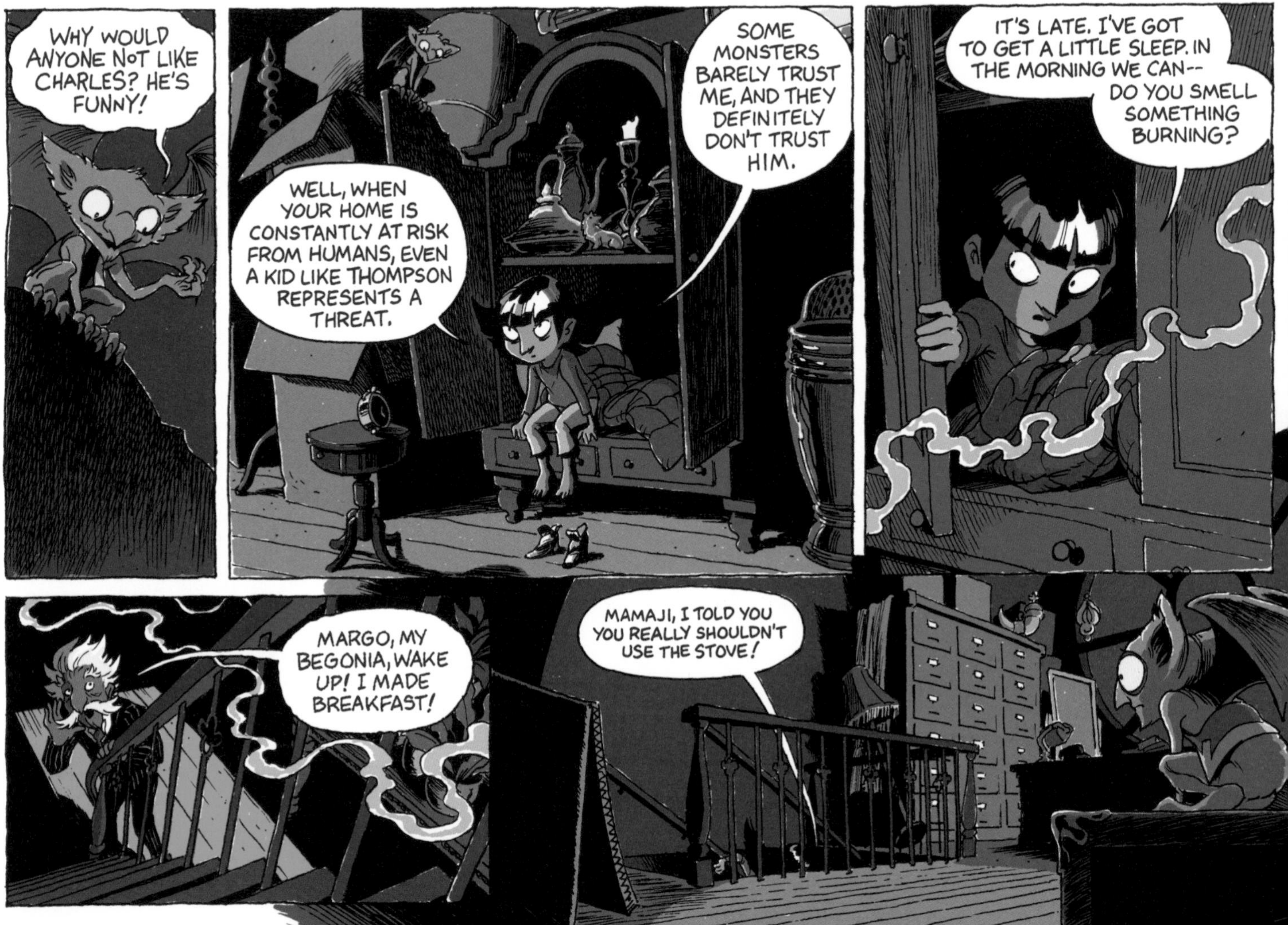
WHY WOULD ANYONE NOT LIKE CHARLES? HE'S FUNNY!
SOME MONSTERS BARELY TRUST ME, AND THEY DEFINITELY DON'T TRUST HIM.
WELL, WHEN YOUR HOME IS CONSTANTLY AT RISK FROM HUMANS, EVEN A KID LIKE THOMPSON REPRESENTS A THREAT.
IT'S LATE. I'VE GOT TO GET A LITTLE SLEEP. IN THE MORNING WE CAN--
DO YOU SMELL SOMETHING BURNING?
MARGO, MY BEGONIA, WAKE UP! I MADE BREAKFAST!
MAMAJI, I TOLD YOU YOU REALLY SHOULDN'T USE THE STOVE!

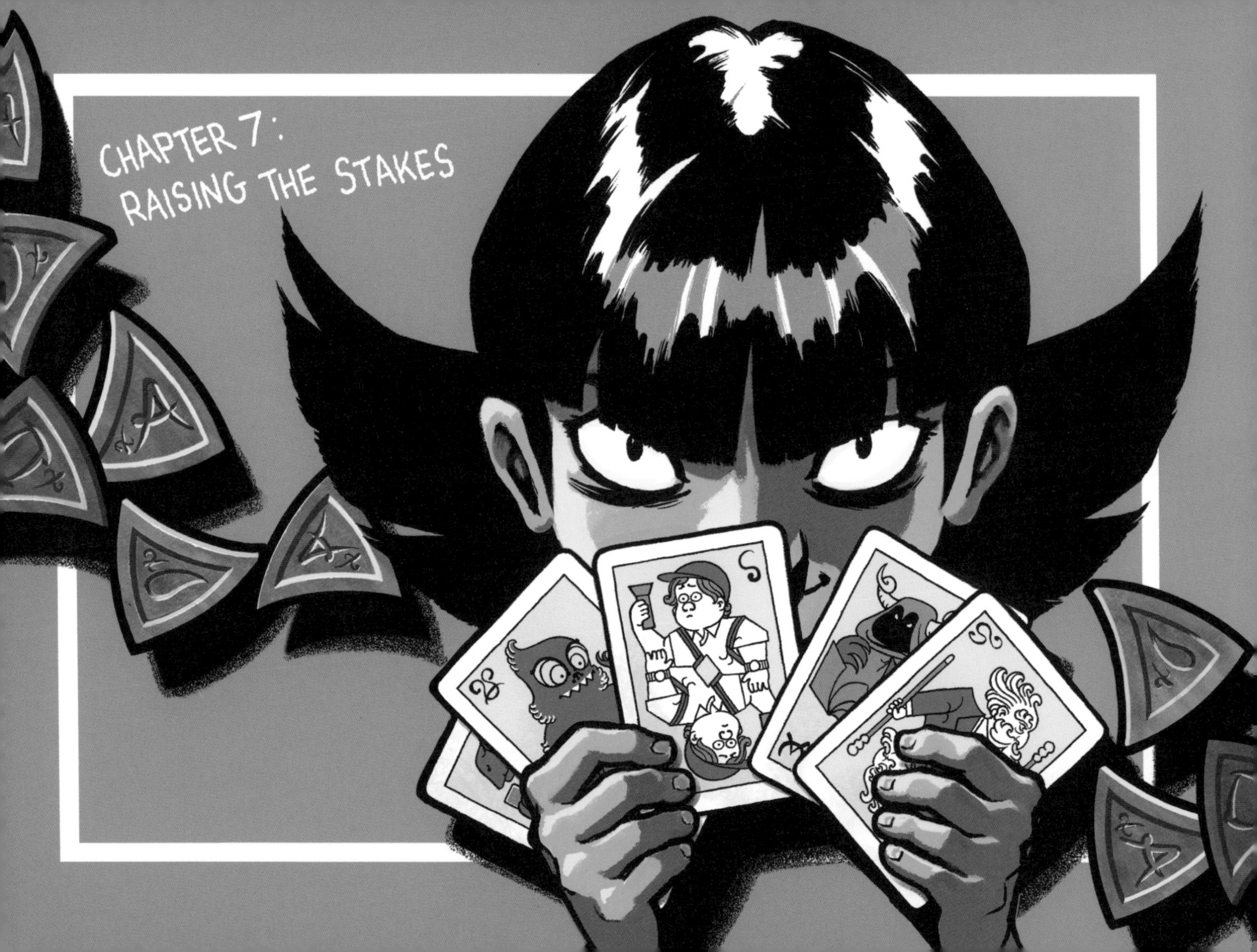
CHAPTER 7:
RAISING THE STAKES

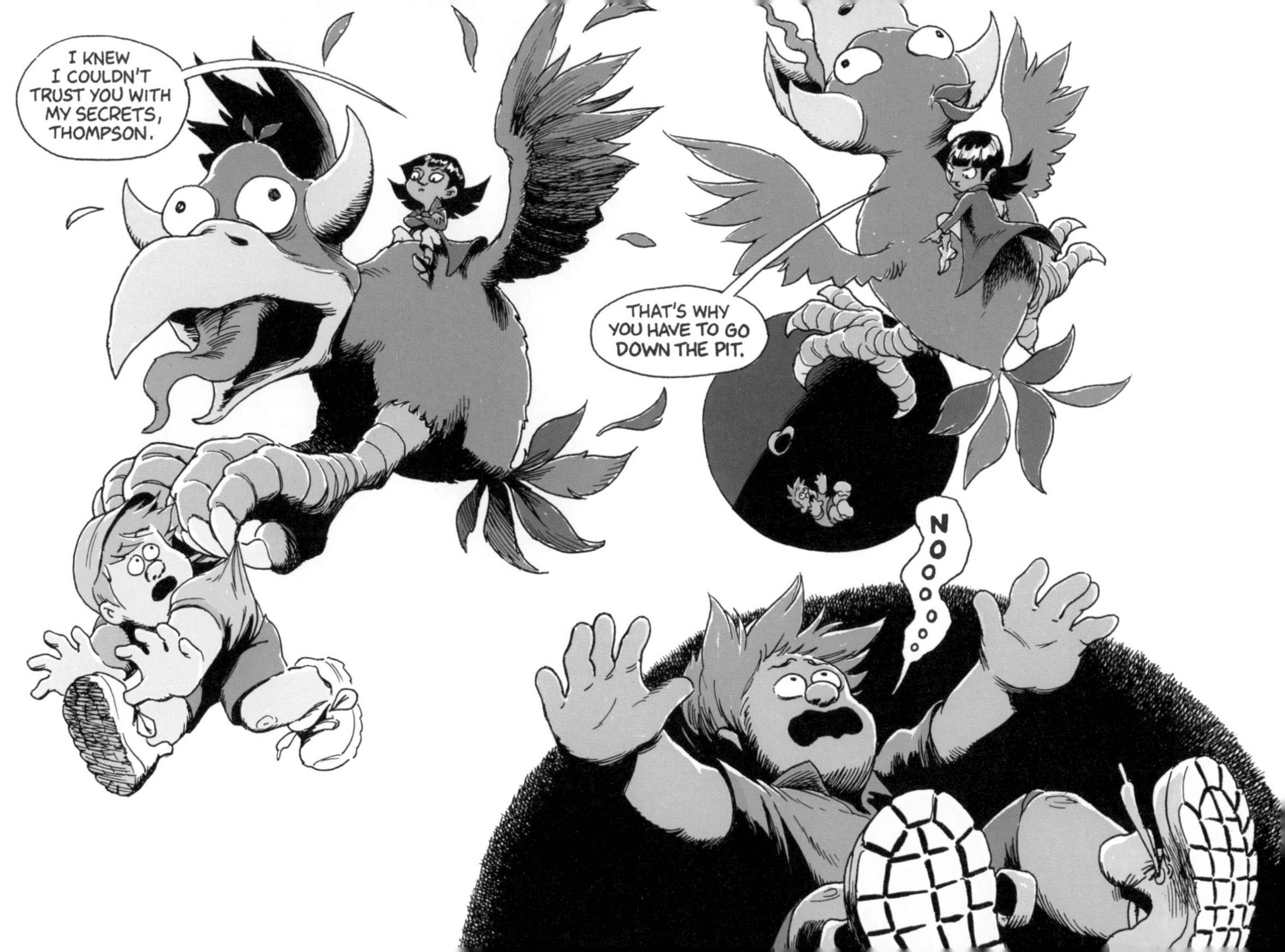
I KNEW I COULDN'T TRUST YOU WITH MY SECRETS, THOMPSON.
THAT'S WHY YOU HAVE TO GO DOWN THE PIT.
NOOOOOO

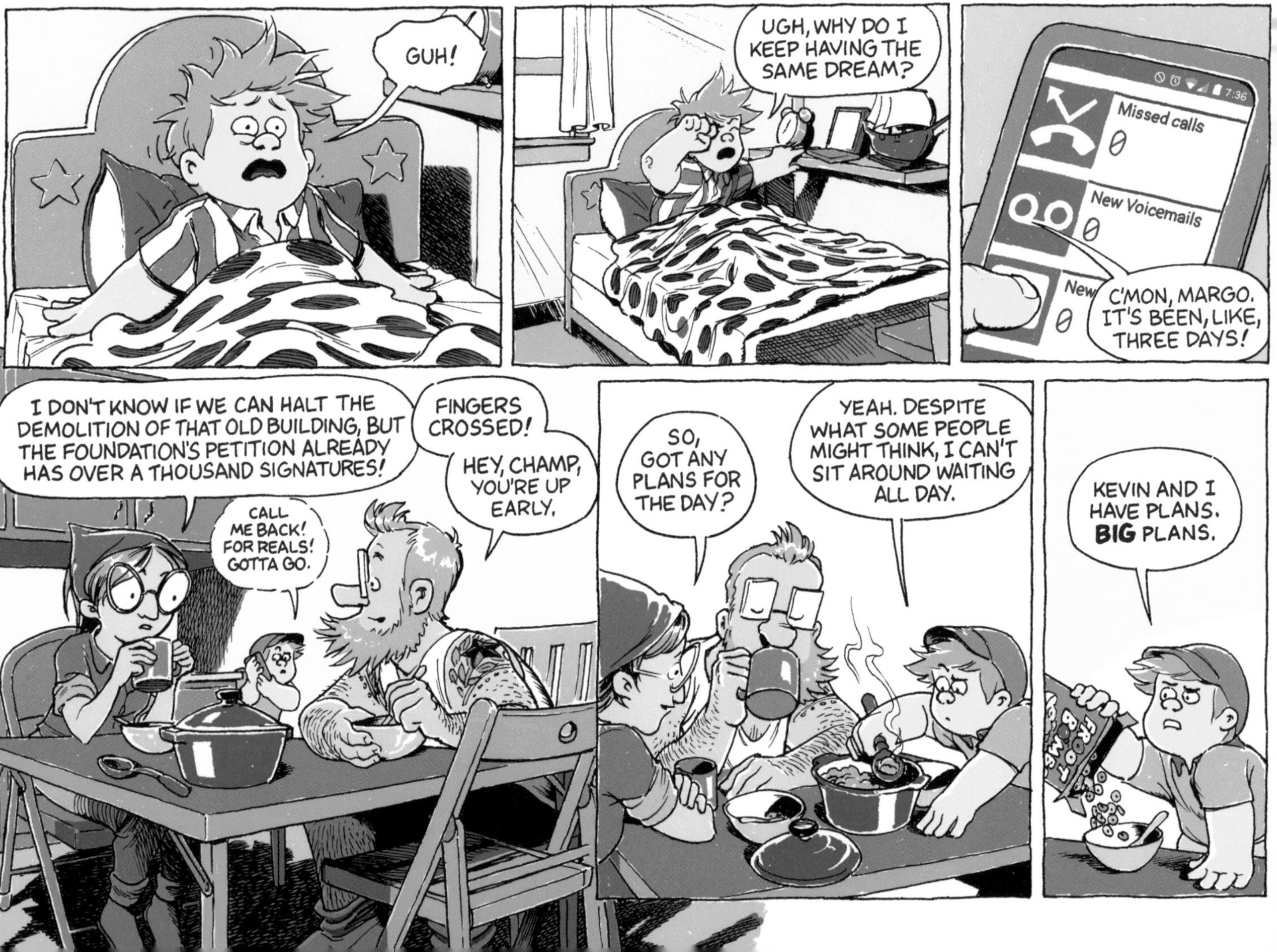
GUH!
UGH, WHY DO I KEEP HAVING THE SAME DREAM?
7:36
Missed calls
0
New Voicemails
0
New
0
C'MON, MARGO. IT'S BEEN, LIKE, THREE DAYS!
I DON'T KNOW IF WE CAN HALT THE DEMOLITION OF THAT OLD BUILDING, BUT THE FOUNDATION'S PETITION ALREADY HAS OVER A THOUSAND SIGNATURES!
FINGERS CROSSED!
HEY, CHAMP, YOU'RE UP EARLY.
CALL ME BACK! FOR REALS! GOTTA GO.
SO, GOT ANY PLANS FOR THE DAY?
YEAH. DESPITE WHAT SOME PEOPLE MIGHT THINK, I CAN'T SIT AROUND WAITING ALL DAY.
KEVIN AND I HAVE PLANS. **BIG** PLANS.
FROOT BOMBS

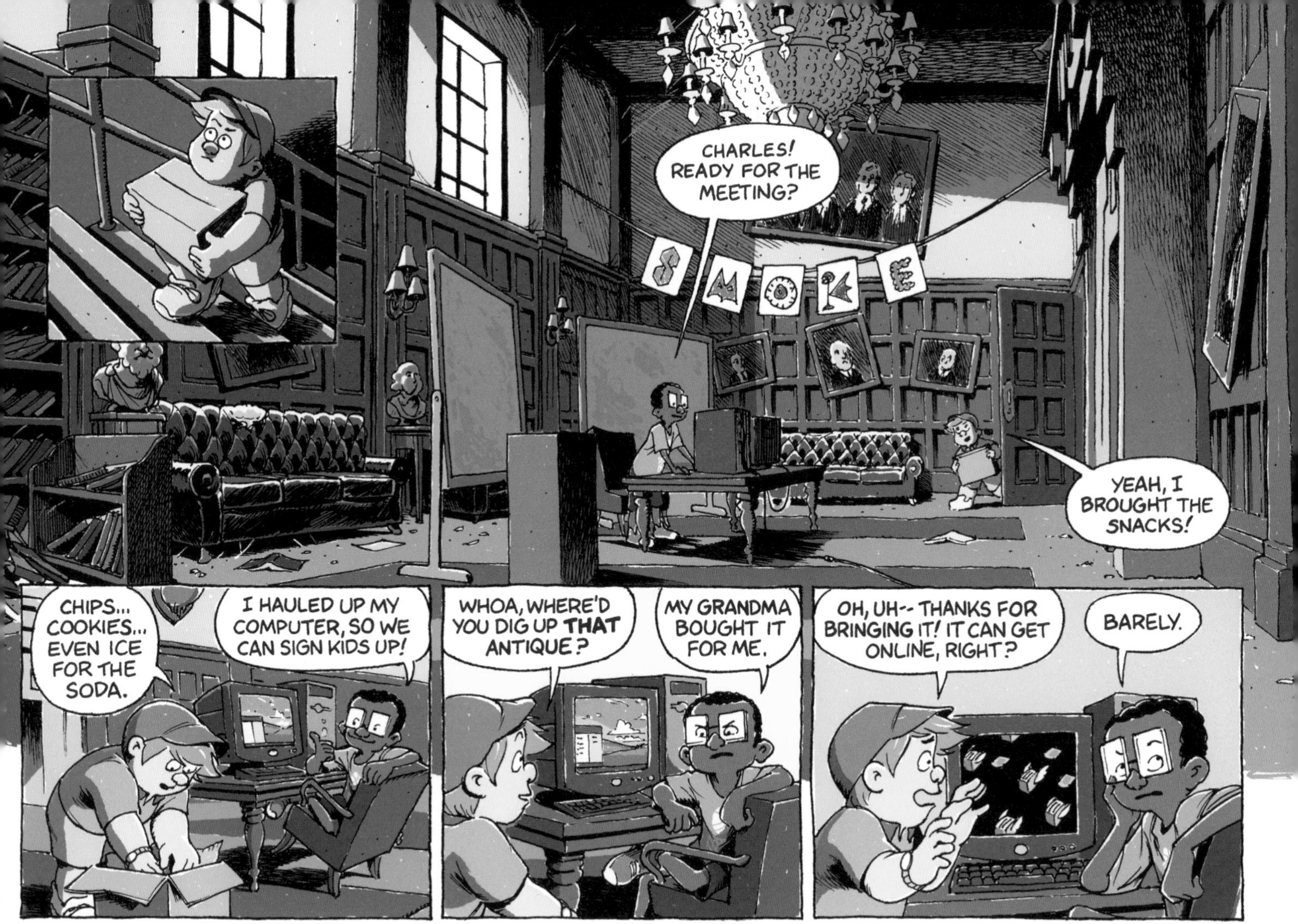
CHARLES! READY FOR THE MEETING?
YEAH, I BROUGHT THE SNACKS!
CHIPS... COOKIES... EVEN ICE FOR THE SODA.
I HAULED UP MY COMPUTER, SO WE CAN SIGN KIDS UP!
WHOA, WHERE'D YOU DIG UP **THAT** ANTIQUE?
MY GRANDMA BOUGHT IT FOR ME.
OH, UH-- THANKS FOR BRINGING IT! IT CAN GET ONLINE, RIGHT?
BARELY.

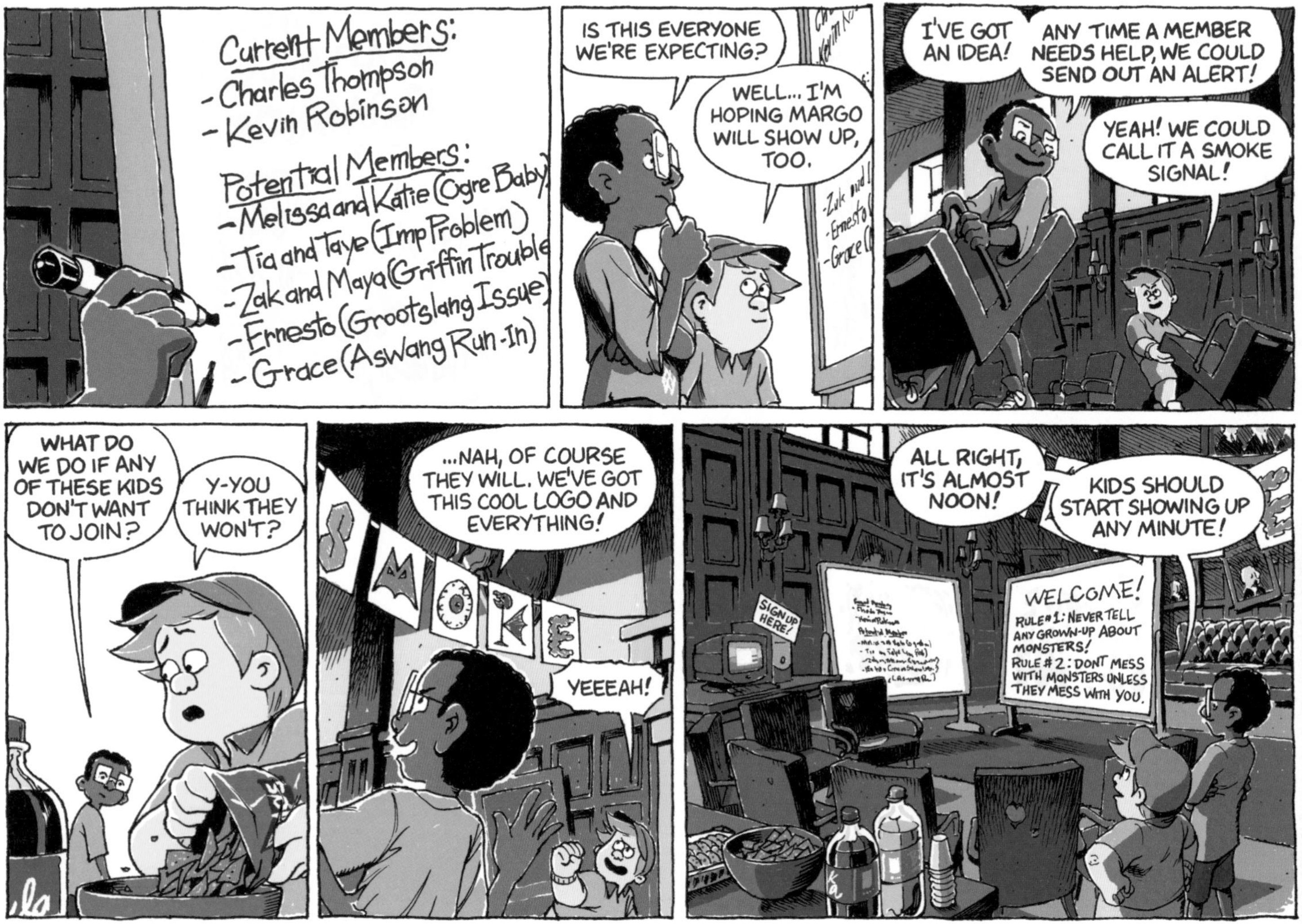
Current Members:
- Charles Thompson
- Kevin Robinson
Potential Members:
- Melissa and Katie (Ogre Baby)
- Tia and Taye (Imp Problem)
- Zak and Maya (Griffin Trouble)
- Ernesto (Grootslang Issue)
- Grace (Aswang Run-In)
IS THIS EVERYONE WE'RE EXPECTING?
WELL... I'M HOPING MARGO WILL SHOW UP, TOO.
I'VE GOT AN IDEA!
ANY TIME A MEMBER NEEDS HELP, WE COULD SEND OUT AN ALERT!
YEAH! WE COULD CALL IT A SMOKE SIGNAL!
WHAT DO WE DO IF ANY OF THESE KIDS DON'T WANT TO JOIN?
Y-YOU THINK THEY WON'T?
...NAH, OF COURSE THEY WILL. WE'VE GOT THIS COOL LOGO AND EVERYTHING!
YEEEAH!
ALL RIGHT, IT'S ALMOST NOON!
KIDS SHOULD START SHOWING UP ANY MINUTE!
SIGN UP HERE!
WELCOME!
RULE #1: NEVER TELL ANY GROWN-UP ABOUT MONSTERS!
RULE #2: DONT MESS WITH MONSTERS UNLESS THEY MESS WITH YOU.

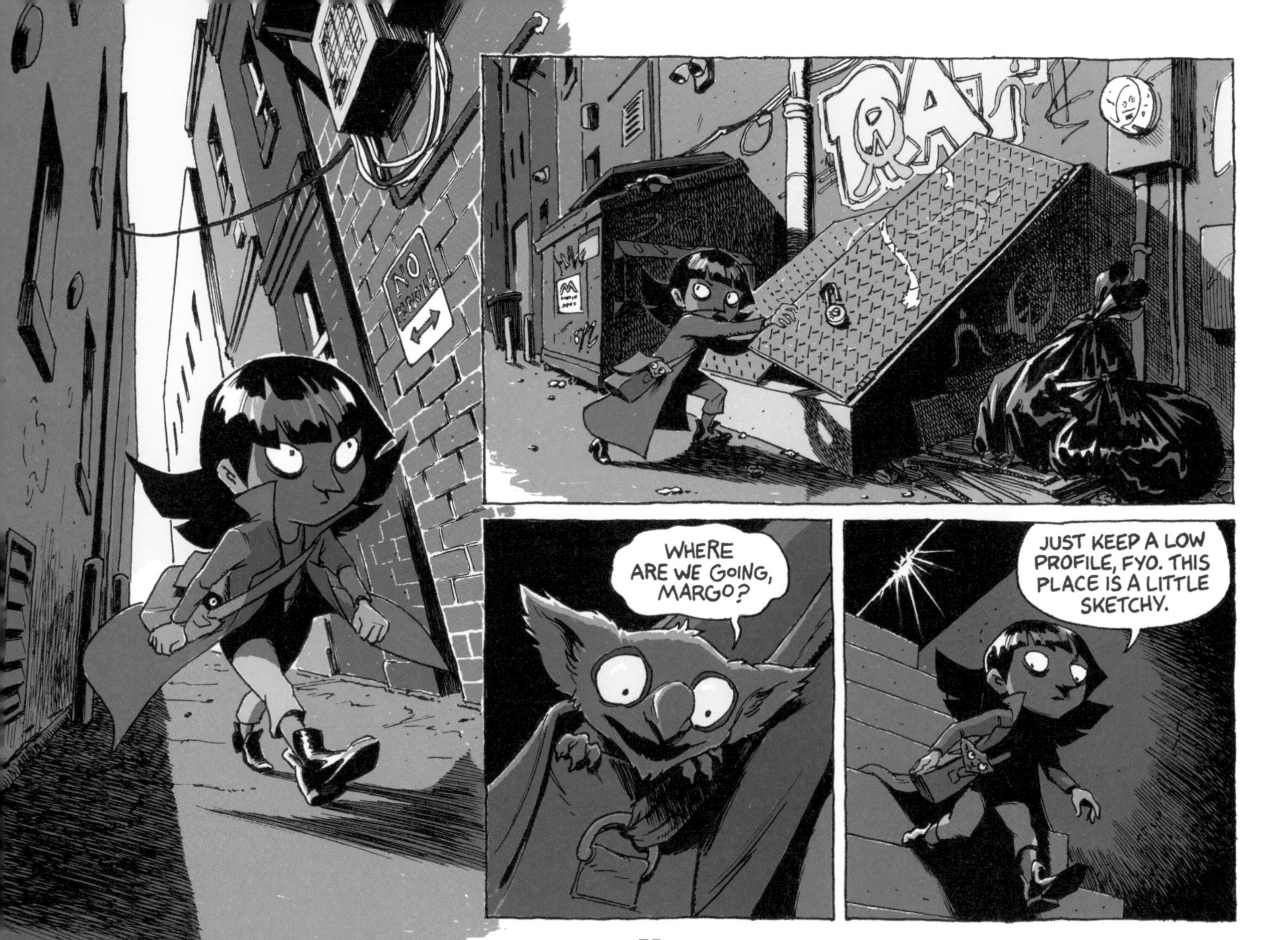
NO PARKING
WHERE ARE WE GOING, MARGO?
JUST KEEP A LOW PROFILE, FYO. THIS PLACE IS A LITTLE SKETCHY.

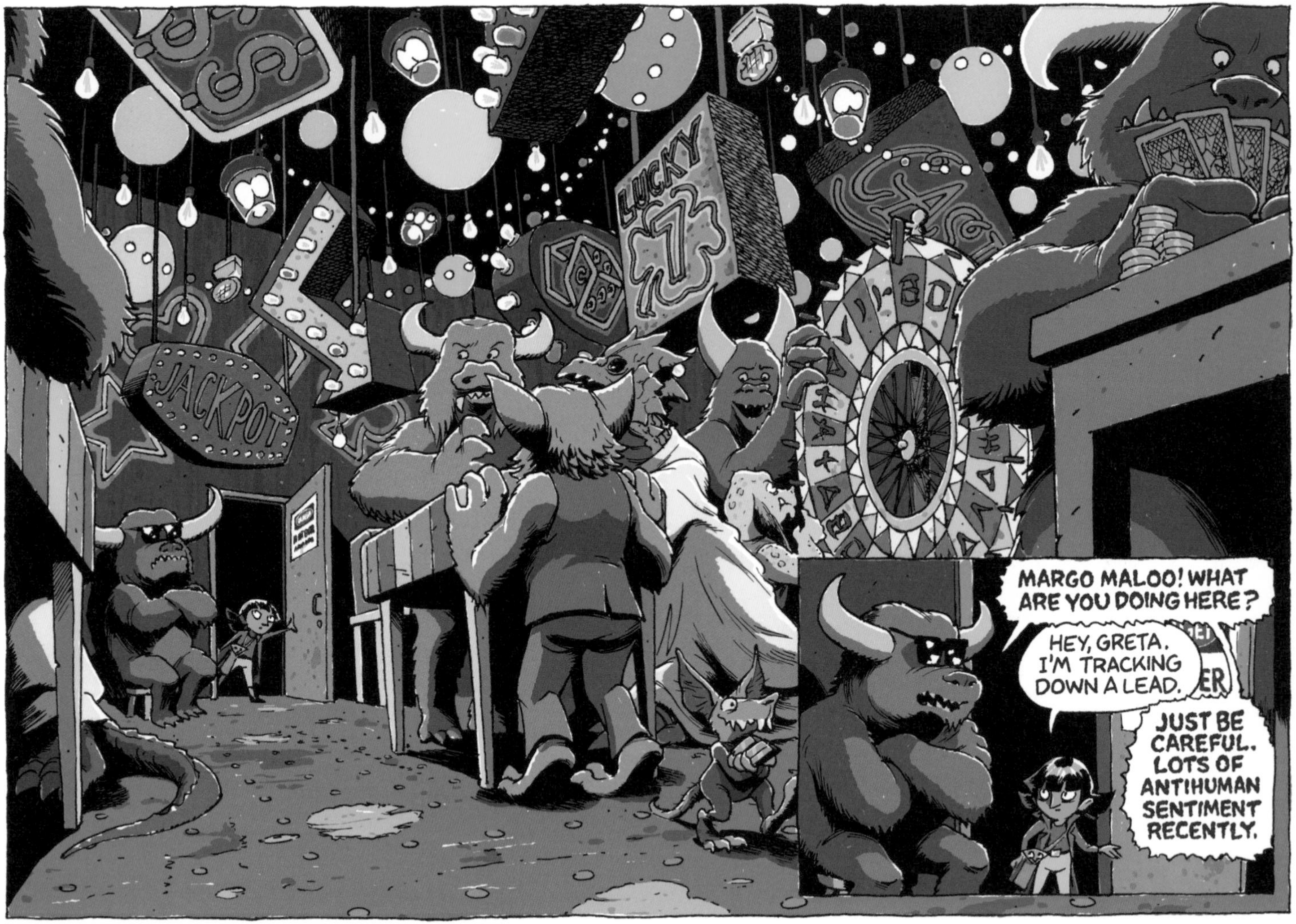
JACKPOT
LUCKY 7
MARGO MALOO! WHAT ARE YOU DOING HERE?
HEY, GRETA. I'M TRACKING DOWN A LEAD.
JUST BE CAREFUL. LOTS OF ANTIHUMAN SENTIMENT RECENTLY.

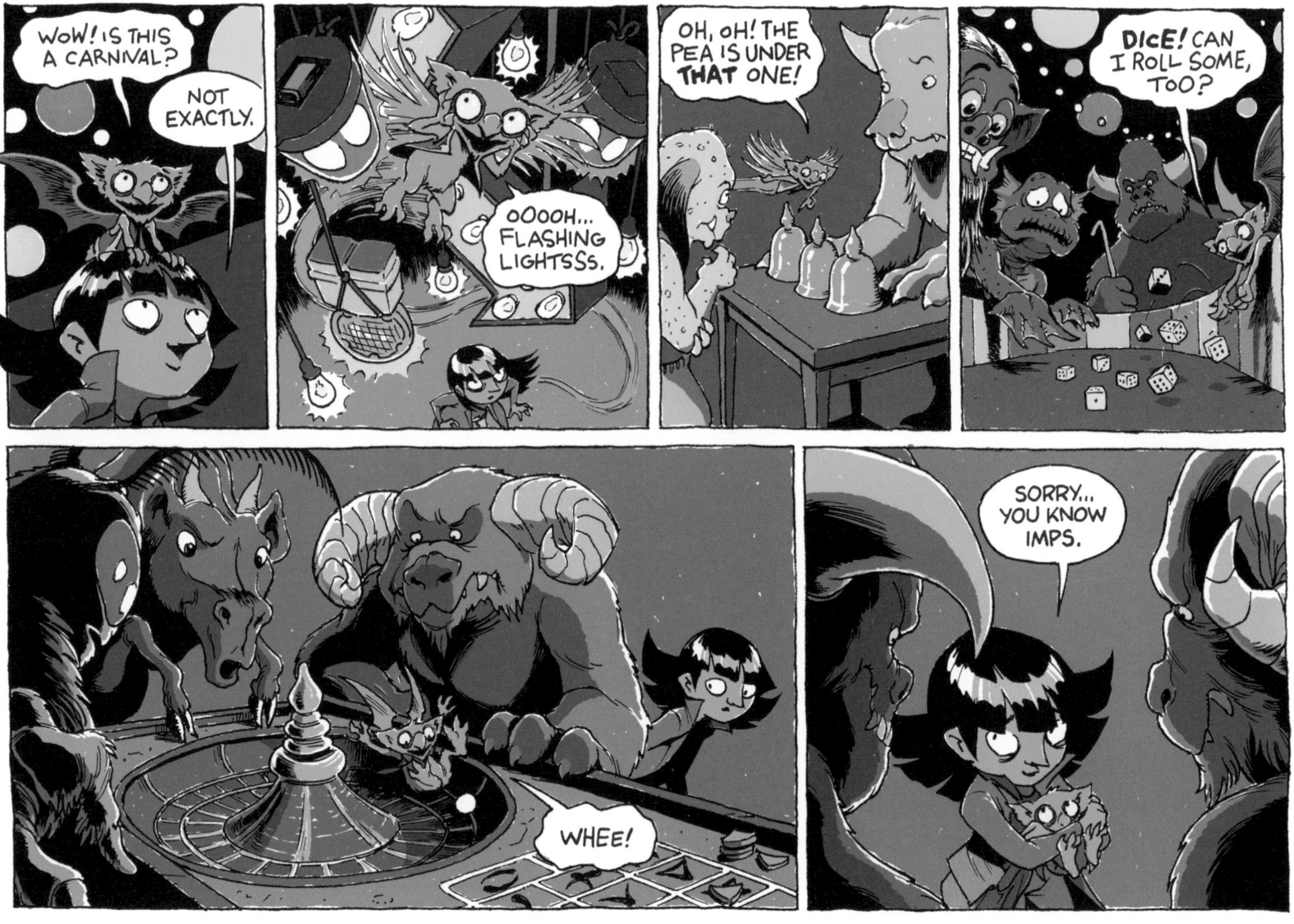
WOW! IS THIS A CARNIVAL?
NOT EXACTLY.
OOOOH... FLASHING LIGHTSSS.
OH, OH! THE PEA IS UNDER **THAT** ONE!
DICE! CAN I ROLL SOME, TOO?
WHEE!
SORRY... YOU KNOW IMPS.

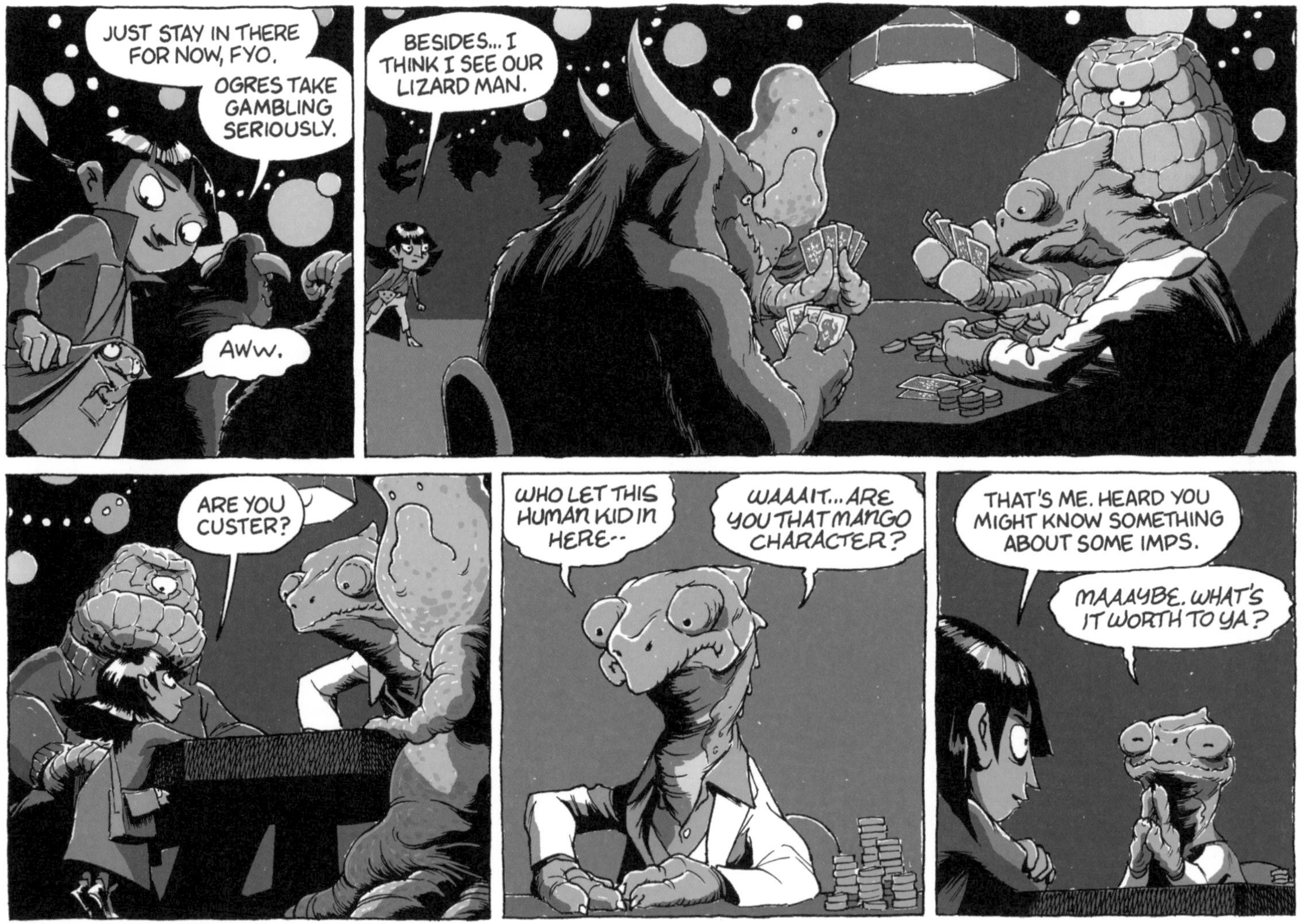
JUST STAY IN THERE FOR NOW, FYO.
OGRES TAKE GAMBLING SERIOUSLY.
AWW.
BESIDES... I THINK I SEE OUR LIZARD MAN.
ARE YOU CUSTER?
WHO LET THIS HUMAN KID IN HERE--
WAAAIT... ARE YOU THAT MANGO CHARACTER?
THAT'S ME. HEARD YOU MIGHT KNOW SOMETHING ABOUT SOME IMPS.
MAAAYBE. WHAT'S IT WORTH TO YA?

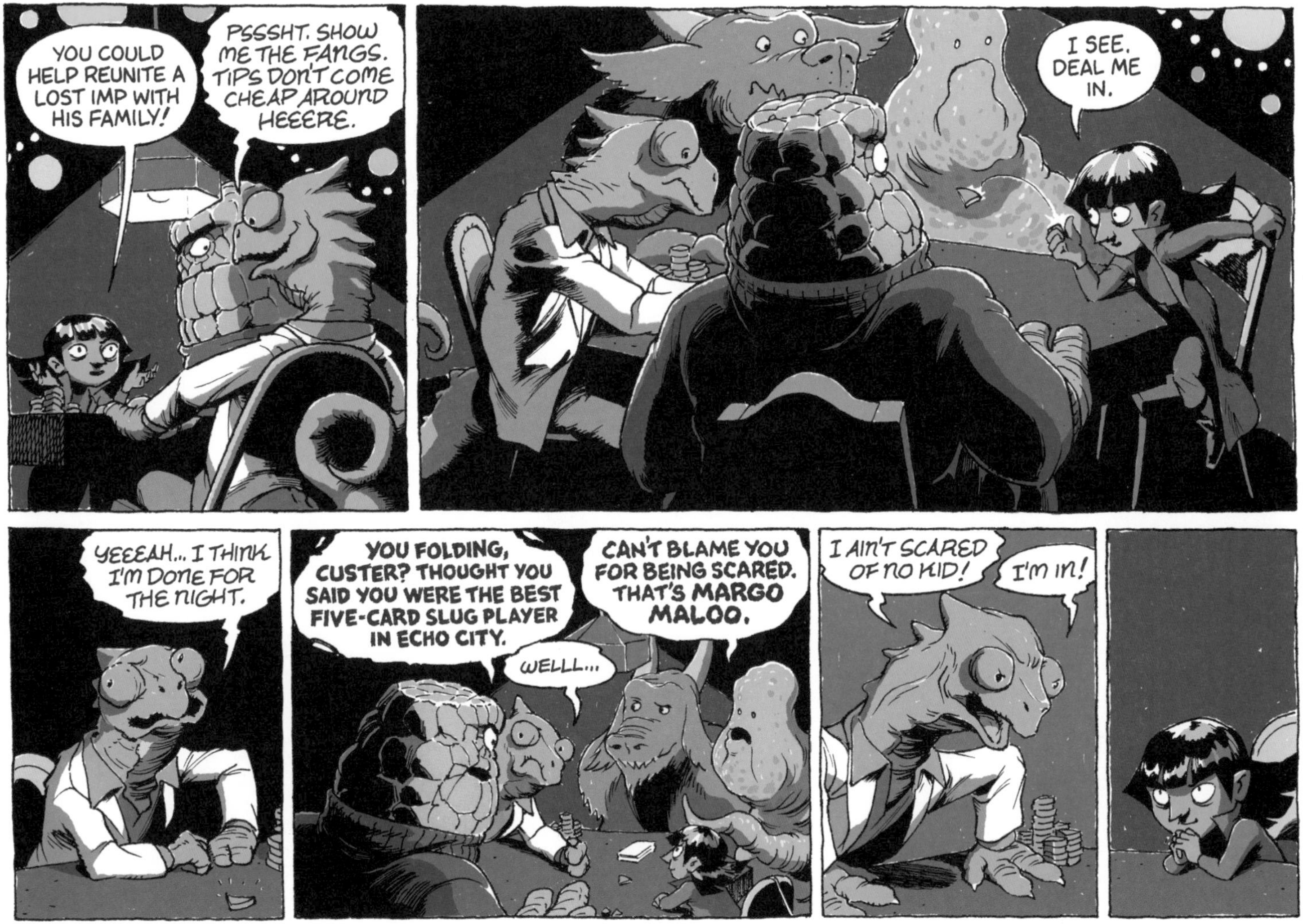

YOU COULD HELP REUNITE A LOST IMP WITH HIS FAMILY!
PSSSHT. SHOW ME THE FANGS. TIPS DON'T COME CHEAP AROUND HEEERE.
I SEE. DEAL ME IN.
YEEEAH... I THINK I'M DONE FOR THE NIGHT.
YOU FOLDING, CUSTER? THOUGHT YOU SAID YOU WERE THE BEST FIVE-CARD SLUG PLAYER IN ECHO CITY.
WELLL...
CAN'T BLAME YOU FOR BEING SCARED. THAT'S MARGO MALOO.
I AIN'T SCARED OF NO KID!
I'M IN!

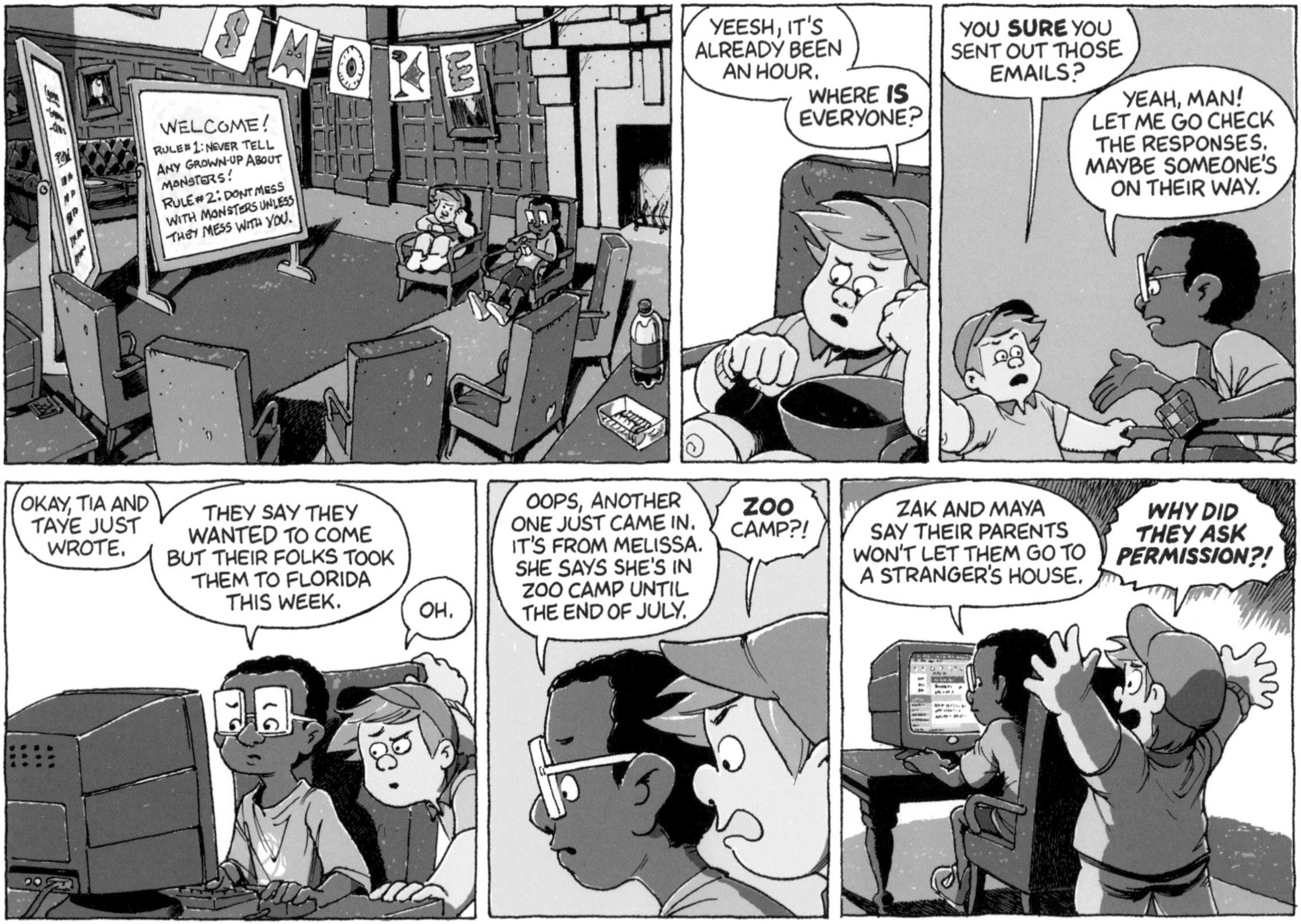
SMOKE
WELCOME! RULE#1: NEVER TELL ANY GROWN-UP ABOUT MONSTERS! RULE#2: DONT MESS WITH MONSTERS UNLESS THEY MESS WITH YOU.
YEESH, IT'S ALREADY BEEN AN HOUR.
WHERE **IS** EVERYONE?
YOU **SURE** YOU SENT OUT THOSE EMAILS?
YEAH, MAN! LET ME GO CHECK THE RESPONSES. MAYBE SOMEONE'S ON THEIR WAY.
OKAY, TIA AND TAYE JUST WROTE.
THEY SAY THEY WANTED TO COME BUT THEIR FOLKS TOOK THEM TO FLORIDA THIS WEEK.
OH.
OOPS, ANOTHER ONE JUST CAME IN. IT'S FROM MELISSA. SHE SAYS SHE'S IN ZOO CAMP UNTIL THE END OF JULY.
ZOO CAMP?!
ZAK AND MAYA SAY THEIR PARENTS WON'T LET THEM GO TO A STRANGER'S HOUSE.
WHY DID THEY ASK PERMISSION?!

WELL, GREAT. WHAT KIND OF A SECRET ORGANIZATION ONLY HAS TWO MEMBERS?!

SORRY, MAN. MOST KIDS JUST DON'T GET TO RUN WILD AROUND THE CITY LIKE YOU!

SIGN UP HERE

HEY, GUYS!

YO, MARCUS, WHAT'S UP?

I KEEP FORGETTING YOU GUYS KNOW EACH OTHER NOW.

ARE YOU HAVING A PARTY? WHAT'S SMOKE?

SMOK

rent Members:

IT'S THE SECRET MONSTER ORGANIZATION FOR KIDS EVERYWHERE. AT LEAST THAT'S WHAT IT'S **SUPPOSED** TO BE.

OOH, CAN I JOIN?

UHHH...

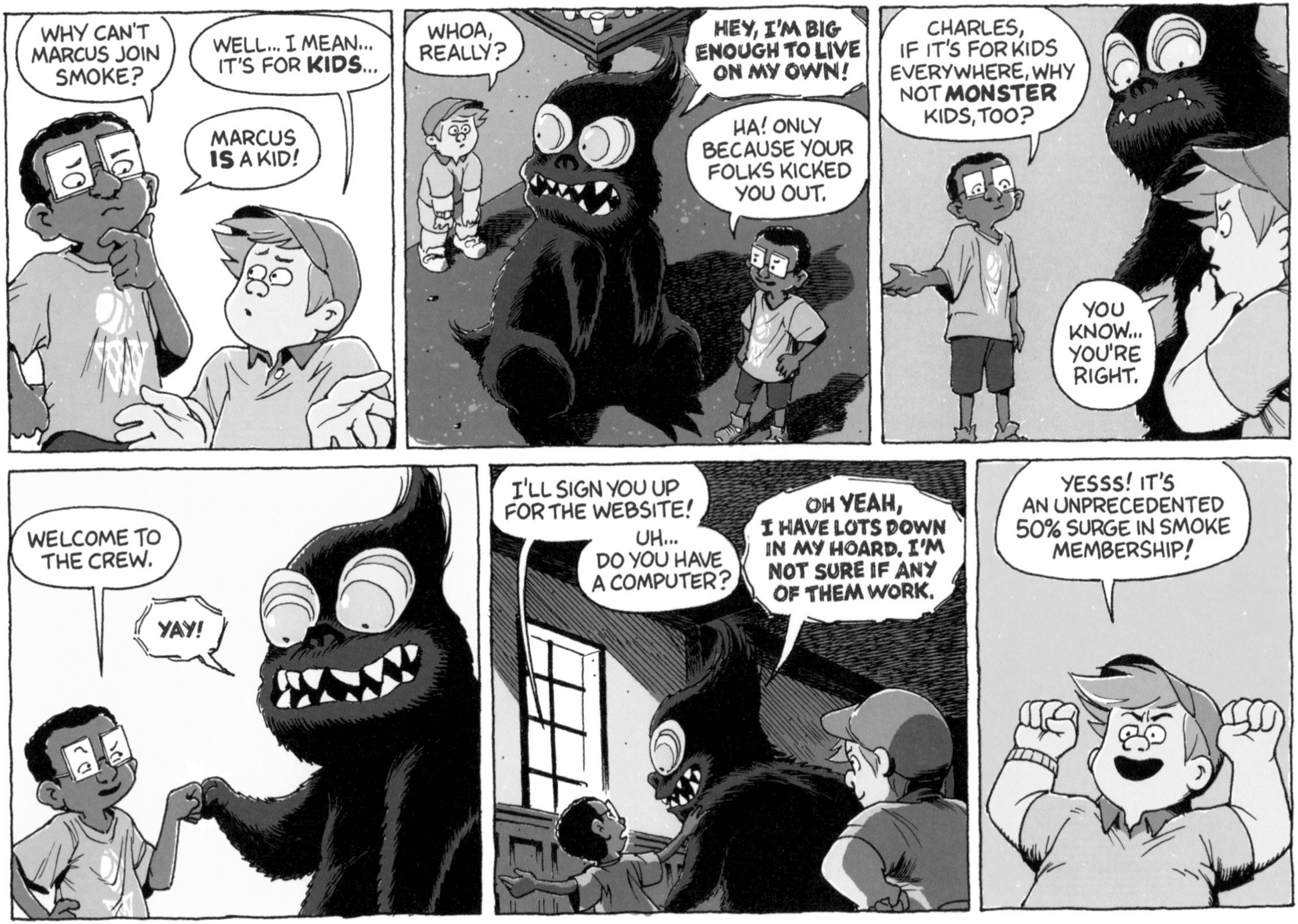
WHY CAN'T MARCUS JOIN SMOKE?
WELL... I MEAN... IT'S FOR **KIDS**...
MARCUS **IS** A KID!
WHOA, REALLY?
HEY, I'M BIG ENOUGH TO LIVE ON MY OWN!
HA! ONLY BECAUSE YOUR FOLKS KICKED YOU OUT.
CHARLES, IF IT'S FOR KIDS EVERYWHERE, WHY NOT **MONSTER** KIDS, TOO?
YOU KNOW... YOU'RE RIGHT.
WELCOME TO THE CREW.
YAY!
I'LL SIGN YOU UP FOR THE WEBSITE!
UH... DO YOU HAVE A COMPUTER?
OH YEAH, I HAVE LOTS DOWN IN MY HOARD. I'M NOT SURE IF ANY OF THEM WORK.
YESSS! IT'S AN UNPRECEDENTED 50% SURGE IN SMOKE MEMBERSHIP!

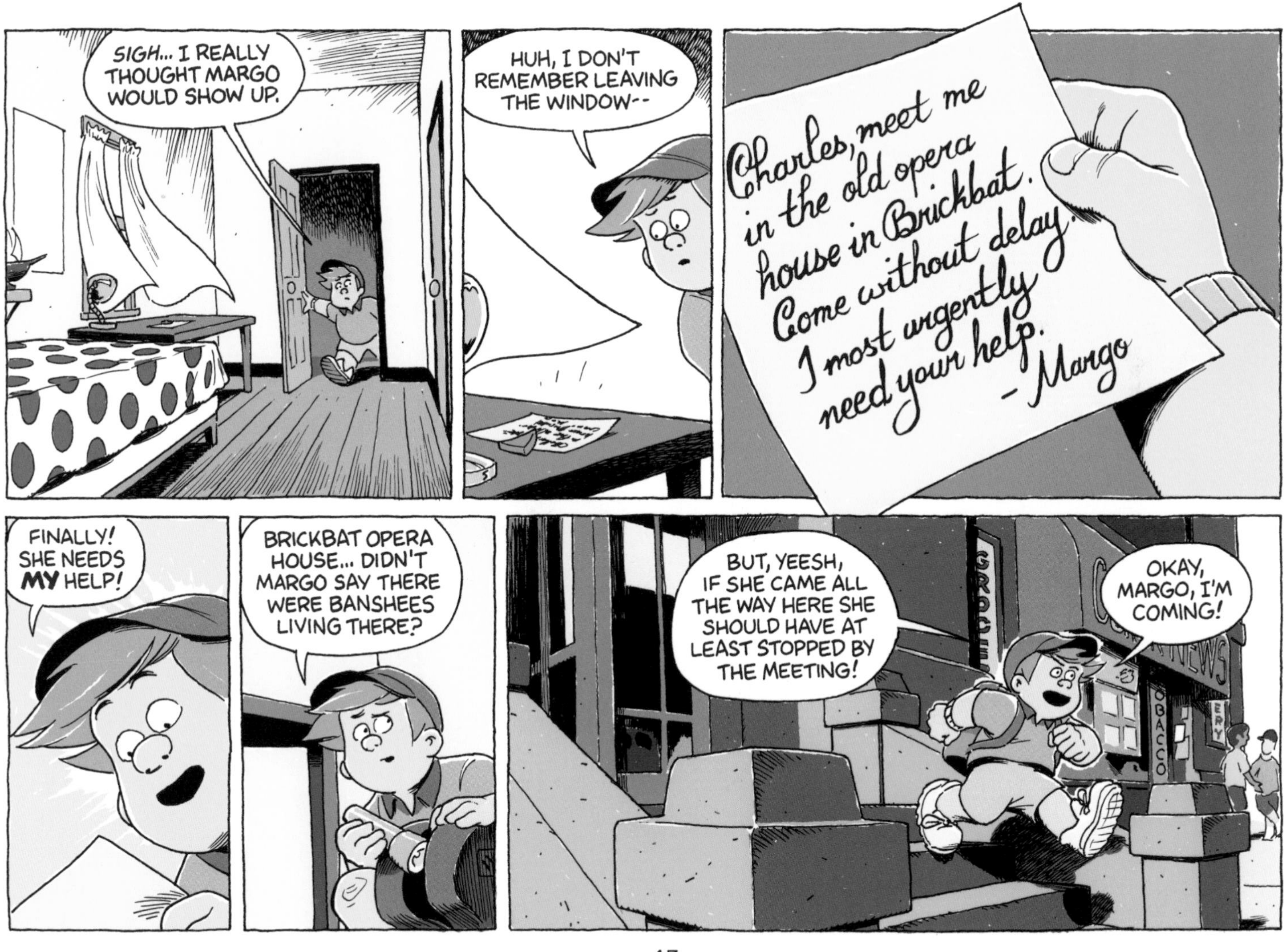
SIGH... I REALLY THOUGHT MARGO WOULD SHOW UP.
HUH, I DON'T REMEMBER LEAVING THE WINDOW--
Charles, meet me in the old opera house in Brickbat. Come without delay. I most urgently need your help. - Margo
FINALLY! SHE NEEDS **MY** HELP!
BRICKBAT OPERA HOUSE... DIDN'T MARGO SAY THERE WERE BANSHEES LIVING THERE?
BUT, YEESH, IF SHE CAME ALL THE WAY HERE SHE SHOULD HAVE AT LEAST STOPPED BY THE MEETING!
OKAY, MARGO, I'M COMING!

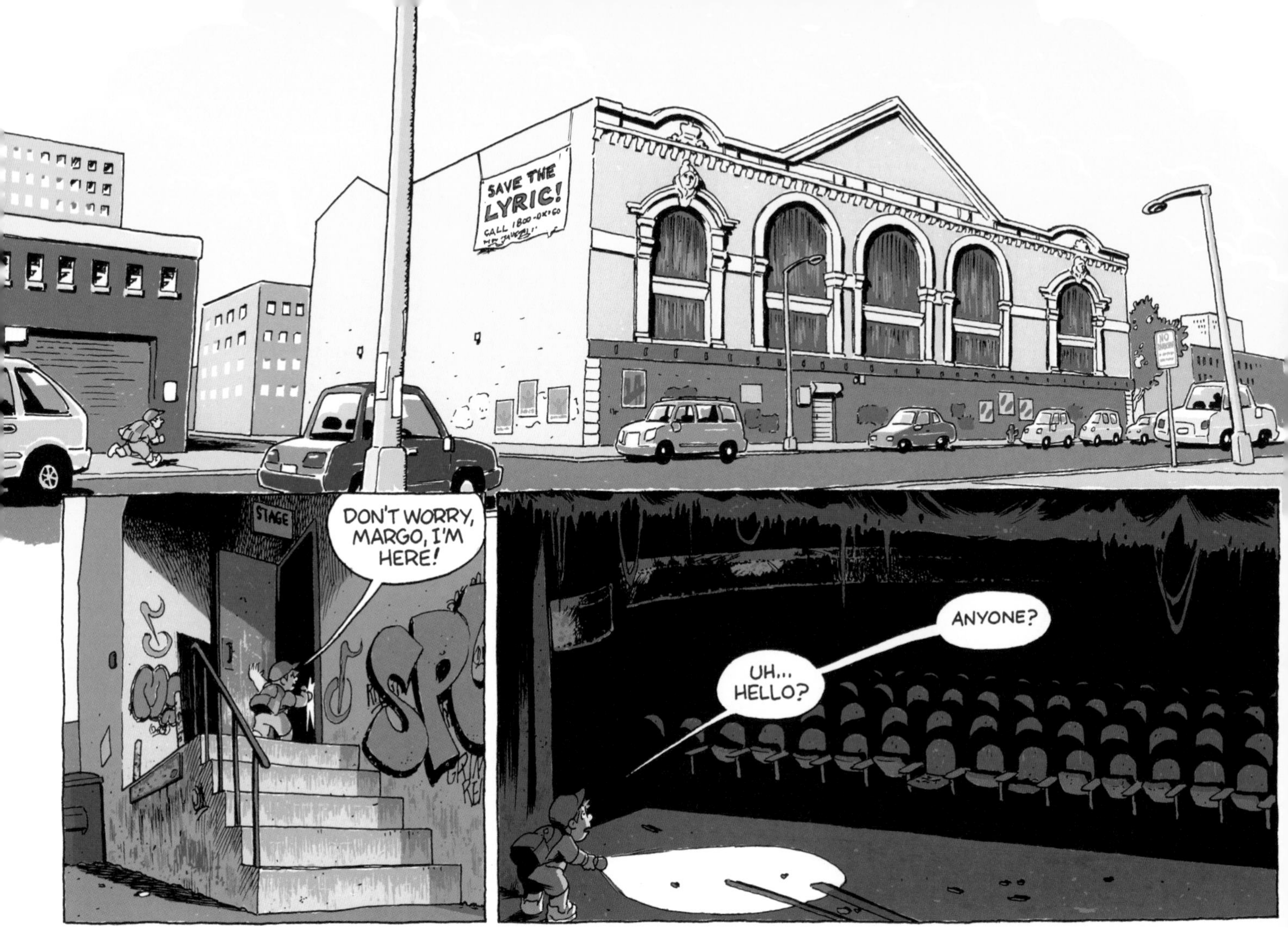
SAVE THE LYRIC!
STAGE
DON'T WORRY, MARGO, I'M HERE!
UH... HELLO?
ANYONE?

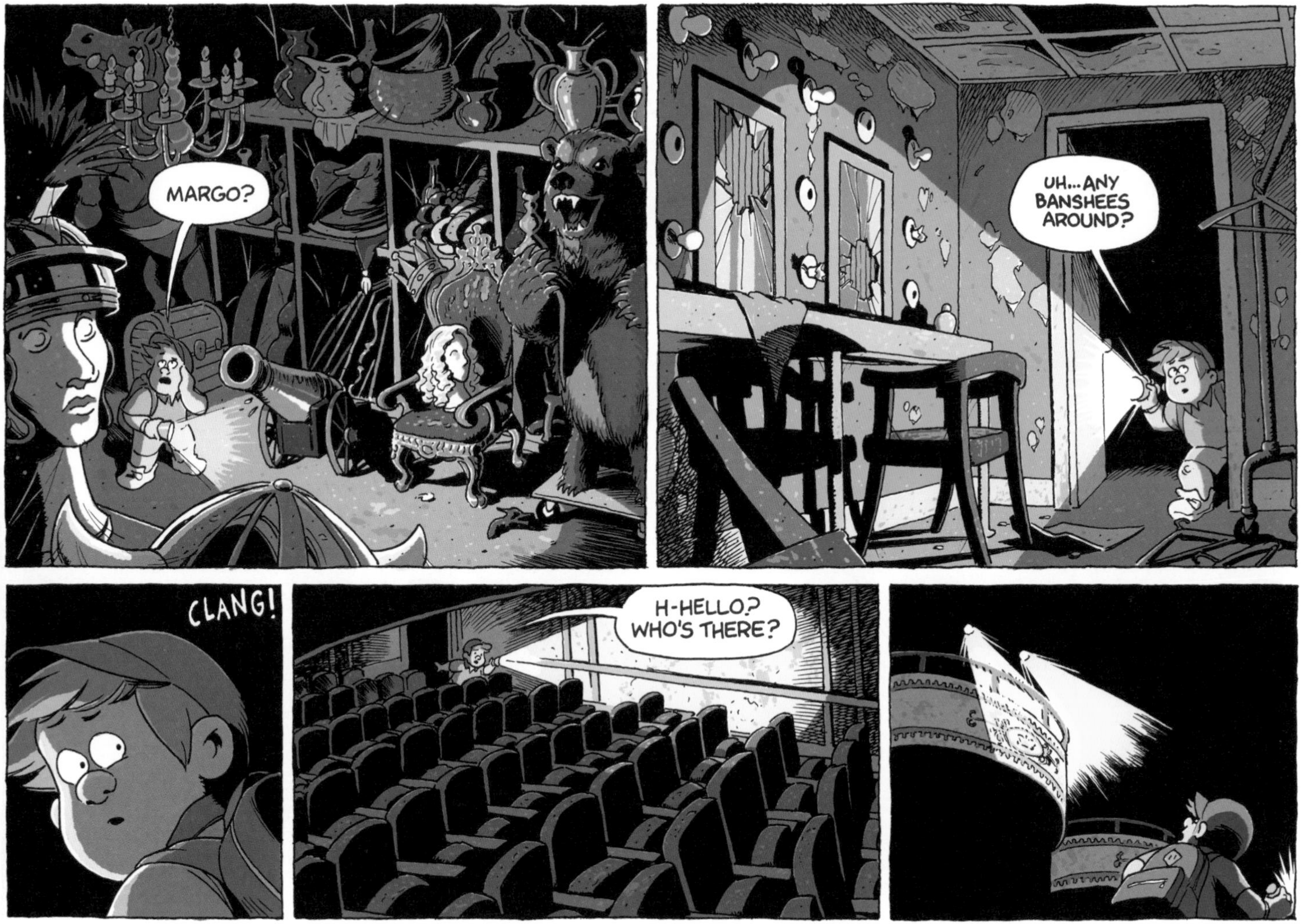
MARGO?
UH... ANY BANSHEES AROUND?
CLANG!
H-HELLO? WHO'S THERE?

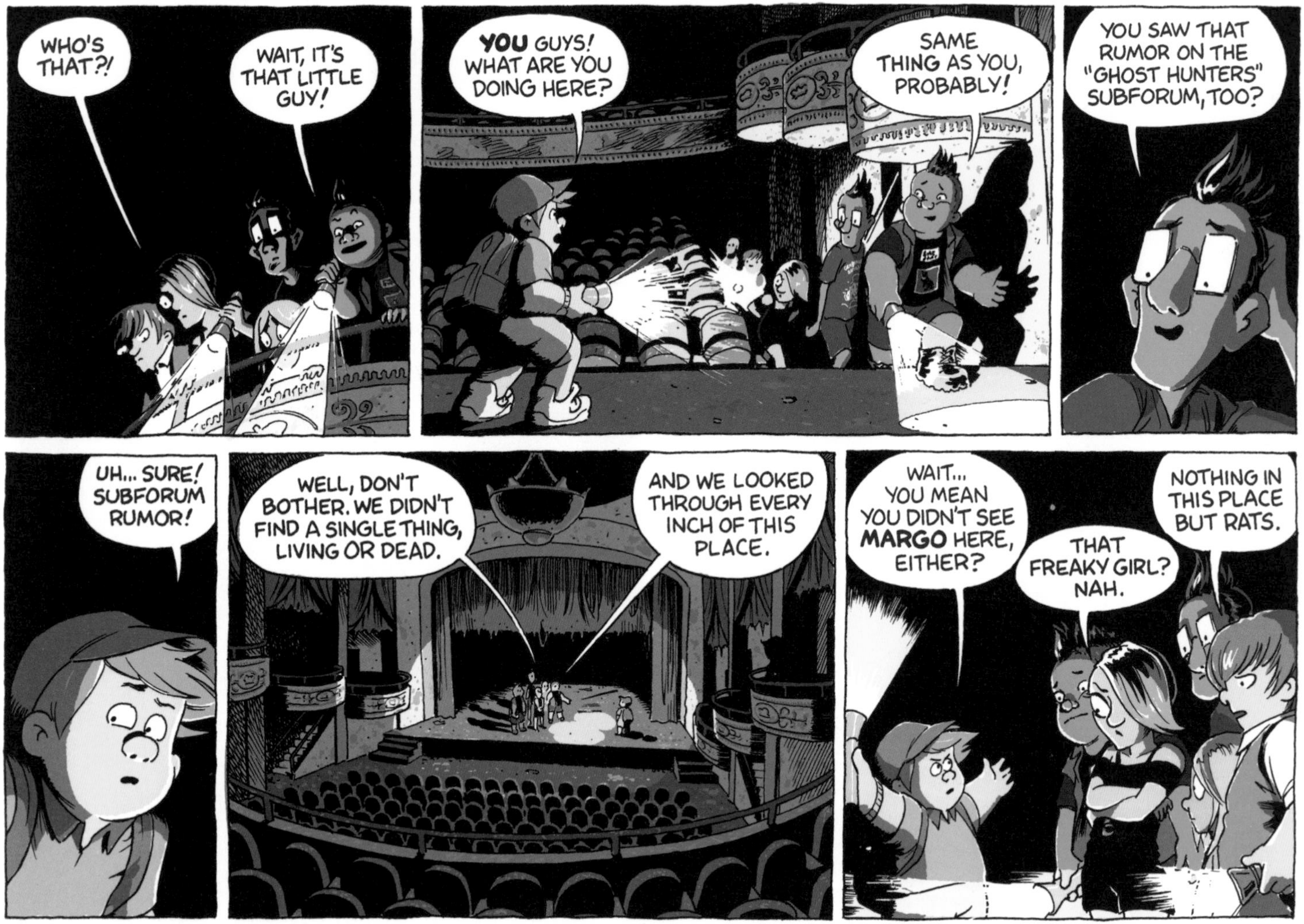
WHO'S THAT?!
WAIT, IT'S THAT LITTLE GUY!
YOU GUYS! WHAT ARE YOU DOING HERE?
SAME THING AS YOU, PROBABLY!
YOU SAW THAT RUMOR ON THE "GHOST HUNTERS" SUBFORUM, TOO?
UH... SURE! SUBFORUM RUMOR!
WELL, DON'T BOTHER. WE DIDN'T FIND A SINGLE THING, LIVING OR DEAD.
AND WE LOOKED THROUGH EVERY INCH OF THIS PLACE.
WAIT... YOU MEAN YOU DIDN'T SEE MARGO HERE, EITHER?
THAT FREAKY GIRL? NAH.
NOTHING IN THIS PLACE BUT RATS.

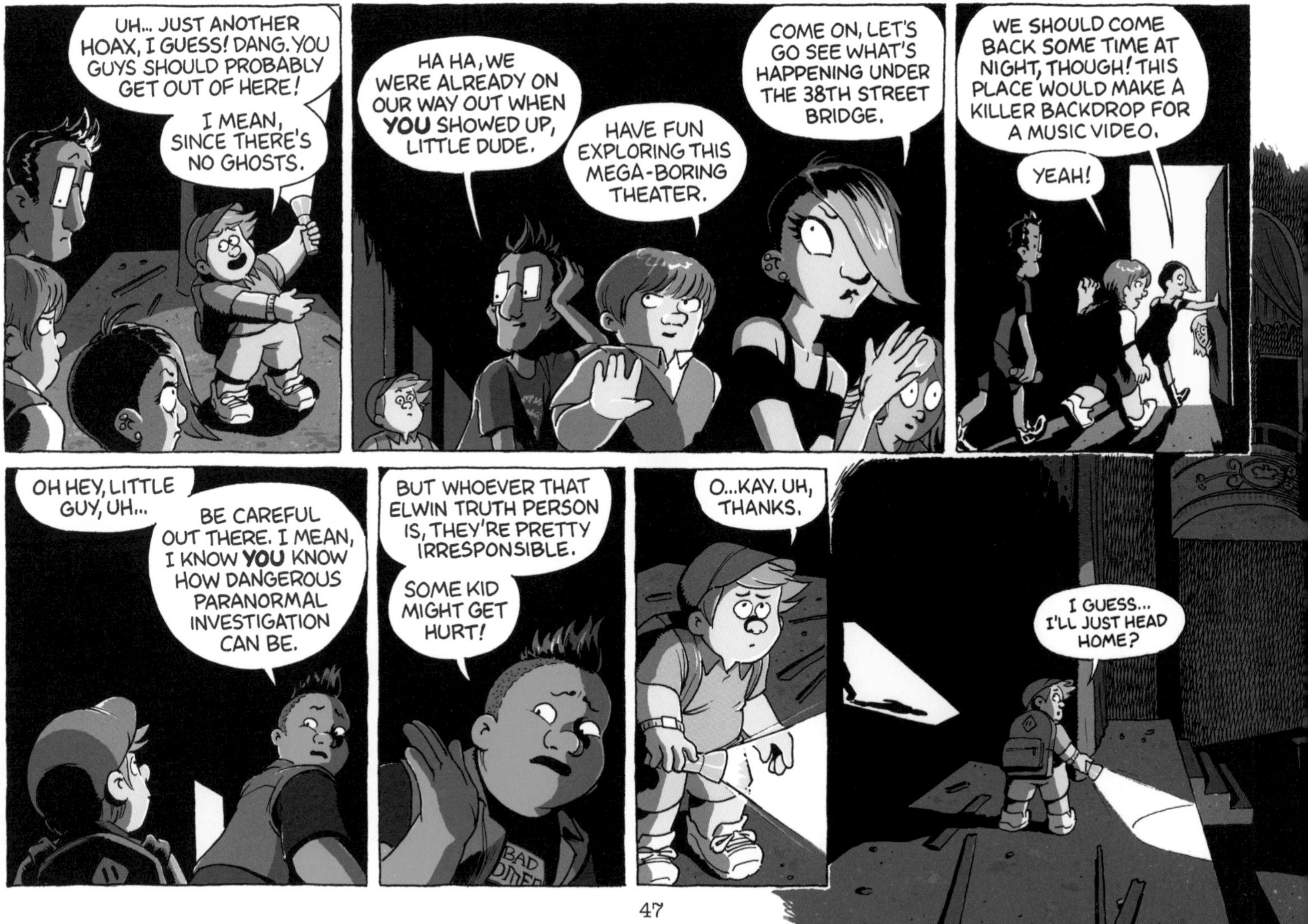
UH... JUST ANOTHER HOAX, I GUESS! DANG. YOU GUYS SHOULD PROBABLY GET OUT OF HERE!
I MEAN, SINCE THERE'S NO GHOSTS.
HA HA, WE WERE ALREADY ON OUR WAY OUT WHEN YOU SHOWED UP, LITTLE DUDE.
HAVE FUN EXPLORING THIS MEGA-BORING THEATER.
COME ON, LET'S GO SEE WHAT'S HAPPENING UNDER THE 38TH STREET BRIDGE.
WE SHOULD COME BACK SOME TIME AT NIGHT, THOUGH! THIS PLACE WOULD MAKE A KILLER BACKDROP FOR A MUSIC VIDEO.
YEAH!
OH HEY, LITTLE GUY, UH...
BE CAREFUL OUT THERE. I MEAN, I KNOW YOU KNOW HOW DANGEROUS PARANORMAL INVESTIGATION CAN BE.
BUT WHOEVER THAT ELWIN TRUTH PERSON IS, THEY'RE PRETTY IRRESPONSIBLE.
SOME KID MIGHT GET HURT!
BAD OMEN
O...KAY. UH, THANKS.
I GUESS... I'LL JUST HEAD HOME?

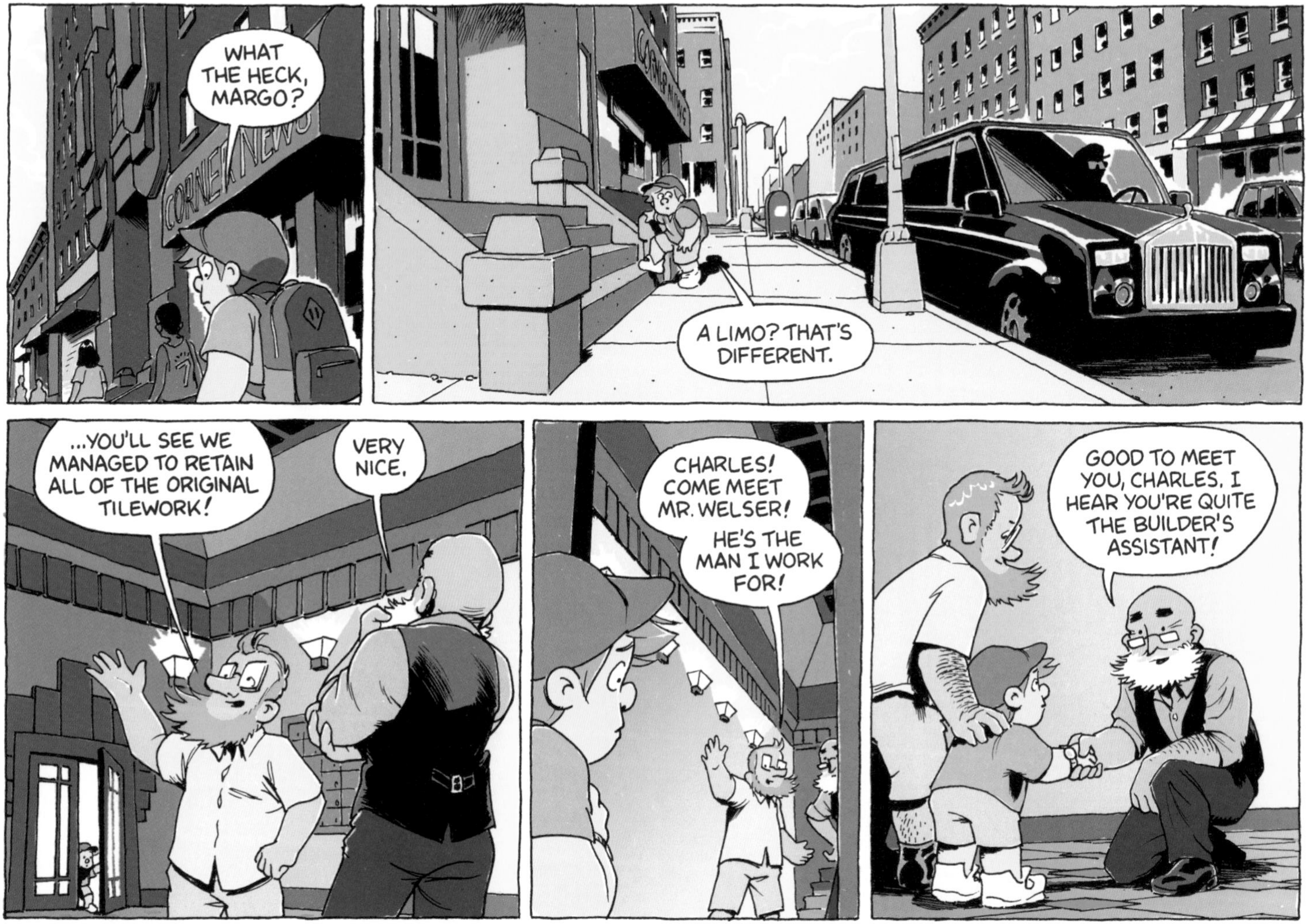
WHAT THE HECK, MARGO?
CORNER NEWS
A LIMO? THAT'S DIFFERENT.
...YOU'LL SEE WE MANAGED TO RETAIN ALL OF THE ORIGINAL TILEWORK!
VERY NICE.
CHARLES! COME MEET MR. WELSER!
HE'S THE MAN I WORK FOR!
GOOD TO MEET YOU, CHARLES. I HEAR YOU'RE QUITE THE BUILDER'S ASSISTANT!

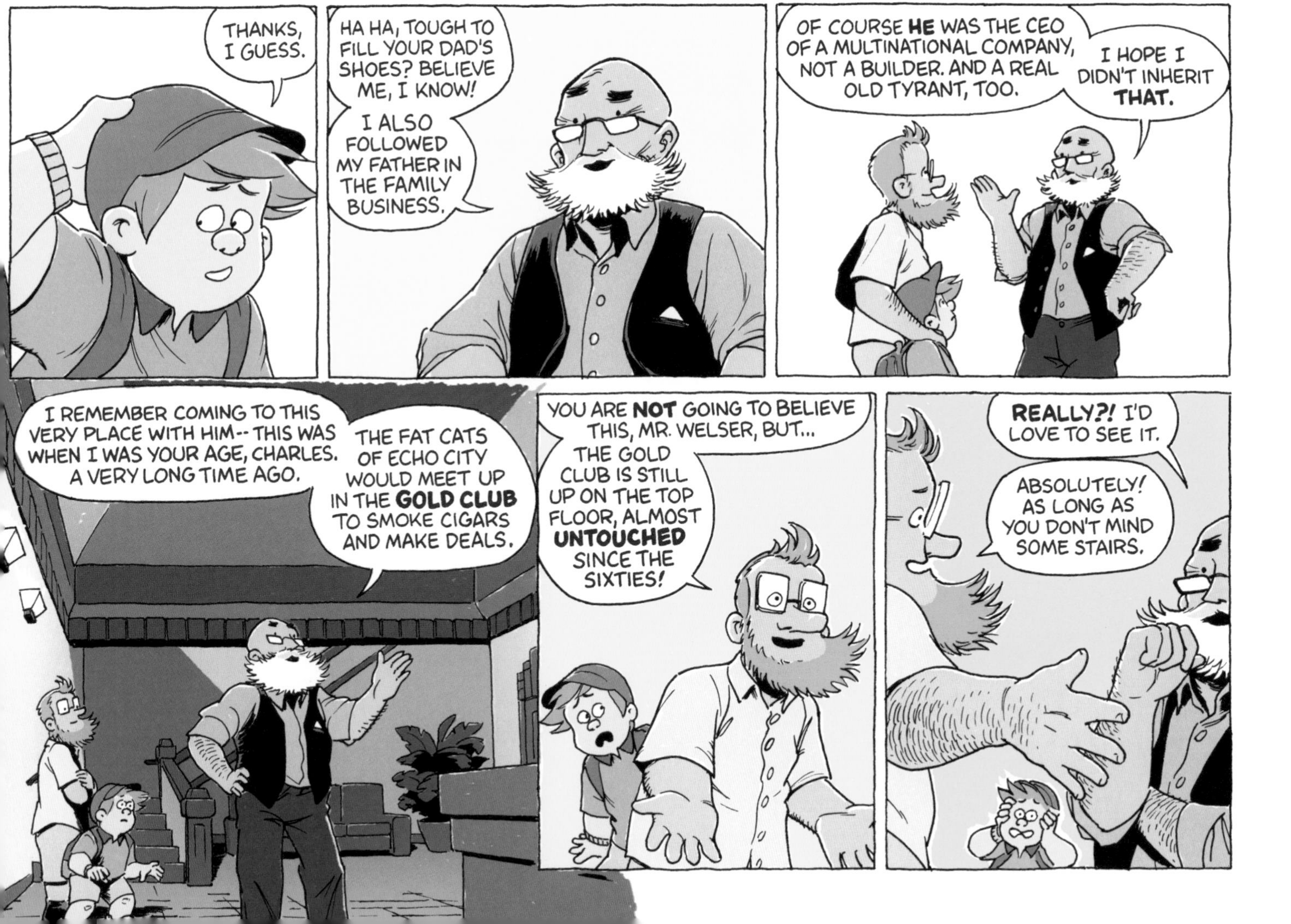
THANKS, I GUESS.
HA HA, TOUGH TO FILL YOUR DAD'S SHOES? BELIEVE ME, I KNOW!
I ALSO FOLLOWED MY FATHER IN THE FAMILY BUSINESS.
OF COURSE **HE** WAS THE CEO OF A MULTINATIONAL COMPANY, NOT A BUILDER. AND A REAL OLD TYRANT, TOO.
I HOPE I DIDN'T INHERIT **THAT.**
I REMEMBER COMING TO THIS VERY PLACE WITH HIM-- THIS WAS WHEN I WAS YOUR AGE, CHARLES. A VERY LONG TIME AGO.
THE FAT CATS OF ECHO CITY WOULD MEET UP IN THE **GOLD CLUB** TO SMOKE CIGARS AND MAKE DEALS.
YOU ARE **NOT** GOING TO BELIEVE THIS, MR. WELSER, BUT...
THE GOLD CLUB IS STILL UP ON THE TOP FLOOR, ALMOST **UNTOUCHED** SINCE THE SIXTIES!
REALLY?! I'D LOVE TO SEE IT.
ABSOLUTELY! AS LONG AS YOU DON'T MIND SOME STAIRS.

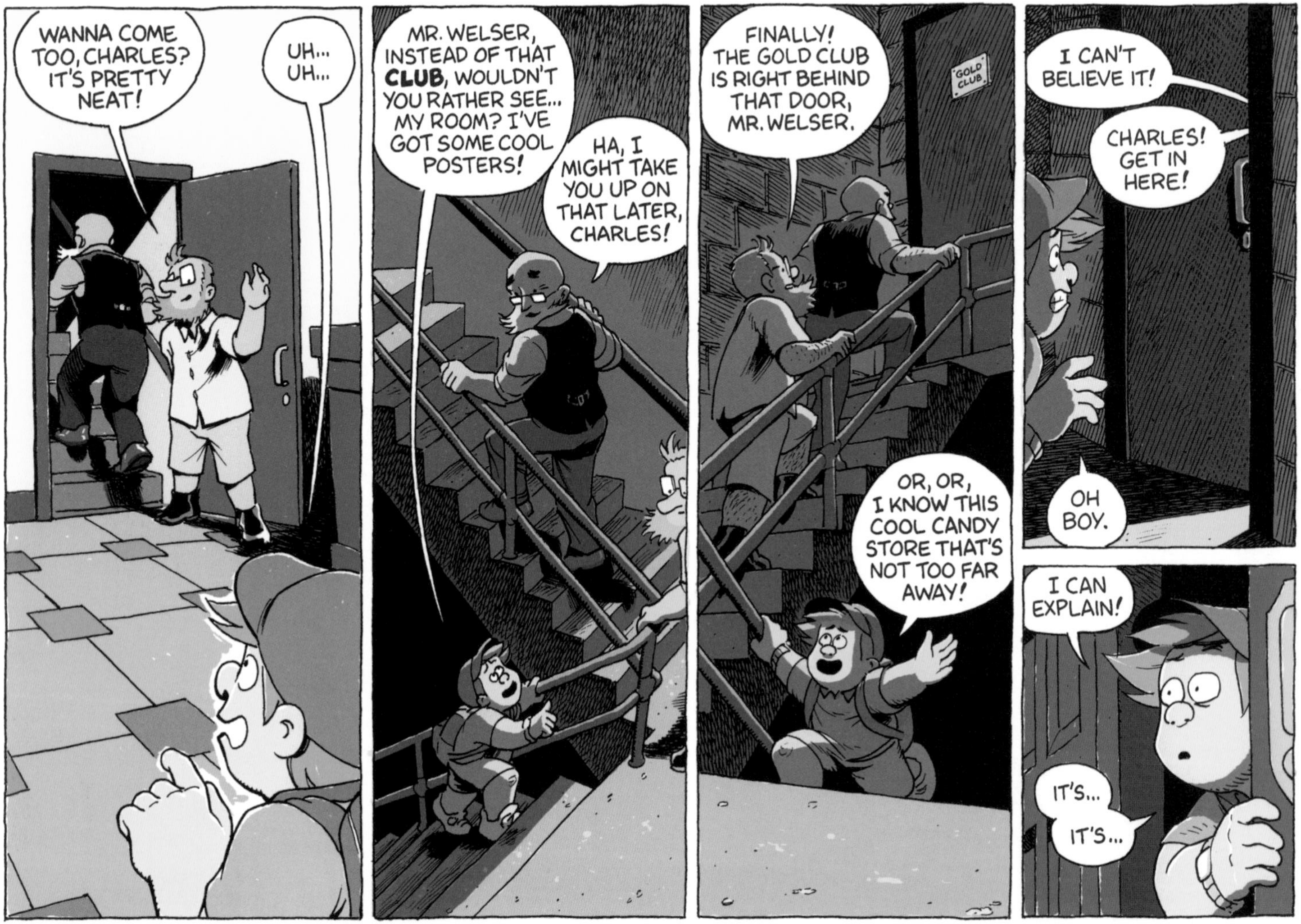
WANNA COME TOO, CHARLES? IT'S PRETTY NEAT!
UH... UH...
MR. WELSER, INSTEAD OF THAT **CLUB**, WOULDN'T YOU RATHER SEE... MY ROOM? I'VE GOT SOME COOL POSTERS!
HA, I MIGHT TAKE YOU UP ON THAT LATER, CHARLES!
FINALLY! THE GOLD CLUB IS RIGHT BEHIND THAT DOOR, MR. WELSER.
GOLD CLUB
OR, OR, I KNOW THIS COOL CANDY STORE THAT'S NOT TOO FAR AWAY!
I CAN'T BELIEVE IT!
CHARLES! GET IN HERE!
OH BOY.
I CAN EXPLAIN!
IT'S...
IT'S...

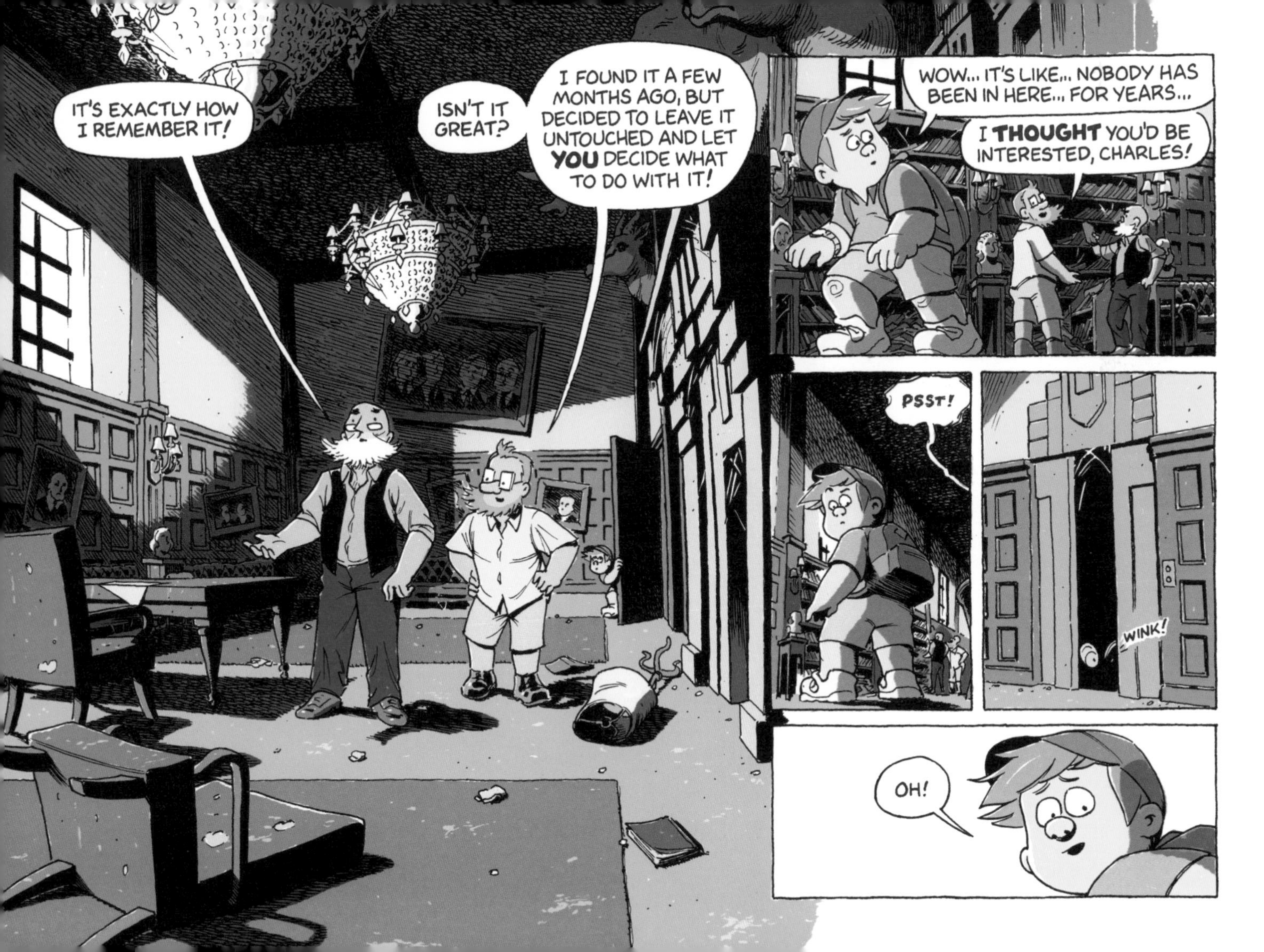
IT'S EXACTLY HOW I REMEMBER IT!
ISN'T IT GREAT?
I FOUND IT A FEW MONTHS AGO, BUT DECIDED TO LEAVE IT UNTOUCHED AND LET YOU DECIDE WHAT TO DO WITH IT!
WOW... IT'S LIKE... NOBODY HAS BEEN IN HERE... FOR YEARS...
I THOUGHT YOU'D BE INTERESTED, CHARLES!
PSST!
WINK!
OH!

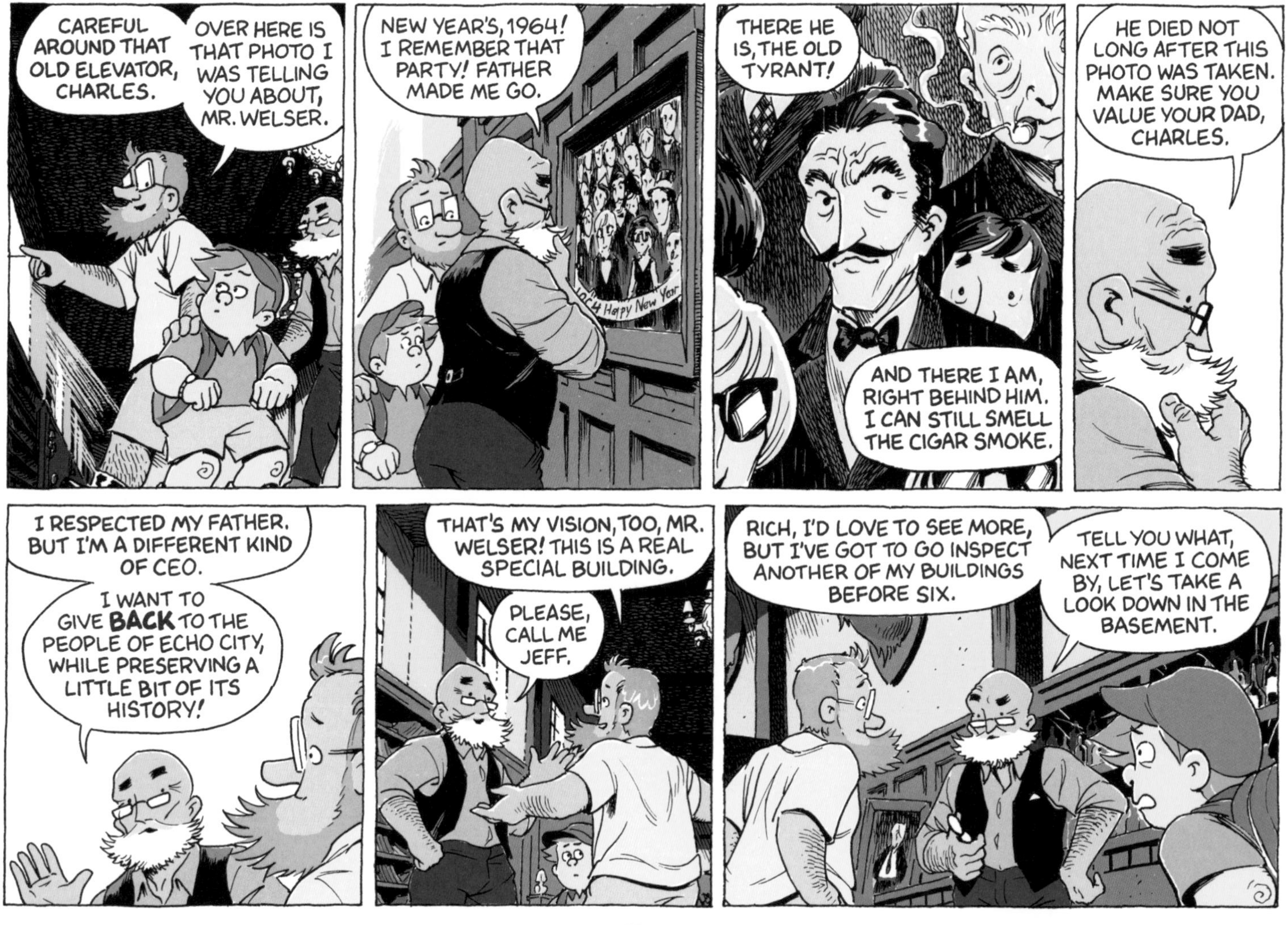
CAREFUL AROUND THAT OLD ELEVATOR, CHARLES.
OVER HERE IS THAT PHOTO I WAS TELLING YOU ABOUT, MR. WELSER.
NEW YEAR'S, 1964! I REMEMBER THAT PARTY! FATHER MADE ME GO.
Happy New Year
THERE HE IS, THE OLD TYRANT!
AND THERE I AM, RIGHT BEHIND HIM. I CAN STILL SMELL THE CIGAR SMOKE.
HE DIED NOT LONG AFTER THIS PHOTO WAS TAKEN. MAKE SURE YOU VALUE YOUR DAD, CHARLES.
I RESPECTED MY FATHER. BUT I'M A DIFFERENT KIND OF CEO.
I WANT TO GIVE BACK TO THE PEOPLE OF ECHO CITY, WHILE PRESERVING A LITTLE BIT OF ITS HISTORY!
THAT'S MY VISION, TOO, MR. WELSER! THIS IS A REAL SPECIAL BUILDING.
PLEASE, CALL ME JEFF.
RICH, I'D LOVE TO SEE MORE, BUT I'VE GOT TO GO INSPECT ANOTHER OF MY BUILDINGS BEFORE SIX.
TELL YOU WHAT, NEXT TIME I COME BY, LET'S TAKE A LOOK DOWN IN THE BASEMENT.

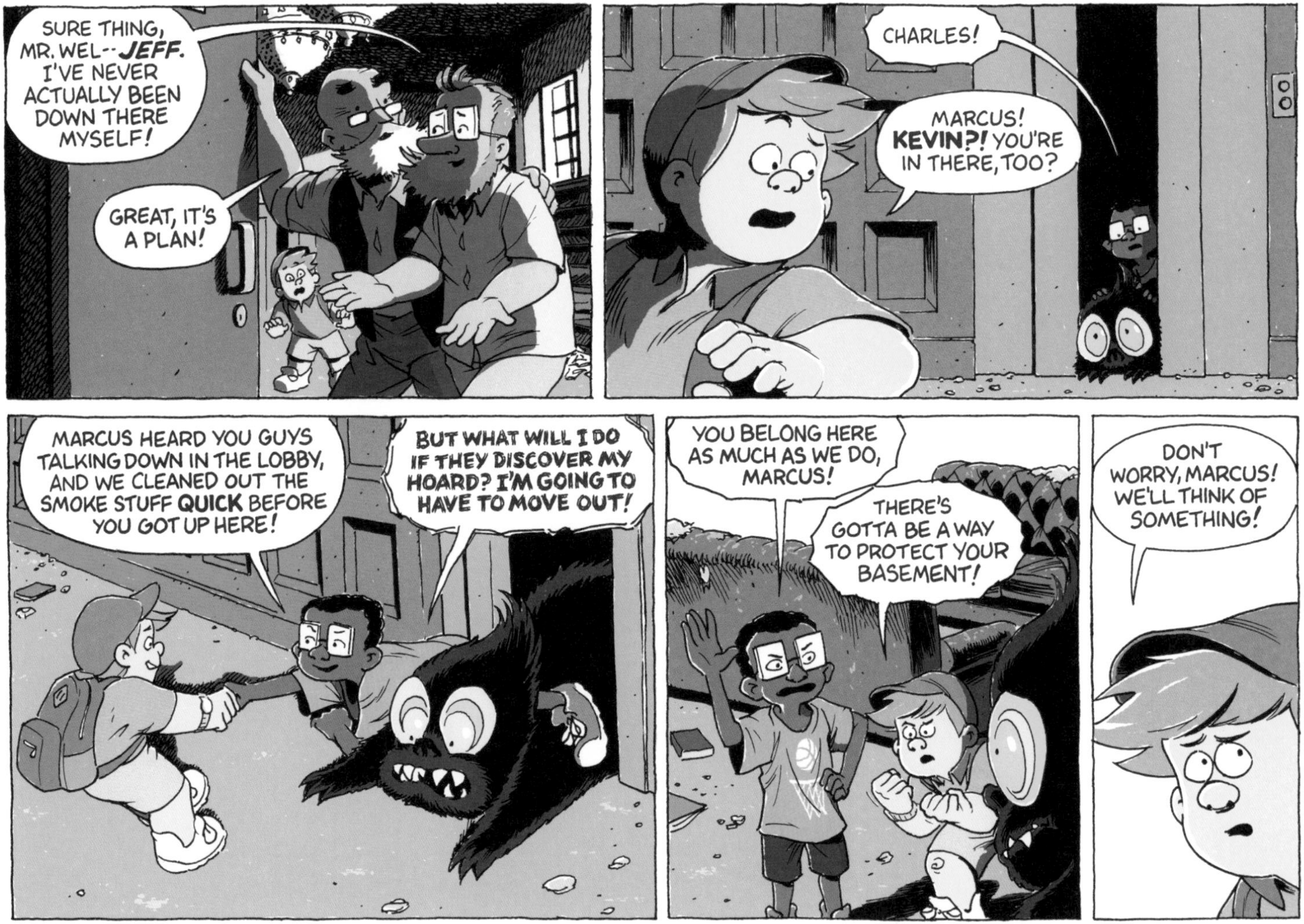
SURE THING, MR. WEL--**JEFF.** I'VE NEVER ACTUALLY BEEN DOWN THERE MYSELF!
GREAT, IT'S A PLAN!
CHARLES!
MARCUS! **KEVIN?!** YOU'RE IN THERE, TOO?
MARCUS HEARD YOU GUYS TALKING DOWN IN THE LOBBY, AND WE CLEANED OUT THE SMOKE STUFF **QUICK** BEFORE YOU GOT UP HERE!
BUT WHAT WILL I DO IF THEY DISCOVER MY HOARD? I'M GOING TO HAVE TO MOVE OUT!
YOU BELONG HERE AS MUCH AS WE DO, MARCUS!
THERE'S GOTTA BE A WAY TO PROTECT YOUR BASEMENT!
DON'T WORRY, MARCUS! WE'LL THINK OF SOMETHING!

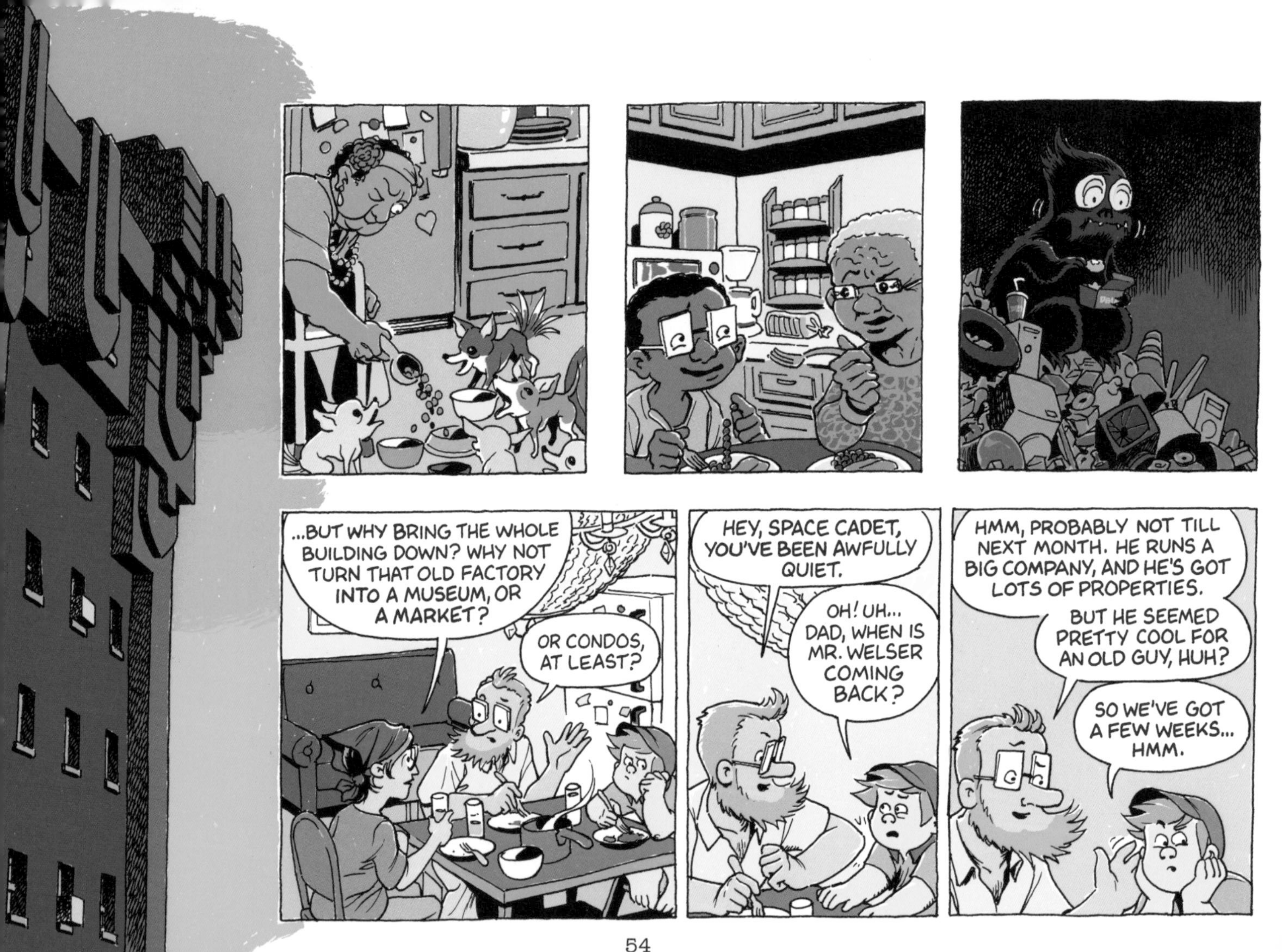
...BUT WHY BRING THE WHOLE BUILDING DOWN? WHY NOT TURN THAT OLD FACTORY INTO A MUSEUM, OR A MARKET?
OR CONDOS, AT LEAST?
HEY, SPACE CADET, YOU'VE BEEN AWFULLY QUIET.
OH! UH... DAD, WHEN IS MR. WELSER COMING BACK?
HMM, PROBABLY NOT TILL NEXT MONTH. HE RUNS A BIG COMPANY, AND HE'S GOT LOTS OF PROPERTIES.
BUT HE SEEMED PRETTY COOL FOR AN OLD GUY, HUH?
SO WE'VE GOT A FEW WEEKS... HMM.

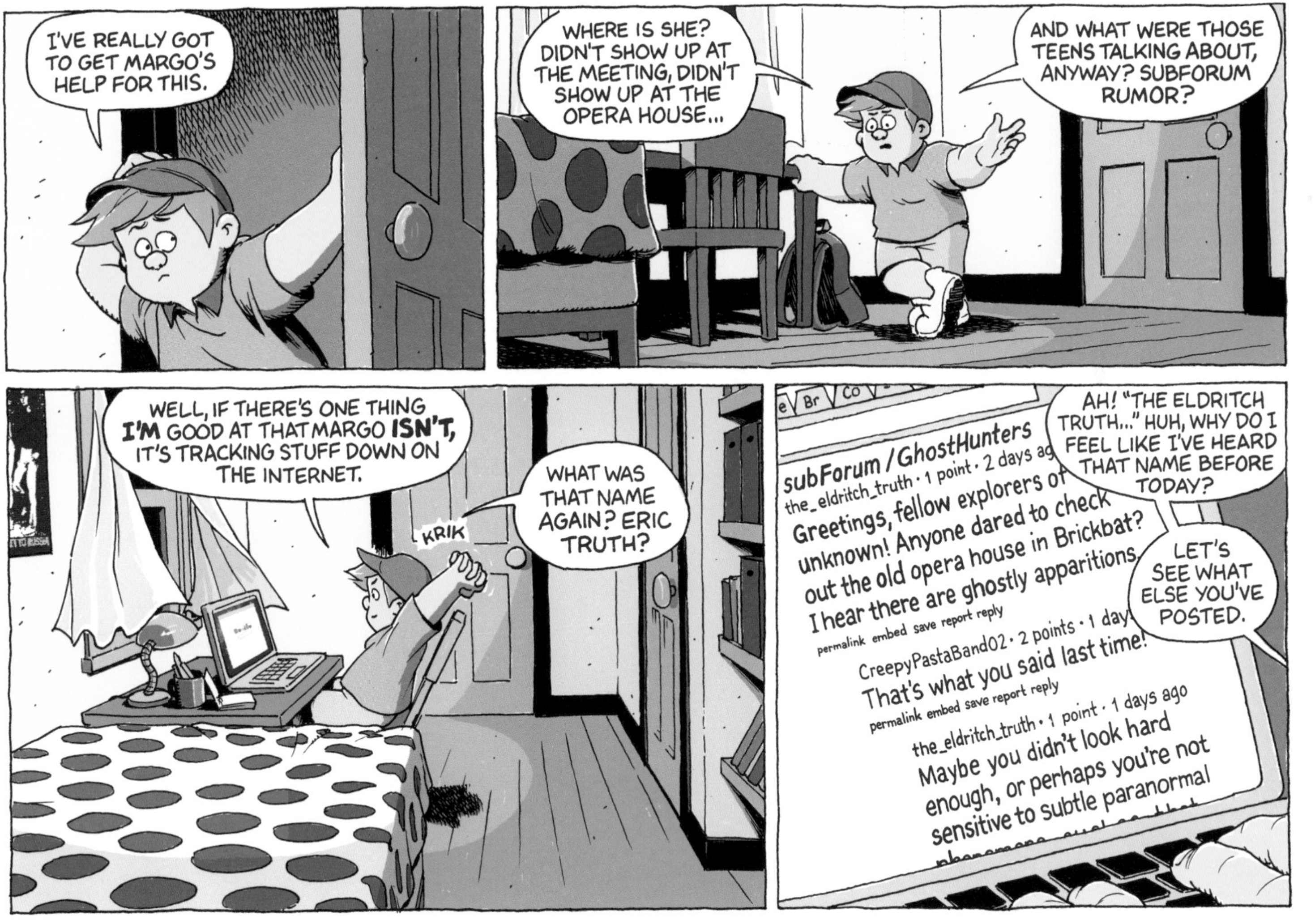
I'VE REALLY GOT TO GET MARGO'S HELP FOR THIS.
WHERE IS SHE? DIDN'T SHOW UP AT THE MEETING, DIDN'T SHOW UP AT THE OPERA HOUSE...
AND WHAT WERE THOSE TEENS TALKING ABOUT, ANYWAY? SUBFORUM RUMOR?
WELL, IF THERE'S ONE THING **I'M** GOOD AT THAT MARGO **ISN'T,** IT'S TRACKING STUFF DOWN ON THE INTERNET.
KRIK
WHAT WAS THAT NAME AGAIN? ERIC TRUTH?
subForum / GhostHunters
the_eldritch_truth · 1 point · 2 days ag
Greetings, fellow explorers of
unknown! Anyone dared to check out the old opera house in Brickbat? I hear there are ghostly apparitions.
permalink embed save report reply
CreepyPastaBand02 · 2 points · 1 day
That's what you said last time!
permalink embed save report reply
the_eldritch_truth · 1 point · 1 days ago
Maybe you didn't look hard enough, or perhaps you're not sensitive to subtle paranormal
AH! "THE ELDRITCH TRUTH..." HUH, WHY DO I FEEL LIKE I'VE HEARD THAT NAME BEFORE TODAY?
LET'S SEE WHAT ELSE YOU'VE POSTED.

subForum / DragonClan
the_eldritch_truth · 2 points · 9 days ago
Hey dragonfans! Do you think there are REAL dragons in the world? I've heard speculation that there's one atop of Echo City's very own Barks Tower!
permalink embed save report reply
fluffyscales · 1 points · 8 days ago
Woah really!!! OwO My whole class is taking a field trip there nxt week!!!!1
permalink embed save report reply
the_eldritch_truth · 1 points · 8 days ago
WAIT, WAIT, ISN'T THIS THOSE DRAGON KIDS? IS... IS THIS ELDRITCH TRUTH PERSON TRYING TO GET KIDS TO GO LOOK FOR MONSTERS?
subForum / AbandonedSpaces
CreepyPastaBand02 · 1 points ·
anyone know some totally dark and gothic abandoned buildings where we could a music video like maybe an old mental asylum ?
permalink embed save report reply
WHOA, THIS IS WHY THOSE TEENS WERE IN THE ECHO POST IN THE FIRST PLACE?
the_eldritch_truth · 2 points · 25 days ago
You simply must check out the old Echo Post building. Rumors abound that it's actually haunted!
permalink embed save report reply
CreepyPastaBand02 · 1 point ·
awesome, thx
WHAT THE HECK IS THIS? HOW WOULD SOMEONE BESIDES ME AND MARGO EVEN KNOW ABOUT ALL THESE PLACES?!
MARGO! I REALLY NEED TO TALK TO YOU! SOMETHING WEIRD IS GOING DOWN ON THE INTERNET!
AND MARCUS NEEDS OUR HELP! IT'S URGENT!
PAST YOUR BEDTIME, KIDDO.
OKAY, MOM!
GOTTA GO. CALL ME!
WHERE IS SHE?
IF I DON'T HEAR FROM HER BY TOMORROW MORNING, I'M GOING TO GO OUT TO HER HOUSE AND TALK TO HER IN PERSON.

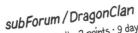

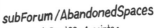

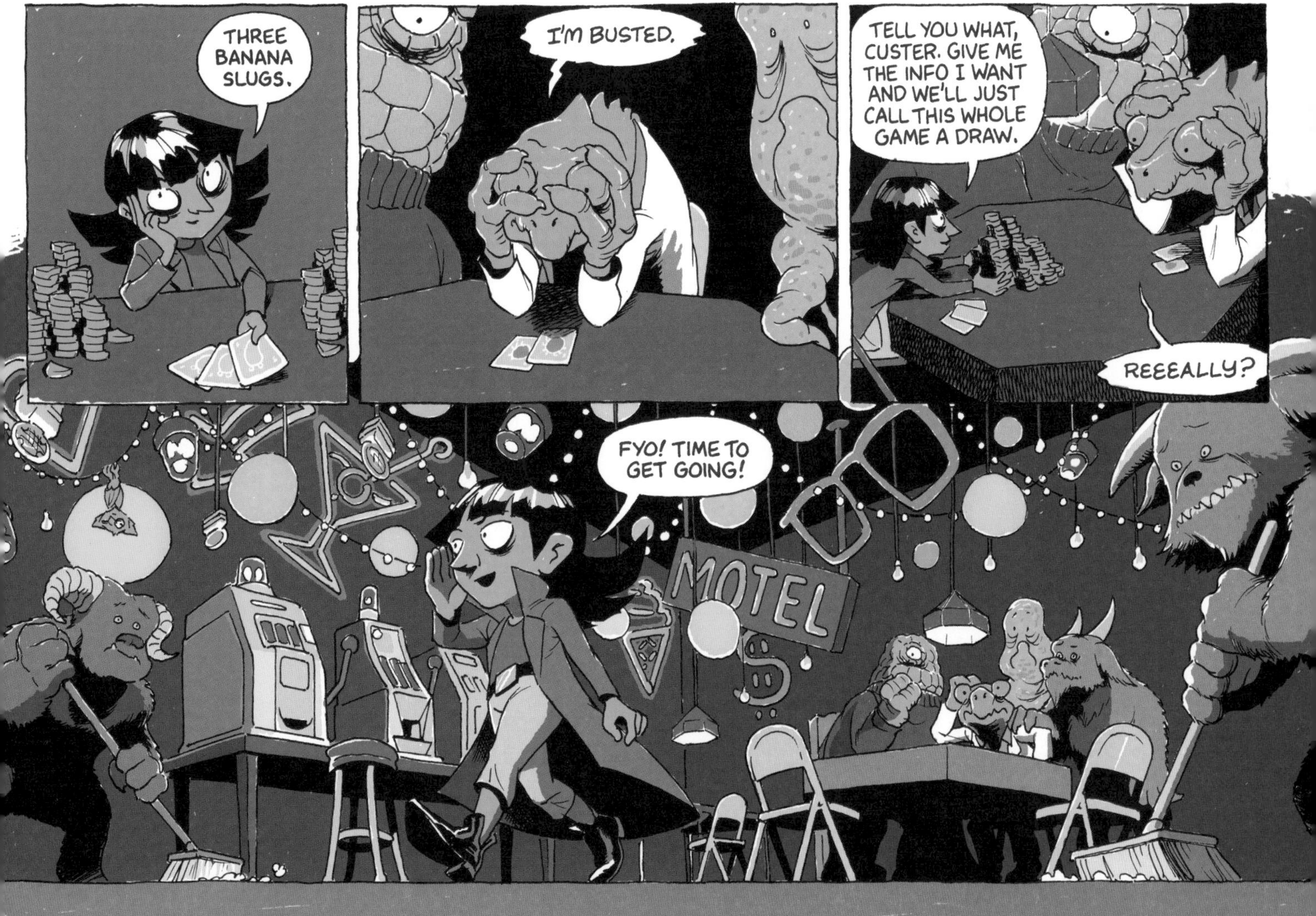
THREE BANANA SLUGS.
I'M BUSTED.
TELL YOU WHAT, CUSTER. GIVE ME THE INFO I WANT AND WE'LL JUST CALL THIS WHOLE GAME A DRAW.
REEEALLY?
FYO! TIME TO GET GOING!
MOTEL

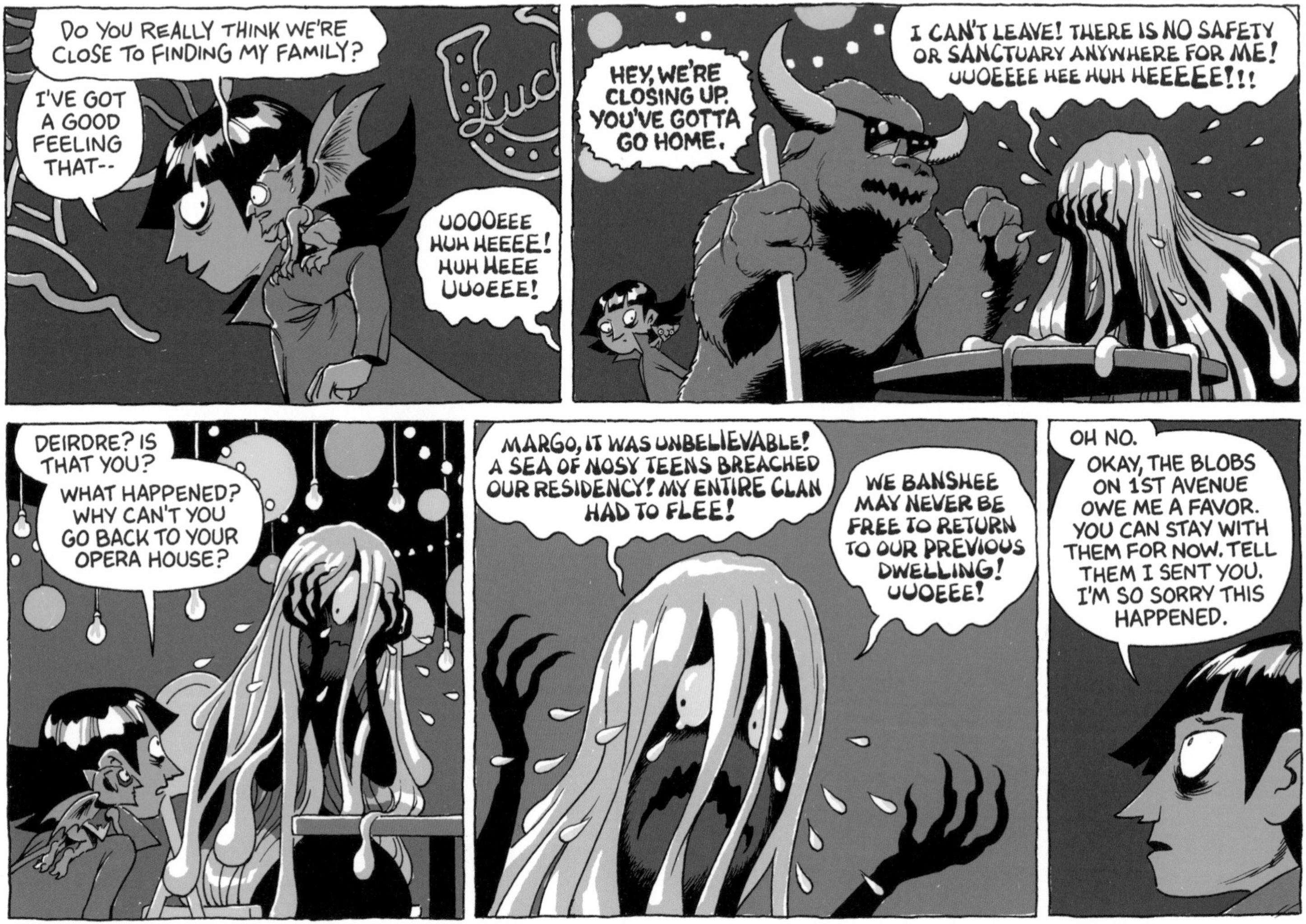
DO YOU REALLY THINK WE'RE CLOSE TO FINDING MY FAMILY?
I'VE GOT A GOOD FEELING THAT--
UOOOEEE HUH HEEEE! HUH HEEE UUOEEE!
HEY, WE'RE CLOSING UP. YOU'VE GOTTA GO HOME.
I CAN'T LEAVE! THERE IS NO SAFETY OR SANCTUARY ANYWHERE FOR ME! UUOEEEE HEE HUH HEEEEE!!!
DEIRDRE? IS THAT YOU?
WHAT HAPPENED? WHY CAN'T YOU GO BACK TO YOUR OPERA HOUSE?
MARGO, IT WAS UNBELIEVABLE! A SEA OF NOSY TEENS BREACHED OUR RESIDENCY! MY ENTIRE CLAN HAD TO FLEE!
WE BANSHEE MAY NEVER BE FREE TO RETURN TO OUR PREVIOUS DWELLING! UUOEEE!
OH NO.
OKAY, THE BLOBS ON 1ST AVENUE OWE ME A FAVOR. YOU CAN STAY WITH THEM FOR NOW. TELL THEM I SENT YOU. I'M SO SORRY THIS HAPPENED.

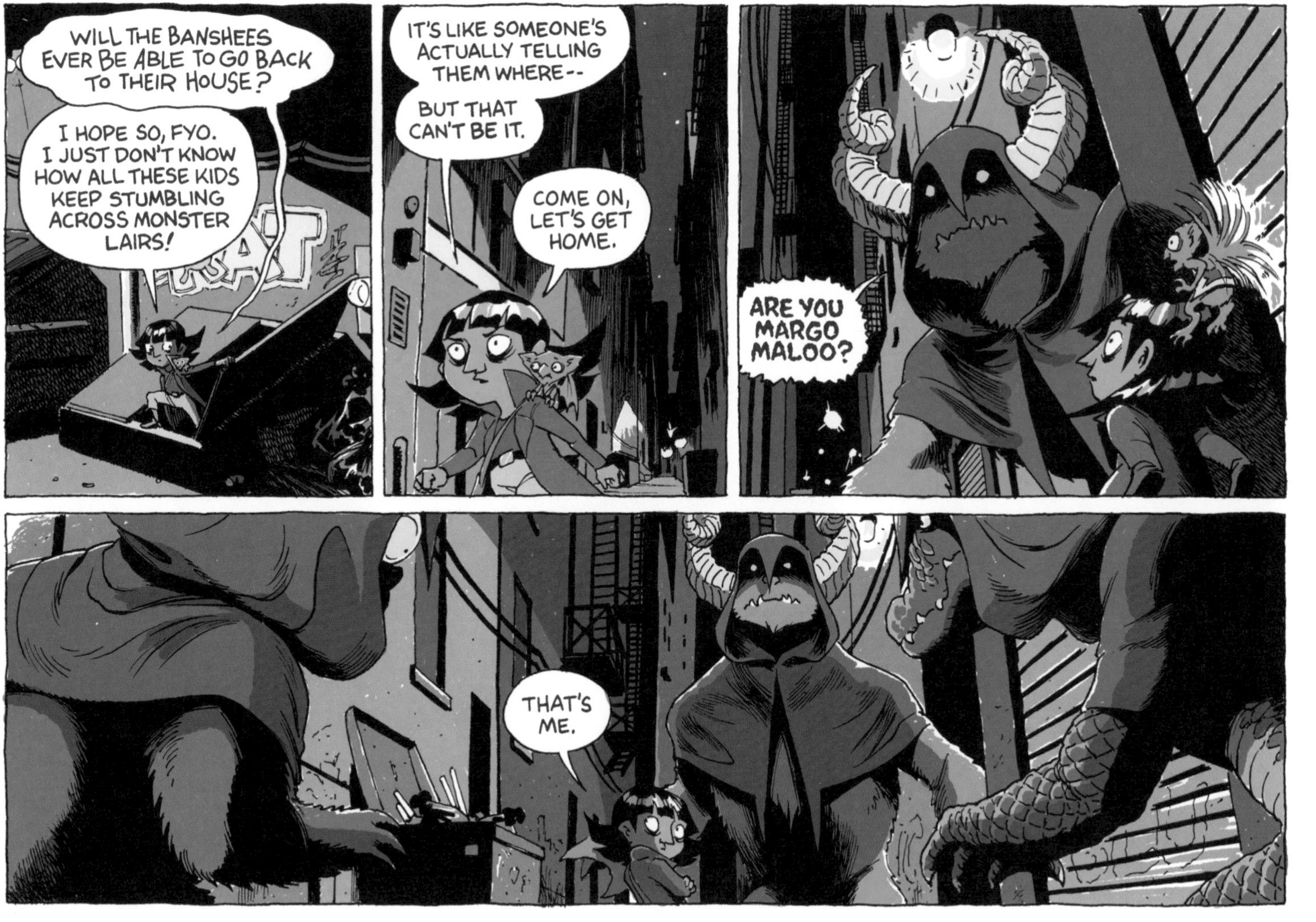
WILL THE BANSHEES EVER BE ABLE TO GO BACK TO THEIR HOUSE?
I HOPE SO, FYO. I JUST DON'T KNOW HOW ALL THESE KIDS KEEP STUMBLING ACROSS MONSTER LAIRS!
IT'S LIKE SOMEONE'S ACTUALLY TELLING THEM WHERE--
BUT THAT CAN'T BE IT.
COME ON, LET'S GET HOME.
ARE YOU MARGO MALOO?
THAT'S ME.

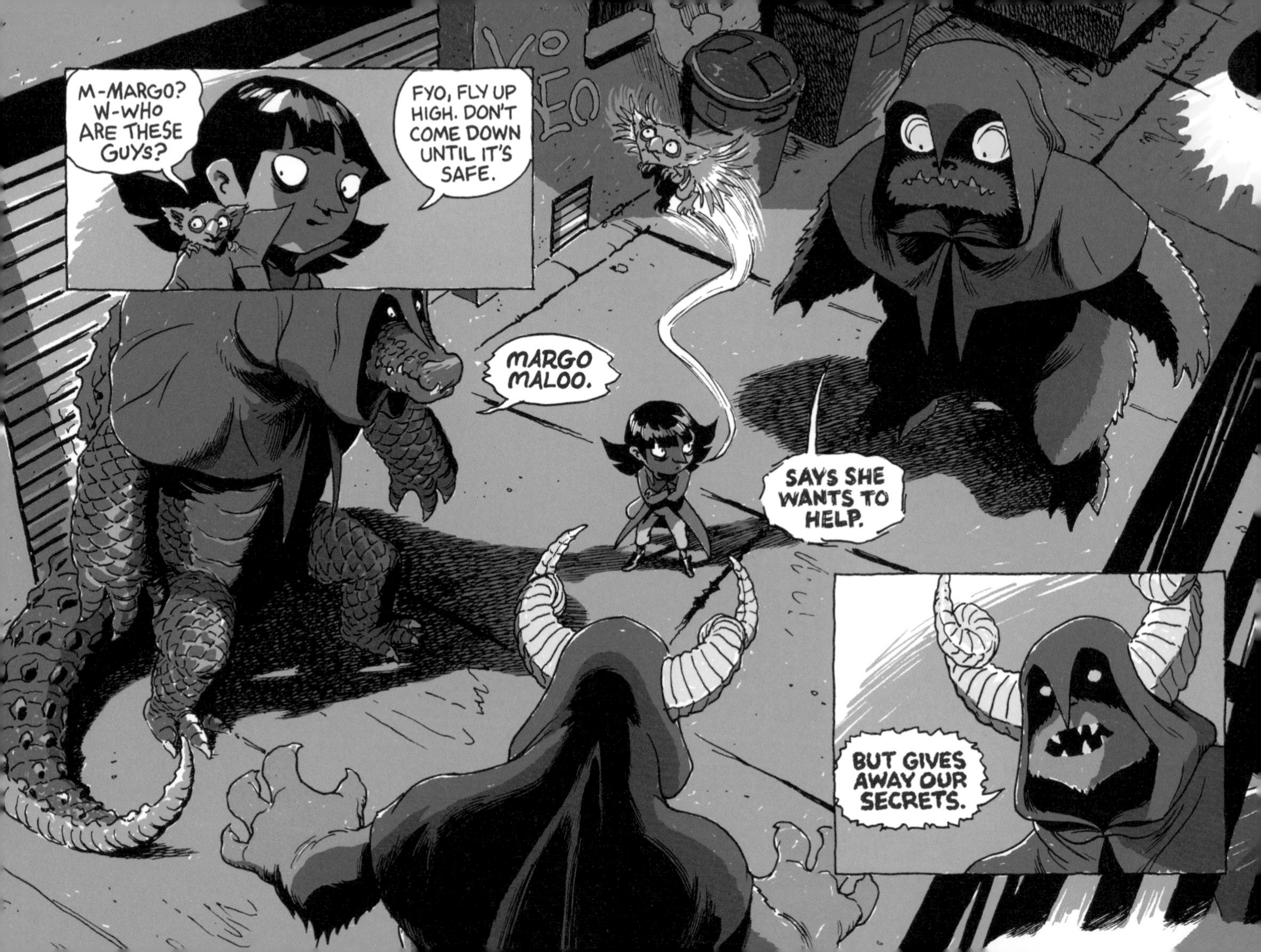
M-MARGO? W-WHO ARE THESE GUYS?
FYO, FLY UP HIGH. DON'T COME DOWN UNTIL IT'S SAFE.
MARGO MALOO.
SAYS SHE WANTS TO HELP.
BUT GIVES AWAY OUR SECRETS.

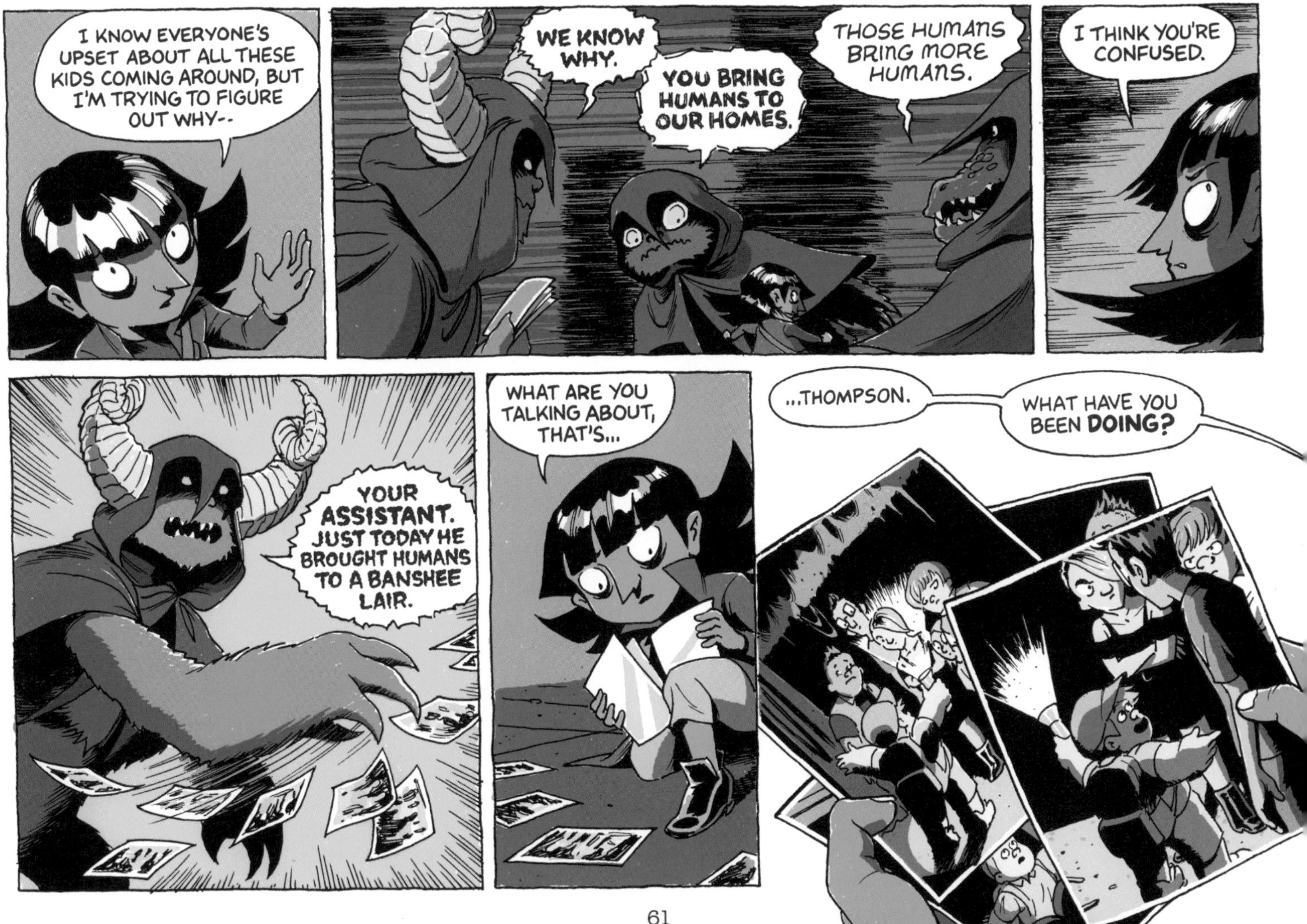
I KNOW EVERYONE'S UPSET ABOUT ALL THESE KIDS COMING AROUND, BUT I'M TRYING TO FIGURE OUT WHY--
WE KNOW WHY.
YOU BRING HUMANS TO OUR HOMES.
THOSE HUMANS BRING MORE HUMANS.
I THINK YOU'RE CONFUSED.
YOUR ASSISTANT. JUST TODAY HE BROUGHT HUMANS TO A BANSHEE LAIR.
WHAT ARE YOU TALKING ABOUT, THAT'S...
...THOMPSON.
WHAT HAVE YOU BEEN DOING?

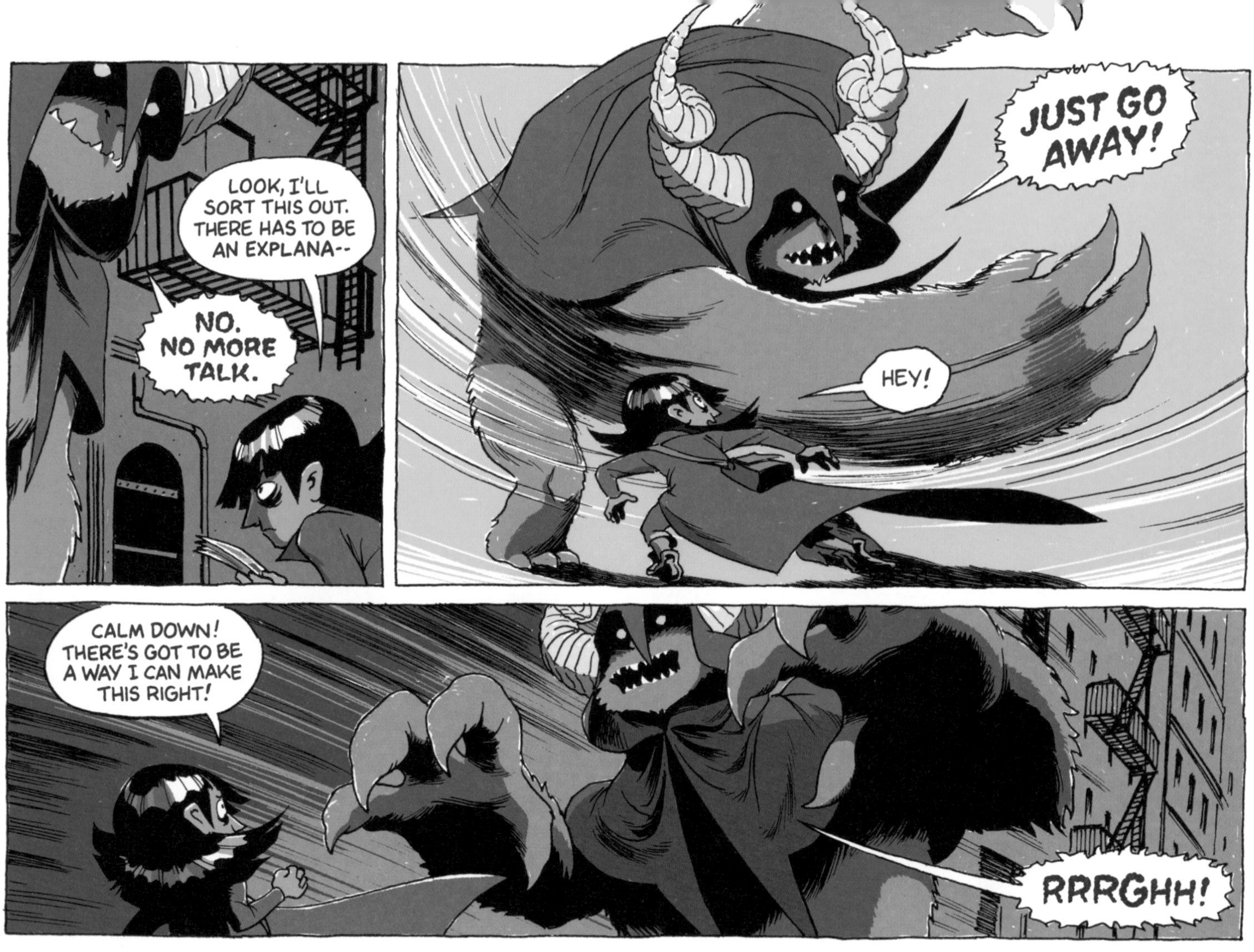

LOOK, I'LL SORT THIS OUT. THERE HAS TO BE AN EXPLANA--
NO. NO MORE TALK.
JUST GO AWAY!
HEY!
CALM DOWN! THERE'S GOT TO BE A WAY I CAN MAKE THIS RIGHT!
RRRGHH!

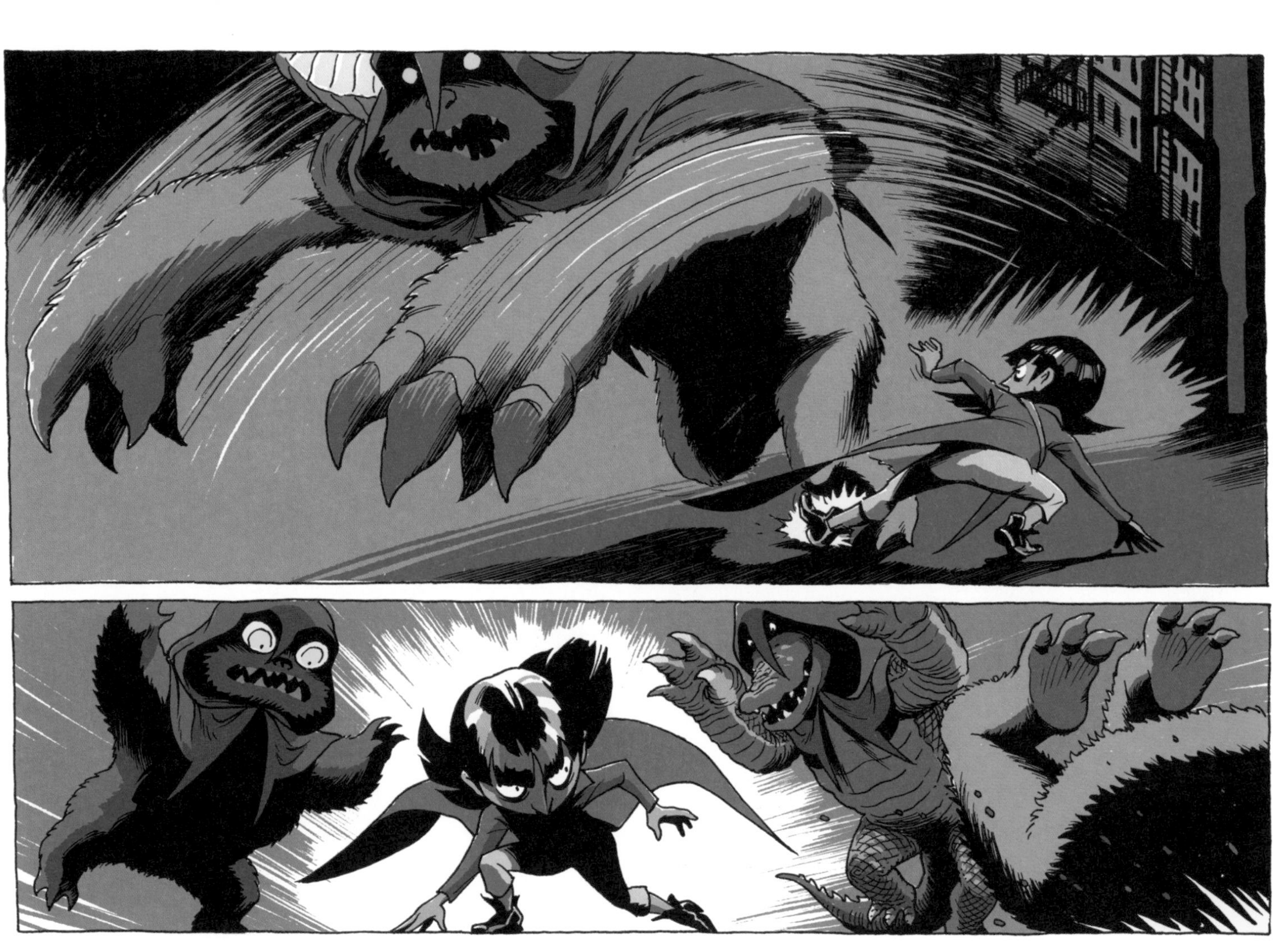

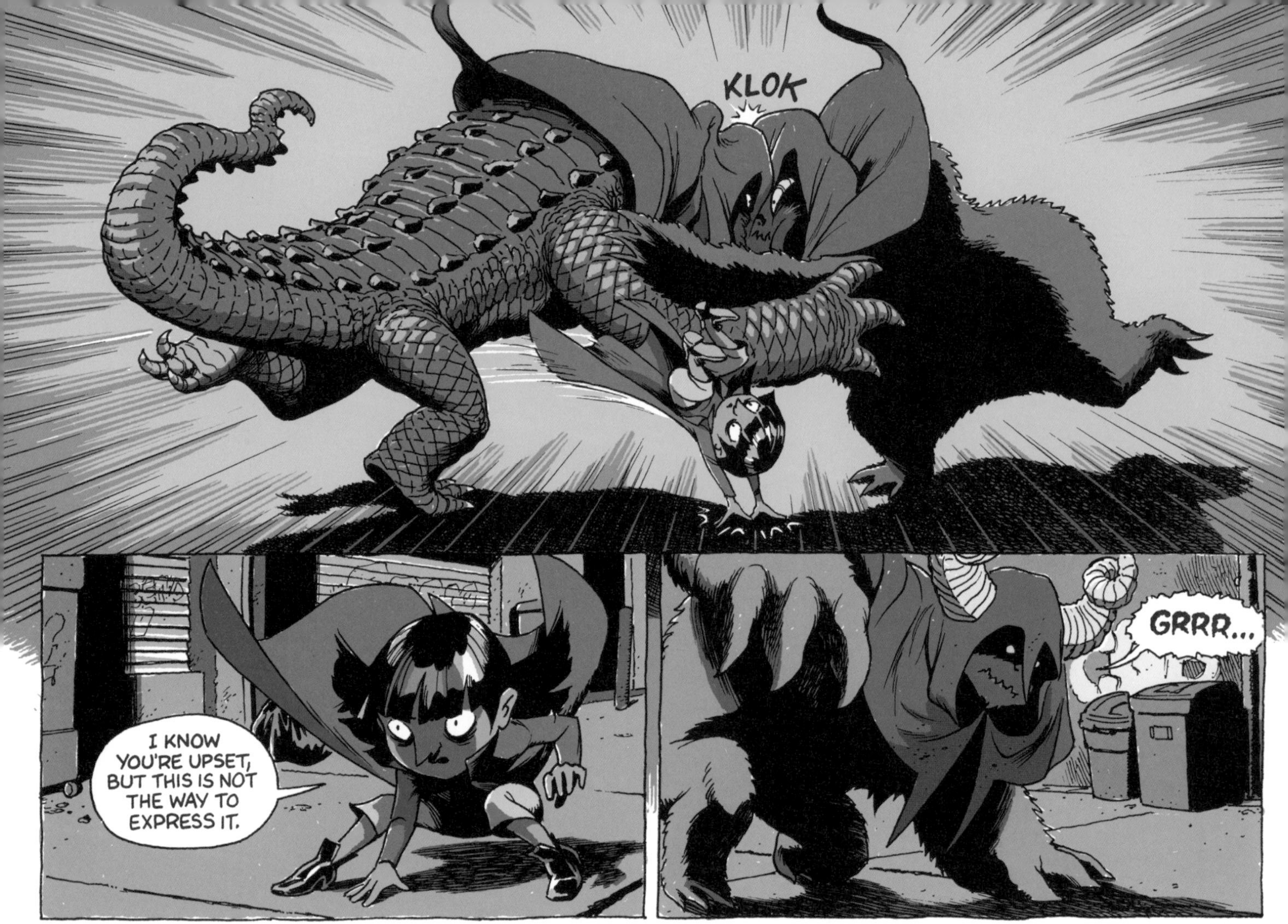
KLOK
I KNOW YOU'RE UPSET, BUT THIS IS NOT THE WAY TO EXPRESS IT.
GRRR...

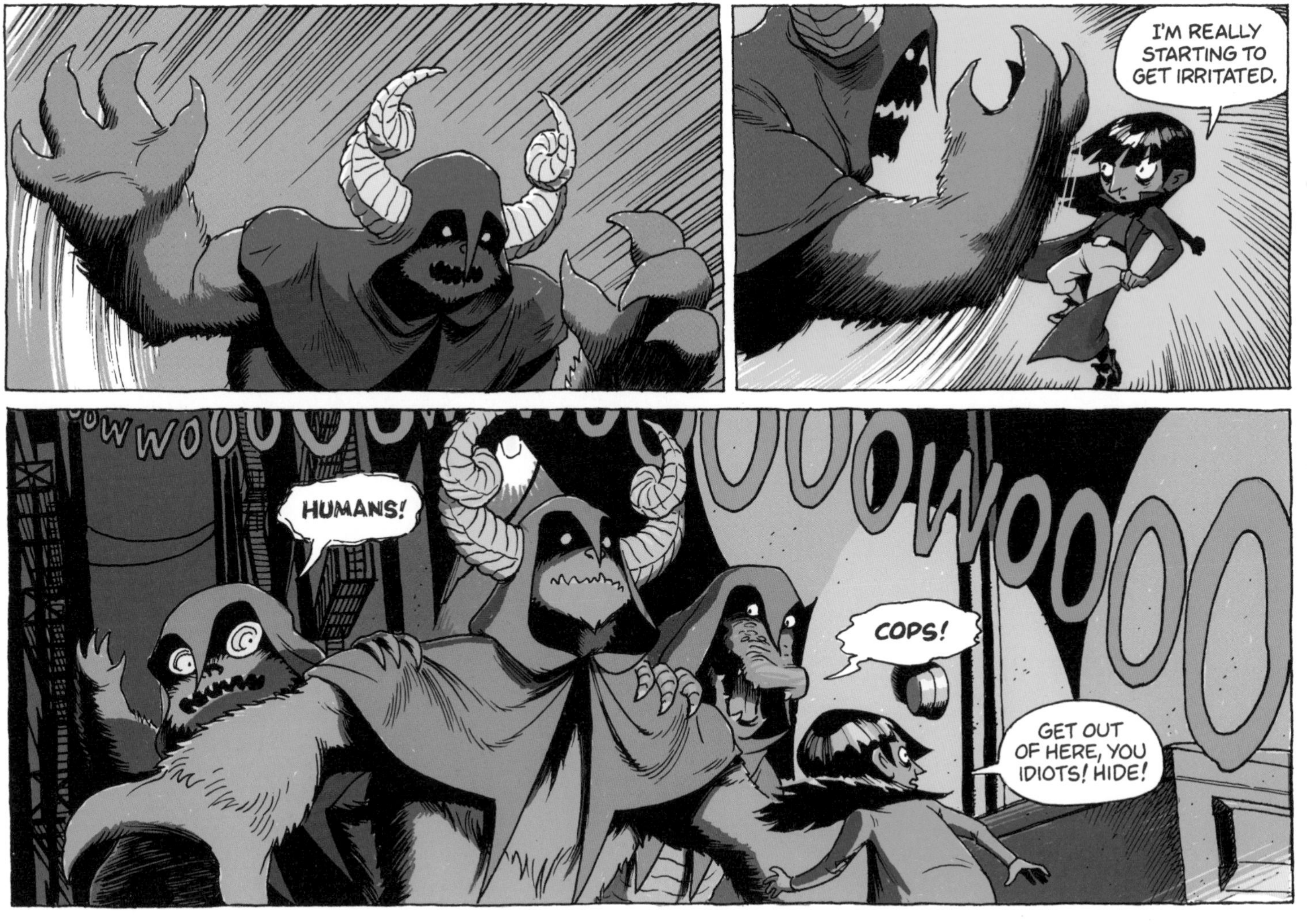
I'M REALLY STARTING TO GET IRRITATED.
OWWOOOOOOOOOOOOOOWOOOOO
HUMANS!
COPS!
GET OUT OF HERE, YOU IDIOTS! HIDE!

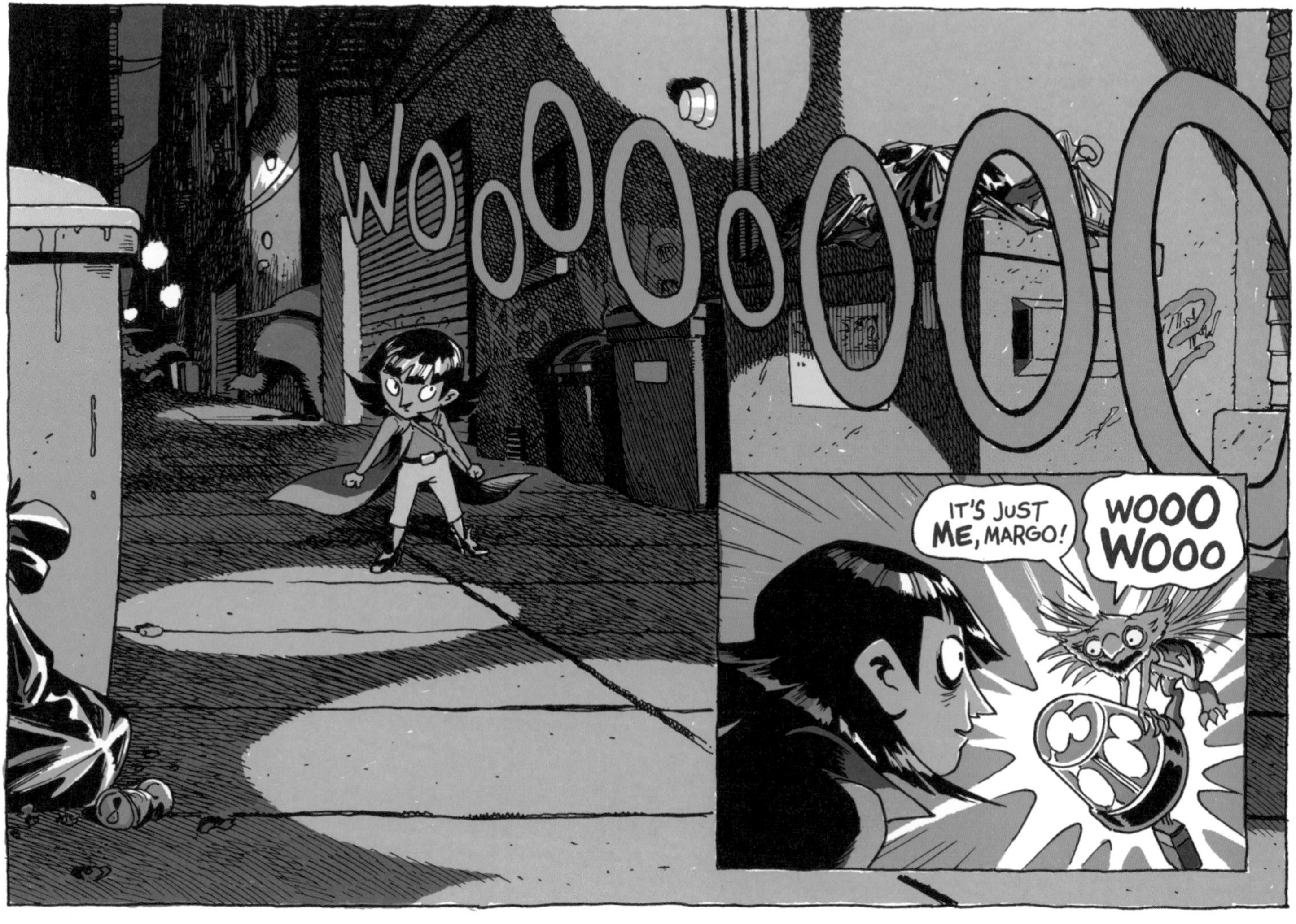
WOoOOoOOOO
IT'S JUST ME, MARGO!
WOOO WOOO

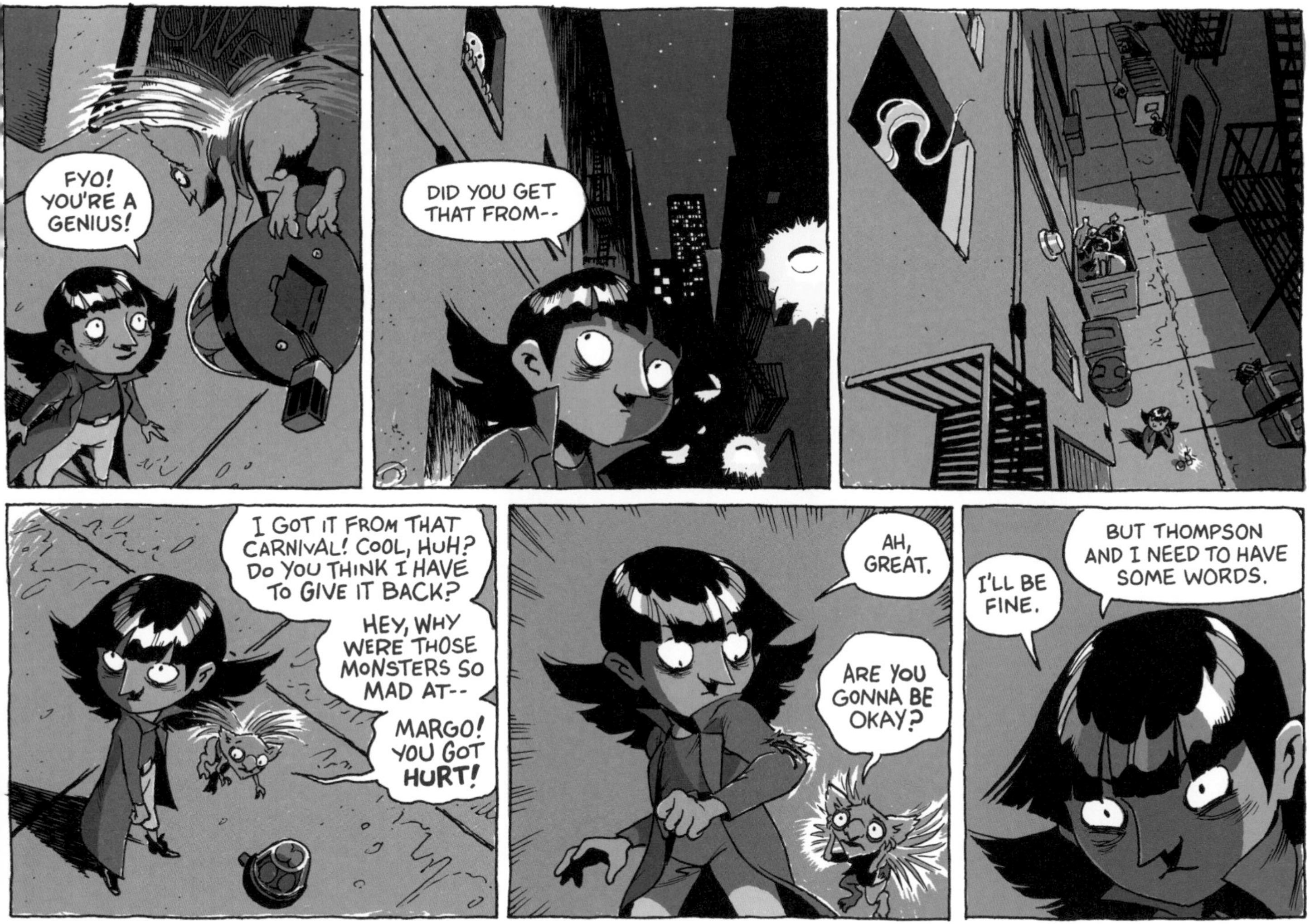
FYO! YOU'RE A GENIUS!
DID YOU GET THAT FROM--
I GOT IT FROM THAT CARNIVAL! COOL, HUH? DO YOU THINK I HAVE TO GIVE IT BACK?
HEY, WHY WERE THOSE MONSTERS SO MAD AT--
MARGO! YOU GOT HURT!
AH, GREAT.
ARE YOU GONNA BE OKAY?
I'LL BE FINE.
BUT THOMPSON AND I NEED TO HAVE SOME WORDS.

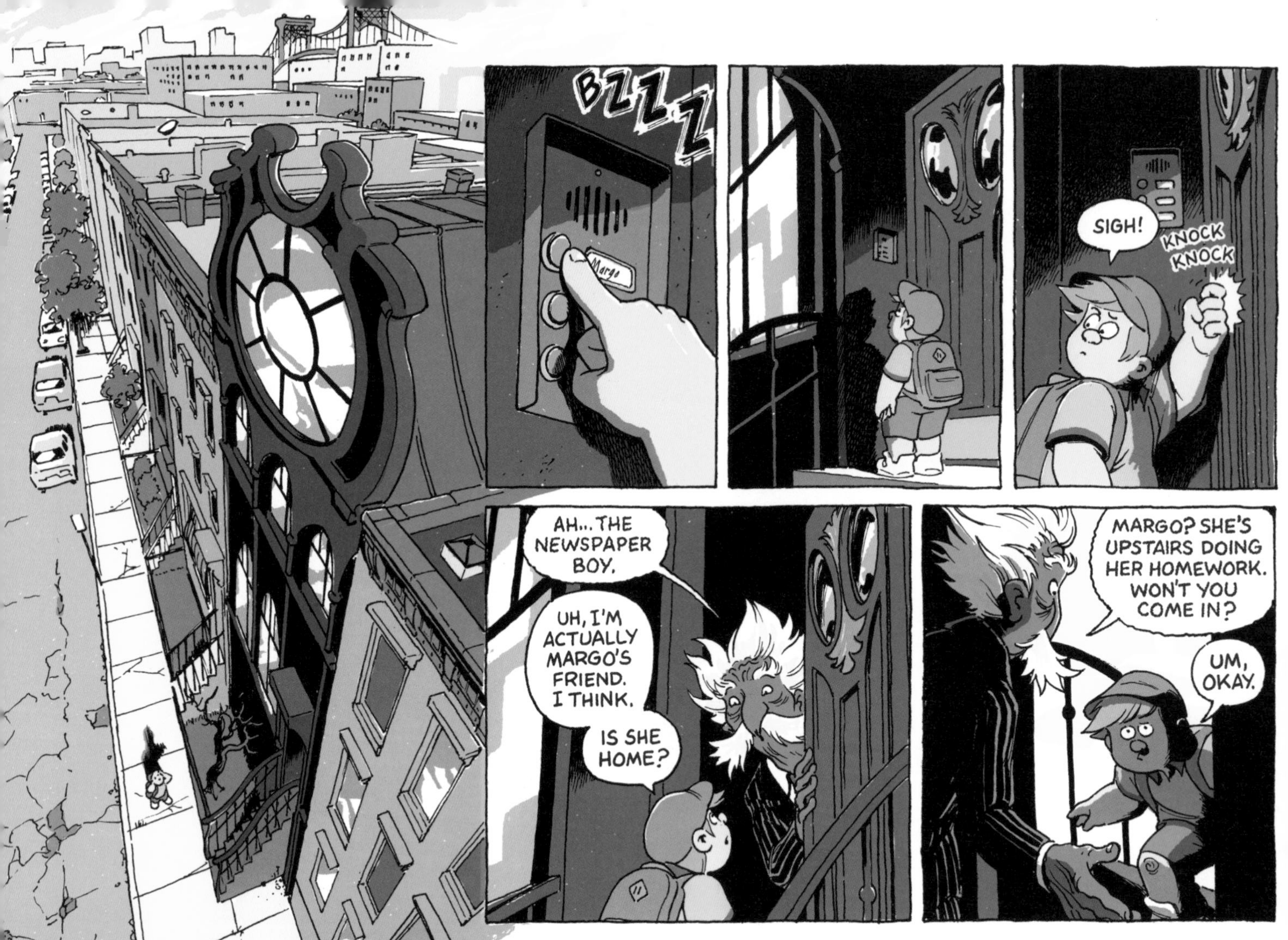

BZZZZ
Margo
SIGH!
KNOCK KNOCK
AH... THE NEWSPAPER BOY.
UH, I'M ACTUALLY MARGO'S FRIEND. I THINK.
IS SHE HOME?
MARGO? SHE'S UPSTAIRS DOING HER HOMEWORK. WON'T YOU COME IN?
UM, OKAY.

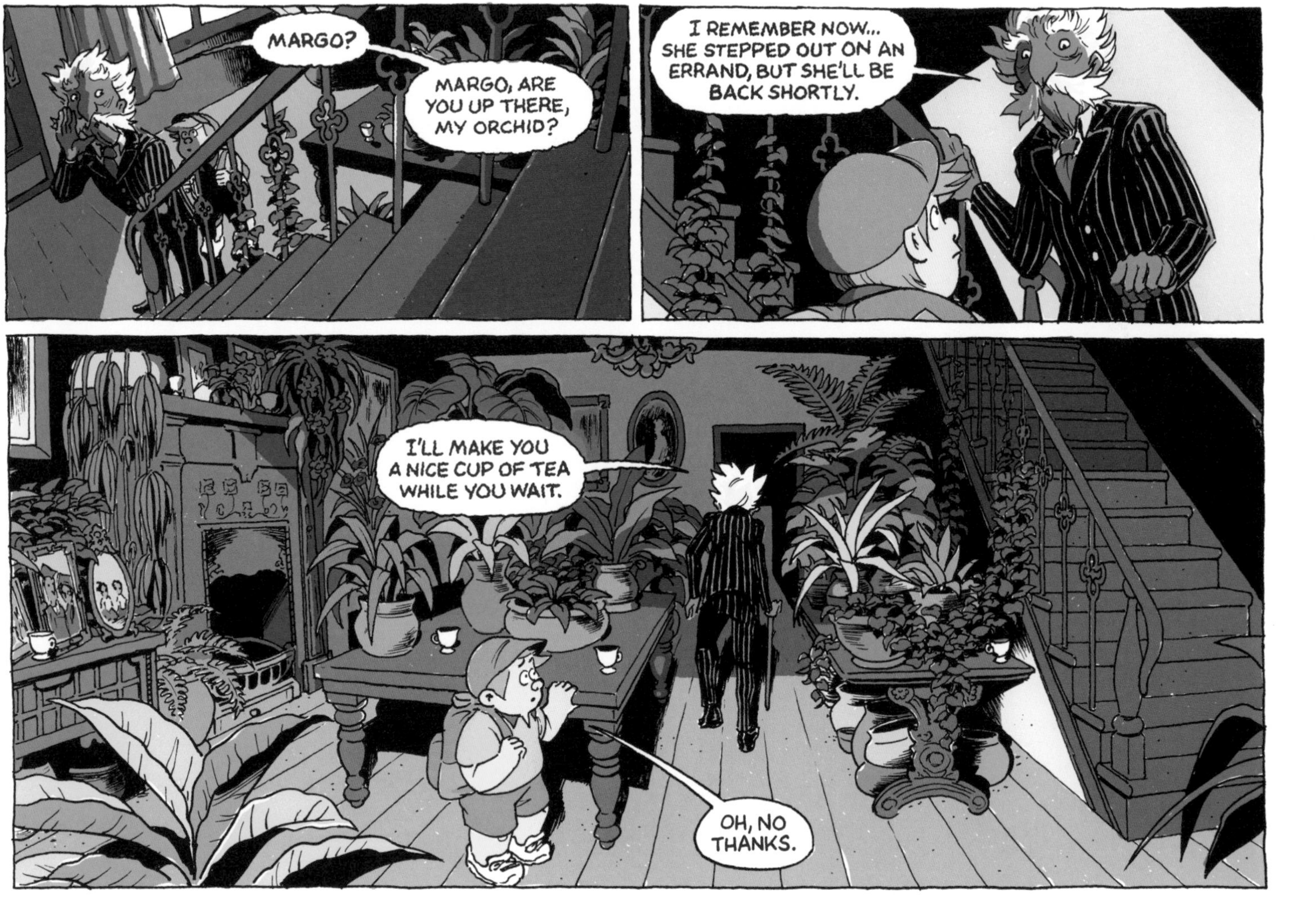
MARGO?
MARGO, ARE YOU UP THERE, MY ORCHID?
I REMEMBER NOW... SHE STEPPED OUT ON AN ERRAND, BUT SHE'LL BE BACK SHORTLY.
I'LL MAKE YOU A NICE CUP OF TEA WHILE YOU WAIT.
OH, NO THANKS.

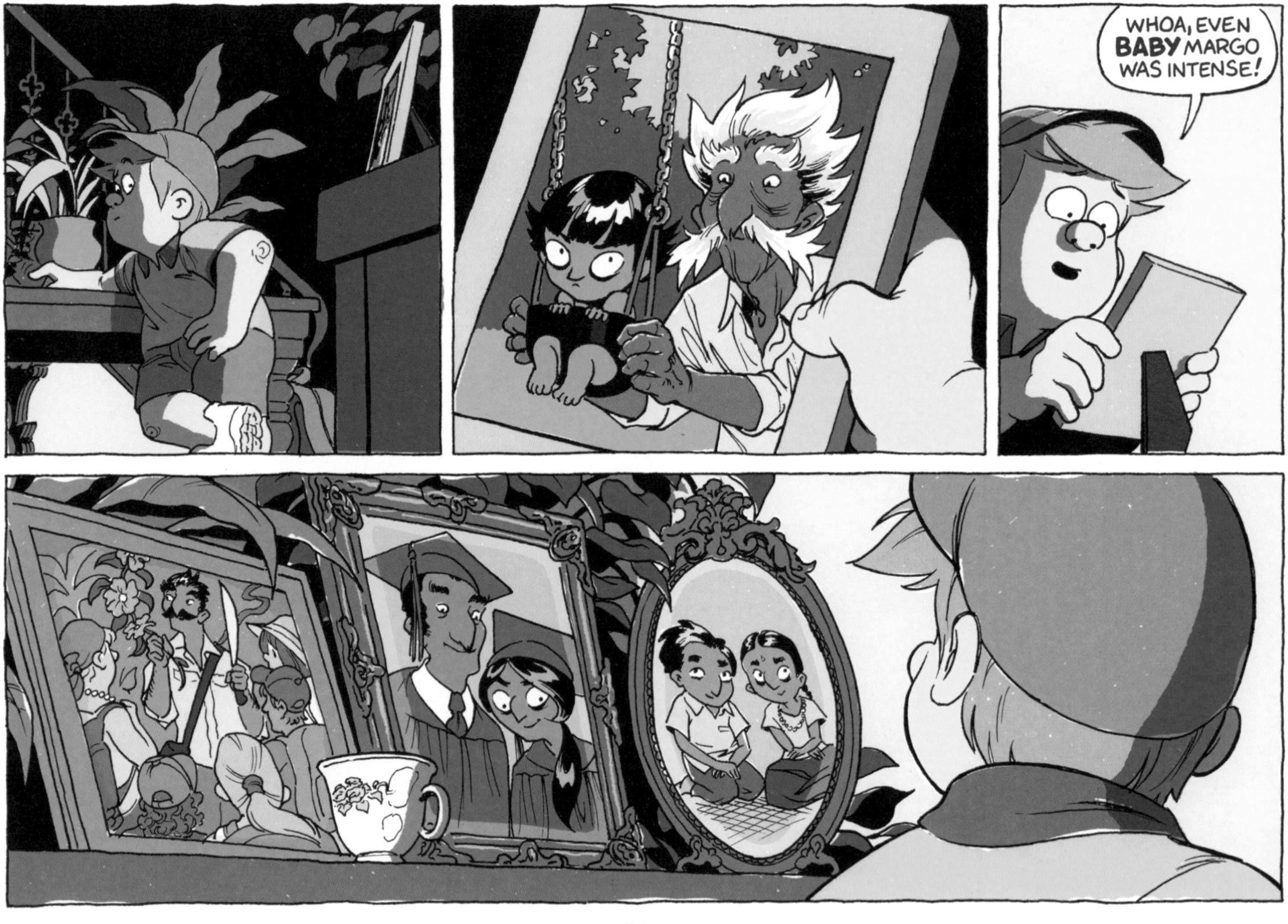
WHOA, EVEN BABY MARGO WAS INTENSE!

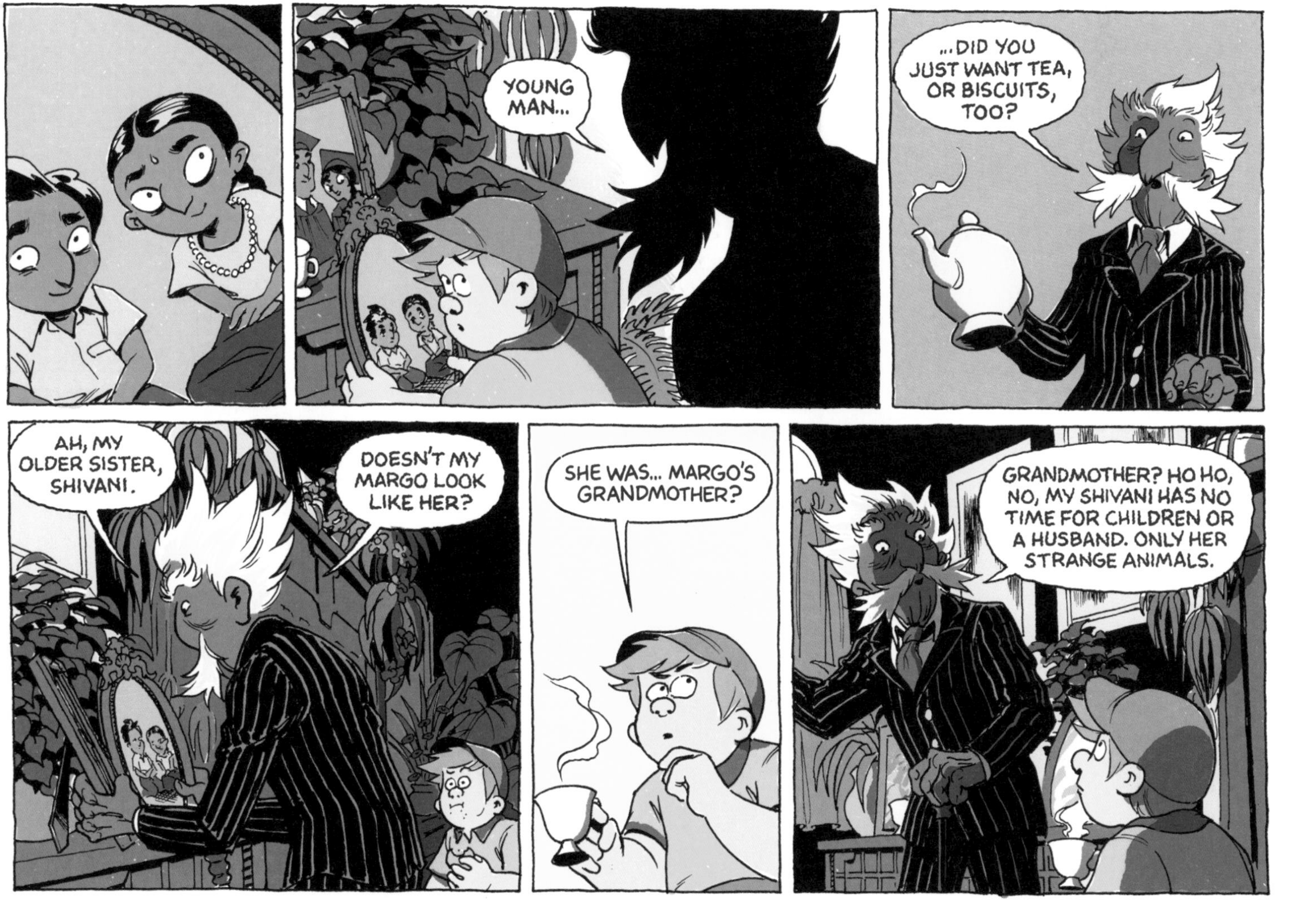
YOUNG MAN...
...DID YOU JUST WANT TEA, OR BISCUITS, TOO?
AH, MY OLDER SISTER, SHIVANI.
DOESN'T MY MARGO LOOK LIKE HER?
SHE WAS... MARGO'S GRANDMOTHER?
GRANDMOTHER? HO HO, NO, MY SHIVANI HAS NO TIME FOR CHILDREN OR A HUSBAND. ONLY HER STRANGE ANIMALS.

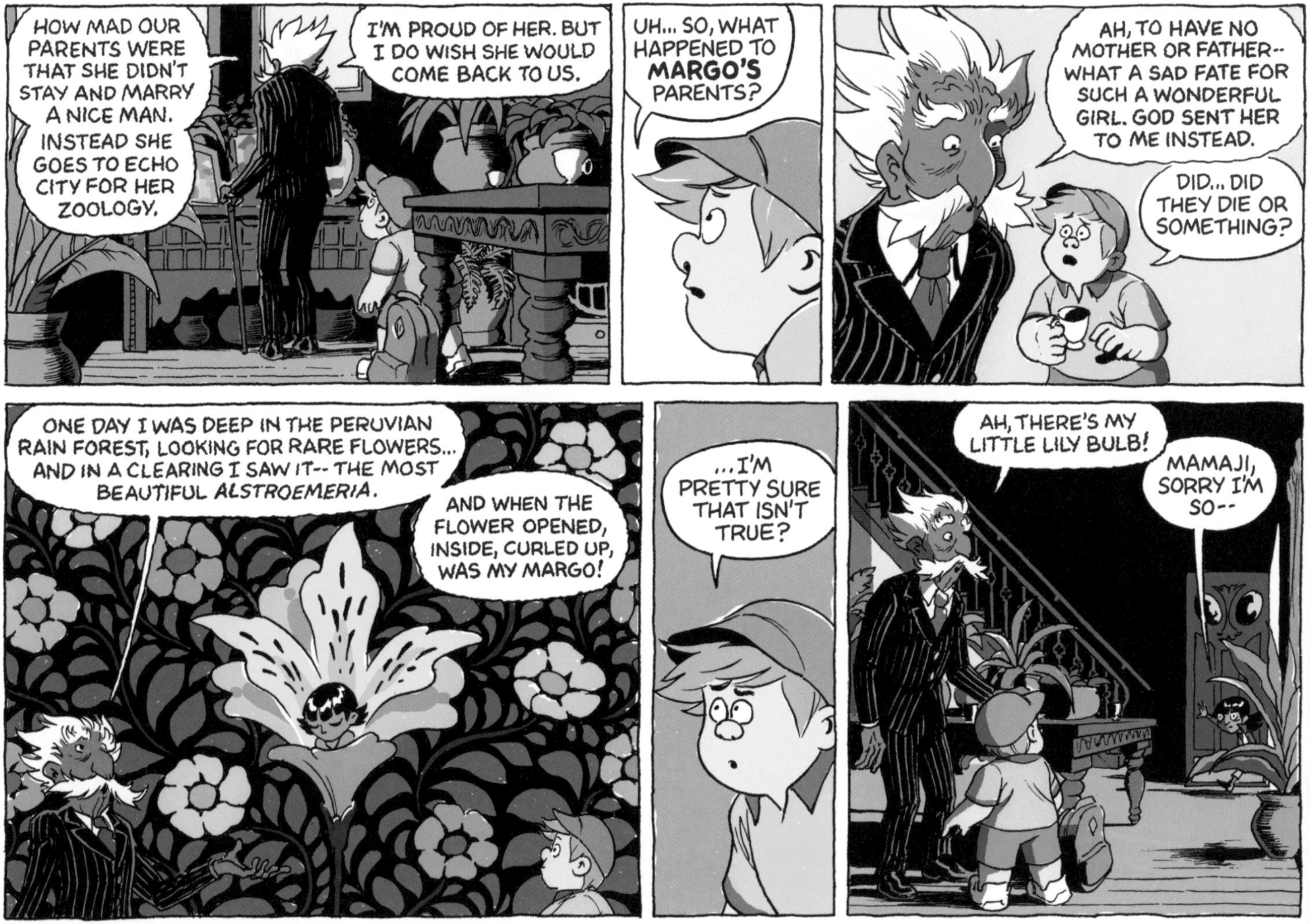
HOW MAD OUR PARENTS WERE THAT SHE DIDN'T STAY AND MARRY A NICE MAN. INSTEAD SHE GOES TO ECHO CITY FOR HER ZOOLOGY.
I'M PROUD OF HER. BUT I DO WISH SHE WOULD COME BACK TO US.
UH... SO, WHAT HAPPENED TO **MARGO'S** PARENTS?
AH, TO HAVE NO MOTHER OR FATHER-- WHAT A SAD FATE FOR SUCH A WONDERFUL GIRL. GOD SENT HER TO ME INSTEAD.
DID... DID THEY DIE OR SOMETHING?
ONE DAY I WAS DEEP IN THE PERUVIAN RAIN FOREST, LOOKING FOR RARE FLOWERS... AND IN A CLEARING I SAW IT-- THE MOST BEAUTIFUL *ALSTROEMERIA*.
AND WHEN THE FLOWER OPENED, INSIDE, CURLED UP, WAS MY MARGO!
...I'M PRETTY SURE THAT ISN'T TRUE?
AH, THERE'S MY LITTLE LILY BULB!
MAMAJI, SORRY I'M SO--

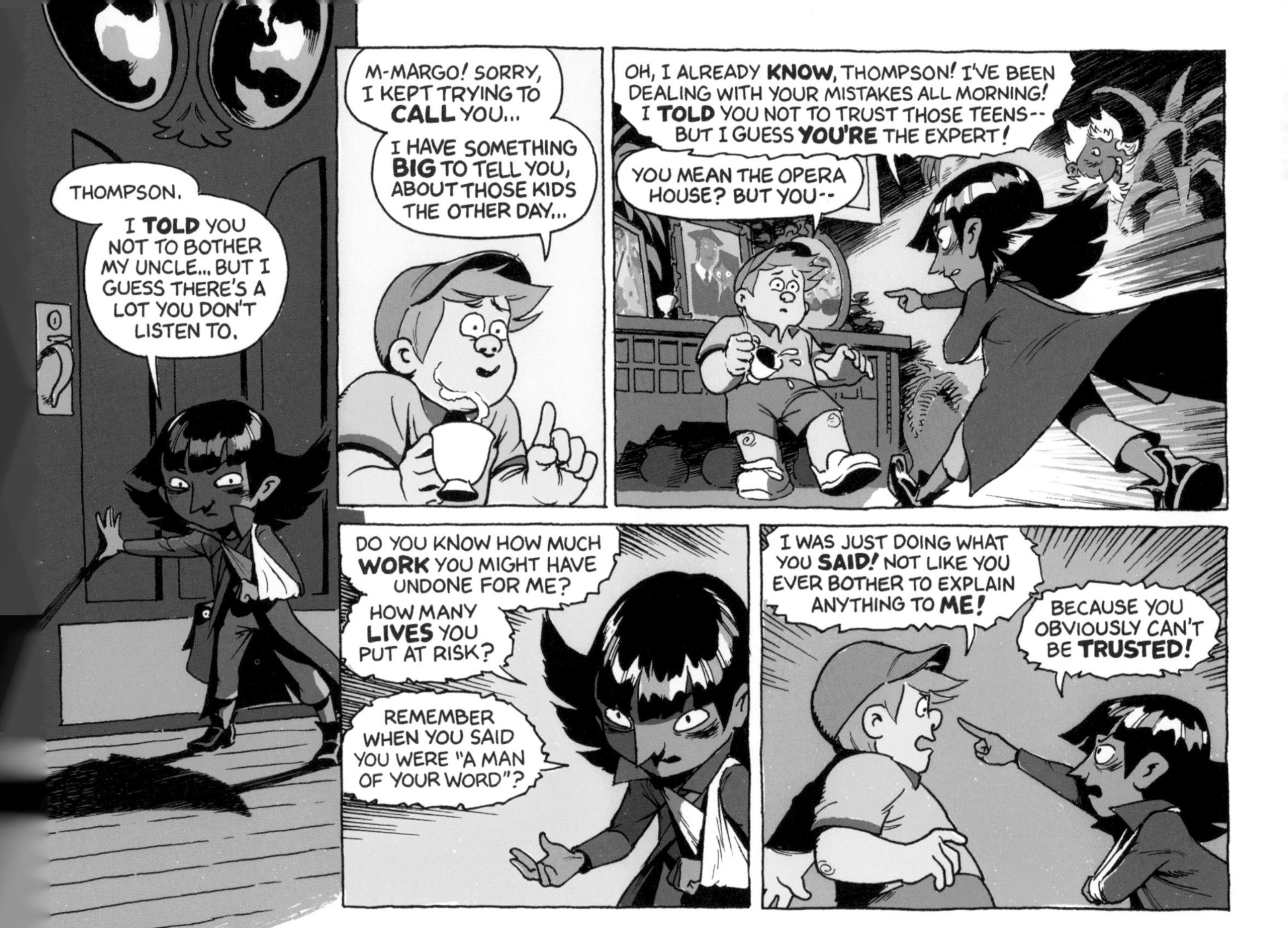
THOMPSON.
I TOLD YOU NOT TO BOTHER MY UNCLE... BUT I GUESS THERE'S A LOT YOU DON'T LISTEN TO.
M-MARGO! SORRY, I KEPT TRYING TO CALL YOU...
I HAVE SOMETHING BIG TO TELL YOU, ABOUT THOSE KIDS THE OTHER DAY...
OH, I ALREADY KNOW, THOMPSON! I'VE BEEN DEALING WITH YOUR MISTAKES ALL MORNING! I TOLD YOU NOT TO TRUST THOSE TEENS-- BUT I GUESS YOU'RE THE EXPERT!
YOU MEAN THE OPERA HOUSE? BUT YOU--
DO YOU KNOW HOW MUCH WORK YOU MIGHT HAVE UNDONE FOR ME?
HOW MANY LIVES YOU PUT AT RISK?
REMEMBER WHEN YOU SAID YOU WERE "A MAN OF YOUR WORD"?
I WAS JUST DOING WHAT YOU SAID! NOT LIKE YOU EVER BOTHER TO EXPLAIN ANYTHING TO ME!
BECAUSE YOU OBVIOUSLY CAN'T BE TRUSTED!

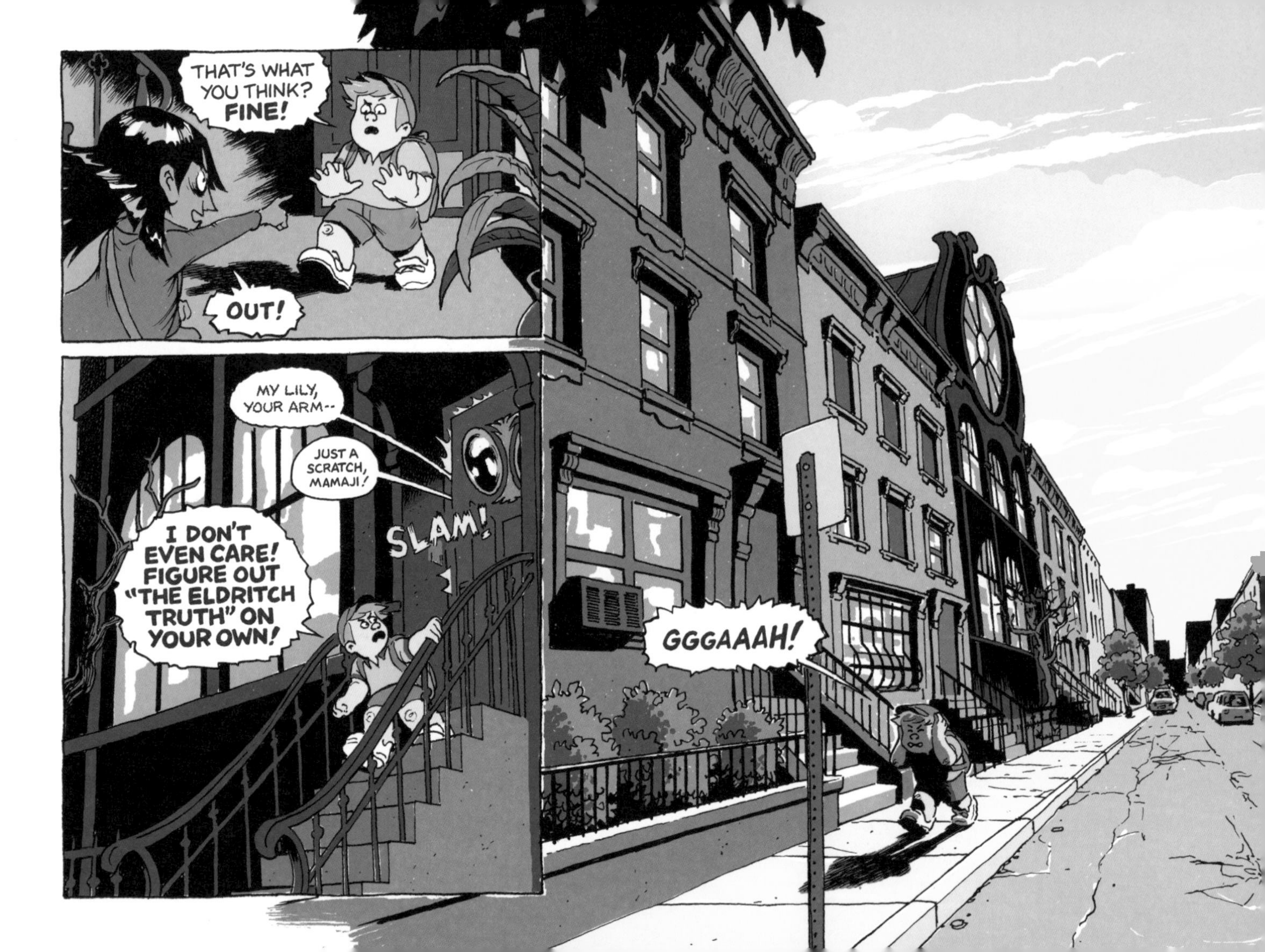
THAT'S WHAT YOU THINK? FINE!
OUT!
MY LILY, YOUR ARM--
JUST A SCRATCH, MAMAJI!
SLAM!
I DON'T EVEN CARE! FIGURE OUT "THE ELDRITCH TRUTH" ON YOUR OWN!
GGGAAAH!

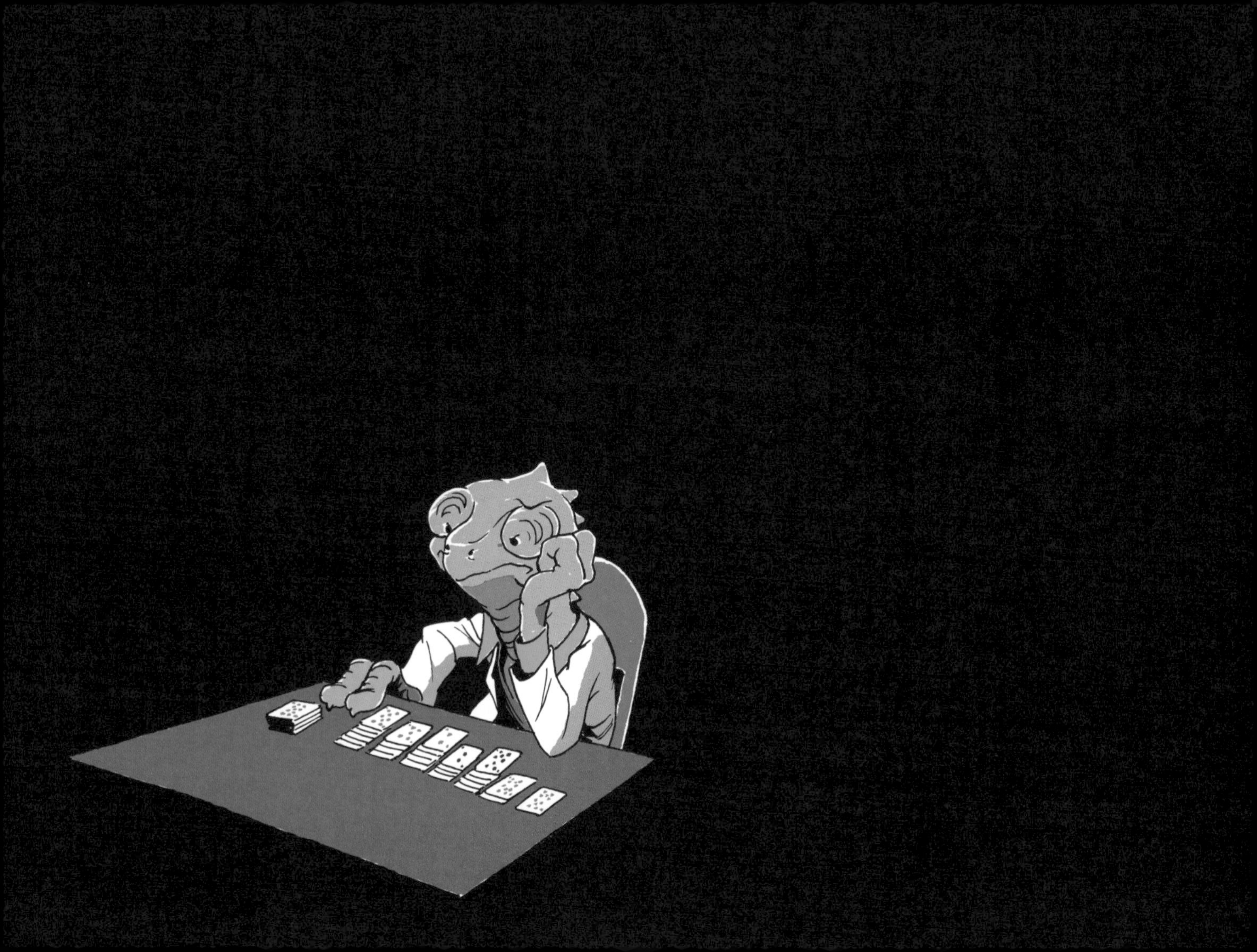

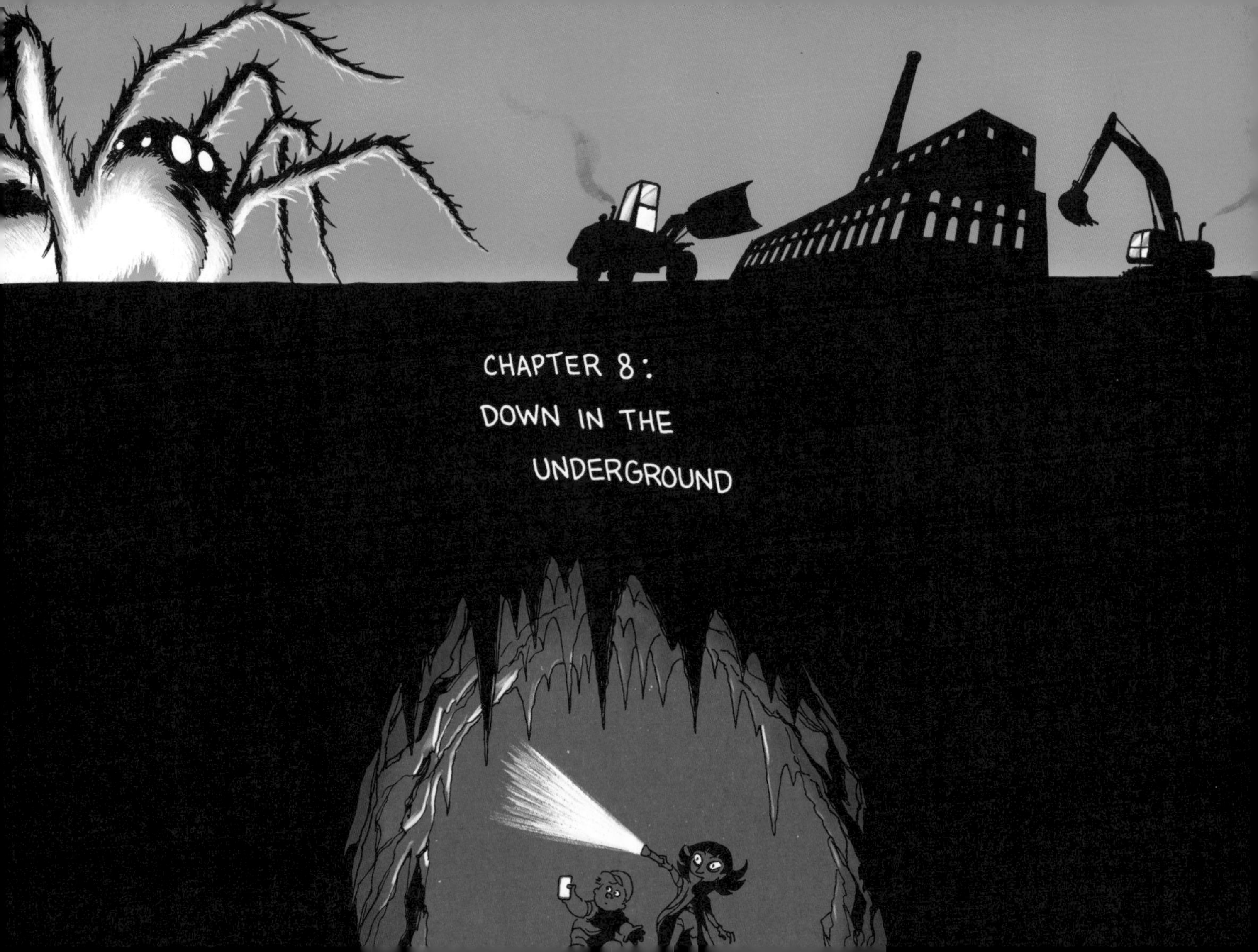
CHAPTER 8:
DOWN IN THE
UNDERGROUND

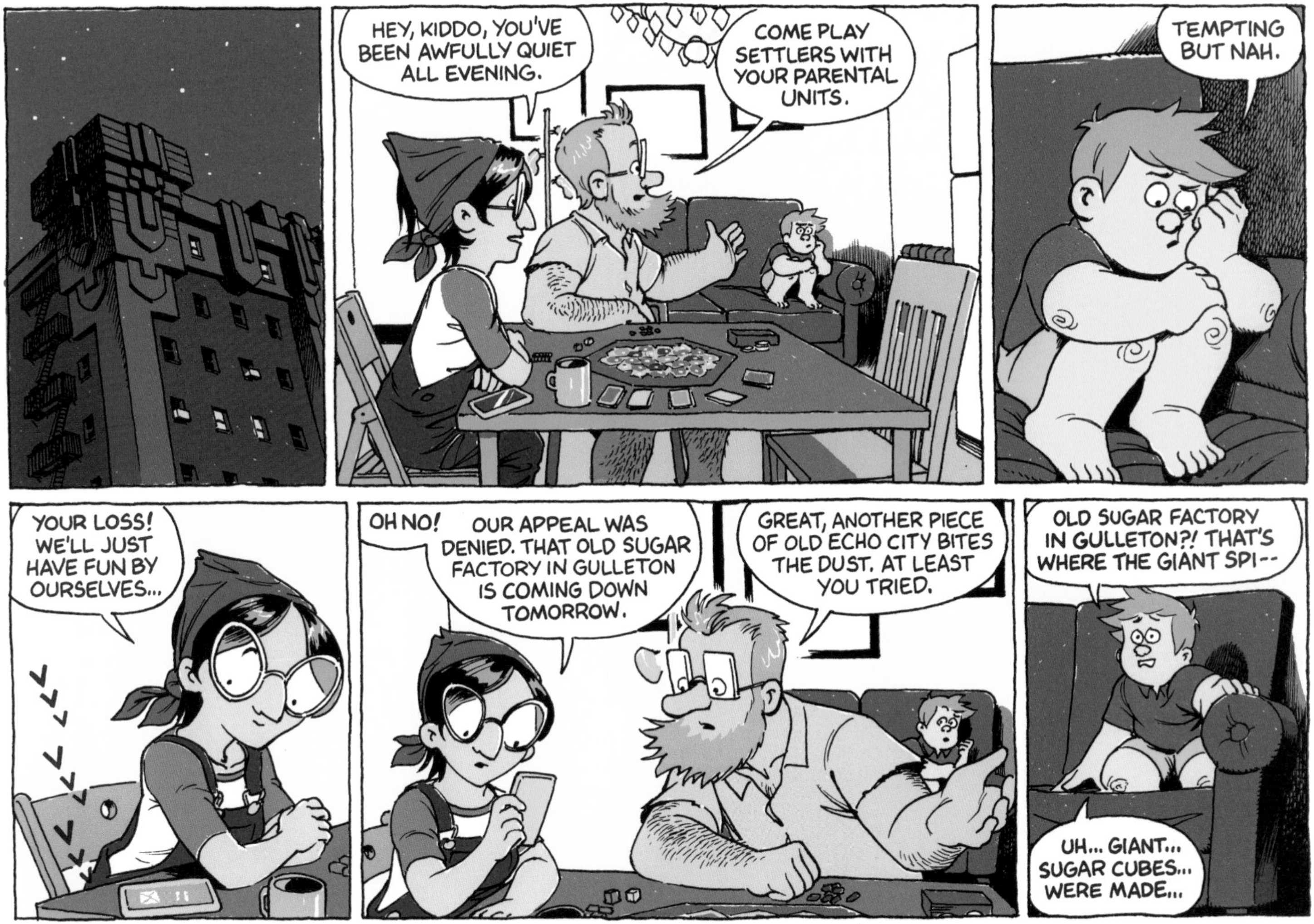

HEY, KIDDO, YOU'VE BEEN AWFULLY QUIET ALL EVENING.
COME PLAY SETTLERS WITH YOUR PARENTAL UNITS.
TEMPTING BUT NAH.
YOUR LOSS! WE'LL JUST HAVE FUN BY OURSELVES...
OH NO!
OUR APPEAL WAS DENIED. THAT OLD SUGAR FACTORY IN GULLETON IS COMING DOWN TOMORROW.
GREAT, ANOTHER PIECE OF OLD ECHO CITY BITES THE DUST. AT LEAST YOU TRIED.
OLD SUGAR FACTORY IN GULLETON?! THAT'S WHERE THE GIANT SPI--
UH... GIANT... SUGAR CUBES... WERE MADE...

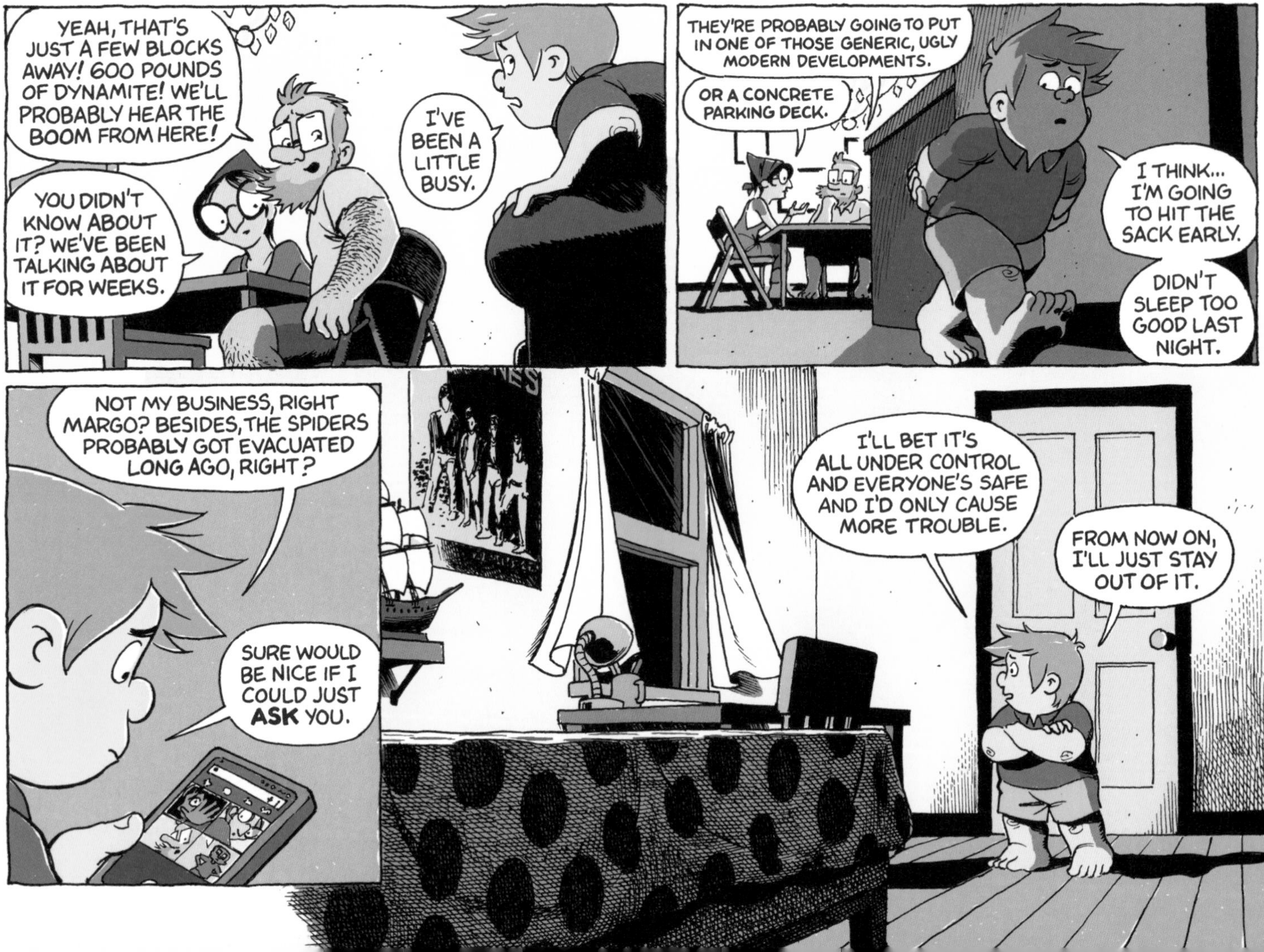
YEAH, THAT'S JUST A FEW BLOCKS AWAY! 600 POUNDS OF DYNAMITE! WE'LL PROBABLY HEAR THE BOOM FROM HERE!
YOU DIDN'T KNOW ABOUT IT? WE'VE BEEN TALKING ABOUT IT FOR WEEKS.
I'VE BEEN A LITTLE BUSY.
THEY'RE PROBABLY GOING TO PUT IN ONE OF THOSE GENERIC, UGLY MODERN DEVELOPMENTS.
OR A CONCRETE PARKING DECK.
I THINK... I'M GOING TO HIT THE SACK EARLY.
DIDN'T SLEEP TOO GOOD LAST NIGHT.
NOT MY BUSINESS, RIGHT MARGO? BESIDES, THE SPIDERS PROBABLY GOT EVACUATED LONG AGO, RIGHT?
SURE WOULD BE NICE IF I COULD JUST **ASK** YOU.
I'LL BET IT'S ALL UNDER CONTROL AND EVERYONE'S SAFE AND I'D ONLY CAUSE MORE TROUBLE.
FROM NOW ON, I'LL JUST STAY OUT OF IT.

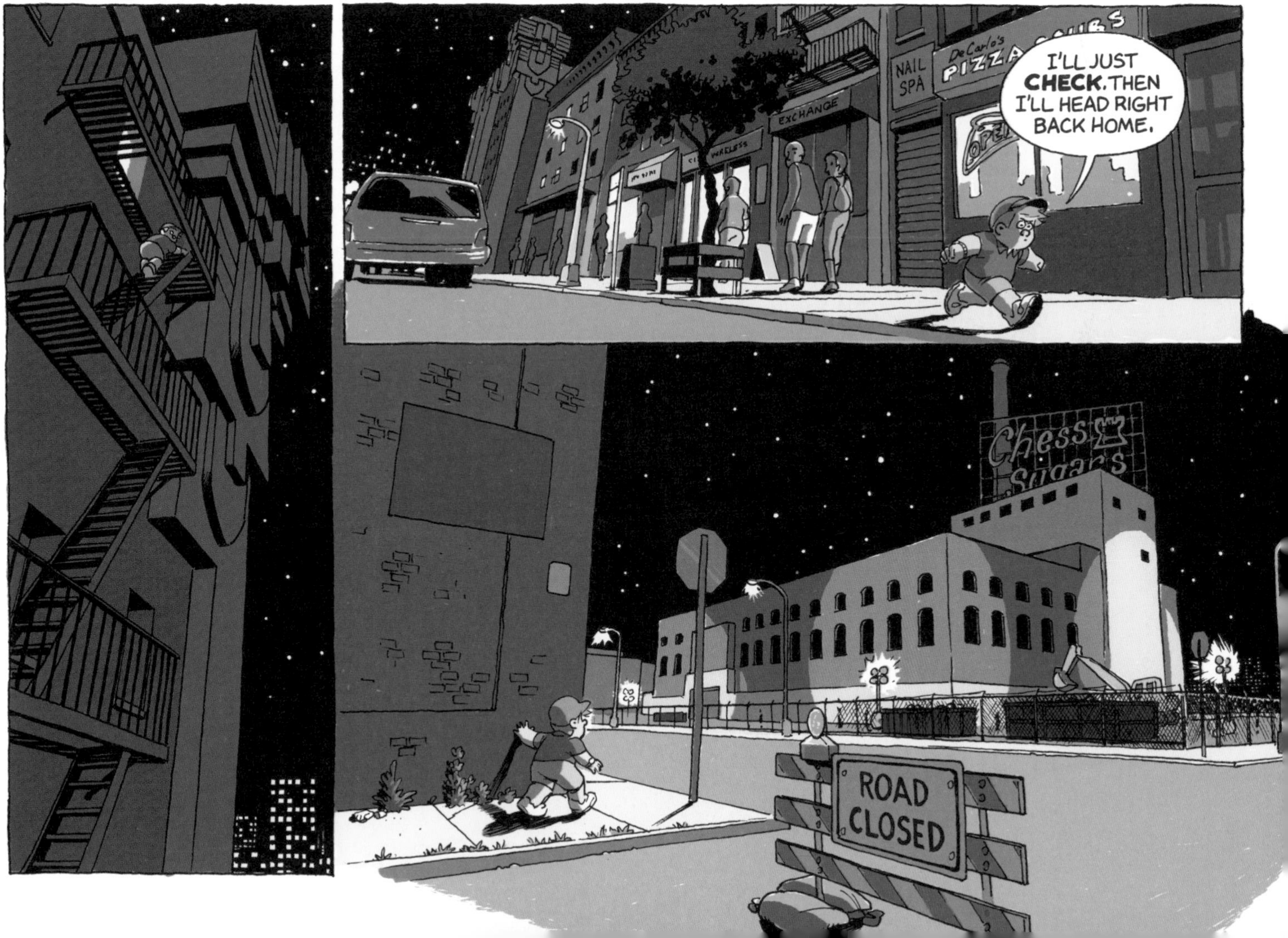
NAIL SPA
De Carlo's
EXCHANGE
I'LL JUST CHECK. THEN I'LL HEAD RIGHT BACK HOME.
Chess
ROAD CLOSED

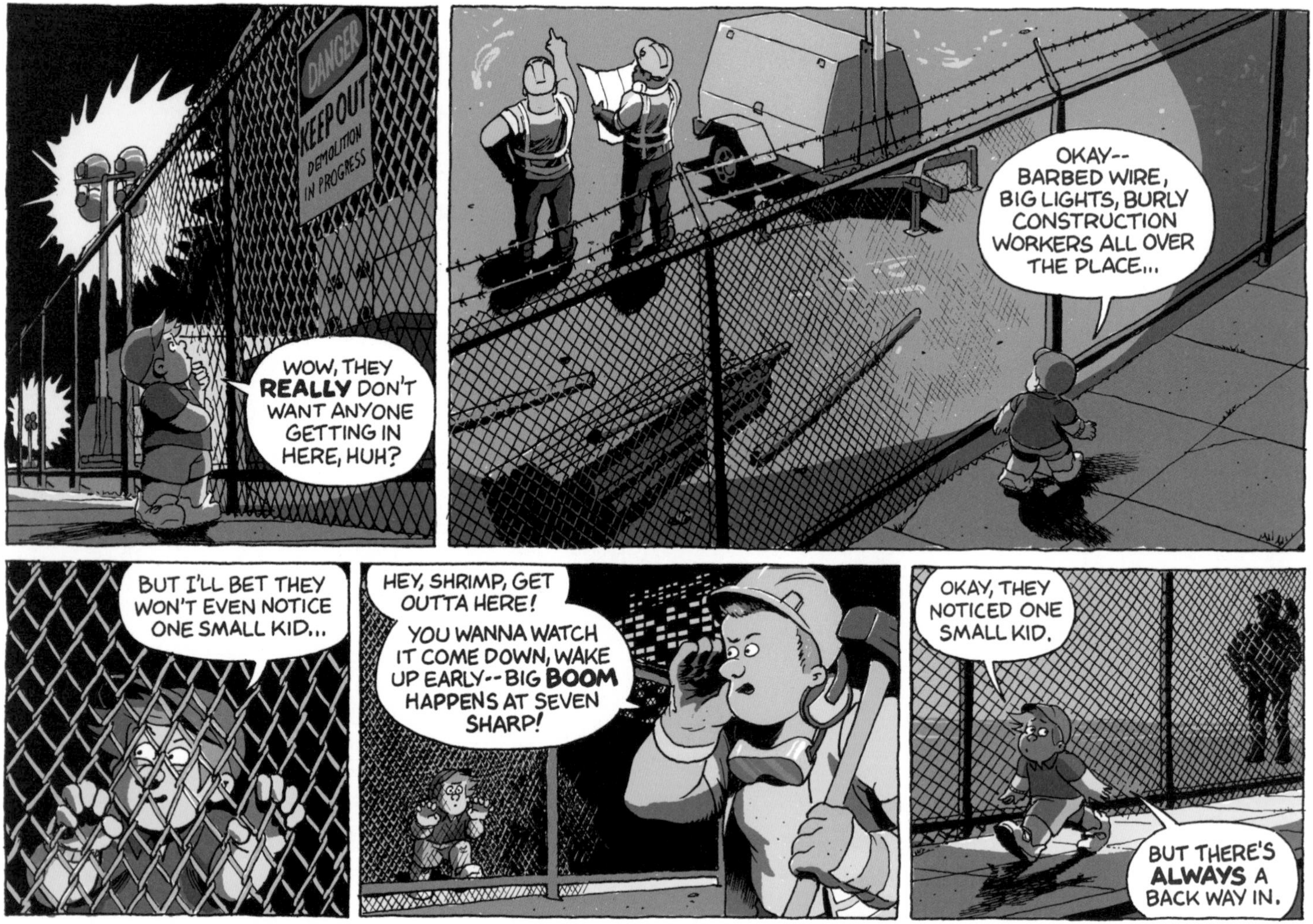
DANGER
KEEP OUT
DEMOLITION IN PROGRESS
WOW, THEY **REALLY** DON'T WANT ANYONE GETTING IN HERE, HUH?
OKAY-- BARBED WIRE, BIG LIGHTS, BURLY CONSTRUCTION WORKERS ALL OVER THE PLACE...
BUT I'LL BET THEY WON'T EVEN NOTICE ONE SMALL KID...
HEY, SHRIMP, GET OUTTA HERE!
YOU WANNA WATCH IT COME DOWN, WAKE UP EARLY--BIG **BOOM** HAPPENS AT SEVEN SHARP!
OKAY, THEY NOTICED ONE SMALL KID.
BUT THERE'S **ALWAYS** A BACK WAY IN.

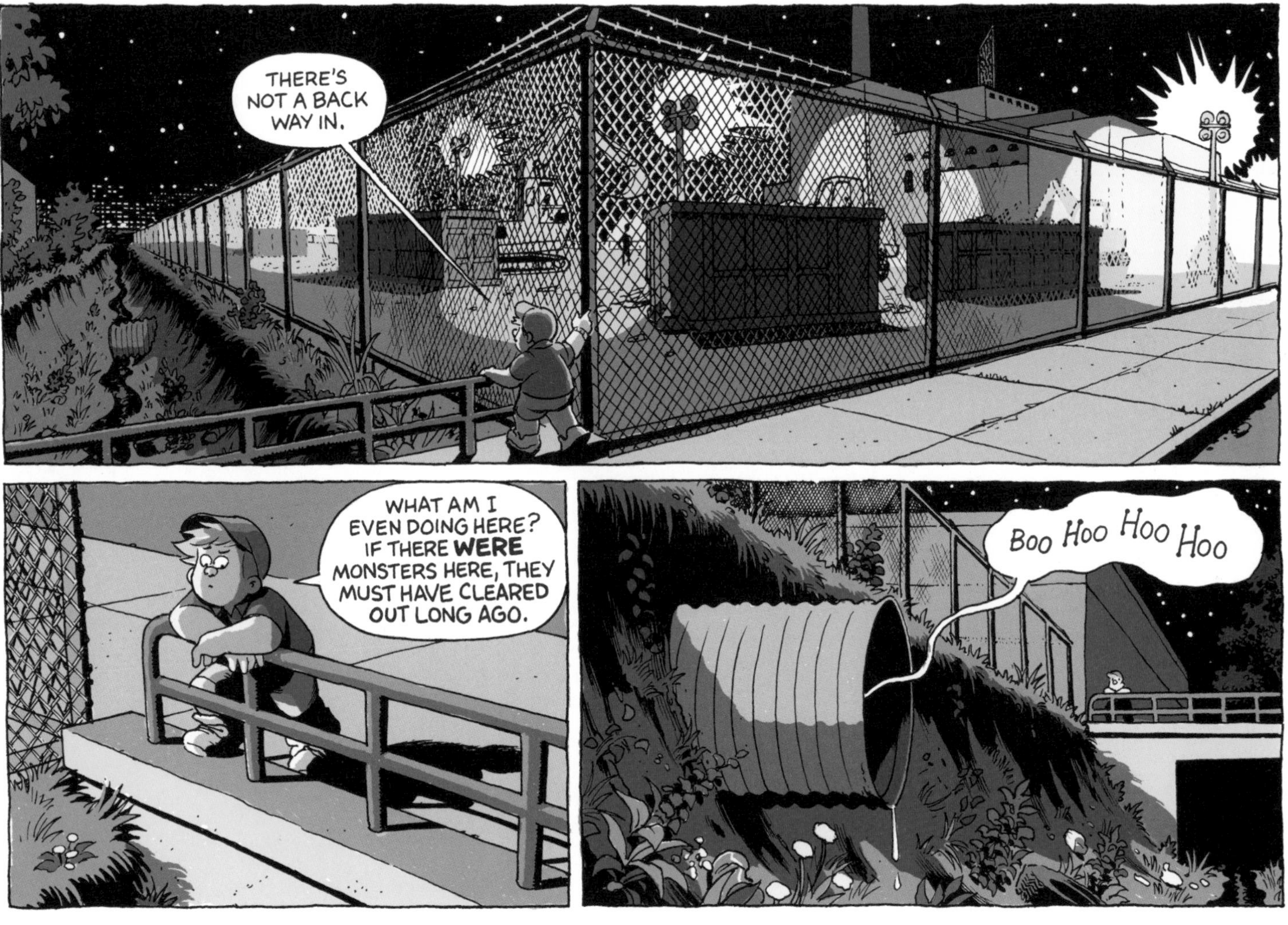
THERE'S NOT A BACK WAY IN.
WHAT AM I EVEN DOING HERE? IF THERE **WERE** MONSTERS HERE, THEY MUST HAVE CLEARED OUT LONG AGO.
Boo Hoo Hoo Hoo

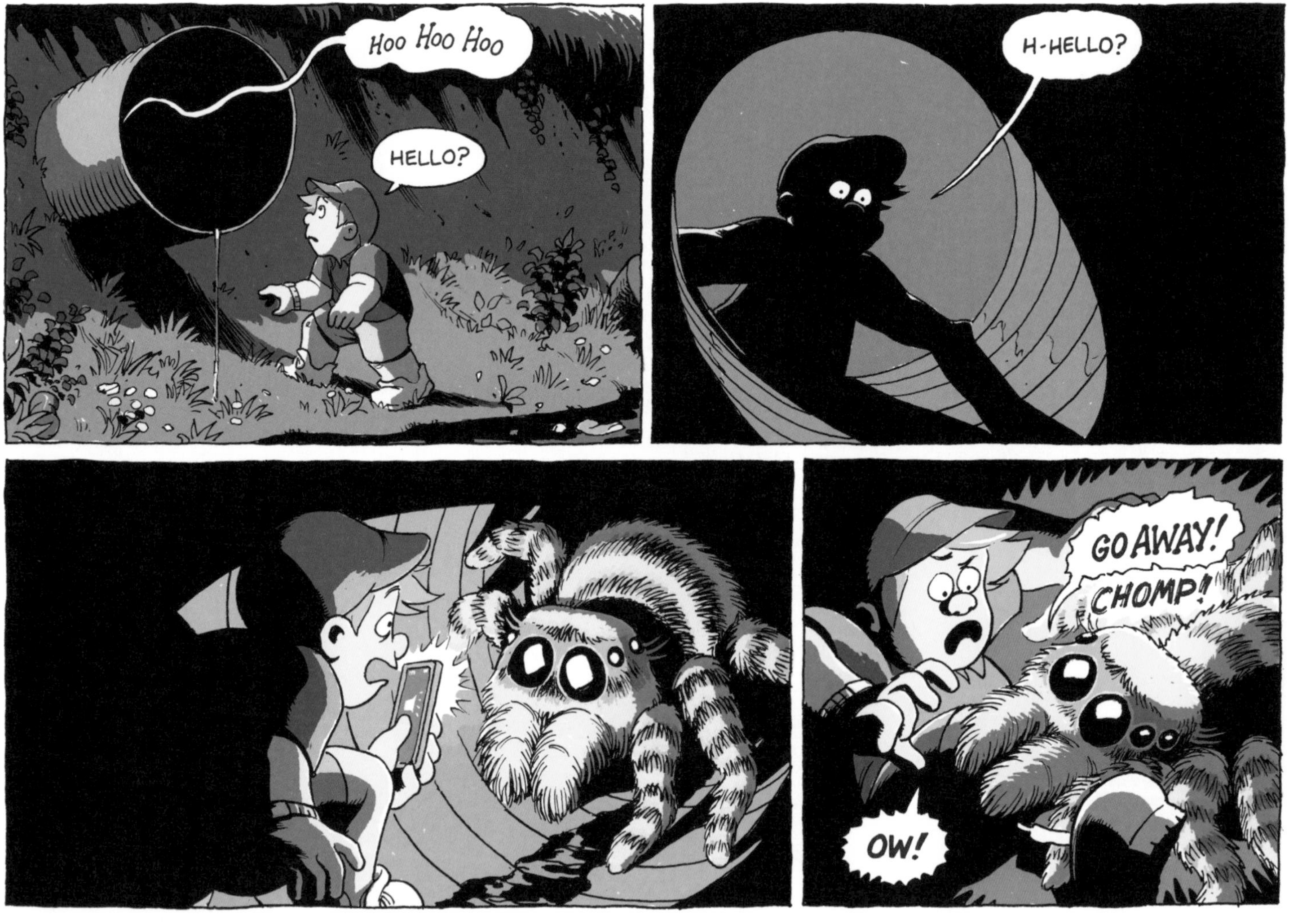
Hoo Hoo Hoo
HELLO?
H-HELLO?
GO AWAY!
CHOMP!
OW!

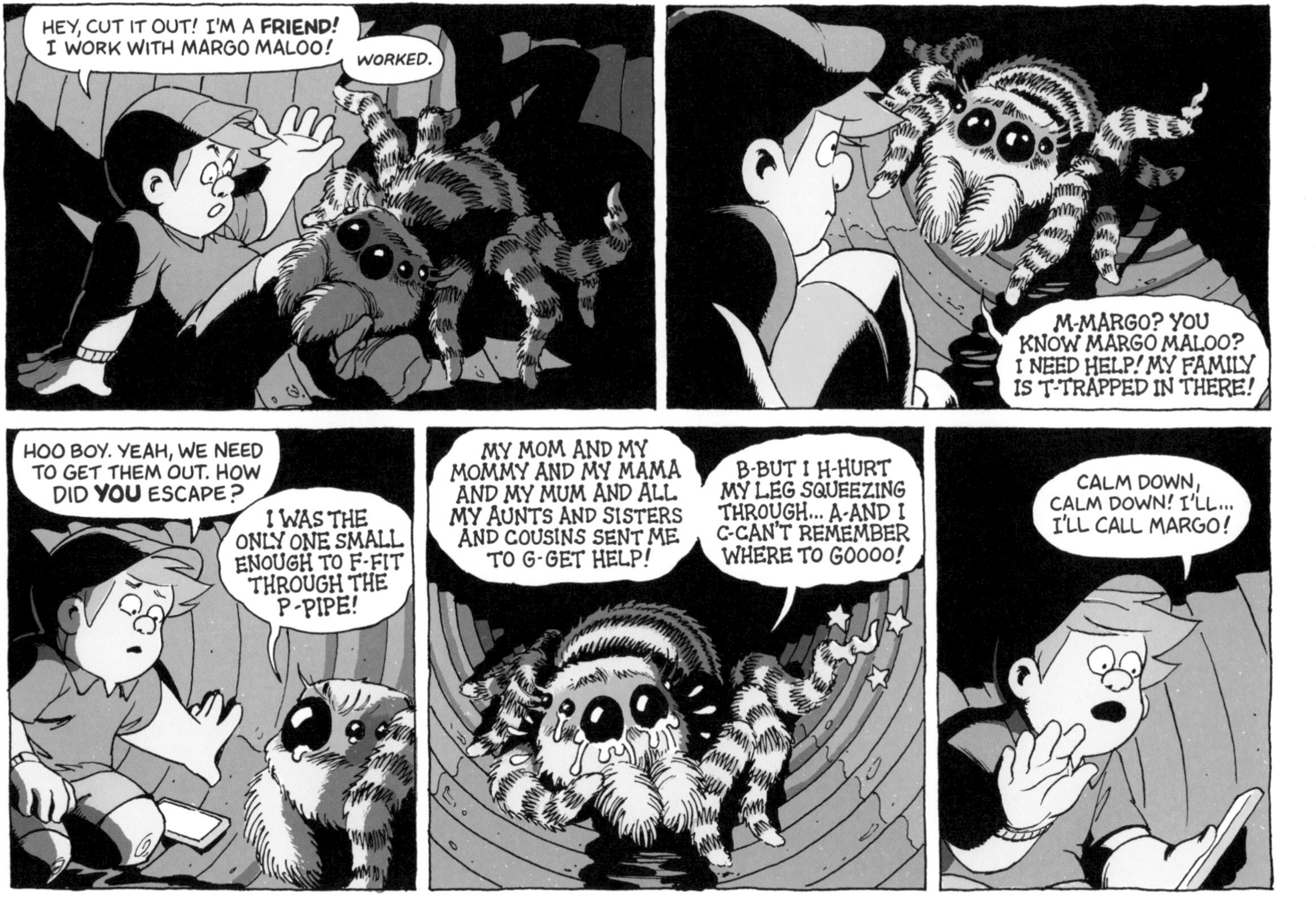
HEY, CUT IT OUT! I'M A FRIEND! I WORK WITH MARGO MALOO!
WORKED.
M-MARGO? YOU KNOW MARGO MALOO? I NEED HELP! MY FAMILY IS T-TRAPPED IN THERE!
HOO BOY. YEAH, WE NEED TO GET THEM OUT. HOW DID YOU ESCAPE?
I WAS THE ONLY ONE SMALL ENOUGH TO F-FIT THROUGH THE P-PIPE!
MY MOM AND MY MOMMY AND MY MAMA AND MY MUM AND ALL MY AUNTS AND SISTERS AND COUSINS SENT ME TO G-GET HELP!
B-BUT I H-HURT MY LEG SQUEEZING THROUGH... A-AND I C-CAN'T REMEMBER WHERE TO GOOOO!
CALM DOWN, CALM DOWN! I'LL... I'LL CALL MARGO!

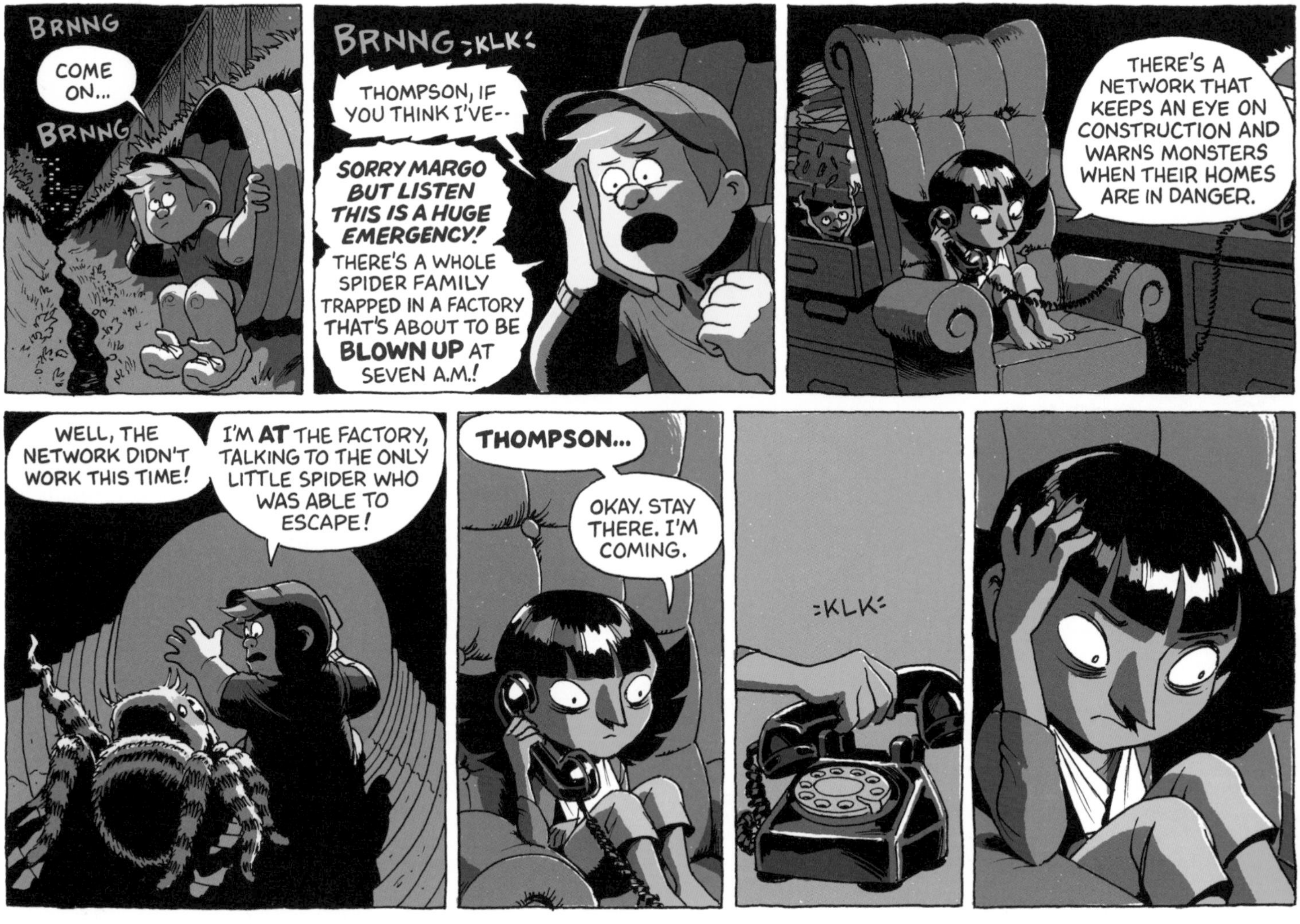
BRNNG
COME ON...
BRNNG
BRNNG =KLK=
THOMPSON, IF YOU THINK I'VE--
SORRY MARGO BUT LISTEN THIS IS A HUGE EMERGENCY! THERE'S A WHOLE SPIDER FAMILY TRAPPED IN A FACTORY THAT'S ABOUT TO BE BLOWN UP AT SEVEN A.M.!
THERE'S A NETWORK THAT KEEPS AN EYE ON CONSTRUCTION AND WARNS MONSTERS WHEN THEIR HOMES ARE IN DANGER.
WELL, THE NETWORK DIDN'T WORK THIS TIME!
I'M AT THE FACTORY, TALKING TO THE ONLY LITTLE SPIDER WHO WAS ABLE TO ESCAPE!
THOMPSON...
OKAY. STAY THERE. I'M COMING.
=KLK=

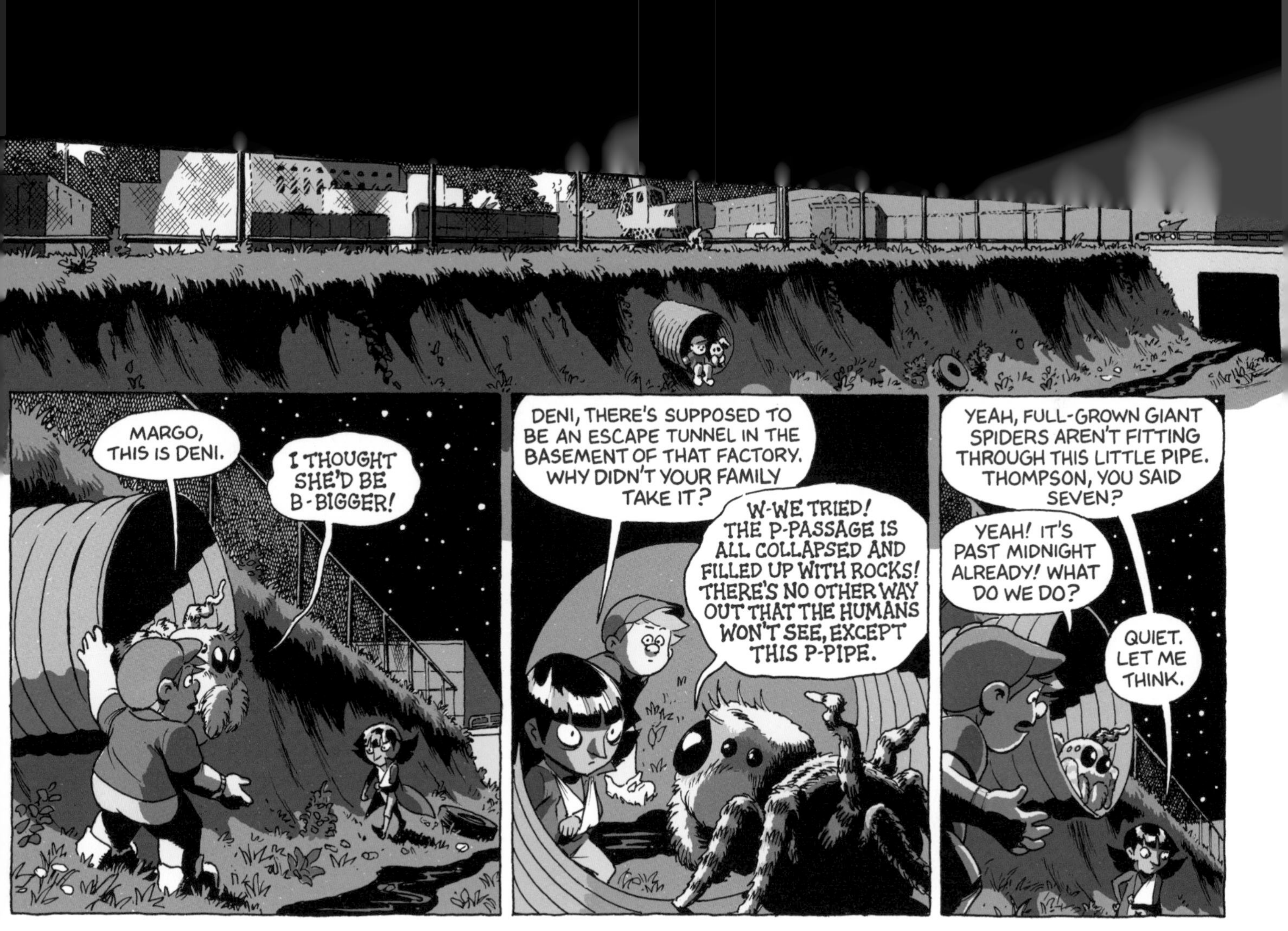
MARGO, THIS IS DENI.
I THOUGHT SHE'D BE B-BIGGER!
DENI, THERE'S SUPPOSED TO BE AN ESCAPE TUNNEL IN THE BASEMENT OF THAT FACTORY. WHY DIDN'T YOUR FAMILY TAKE IT?
W-WE TRIED! THE P-PASSAGE IS ALL COLLAPSED AND FILLED UP WITH ROCKS! THERE'S NO OTHER WAY OUT THAT THE HUMANS WON'T SEE, EXCEPT THIS P-PIPE.
YEAH, FULL-GROWN GIANT SPIDERS AREN'T FITTING THROUGH THIS LITTLE PIPE. THOMPSON, YOU SAID SEVEN?
YEAH! IT'S PAST MIDNIGHT ALREADY! WHAT DO WE DO?
QUIET. LET ME THINK.

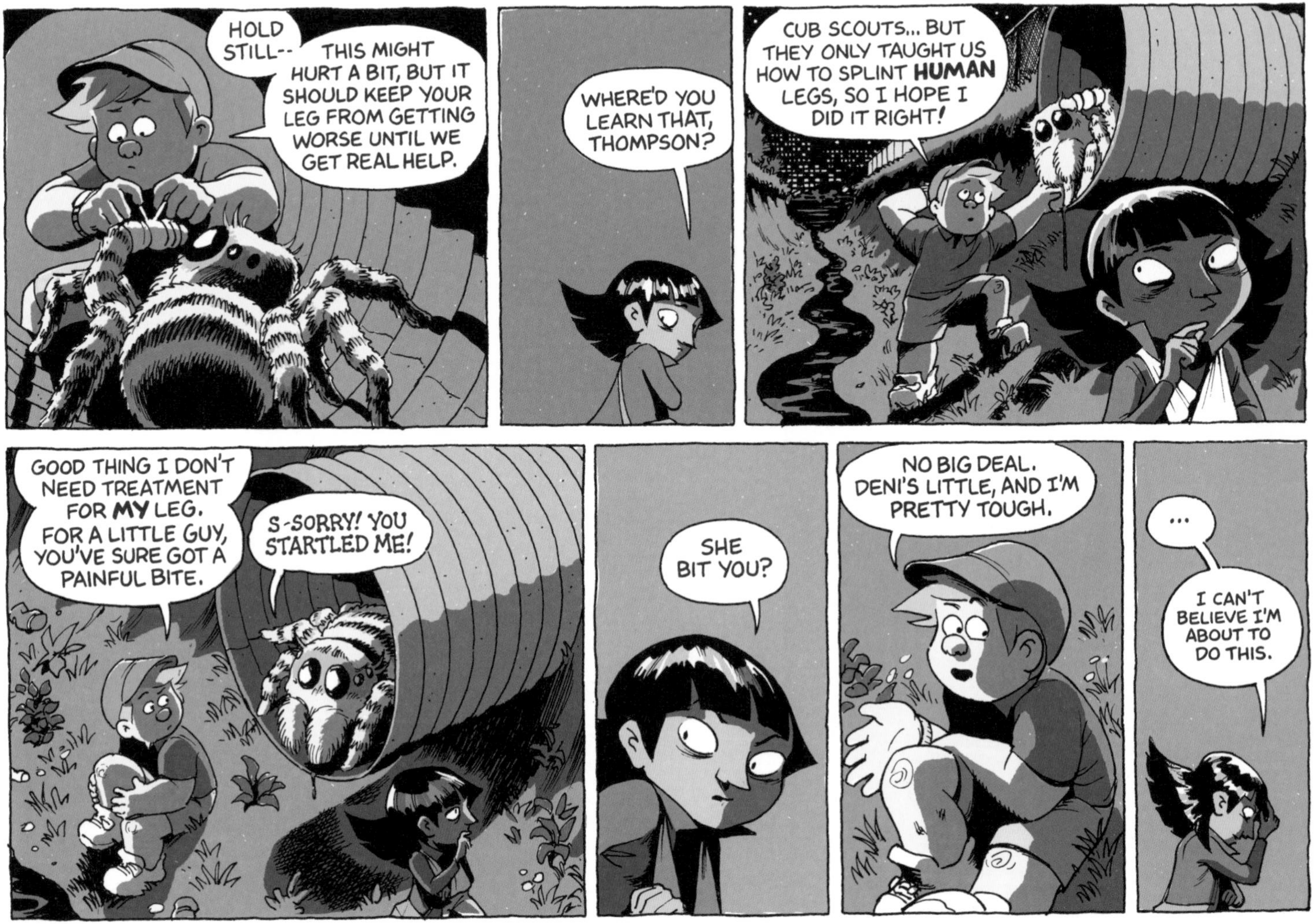

HOLD STILL--
THIS MIGHT HURT A BIT, BUT IT SHOULD KEEP YOUR LEG FROM GETTING WORSE UNTIL WE GET REAL HELP.
WHERE'D YOU LEARN THAT, THOMPSON?
CUB SCOUTS... BUT THEY ONLY TAUGHT US HOW TO SPLINT **HUMAN** LEGS, SO I HOPE I DID IT RIGHT!
GOOD THING I DON'T NEED TREATMENT FOR **MY** LEG. FOR A LITTLE GUY, YOU'VE SURE GOT A PAINFUL BITE.
S-SORRY! YOU STARTLED ME!
SHE BIT YOU?
NO BIG DEAL. DENI'S LITTLE, AND I'M PRETTY TOUGH.
...
I CAN'T BELIEVE I'M ABOUT TO DO THIS.

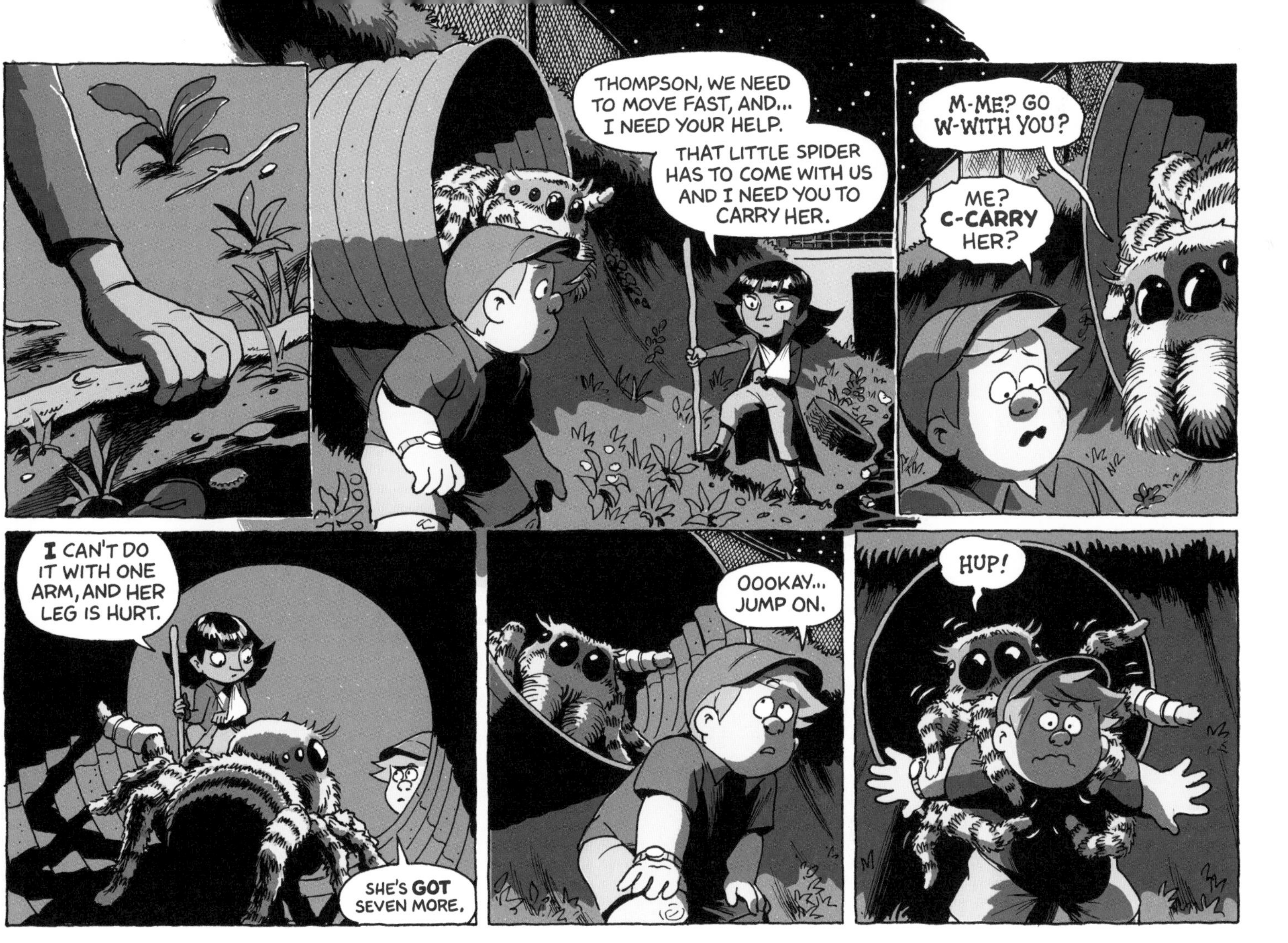
THOMPSON, WE NEED TO MOVE FAST, AND... I NEED YOUR HELP.
THAT LITTLE SPIDER HAS TO COME WITH US AND I NEED YOU TO CARRY HER.
M-ME? GO W-WITH YOU?
ME? **C-CARRY** HER?
I CAN'T DO IT WITH ONE ARM, AND HER LEG IS HURT.
SHE'S **GOT** SEVEN MORE.
OOOKAY... JUMP ON.
HUP!

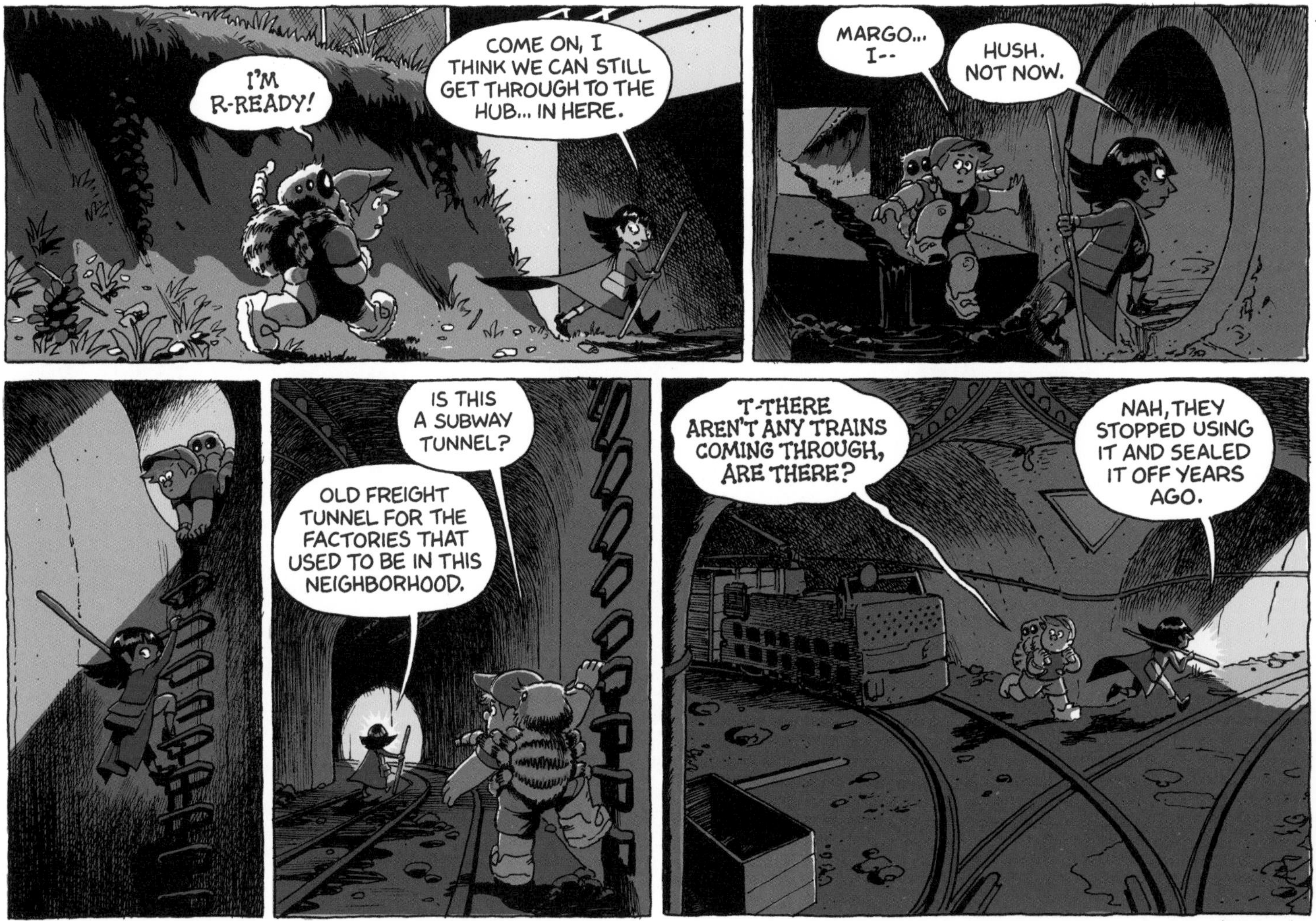
I'M R-READY!
COME ON, I THINK WE CAN STILL GET THROUGH TO THE HUB... IN HERE.
MARGO... I--
HUSH. NOT NOW.
IS THIS A SUBWAY TUNNEL?
OLD FREIGHT TUNNEL FOR THE FACTORIES THAT USED TO BE IN THIS NEIGHBORHOOD.
T-THERE AREN'T ANY TRAINS COMING THROUGH, ARE THERE?
NAH, THEY STOPPED USING IT AND SEALED IT OFF YEARS AGO.

drew weing

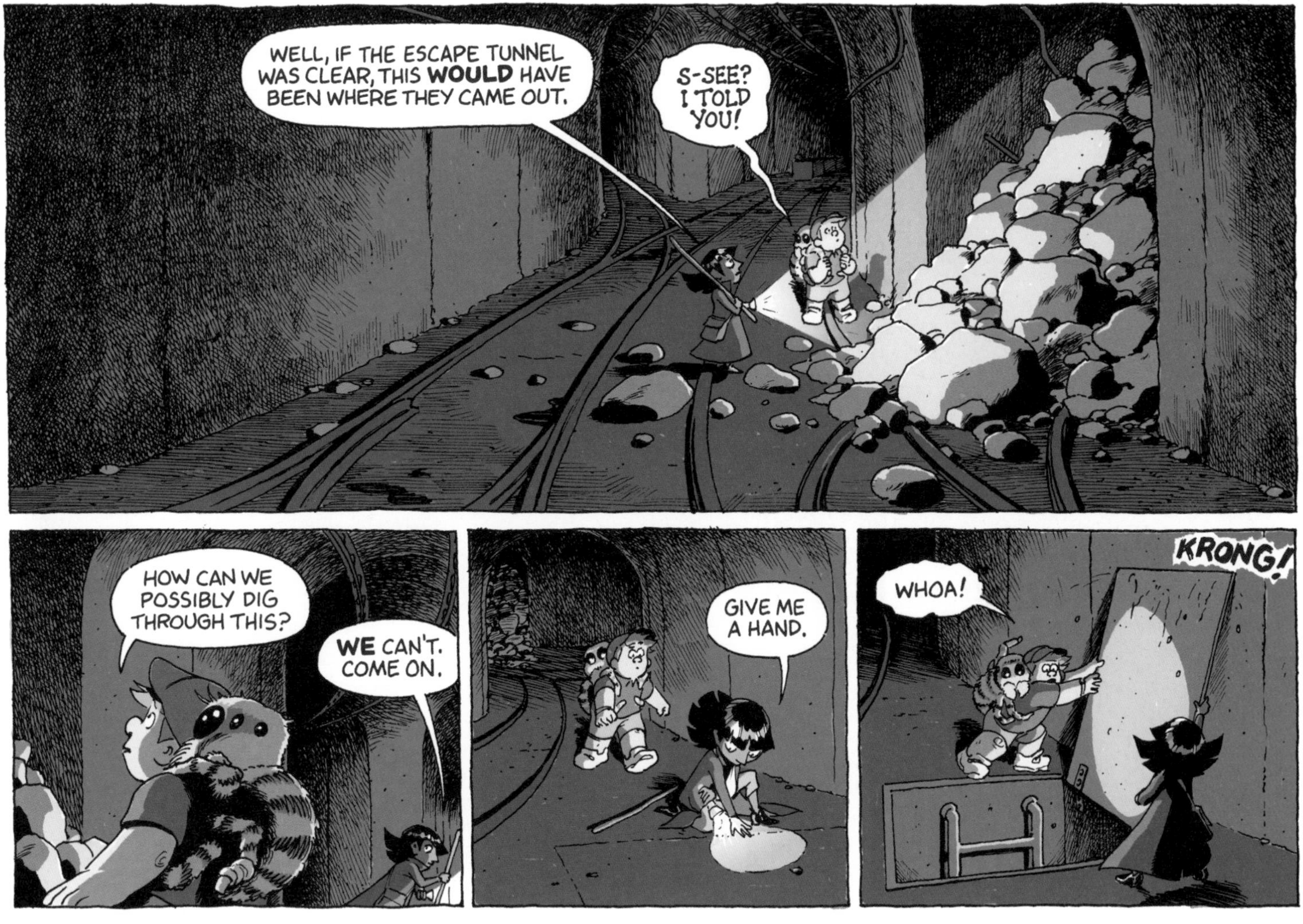
WELL, IF THE ESCAPE TUNNEL WAS CLEAR, THIS **WOULD** HAVE BEEN WHERE THEY CAME OUT.
S-SEE? I TOLD YOU!
HOW CAN WE POSSIBLY DIG THROUGH THIS?
WE CAN'T. COME ON.
GIVE ME A HAND.
WHOA!
KRONG!

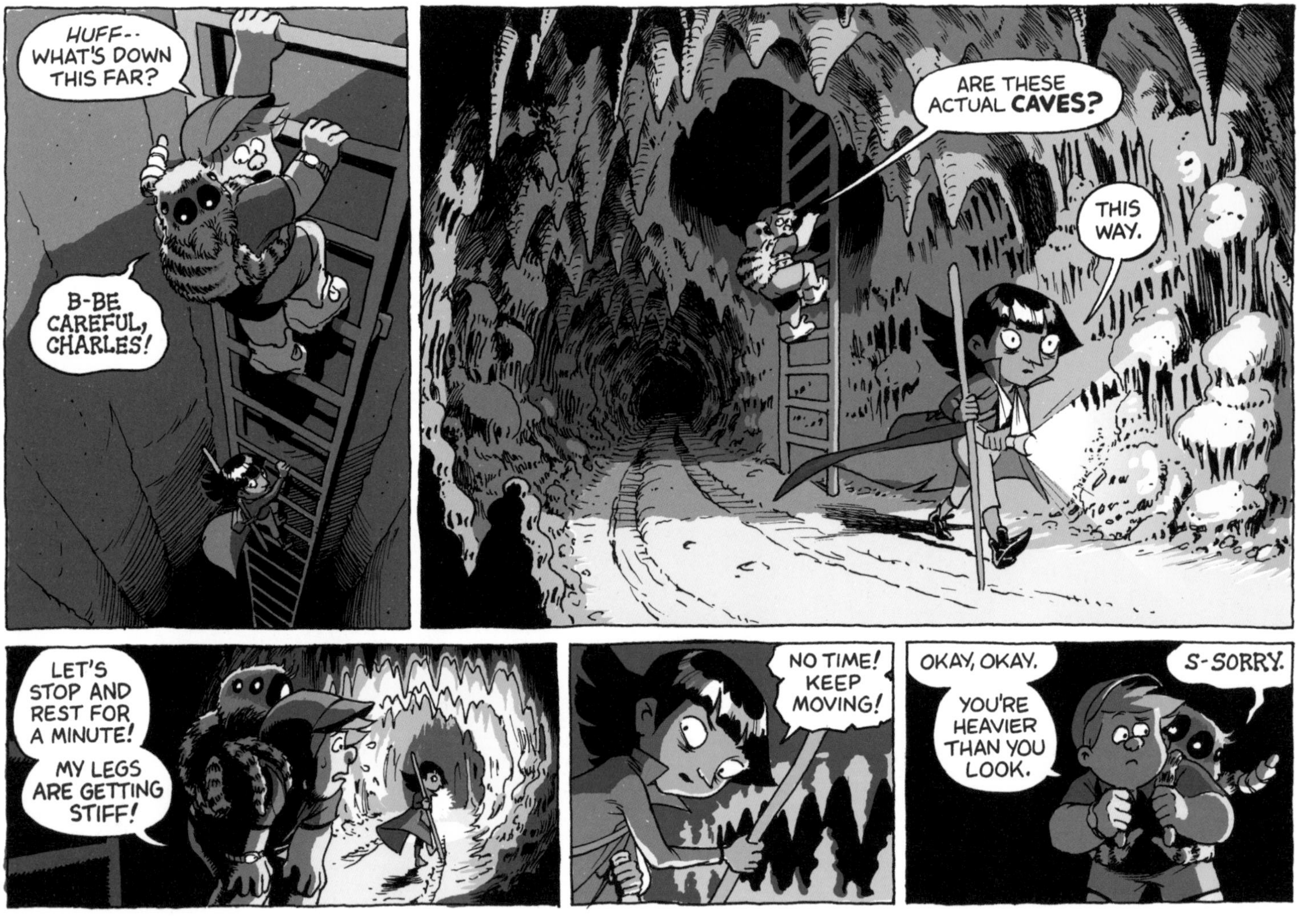
HUFF-- WHAT'S DOWN THIS FAR?
B-BE CAREFUL, CHARLES!
ARE THESE ACTUAL **CAVES?**
THIS WAY.
LET'S STOP AND REST FOR A MINUTE!
MY LEGS ARE GETTING STIFF!
NO TIME! KEEP MOVING!
OKAY, OKAY.
YOU'RE HEAVIER THAN YOU LOOK.
S-SORRY.

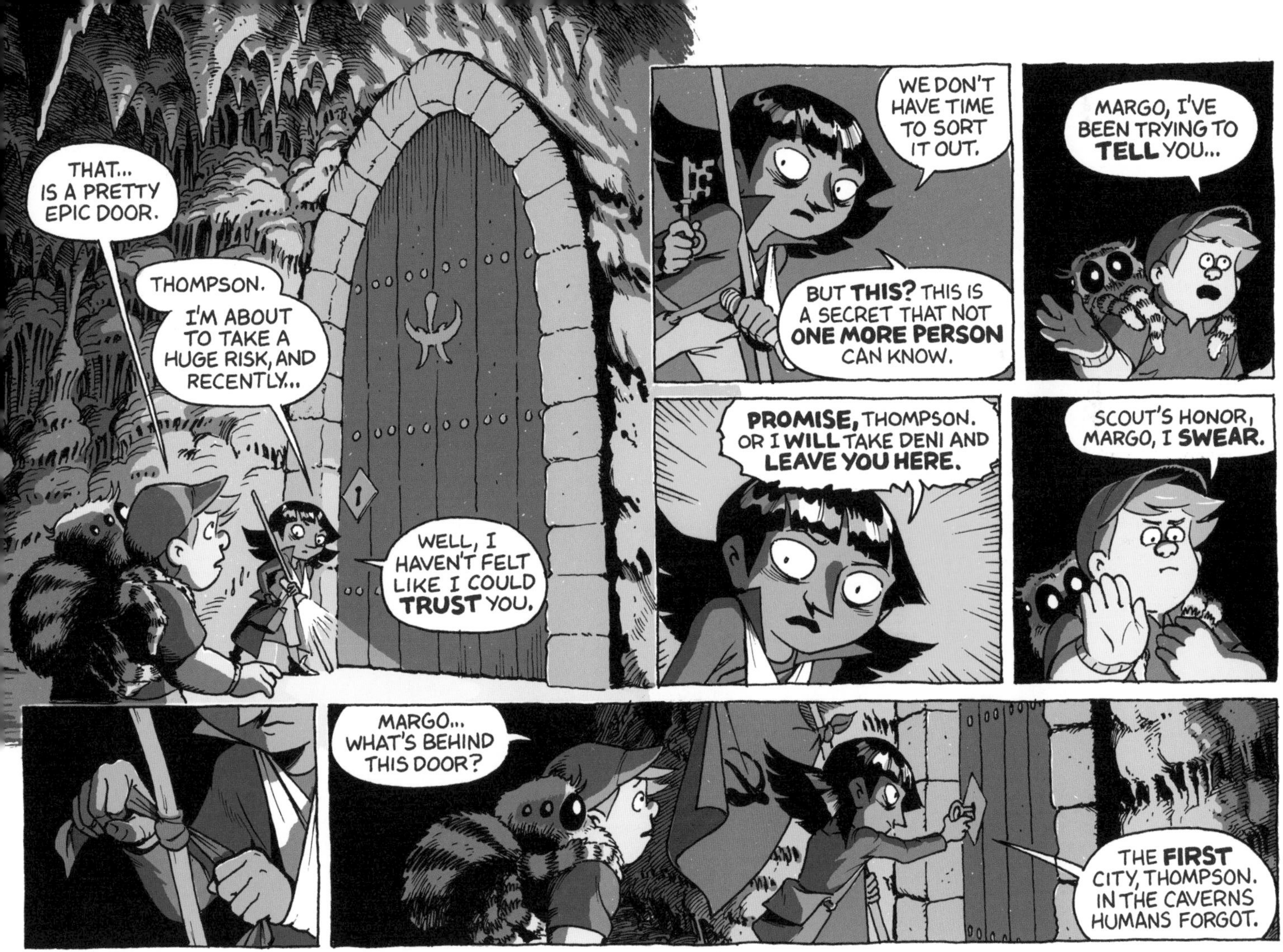
THAT... IS A PRETTY EPIC DOOR.
THOMPSON.
I'M ABOUT TO TAKE A HUGE RISK, AND RECENTLY...
WELL, I HAVEN'T FELT LIKE I COULD **TRUST** YOU.
WE DON'T HAVE TIME TO SORT IT OUT.
BUT **THIS?** THIS IS A SECRET THAT NOT **ONE MORE PERSON** CAN KNOW.
MARGO, I'VE BEEN TRYING TO **TELL** YOU...
PROMISE, THOMPSON. OR I **WILL** TAKE DENI AND **LEAVE YOU HERE.**
SCOUT'S HONOR, MARGO, I **SWEAR.**
MARGO... WHAT'S BEHIND THIS DOOR?
THE **FIRST** CITY, THOMPSON. IN THE CAVERNS HUMANS FORGOT.

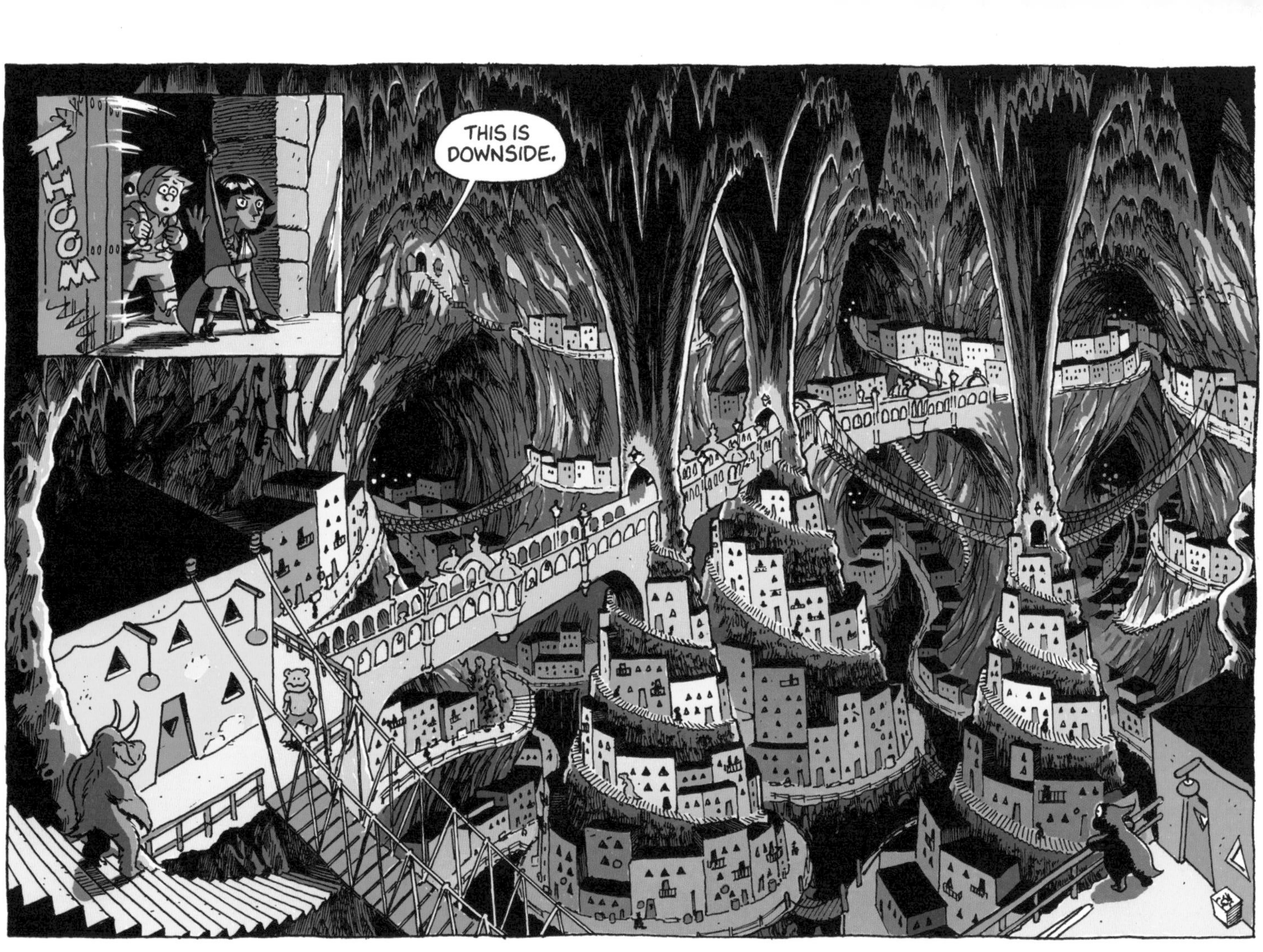
THOOM
THIS IS DOWNSIDE.

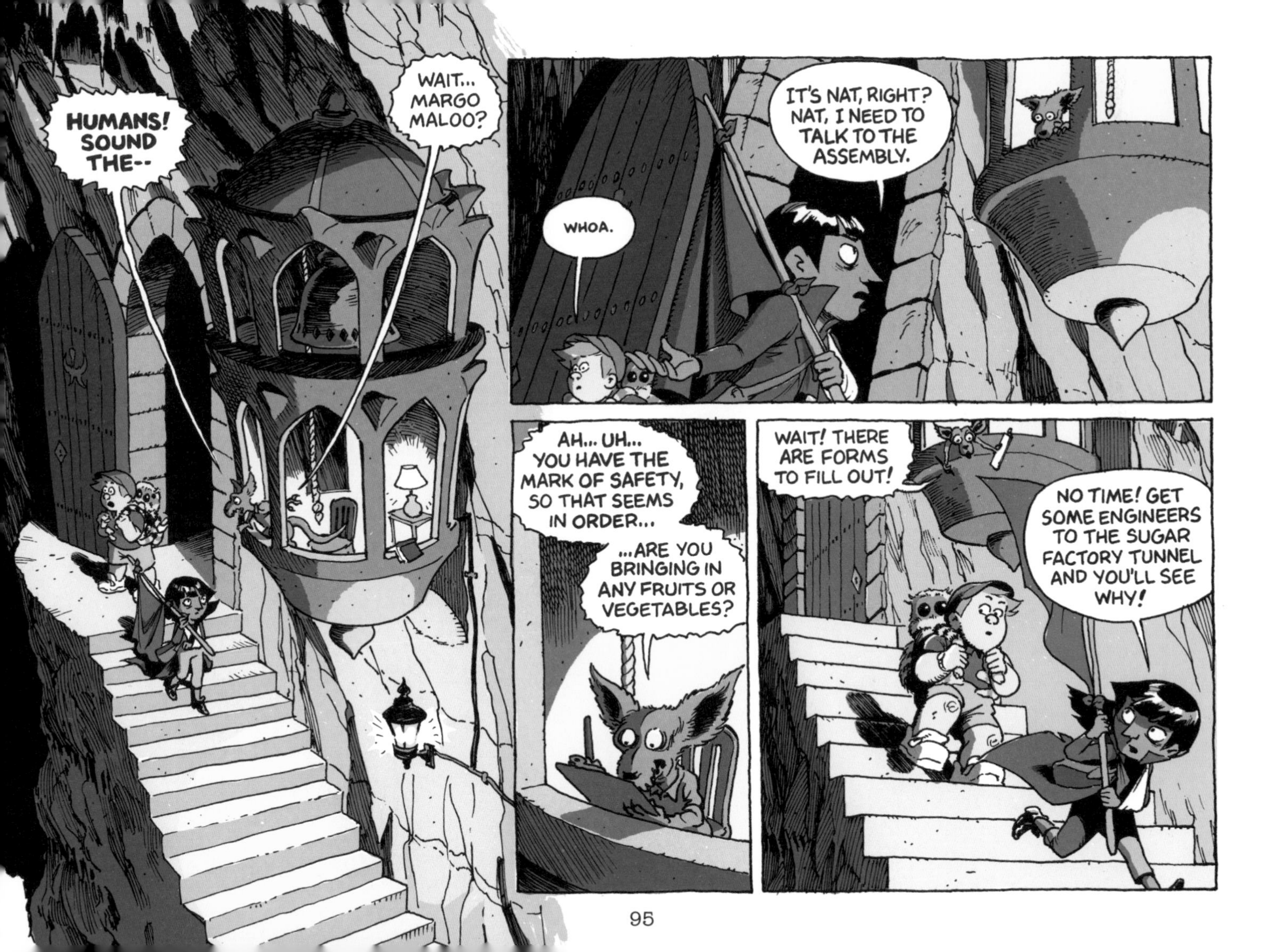
HUMANS! SOUND THE--
WAIT... MARGO MALOO?
WHOA.
IT'S NAT, RIGHT? NAT, I NEED TO TALK TO THE ASSEMBLY.
AH... UH... YOU HAVE THE MARK OF SAFETY, SO THAT SEEMS IN ORDER...
...ARE YOU BRINGING IN ANY FRUITS OR VEGETABLES?
WAIT! THERE ARE FORMS TO FILL OUT!
NO TIME! GET SOME ENGINEERS TO THE SUGAR FACTORY TUNNEL AND YOU'LL SEE WHY!

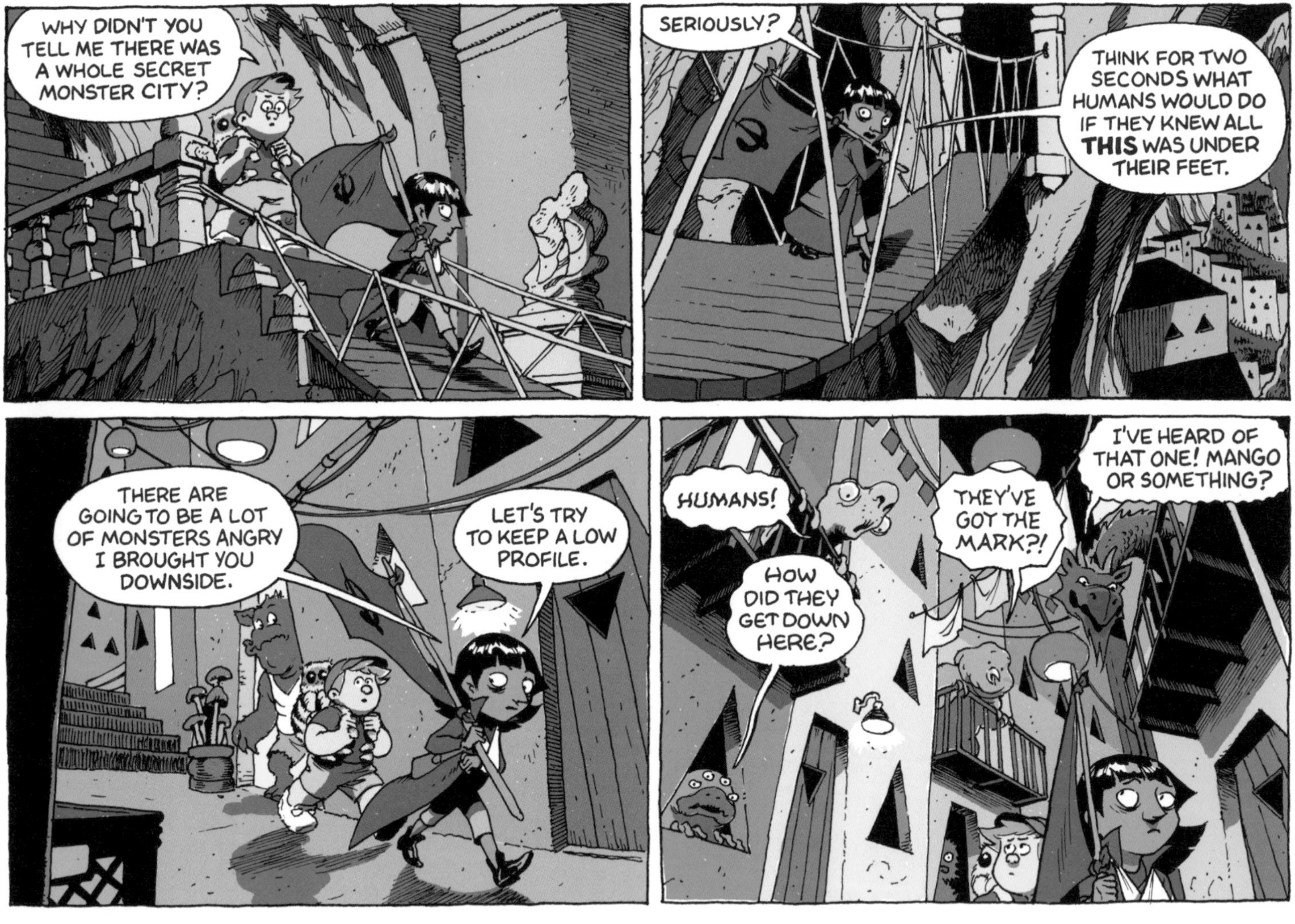
WHY DIDN'T YOU TELL ME THERE WAS A WHOLE SECRET MONSTER CITY?
SERIOUSLY?
THINK FOR TWO SECONDS WHAT HUMANS WOULD DO IF THEY KNEW ALL **THIS** WAS UNDER THEIR FEET.
THERE ARE GOING TO BE A LOT OF MONSTERS ANGRY I BROUGHT YOU DOWNSIDE.
LET'S TRY TO KEEP A LOW PROFILE.
HUMANS!
HOW DID THEY GET DOWN HERE?
THEY'VE GOT THE MARK?!
I'VE HEARD OF THAT ONE! MANGO OR SOMETHING?

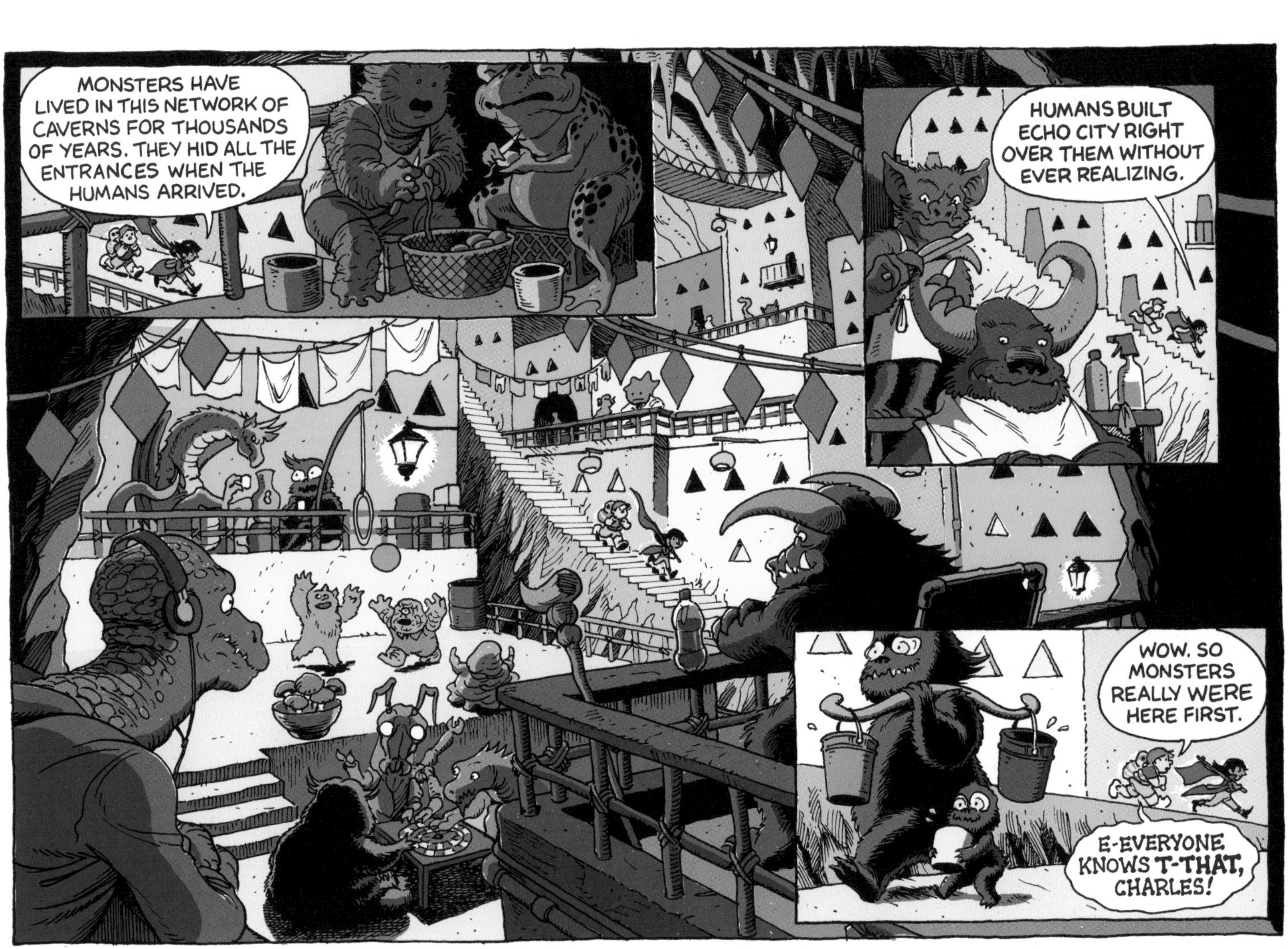
MONSTERS HAVE LIVED IN THIS NETWORK OF CAVERNS FOR THOUSANDS OF YEARS. THEY HID ALL THE ENTRANCES WHEN THE HUMANS ARRIVED.
HUMANS BUILT ECHO CITY RIGHT OVER THEM WITHOUT EVER REALIZING.
WOW. SO MONSTERS REALLY WERE HERE FIRST.
E-EVERYONE KNOWS T-THAT, CHARLES!

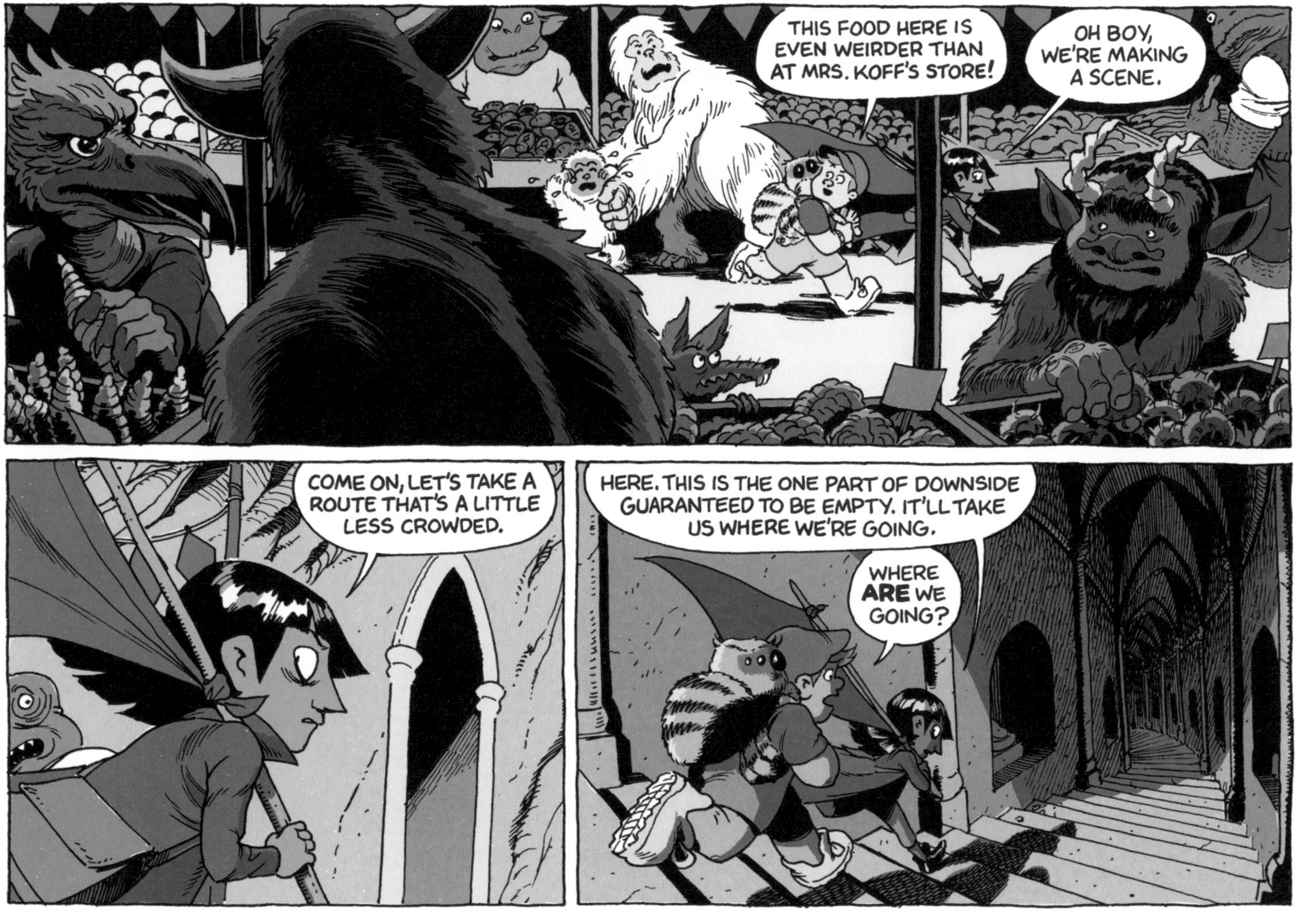
THIS FOOD HERE IS EVEN WEIRDER THAN AT MRS. KOFF'S STORE!
OH BOY, WE'RE MAKING A SCENE.
COME ON, LET'S TAKE A ROUTE THAT'S A LITTLE LESS CROWDED.
HERE. THIS IS THE ONE PART OF DOWNSIDE GUARANTEED TO BE EMPTY. IT'LL TAKE US WHERE WE'RE GOING.
WHERE **ARE** WE GOING?

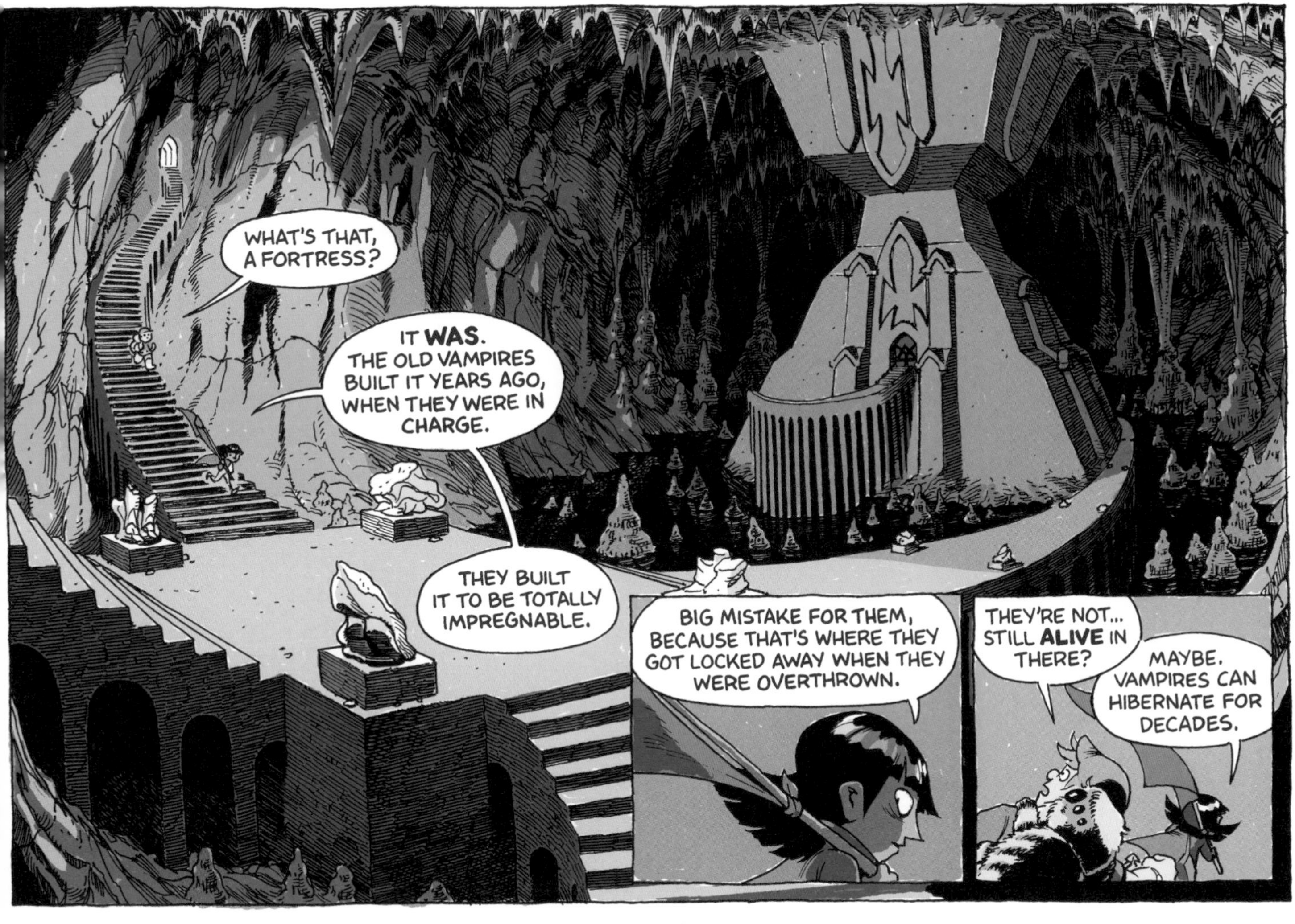
WHAT'S THAT, A FORTRESS?
IT WAS. THE OLD VAMPIRES BUILT IT YEARS AGO, WHEN THEY WERE IN CHARGE.
THEY BUILT IT TO BE TOTALLY IMPREGNABLE.
BIG MISTAKE FOR THEM, BECAUSE THAT'S WHERE THEY GOT LOCKED AWAY WHEN THEY WERE OVERTHROWN.
THEY'RE NOT... STILL ALIVE IN THERE?
MAYBE. VAMPIRES CAN HIBERNATE FOR DECADES.

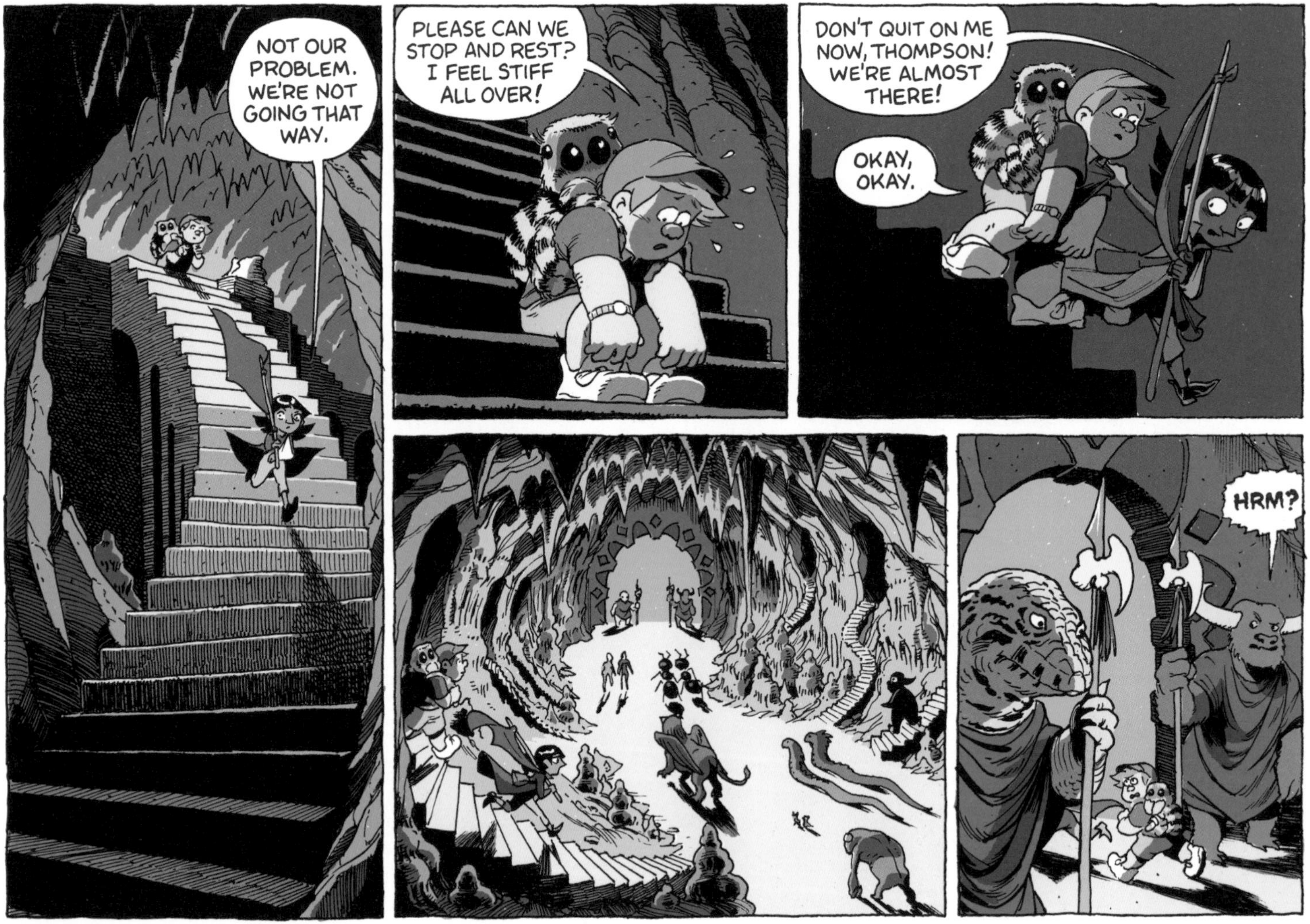
NOT OUR PROBLEM. WE'RE NOT GOING THAT WAY.
PLEASE CAN WE STOP AND REST? I FEEL STIFF ALL OVER!
DON'T QUIT ON ME NOW, THOMPSON! WE'RE ALMOST THERE!
OKAY, OKAY.
HRM?

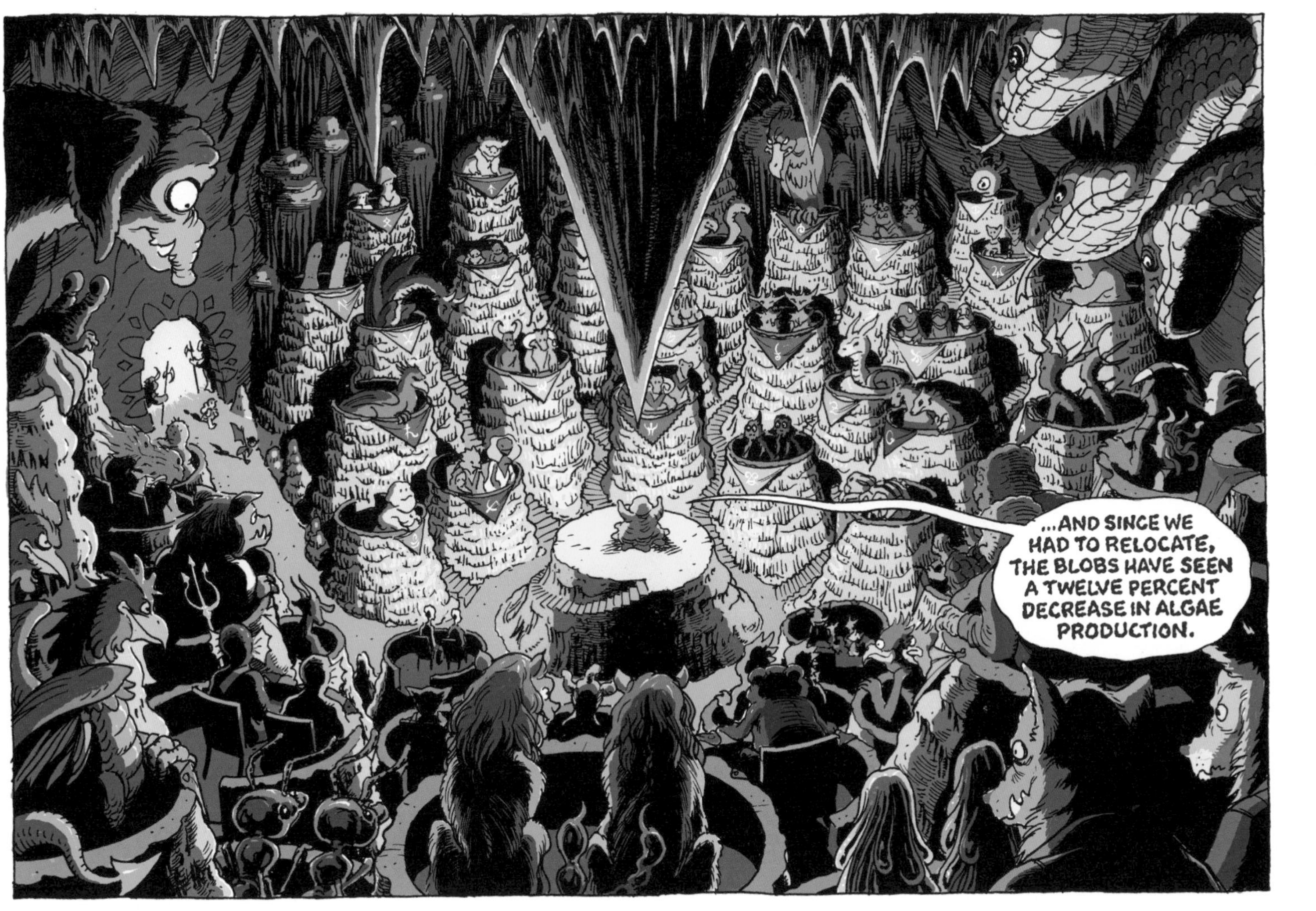
...AND SINCE WE HAD TO RELOCATE, THE BLOBS HAVE SEEN A TWELVE PERCENT DECREASE IN ALGAE PRODUCTION.

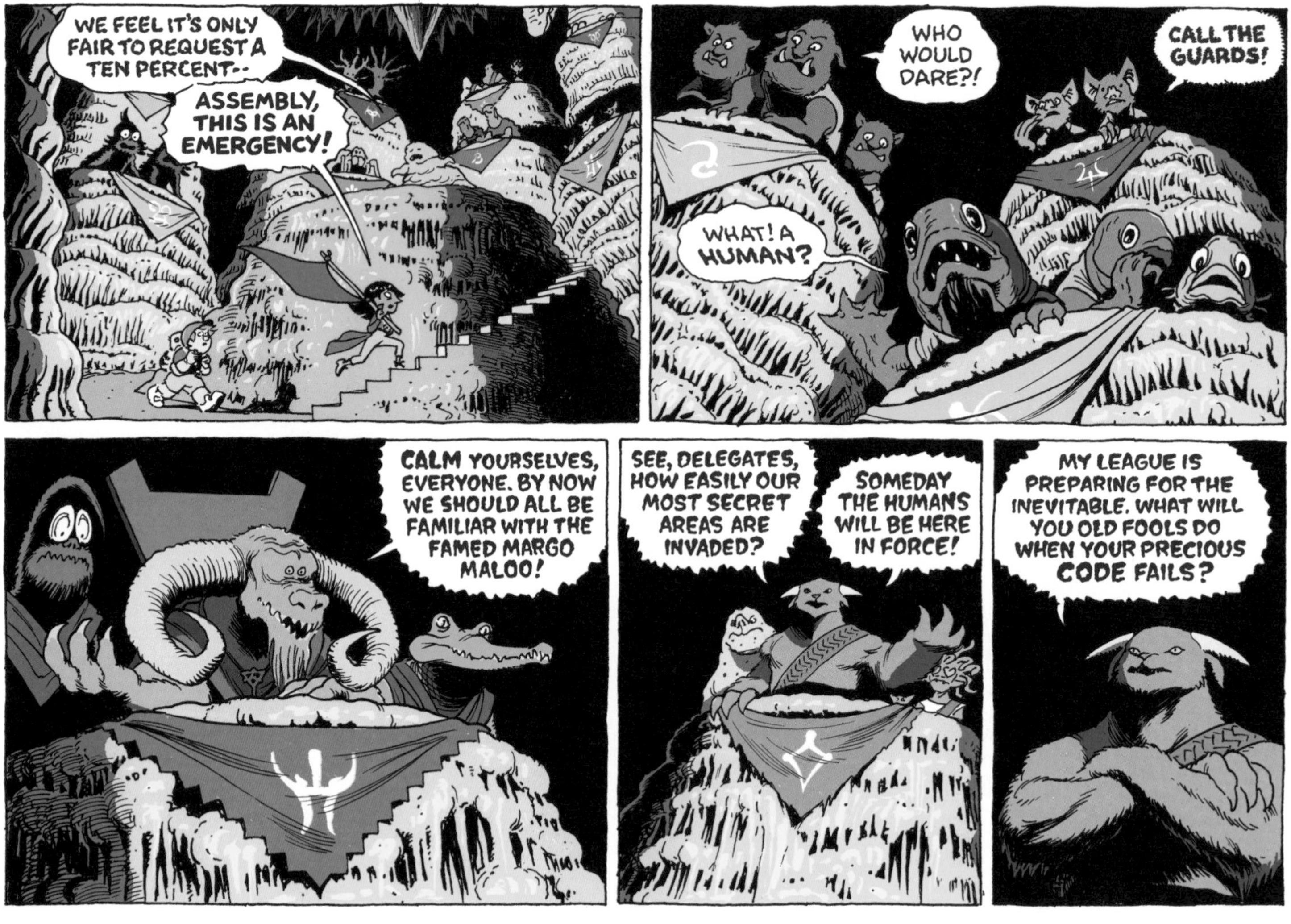
WE FEEL IT'S ONLY FAIR TO REQUEST A TEN PERCENT--
ASSEMBLY, THIS IS AN EMERGENCY!
WHO WOULD DARE?!
CALL THE GUARDS!
WHAT! A HUMAN?
CALM YOURSELVES, EVERYONE. BY NOW WE SHOULD ALL BE FAMILIAR WITH THE FAMED MARGO MALOO!
SEE, DELEGATES, HOW EASILY OUR MOST SECRET AREAS ARE INVADED?
SOMEDAY THE HUMANS WILL BE HERE IN FORCE!
MY LEAGUE IS PREPARING FOR THE INEVITABLE. WHAT WILL YOU OLD FOOLS DO WHEN YOUR PRECIOUS CODE FAILS?

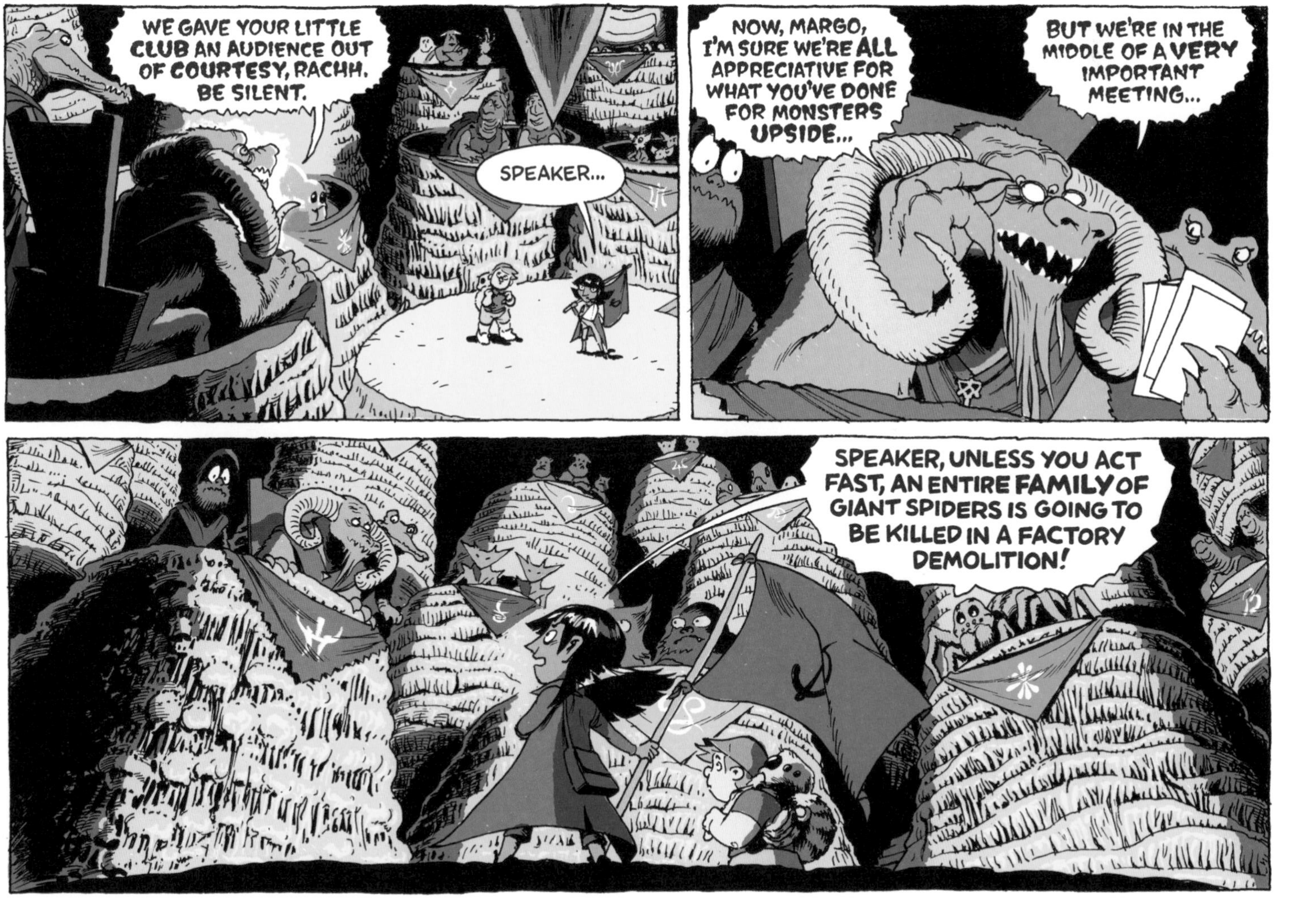
WE GAVE YOUR LITTLE CLUB AN AUDIENCE OUT OF COURTESY, RACHH. BE SILENT.
SPEAKER...
NOW, MARGO, I'M SURE WE'RE ALL APPRECIATIVE FOR WHAT YOU'VE DONE FOR MONSTERS UPSIDE...
BUT WE'RE IN THE MIDDLE OF A VERY IMPORTANT MEETING...
SPEAKER, UNLESS YOU ACT FAST, AN ENTIRE FAMILY OF GIANT SPIDERS IS GOING TO BE KILLED IN A FACTORY DEMOLITION!

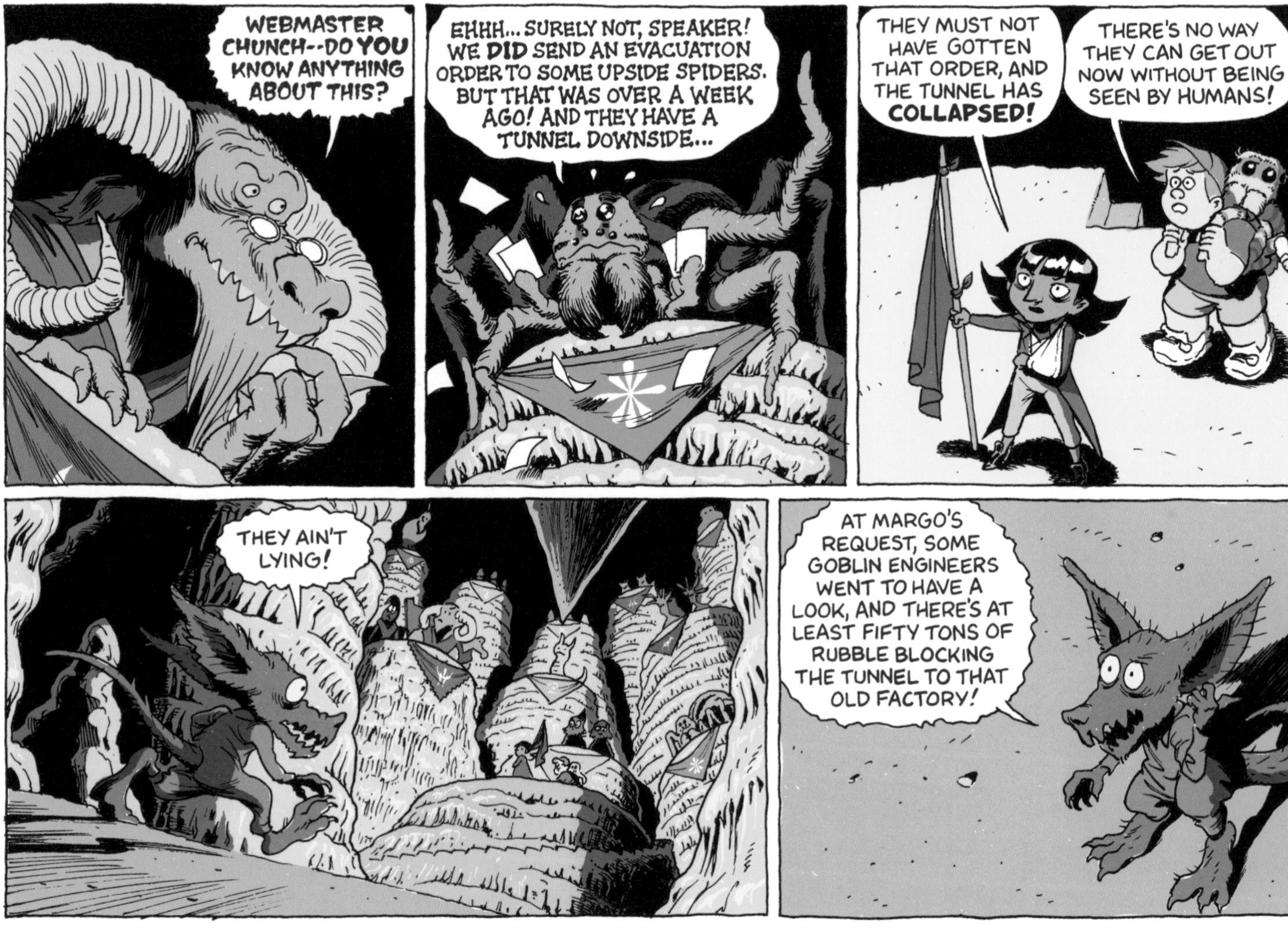
WEBMASTER CHUNCH--DO YOU KNOW ANYTHING ABOUT THIS?
EHHH... SURELY NOT, SPEAKER! WE DID SEND AN EVACUATION ORDER TO SOME UPSIDE SPIDERS. BUT THAT WAS OVER A WEEK AGO! AND THEY HAVE A TUNNEL DOWNSIDE...
THEY MUST NOT HAVE GOTTEN THAT ORDER, AND THE TUNNEL HAS COLLAPSED!
THERE'S NO WAY THEY CAN GET OUT NOW WITHOUT BEING SEEN BY HUMANS!
THEY AIN'T LYING!
AT MARGO'S REQUEST, SOME GOBLIN ENGINEERS WENT TO HAVE A LOOK, AND THERE'S AT LEAST FIFTY TONS OF RUBBLE BLOCKING THE TUNNEL TO THAT OLD FACTORY!

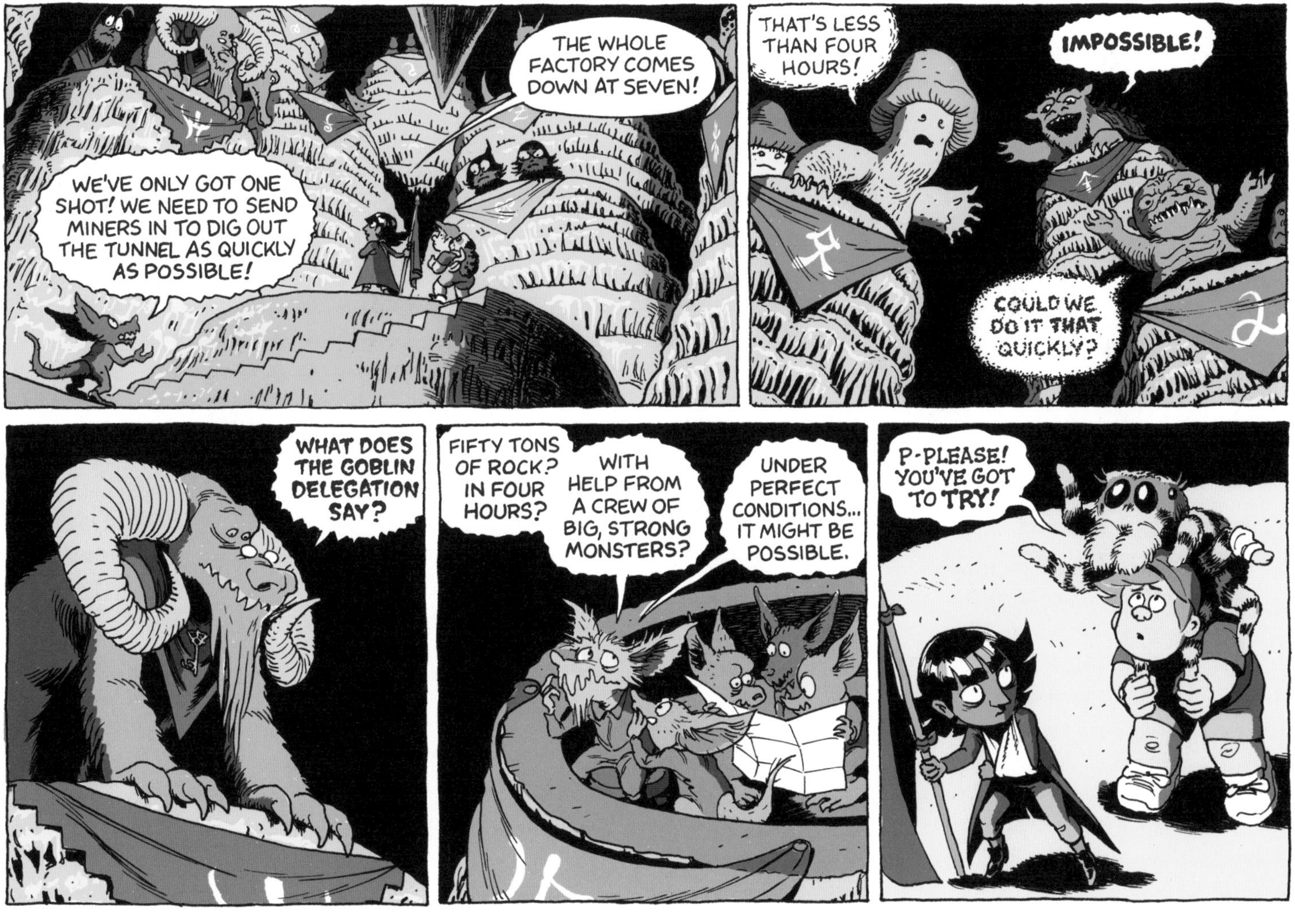
THE WHOLE FACTORY COMES DOWN AT SEVEN!
WE'VE ONLY GOT ONE SHOT! WE NEED TO SEND MINERS IN TO DIG OUT THE TUNNEL AS QUICKLY AS POSSIBLE!
THAT'S LESS THAN FOUR HOURS!
IMPOSSIBLE!
COULD WE DO IT THAT QUICKLY?
WHAT DOES THE GOBLIN DELEGATION SAY?
FIFTY TONS OF ROCK? IN FOUR HOURS?
WITH HELP FROM A CREW OF BIG, STRONG MONSTERS?
UNDER PERFECT CONDITIONS... IT MIGHT BE POSSIBLE.
P-PLEASE! YOU'VE GOT TO TRY!

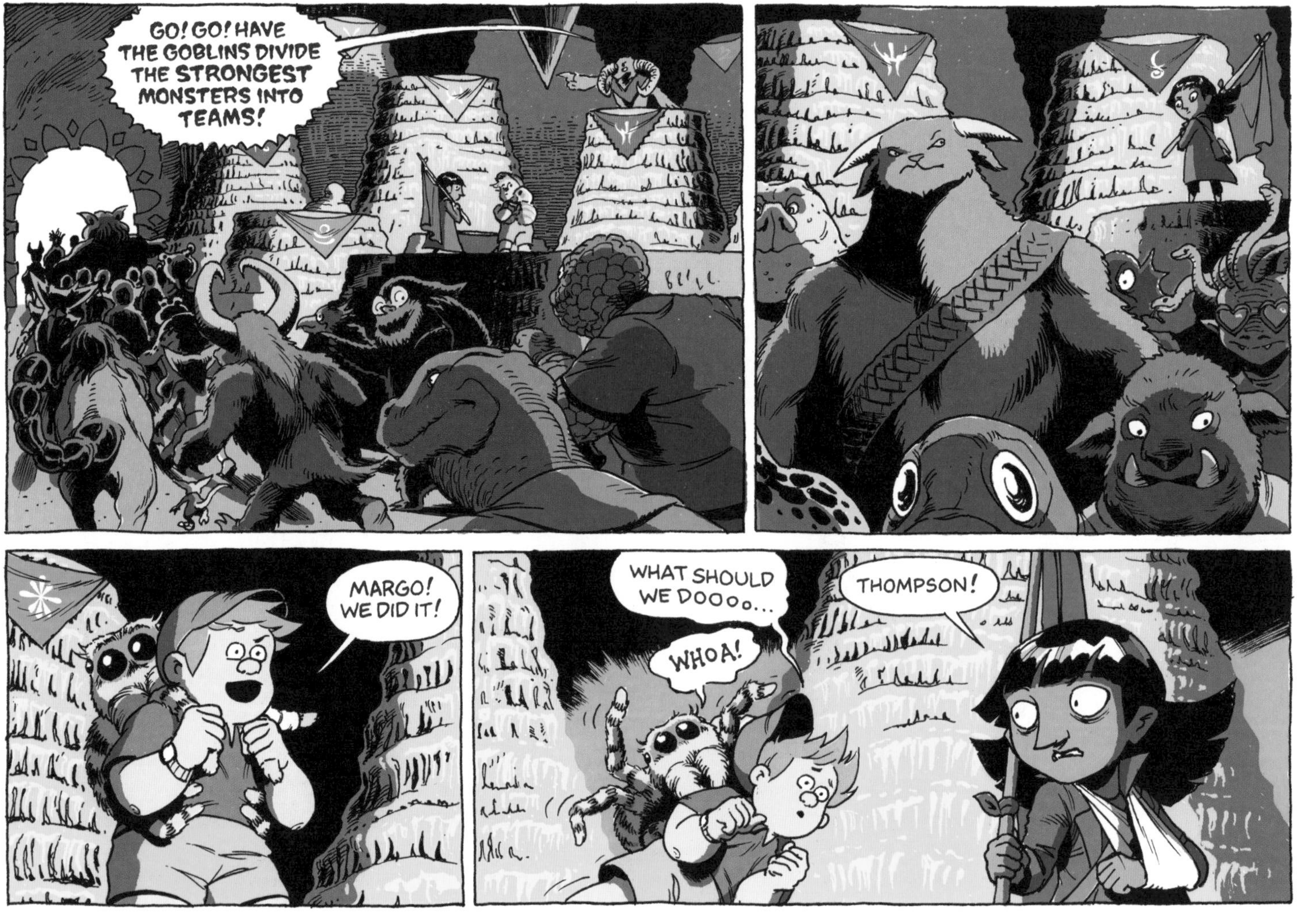
GO! GO! HAVE THE GOBLINS DIVIDE THE STRONGEST MONSTERS INTO TEAMS!
MARGO! WE DID IT!
WHAT SHOULD WE DOOooo...
THOMPSON!
WHOA!

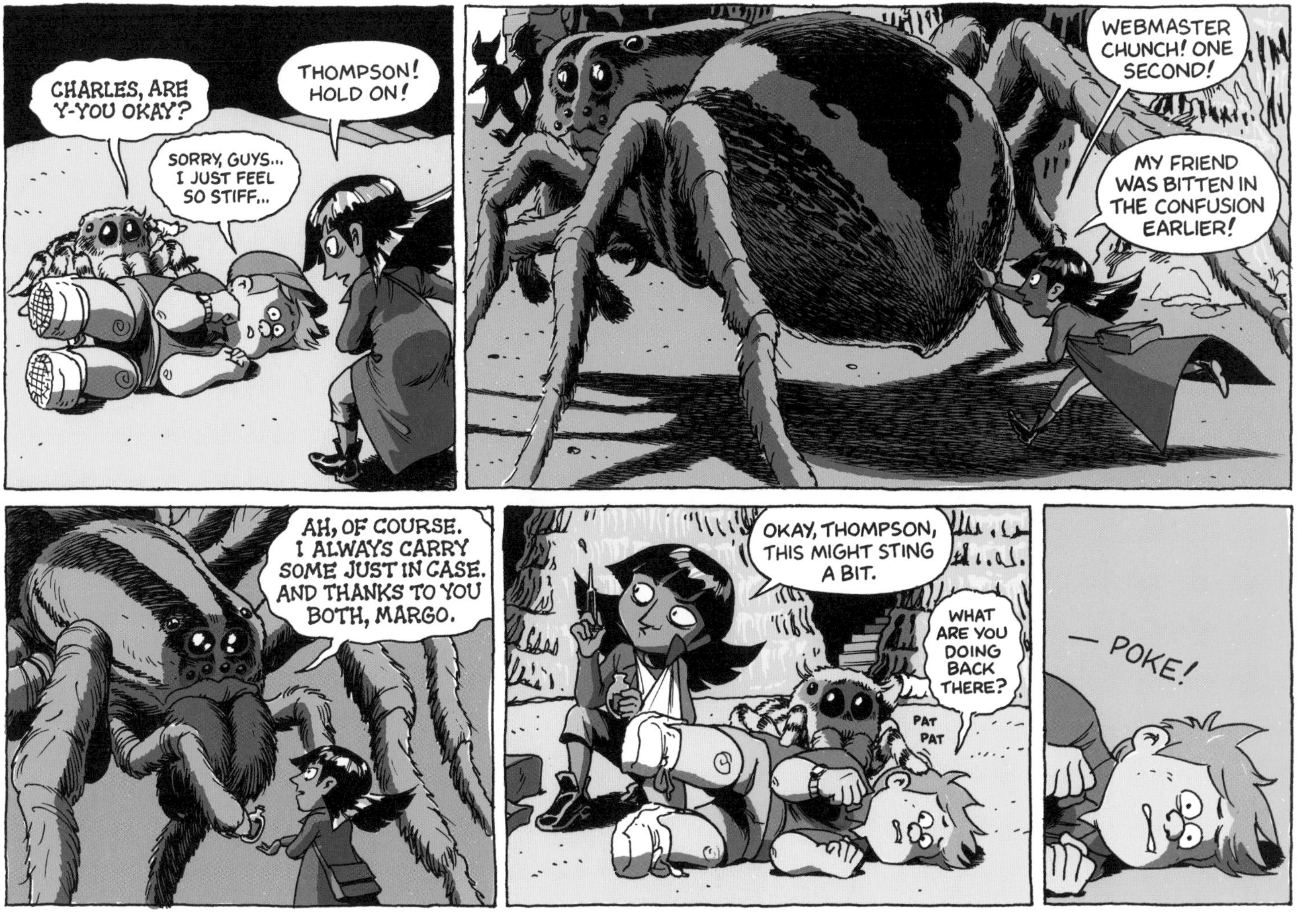
CHARLES, ARE Y-YOU OKAY?
THOMPSON! HOLD ON!
SORRY, GUYS... I JUST FEEL SO STIFF...
WEBMASTER CHUNCH! ONE SECOND!
MY FRIEND WAS BITTEN IN THE CONFUSION EARLIER!
AH, OF COURSE. I ALWAYS CARRY SOME JUST IN CASE. AND THANKS TO YOU BOTH, MARGO.
OKAY, THOMPSON, THIS MIGHT STING A BIT.
WHAT ARE YOU DOING BACK THERE?
PAT PAT
— POKE!

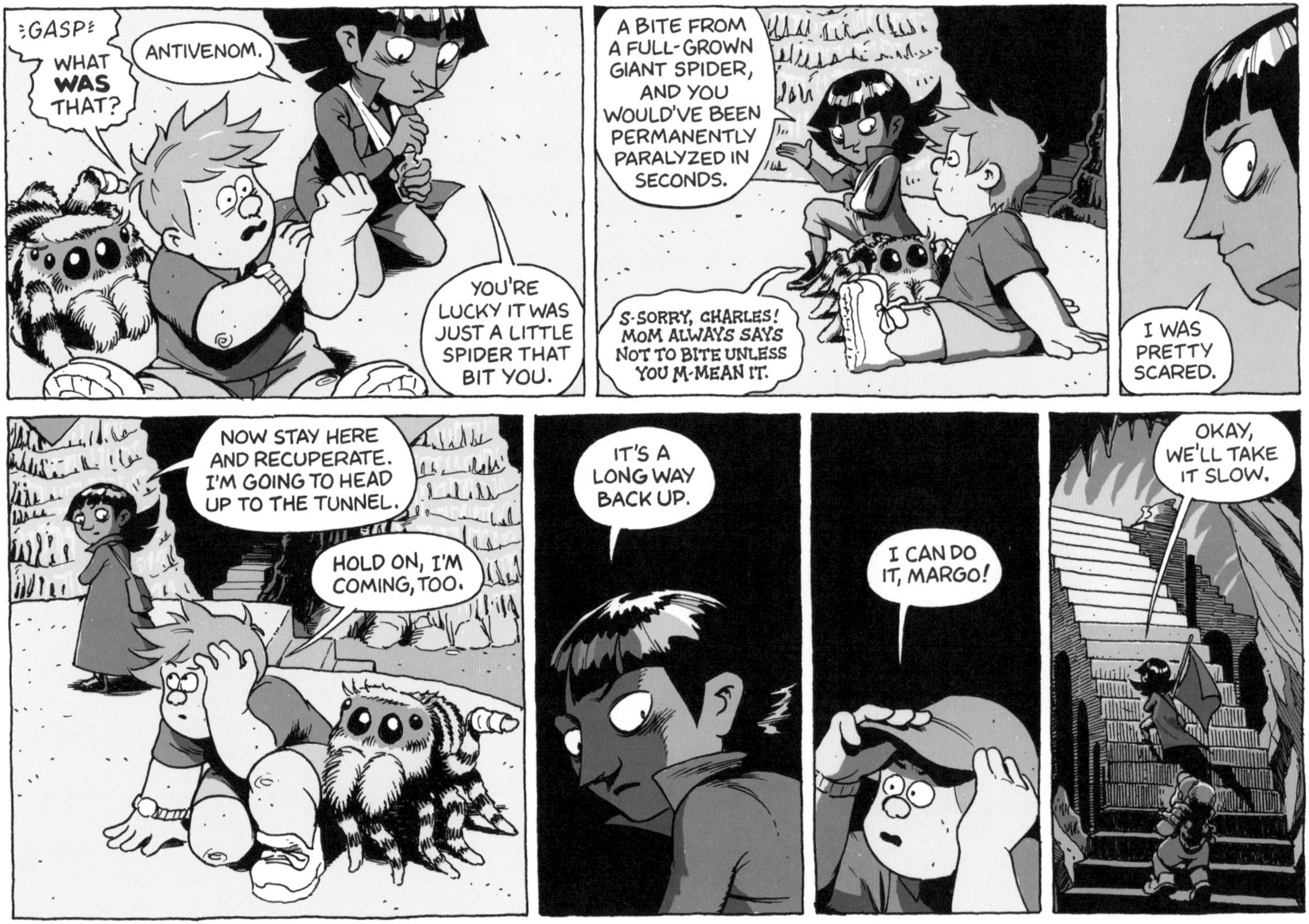
GASP
WHAT WAS THAT?
ANTIVENOM.
YOU'RE LUCKY IT WAS JUST A LITTLE SPIDER THAT BIT YOU.
A BITE FROM A FULL-GROWN GIANT SPIDER, AND YOU WOULD'VE BEEN PERMANENTLY PARALYZED IN SECONDS.
S-SORRY, CHARLES! MOM ALWAYS SAYS NOT TO BITE UNLESS YOU M-MEAN IT.
I WAS PRETTY SCARED.
NOW STAY HERE AND RECUPERATE. I'M GOING TO HEAD UP TO THE TUNNEL.
HOLD ON, I'M COMING, TOO.
IT'S A LONG WAY BACK UP.
I CAN DO IT, MARGO!
OKAY, WE'LL TAKE IT SLOW.

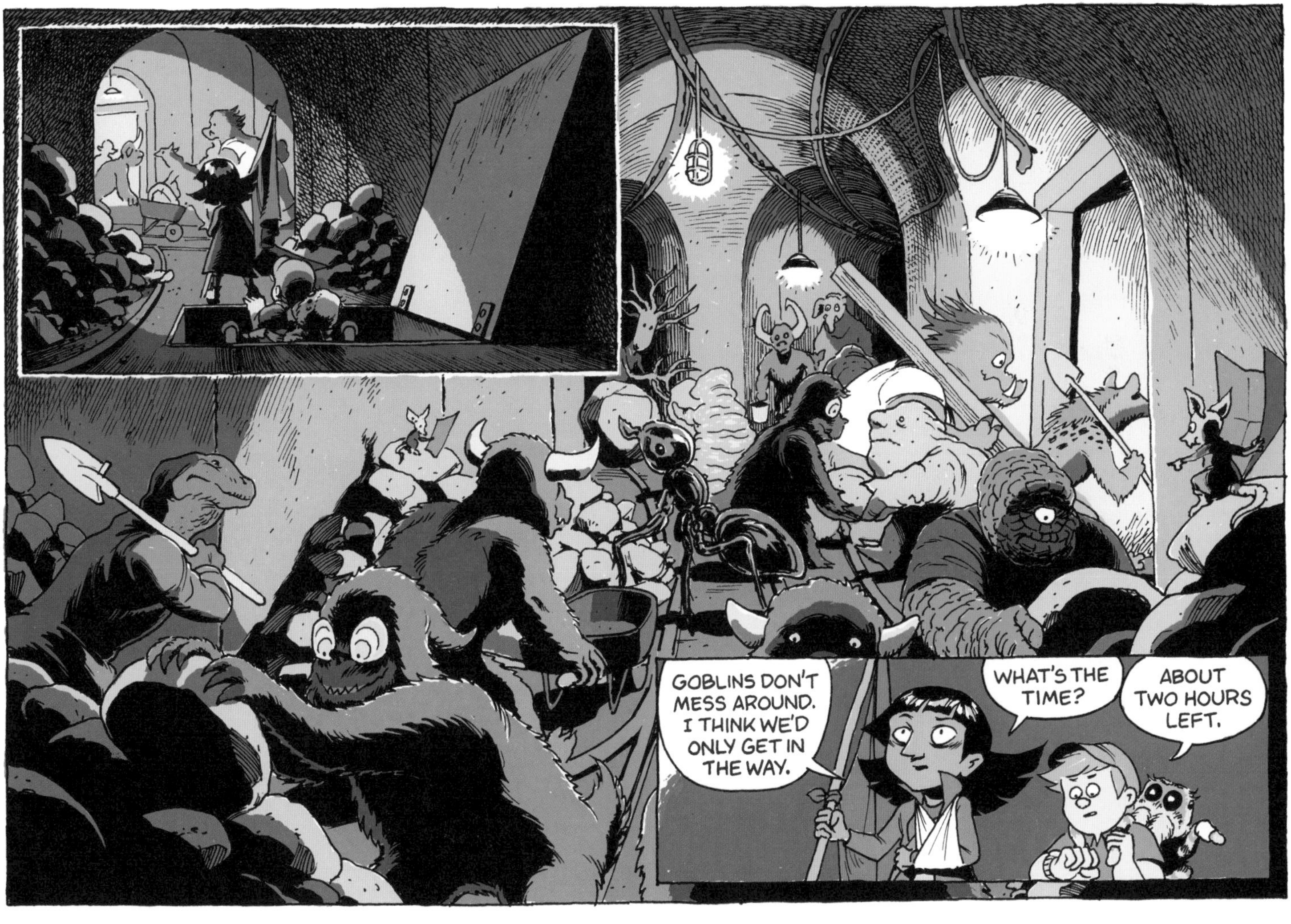
GOBLINS DON'T MESS AROUND. I THINK WE'D ONLY GET IN THE WAY.
WHAT'S THE TIME?
ABOUT TWO HOURS LEFT.

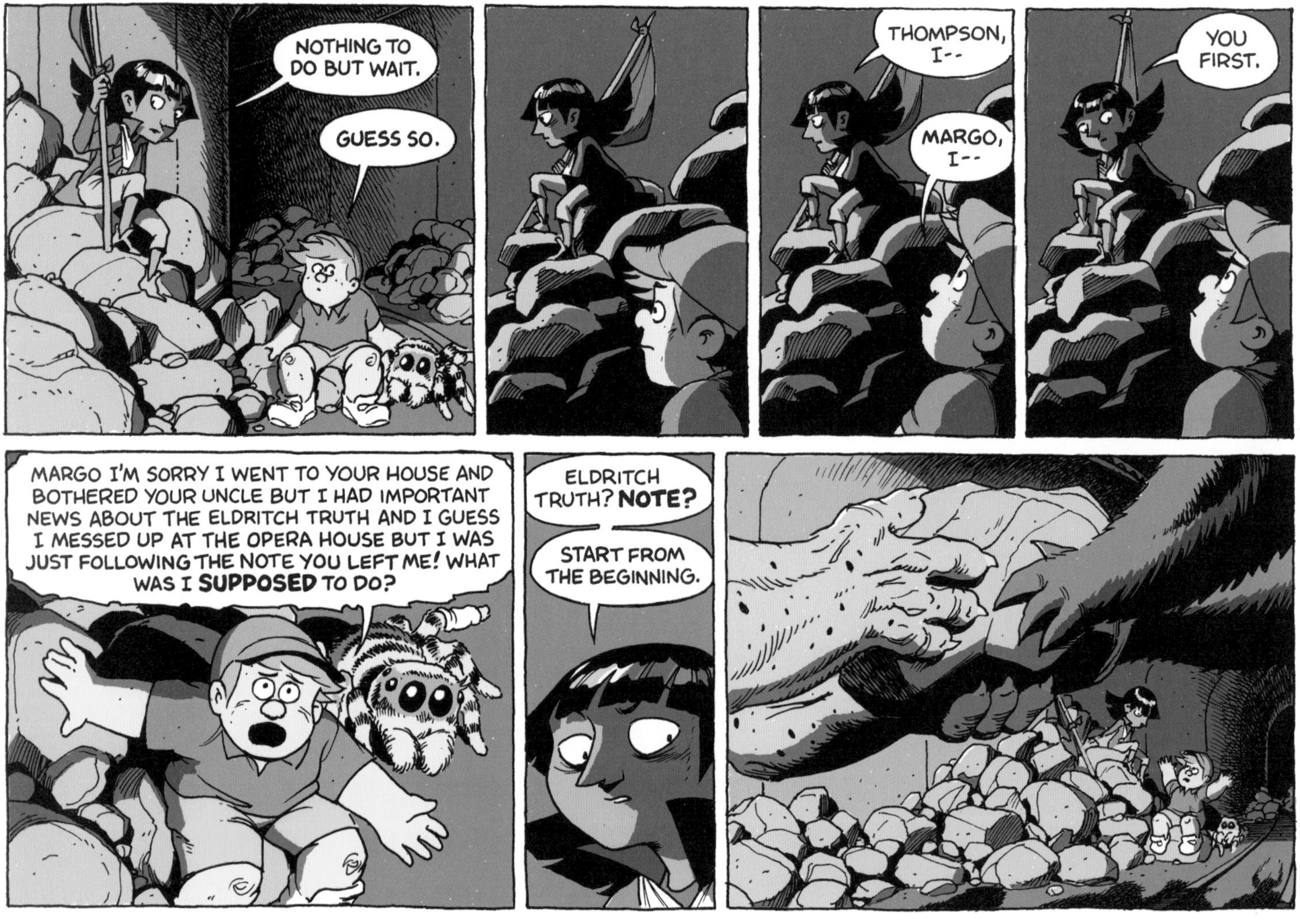
NOTHING TO DO BUT WAIT.
GUESS SO.
THOMPSON, I--
MARGO, I--
YOU FIRST.
MARGO I'M SORRY I WENT TO YOUR HOUSE AND BOTHERED YOUR UNCLE BUT I HAD IMPORTANT NEWS ABOUT THE ELDRITCH TRUTH AND I GUESS I MESSED UP AT THE OPERA HOUSE BUT I WAS JUST FOLLOWING THE NOTE YOU LEFT ME! WHAT WAS I **SUPPOSED** TO DO?
ELDRITCH TRUTH? **NOTE?**
START FROM THE BEGINNING.

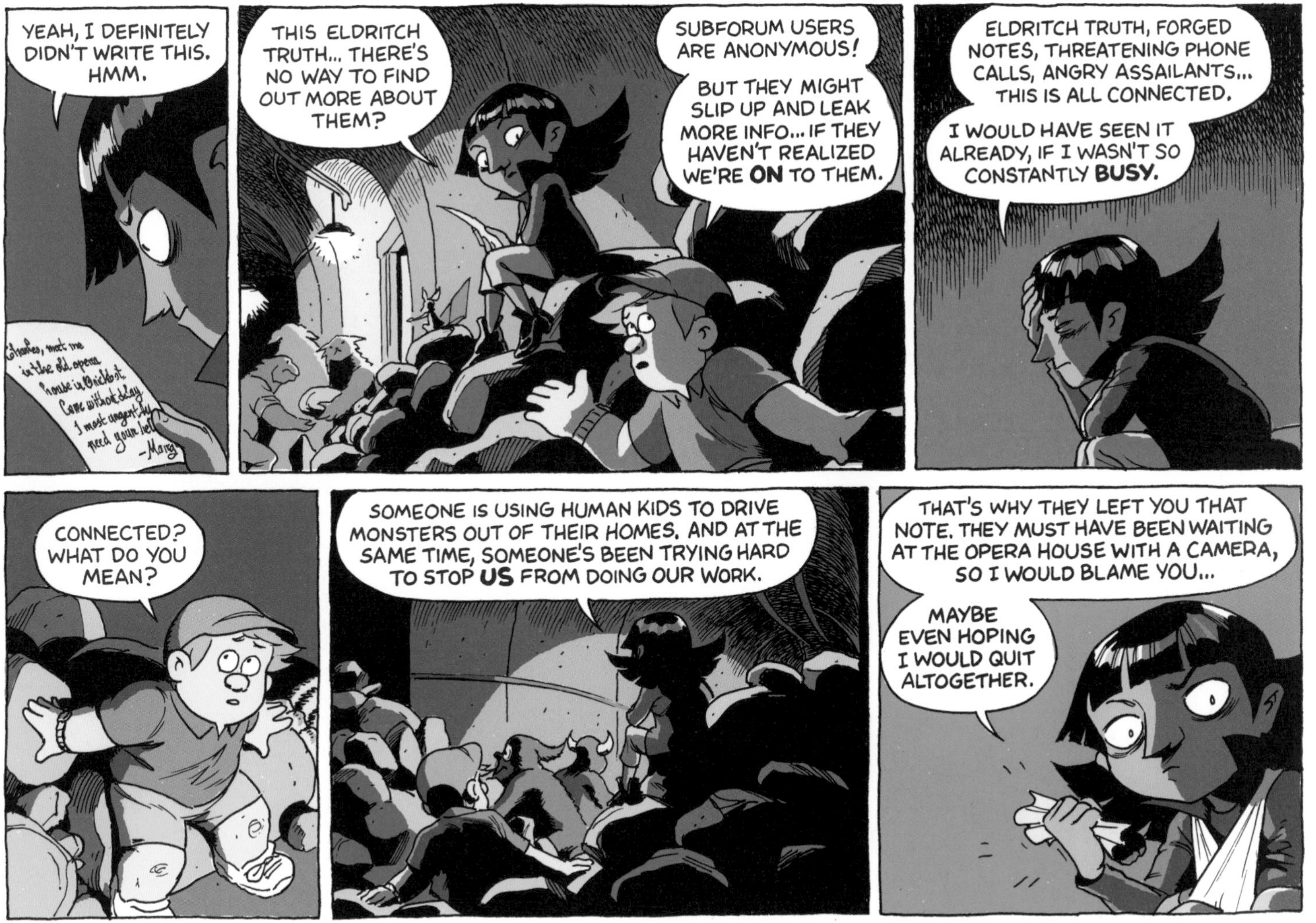
YEAH, I DEFINITELY DIDN'T WRITE THIS. HMM.
THIS ELDRITCH TRUTH... THERE'S NO WAY TO FIND OUT MORE ABOUT THEM?
SUBFORUM USERS ARE ANONYMOUS!
BUT THEY MIGHT SLIP UP AND LEAK MORE INFO... IF THEY HAVEN'T REALIZED WE'RE **ON** TO THEM.
ELDRITCH TRUTH, FORGED NOTES, THREATENING PHONE CALLS, ANGRY ASSAILANTS... THIS IS ALL CONNECTED.
I WOULD HAVE SEEN IT ALREADY, IF I WASN'T SO CONSTANTLY **BUSY.**
CONNECTED? WHAT DO YOU MEAN?
SOMEONE IS USING HUMAN KIDS TO DRIVE MONSTERS OUT OF THEIR HOMES. AND AT THE SAME TIME, SOMEONE'S BEEN TRYING HARD TO STOP **US** FROM DOING OUR WORK.
THAT'S WHY THEY LEFT YOU THAT NOTE. THEY MUST HAVE BEEN WAITING AT THE OPERA HOUSE WITH A CAMERA, SO I WOULD BLAME YOU...
MAYBE EVEN HOPING I WOULD QUIT ALTOGETHER.

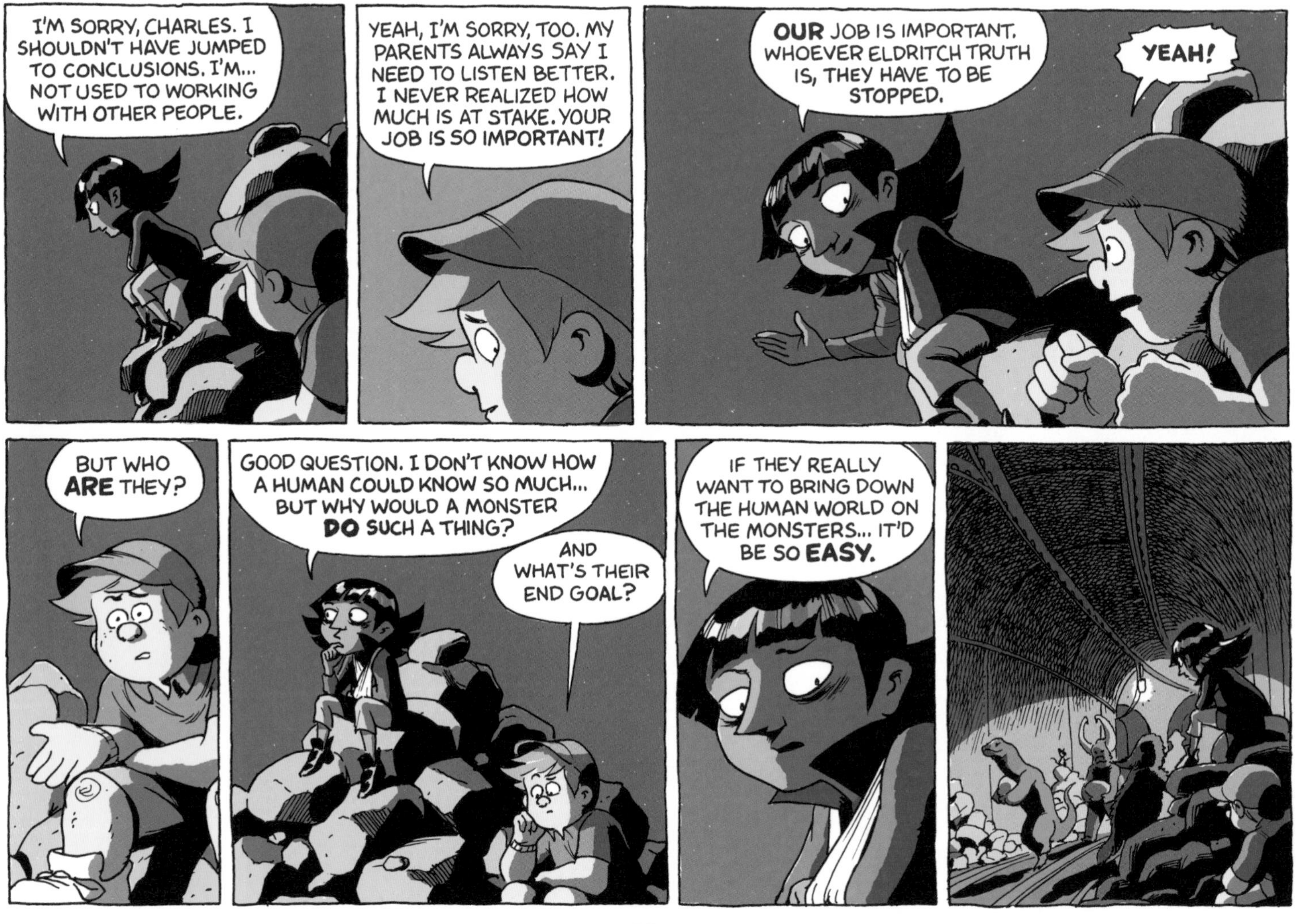
I'M SORRY, CHARLES. I SHOULDN'T HAVE JUMPED TO CONCLUSIONS. I'M... NOT USED TO WORKING WITH OTHER PEOPLE.
YEAH, I'M SORRY, TOO. MY PARENTS ALWAYS SAY I NEED TO LISTEN BETTER. I NEVER REALIZED HOW MUCH IS AT STAKE. YOUR JOB IS SO IMPORTANT!
OUR JOB IS IMPORTANT. WHOEVER ELDRITCH TRUTH IS, THEY HAVE TO BE STOPPED.
YEAH!
BUT WHO ARE THEY?
GOOD QUESTION. I DON'T KNOW HOW A HUMAN COULD KNOW SO MUCH... BUT WHY WOULD A MONSTER DO SUCH A THING?
AND WHAT'S THEIR END GOAL?
IF THEY REALLY WANT TO BRING DOWN THE HUMAN WORLD ON THE MONSTERS... IT'D BE SO EASY.

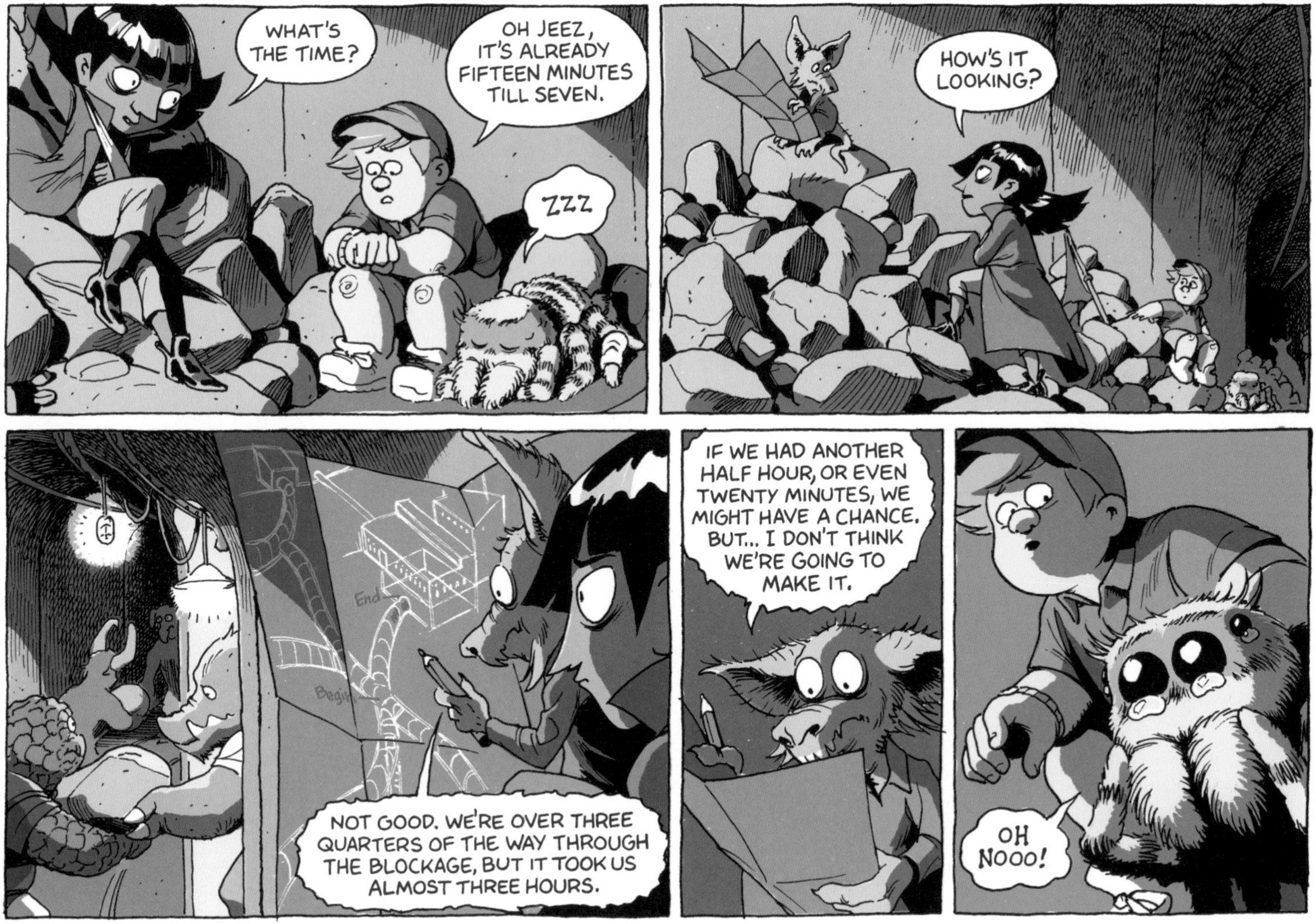
WHAT'S THE TIME?
OH JEEZ, IT'S ALREADY FIFTEEN MINUTES TILL SEVEN.
ZZZ
HOW'S IT LOOKING?
End
Begin
NOT GOOD. WE'RE OVER THREE QUARTERS OF THE WAY THROUGH THE BLOCKAGE, BUT IT TOOK US ALMOST THREE HOURS.
IF WE HAD ANOTHER HALF HOUR, OR EVEN TWENTY MINUTES, WE MIGHT HAVE A CHANCE. BUT... I DON'T THINK WE'RE GOING TO MAKE IT.
OH NOOO!

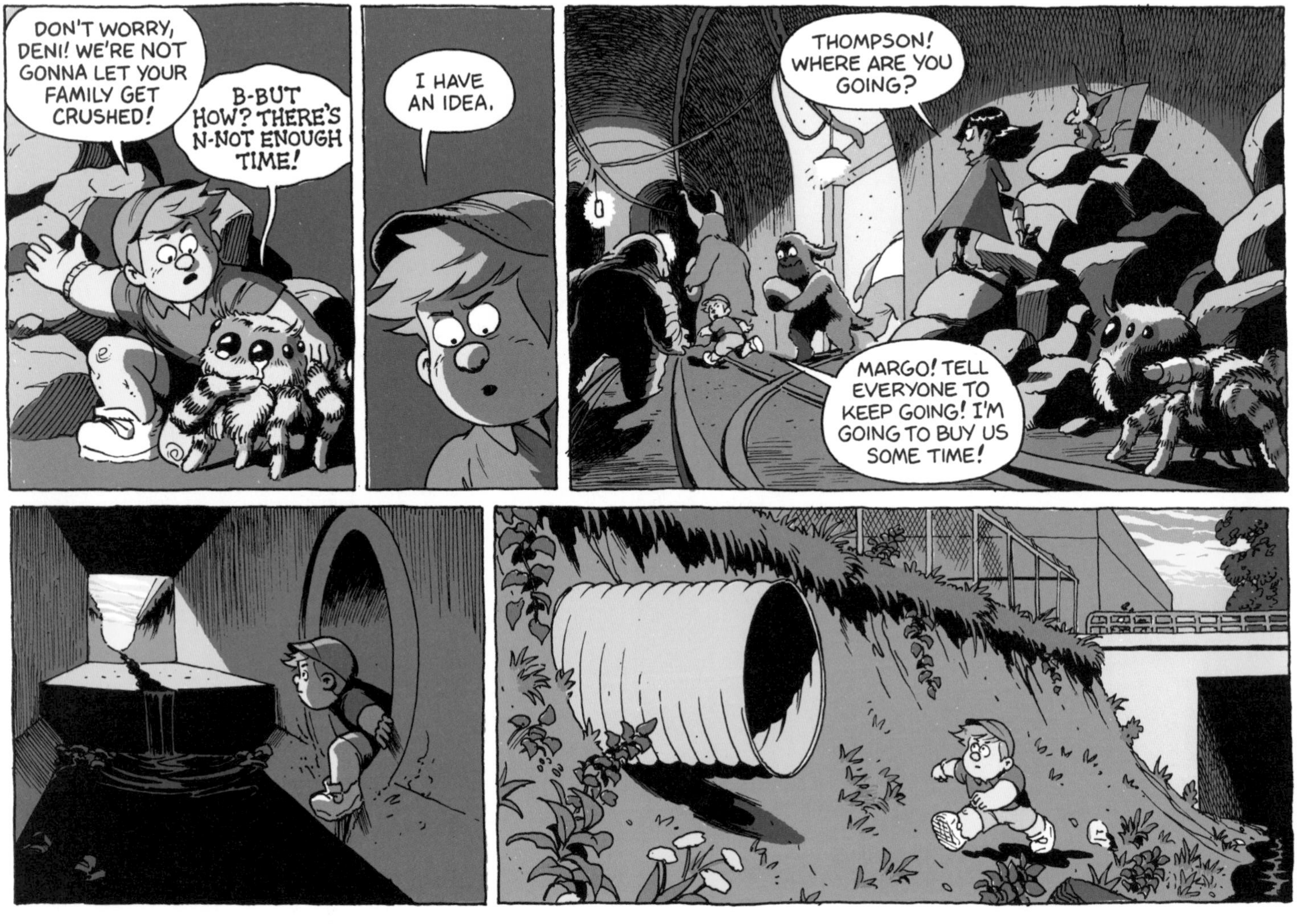
DON'T WORRY, DENI! WE'RE NOT GONNA LET YOUR FAMILY GET CRUSHED!
B-BUT HOW? THERE'S N-NOT ENOUGH TIME!
I HAVE AN IDEA.
THOMPSON! WHERE ARE YOU GOING?
MARGO! TELL EVERYONE TO KEEP GOING! I'M GOING TO BUY US SOME TIME!

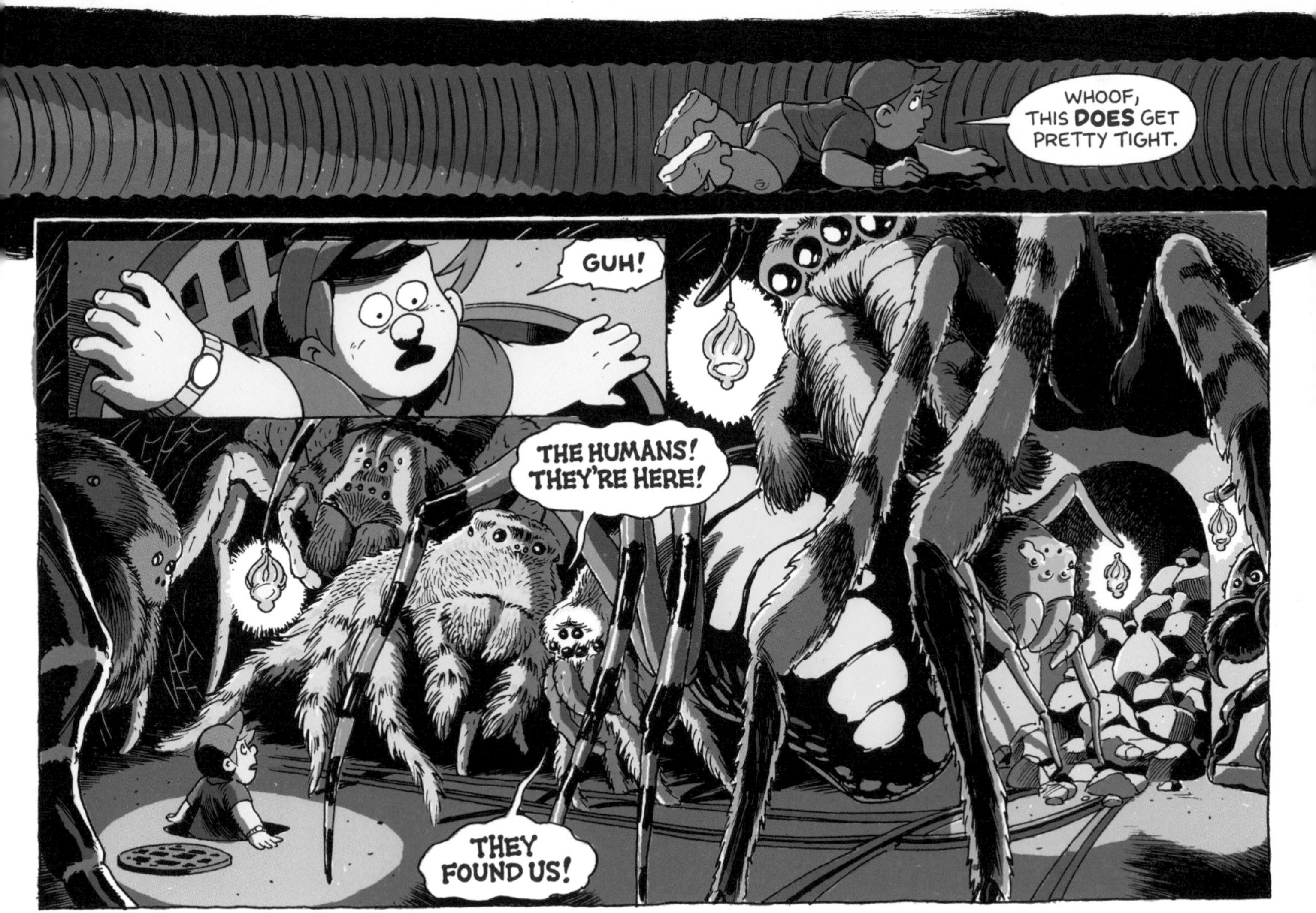
WHOOF, THIS **DOES** GET PRETTY TIGHT.
GUH!
THE HUMANS! THEY'RE HERE!
THEY FOUND US!

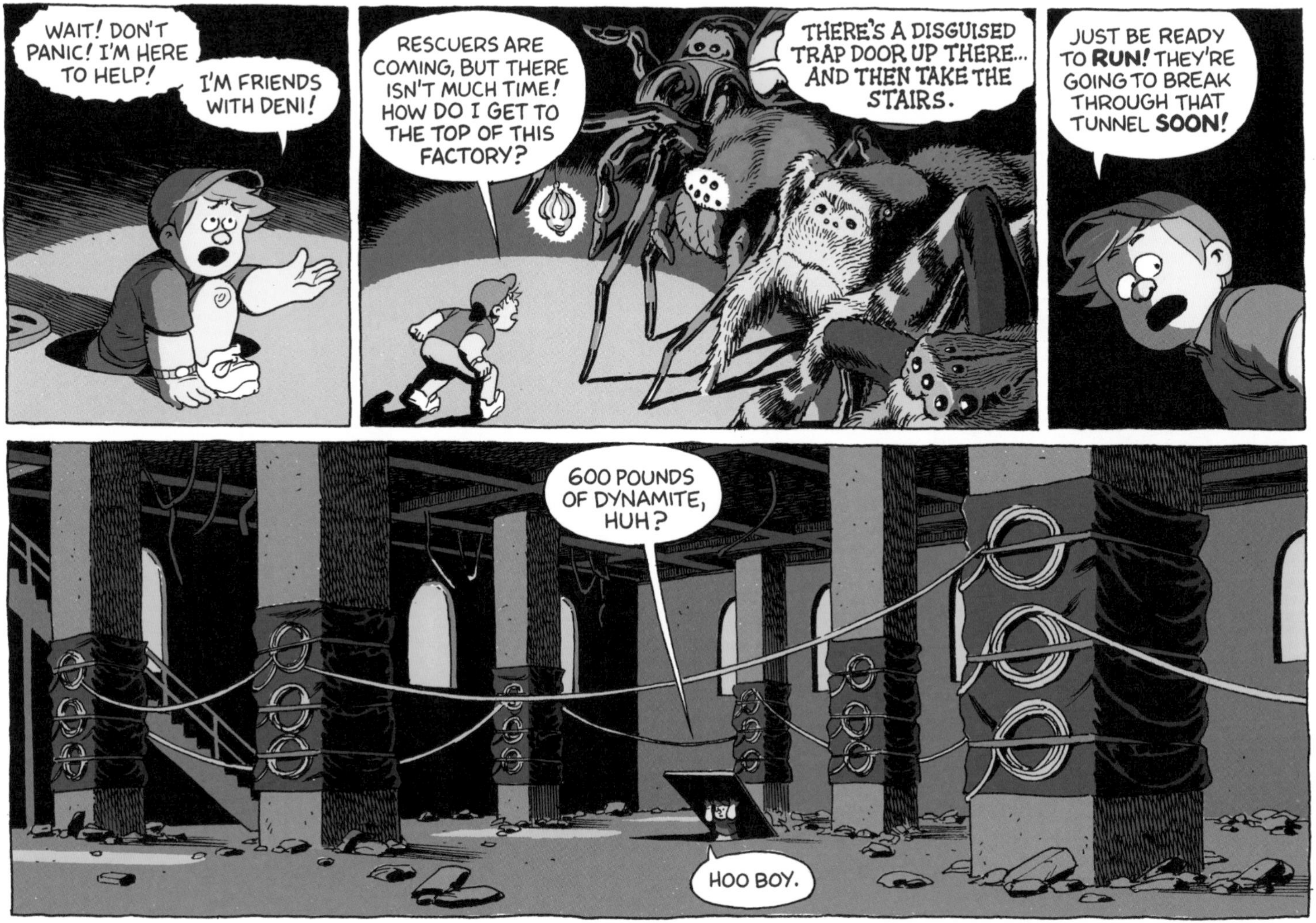

WAIT! DON'T PANIC! I'M HERE TO HELP!
I'M FRIENDS WITH DENI!
RESCUERS ARE COMING, BUT THERE ISN'T MUCH TIME! HOW DO I GET TO THE TOP OF THIS FACTORY?
THERE'S A DISGUISED TRAP DOOR UP THERE... AND THEN TAKE THE STAIRS.
JUST BE READY TO RUN! THEY'RE GOING TO BREAK THROUGH THAT TUNNEL SOON!
600 POUNDS OF DYNAMITE, HUH?
HOO BOY.

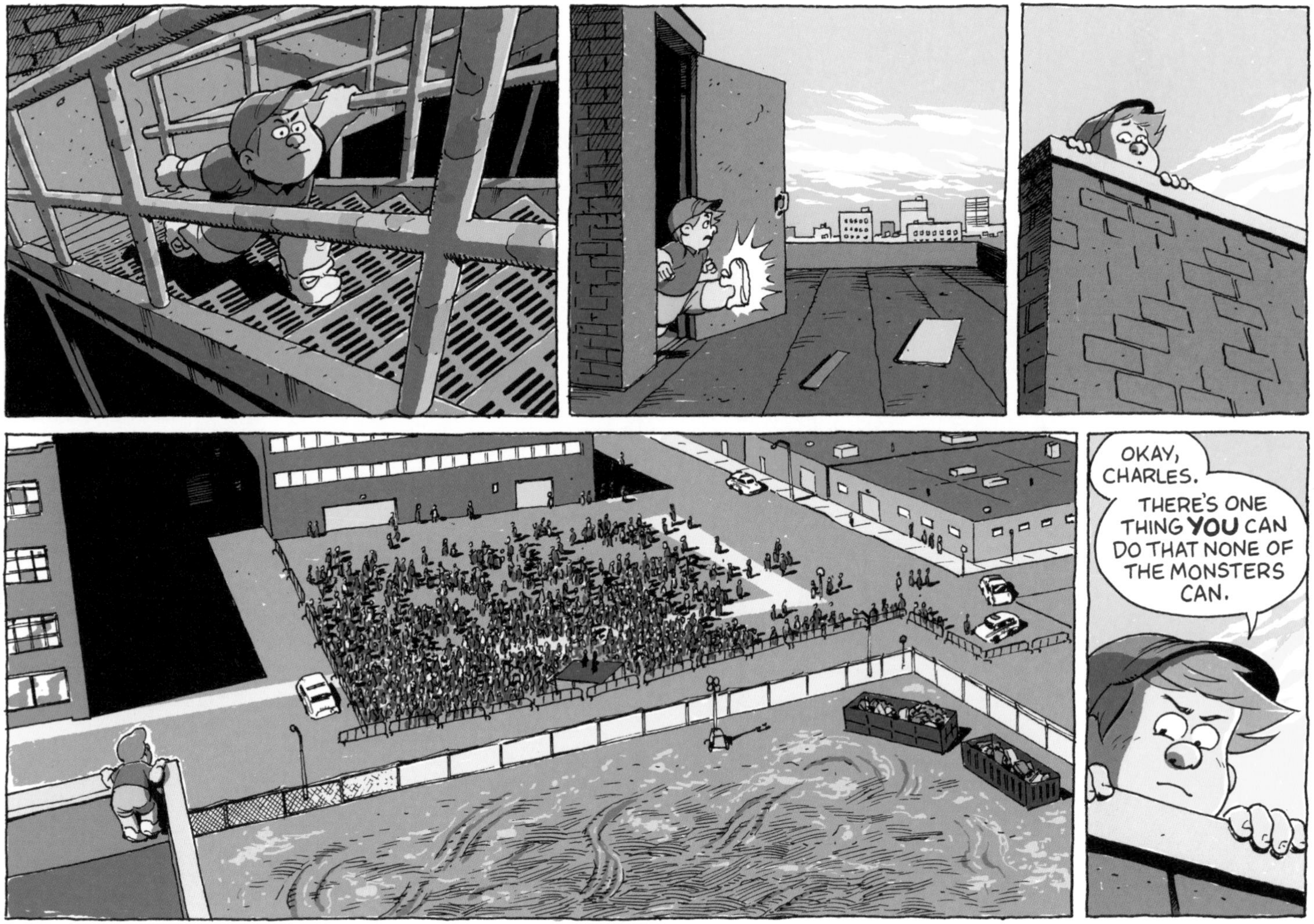
OKAY, CHARLES.
THERE'S ONE THING YOU CAN DO THAT NONE OF THE MONSTERS CAN.

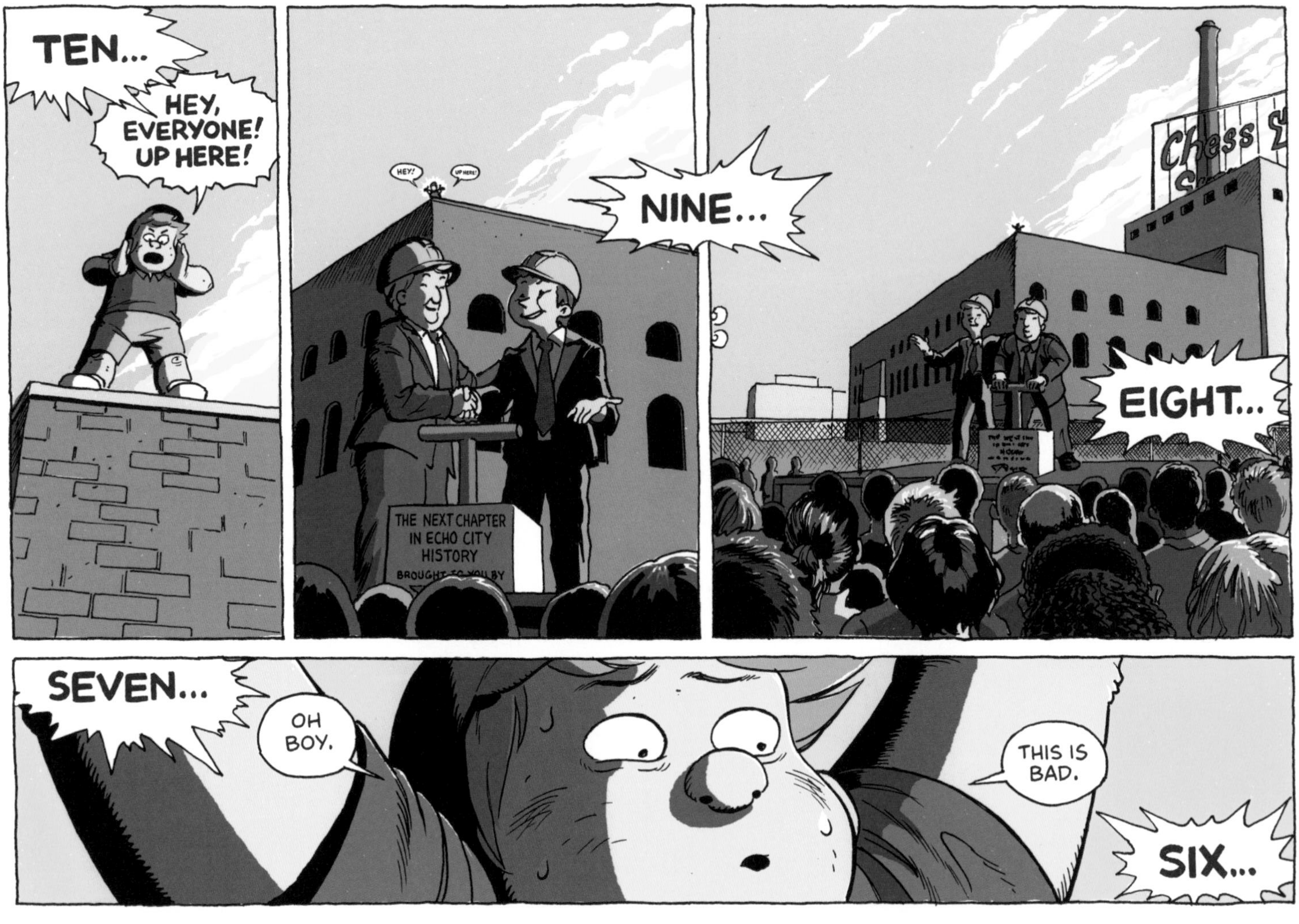
TEN...
HEY, EVERYONE! UP HERE!
HEY!
UP HERE!
NINE...
THE NEXT CHAPTER IN ECHO CITY HISTORY
BROUGHT TO YOU BY
Chess
EIGHT...
SEVEN...
OH BOY.
THIS IS BAD.
SIX...

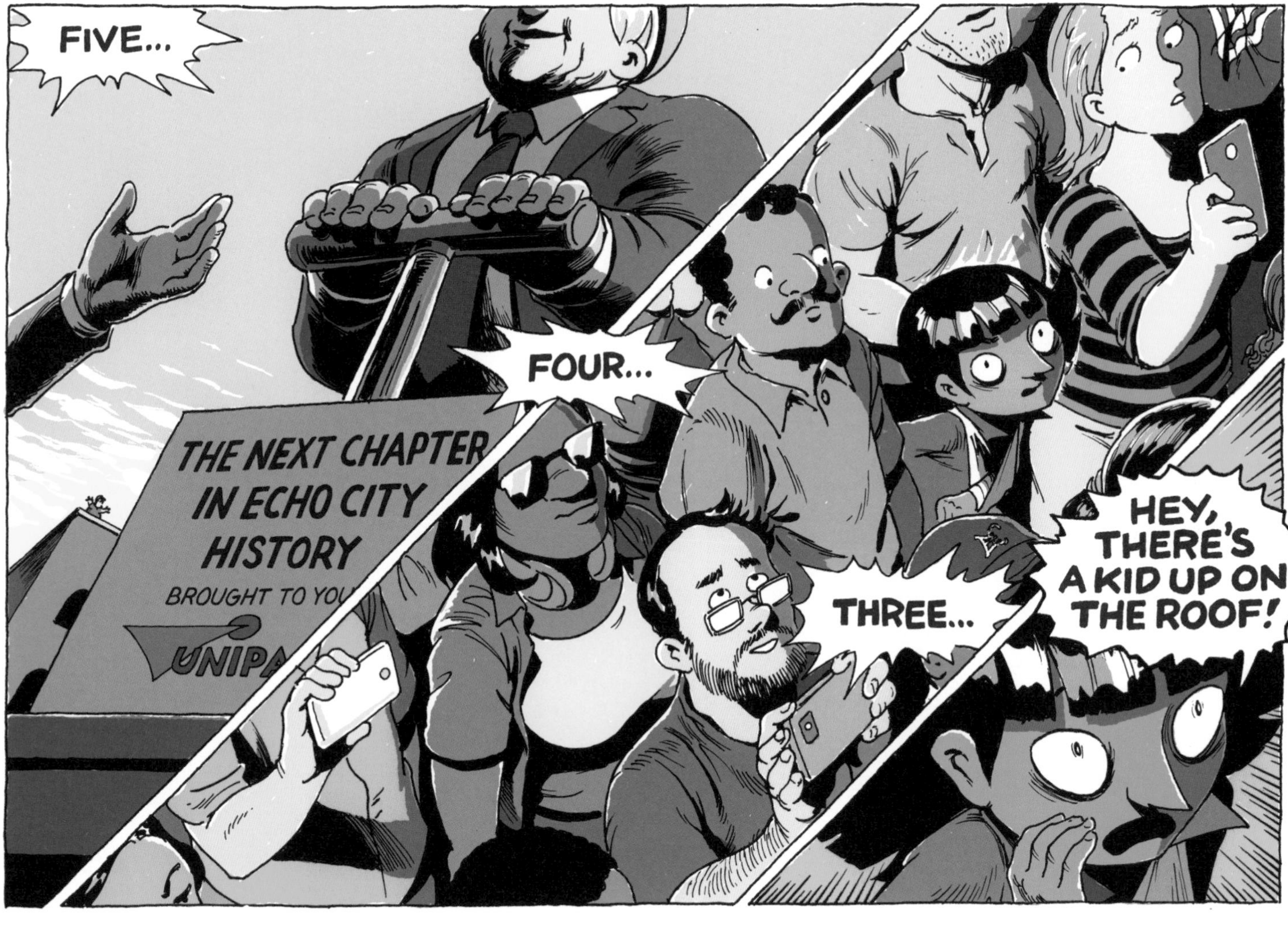
FIVE...
THE NEXT CHAPTER IN ECHO CITY HISTORY
BROUGHT TO YOU
UNIPA
FOUR...
THREE...
HEY, THERE'S A KID UP ON THE ROOF!

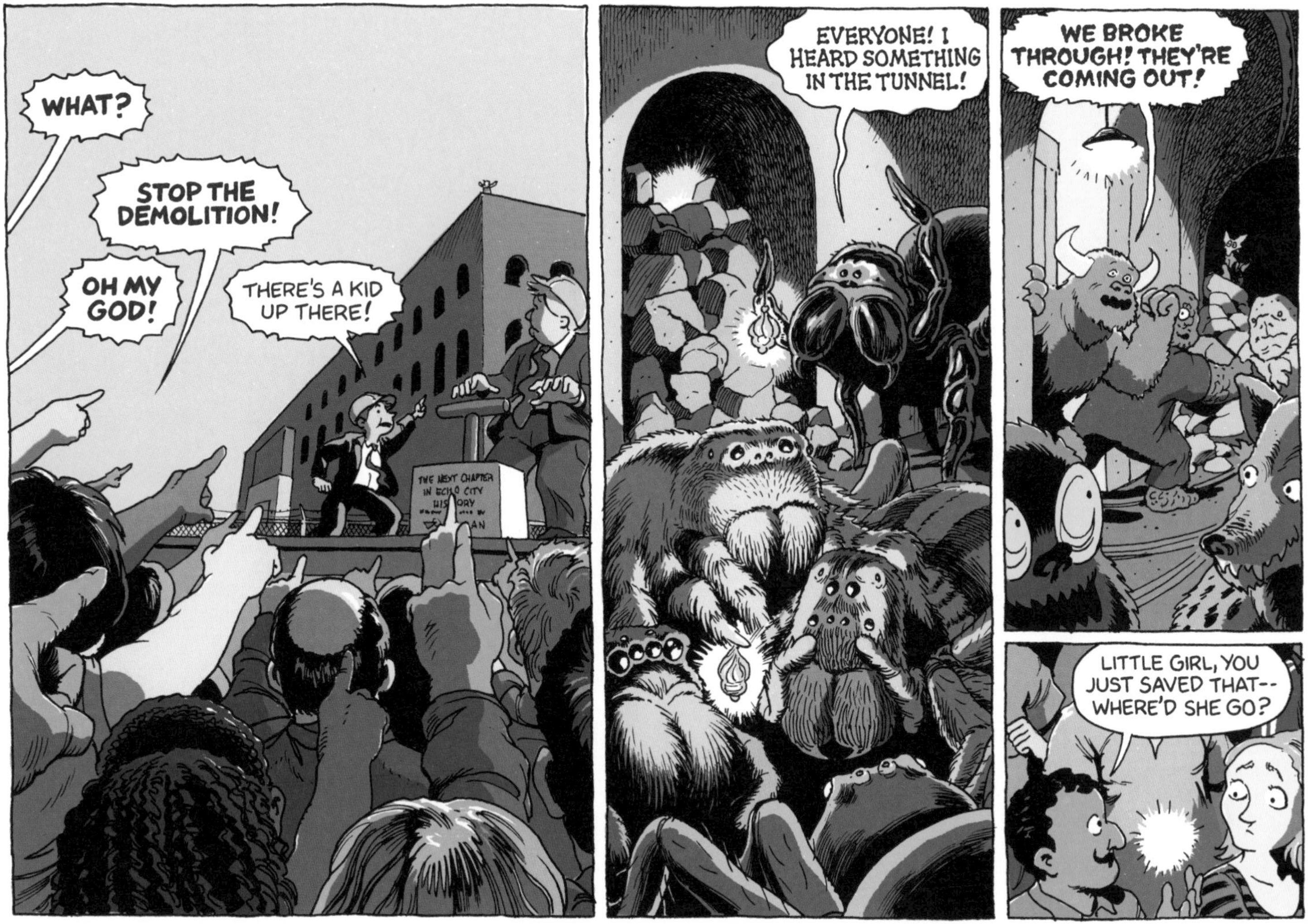
WHAT?
STOP THE DEMOLITION!
OH MY GOD!
THERE'S A KID UP THERE!
THE NEXT CHAPTER
EVERYONE! I HEARD SOMETHING IN THE TUNNEL!
WE BROKE THROUGH! THEY'RE COMING OUT!
LITTLE GIRL, YOU JUST SAVED THAT-- WHERE'D SHE GO?

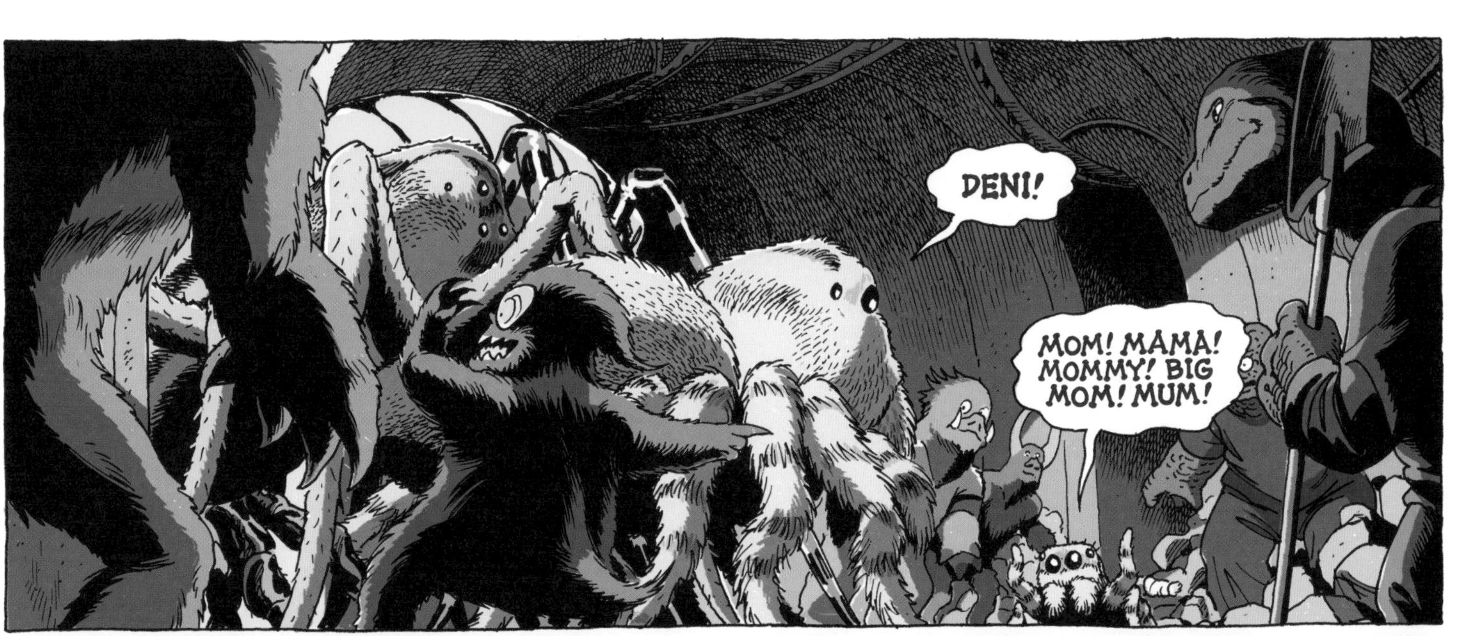
DENI!
MOM! MAMA! MOMMY! BIG MOM! MUM!

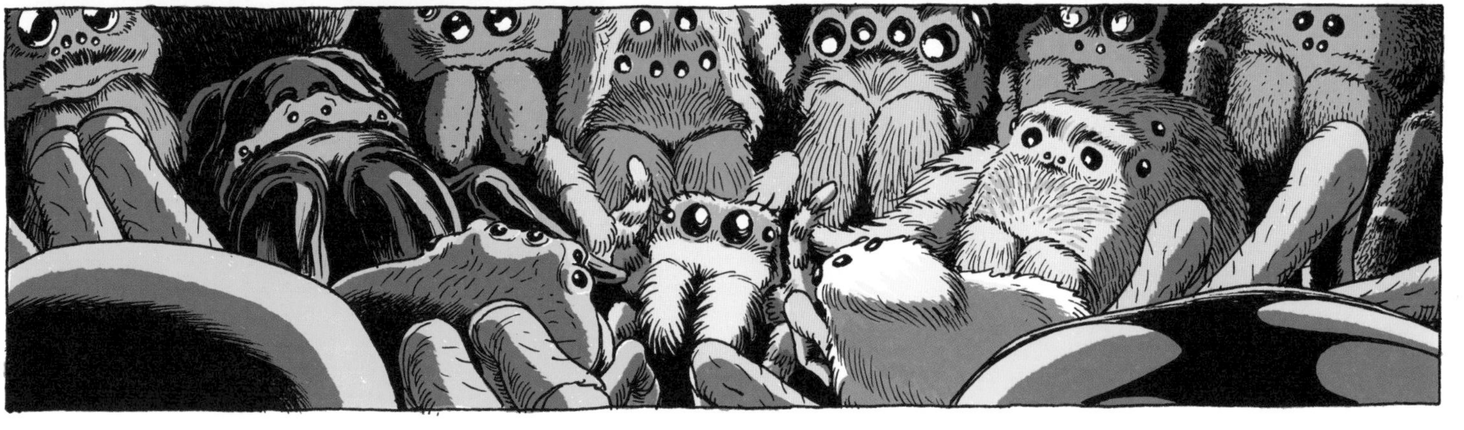

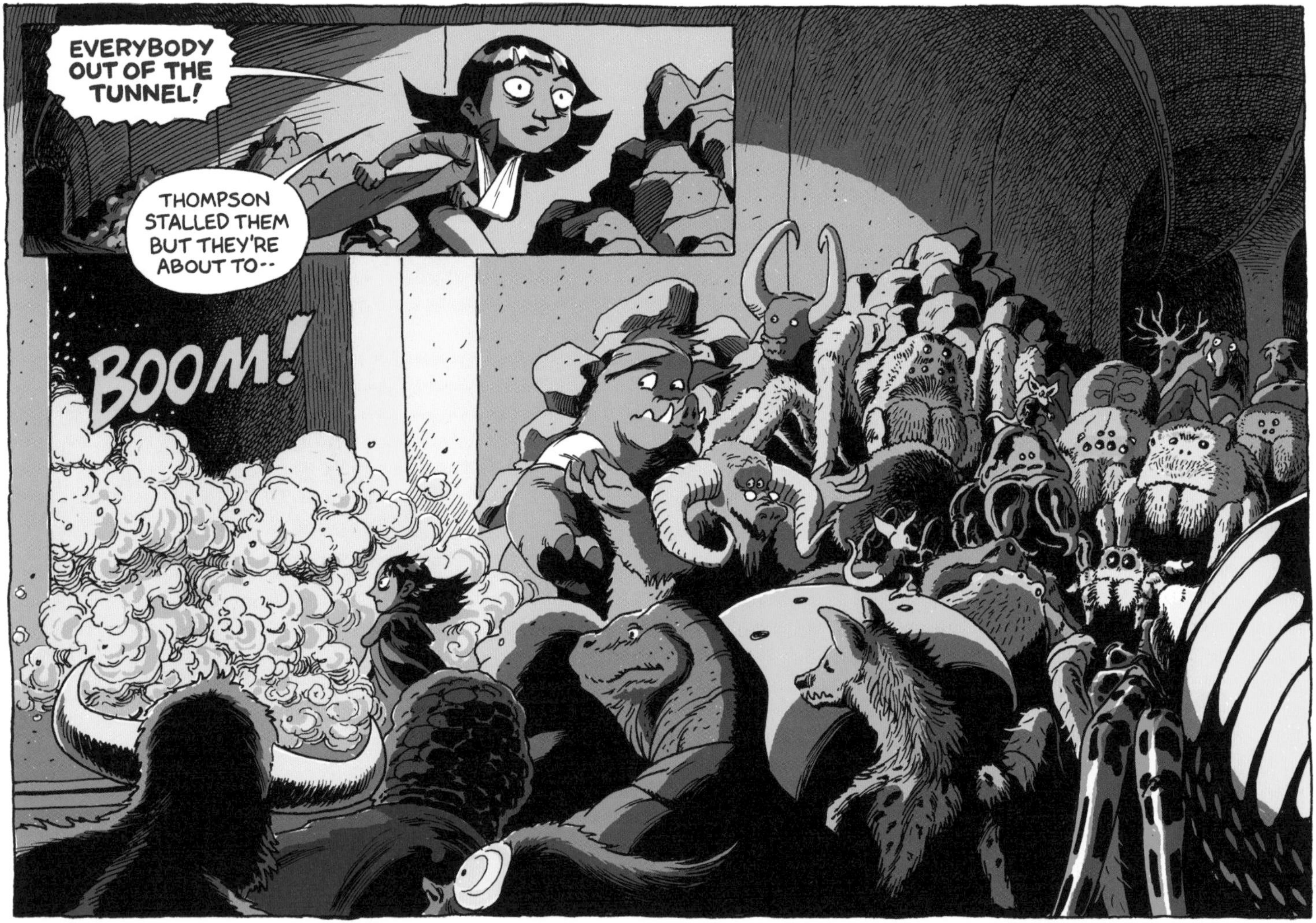
EVERYBODY OUT OF THE TUNNEL!
THOMPSON STALLED THEM BUT THEY'RE ABOUT TO--
BOOM!

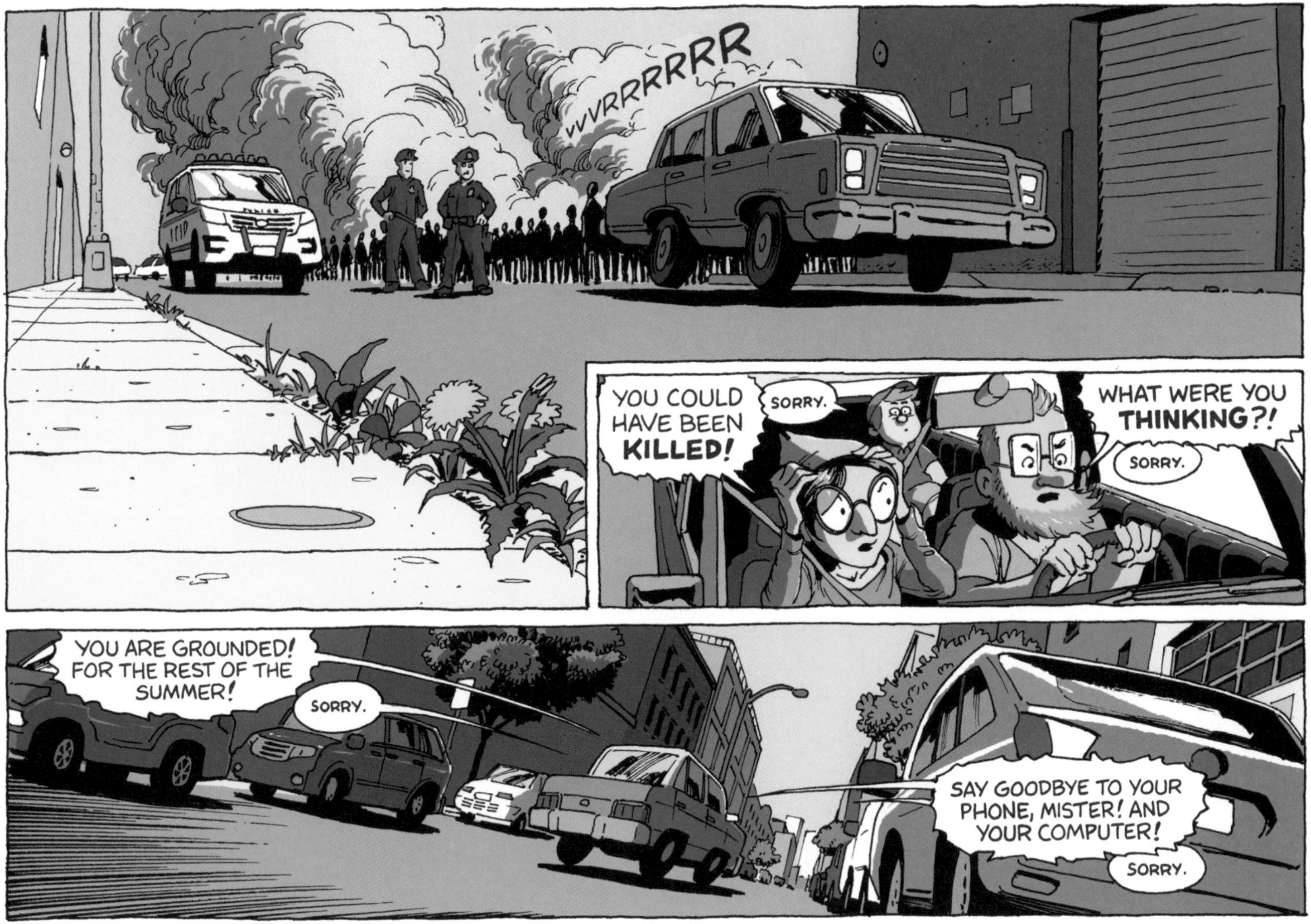
VVVRRRRRRR
YOU COULD HAVE BEEN KILLED!
SORRY.
WHAT WERE YOU THINKING?!
SORRY.
YOU ARE GROUNDED! FOR THE REST OF THE SUMMER!
SORRY.
SAY GOODBYE TO YOUR PHONE, MISTER! AND YOUR COMPUTER!
SORRY.

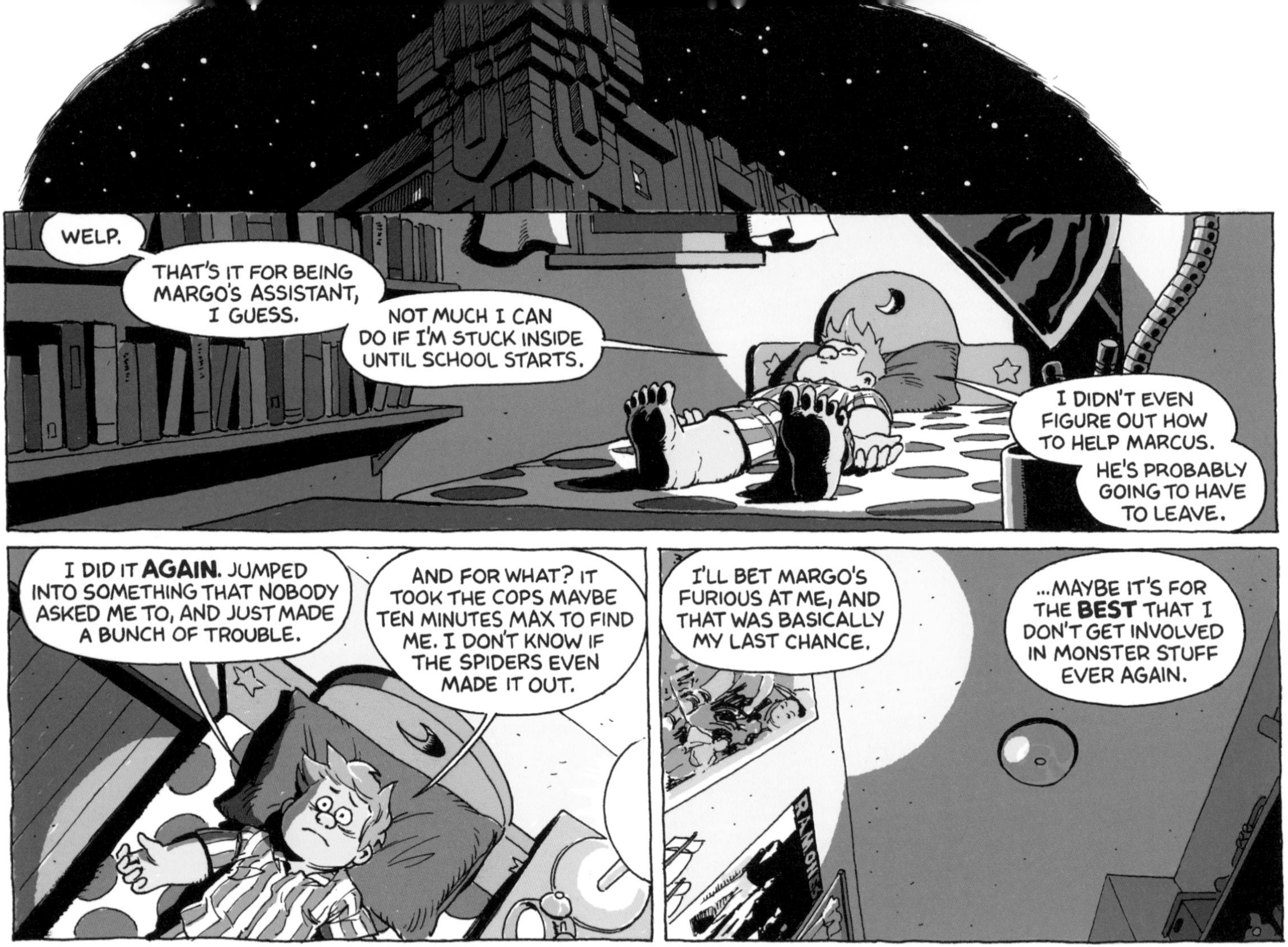
WELP.
THAT'S IT FOR BEING MARGO'S ASSISTANT, I GUESS.
NOT MUCH I CAN DO IF I'M STUCK INSIDE UNTIL SCHOOL STARTS.
I DIDN'T EVEN FIGURE OUT HOW TO HELP MARCUS.
HE'S PROBABLY GOING TO HAVE TO LEAVE.
I DID IT **AGAIN**. JUMPED INTO SOMETHING THAT NOBODY ASKED ME TO, AND JUST MADE A BUNCH OF TROUBLE.
AND FOR WHAT? IT TOOK THE COPS MAYBE TEN MINUTES MAX TO FIND ME. I DON'T KNOW IF THE SPIDERS EVEN MADE IT OUT.
I'LL BET MARGO'S FURIOUS AT ME, AND THAT WAS BASICALLY MY LAST CHANCE.
...MAYBE IT'S FOR THE **BEST** THAT I DON'T GET INVOLVED IN MONSTER STUFF EVER AGAIN.
RAMONES

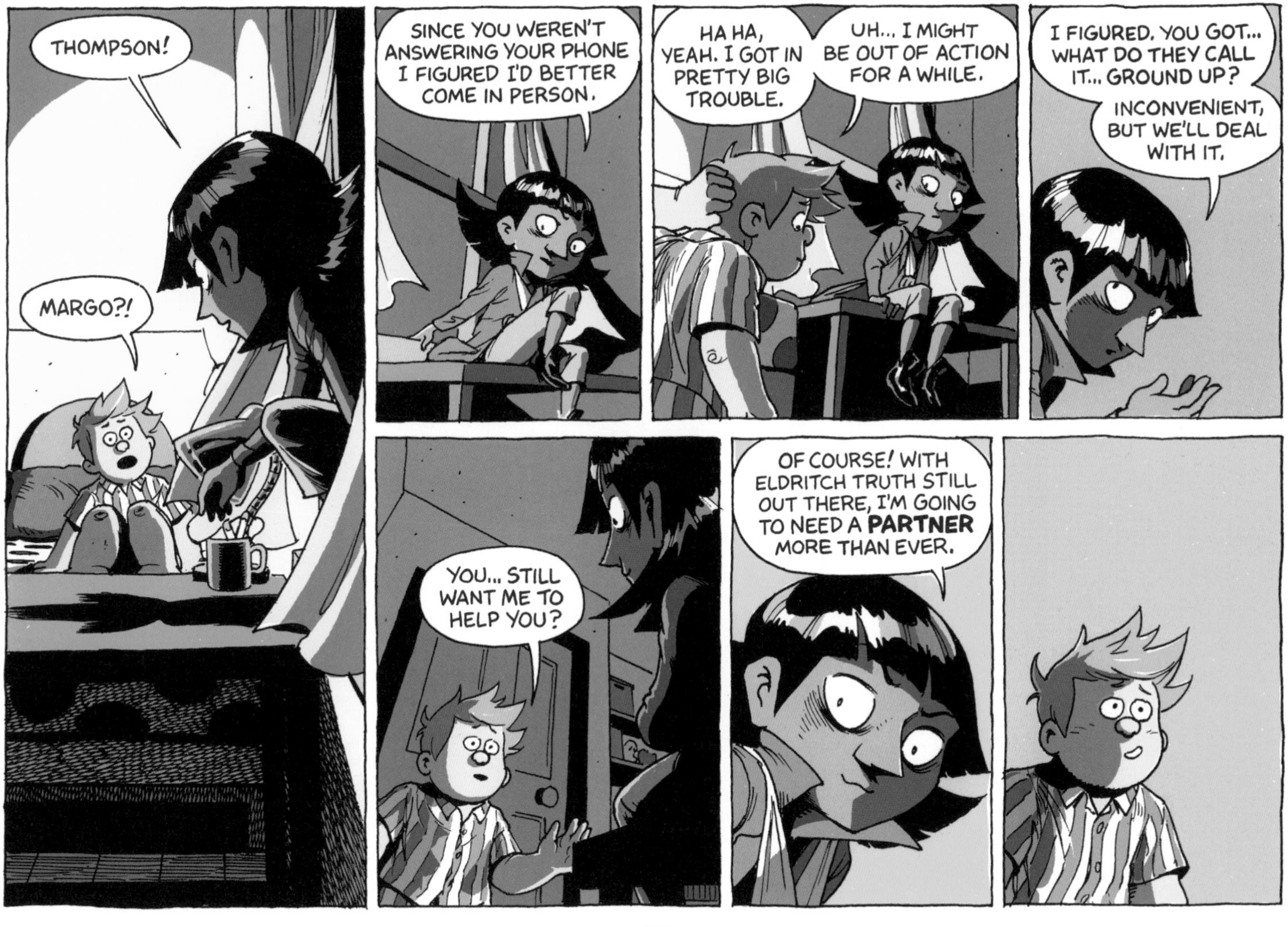
THOMPSON!
MARGO?!
SINCE YOU WEREN'T ANSWERING YOUR PHONE I FIGURED I'D BETTER COME IN PERSON.
HA HA, YEAH. I GOT IN PRETTY BIG TROUBLE.
UH... I MIGHT BE OUT OF ACTION FOR A WHILE.
I FIGURED. YOU GOT... WHAT DO THEY CALL IT... GROUND UP?
INCONVENIENT, BUT WE'LL DEAL WITH IT.
YOU... STILL WANT ME TO HELP YOU?
OF COURSE! WITH ELDRITCH TRUTH STILL OUT THERE, I'M GOING TO NEED A PARTNER MORE THAN EVER.

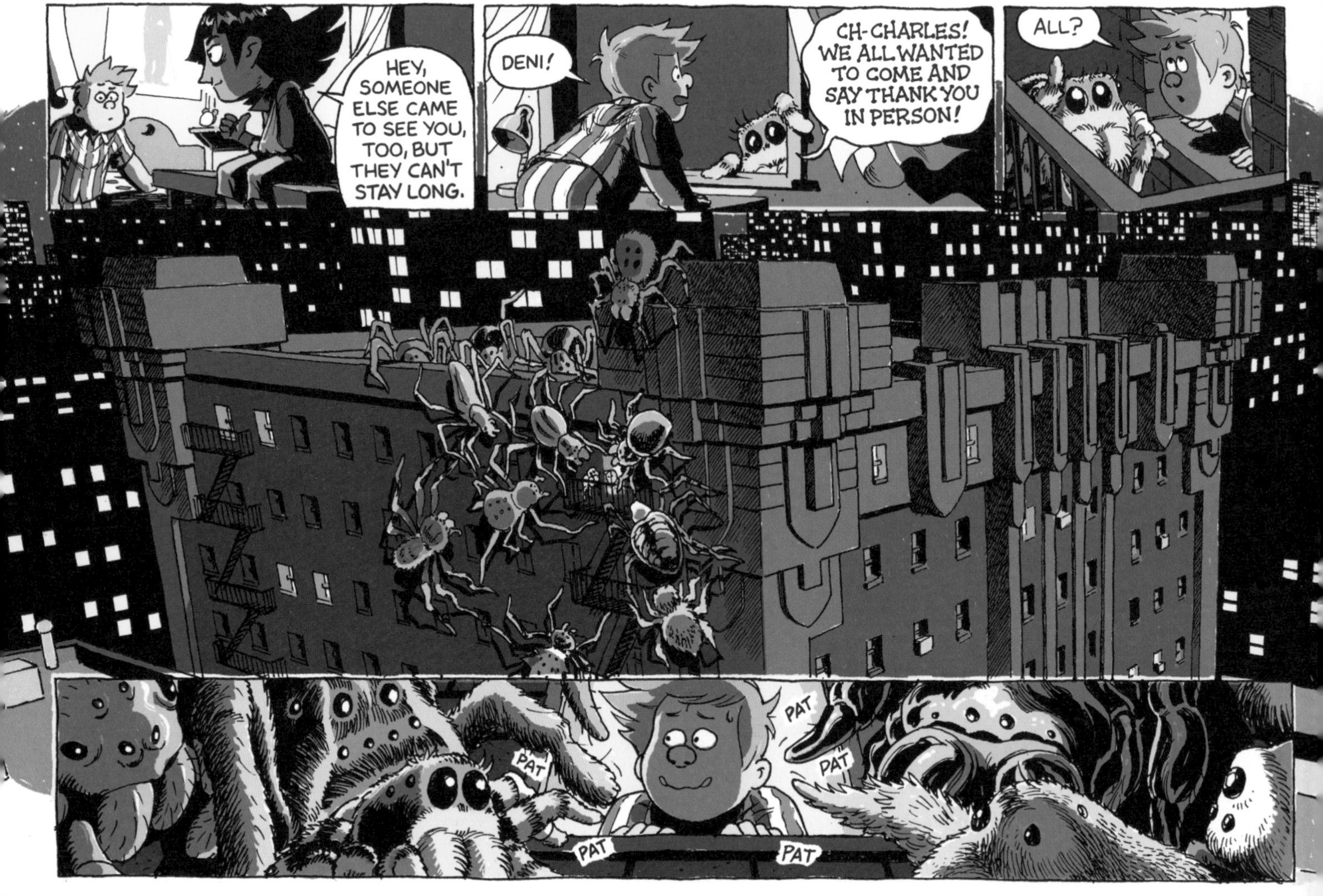
HEY, SOMEONE ELSE CAME TO SEE YOU, TOO, BUT THEY CAN'T STAY LONG.
DENI!
CH-CHARLES! WE ALL WANTED TO COME AND SAY THANK YOU IN PERSON!
ALL?
PAT
PAT
PAT
PAT
PAT
PAT

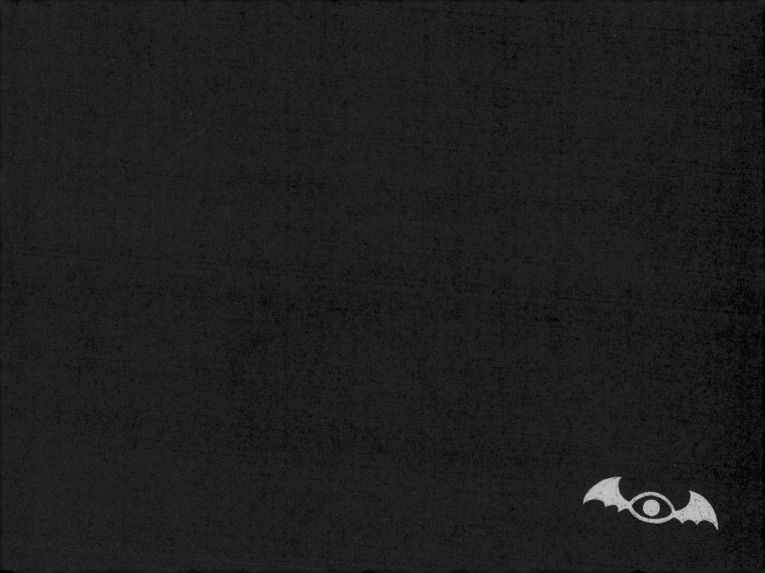

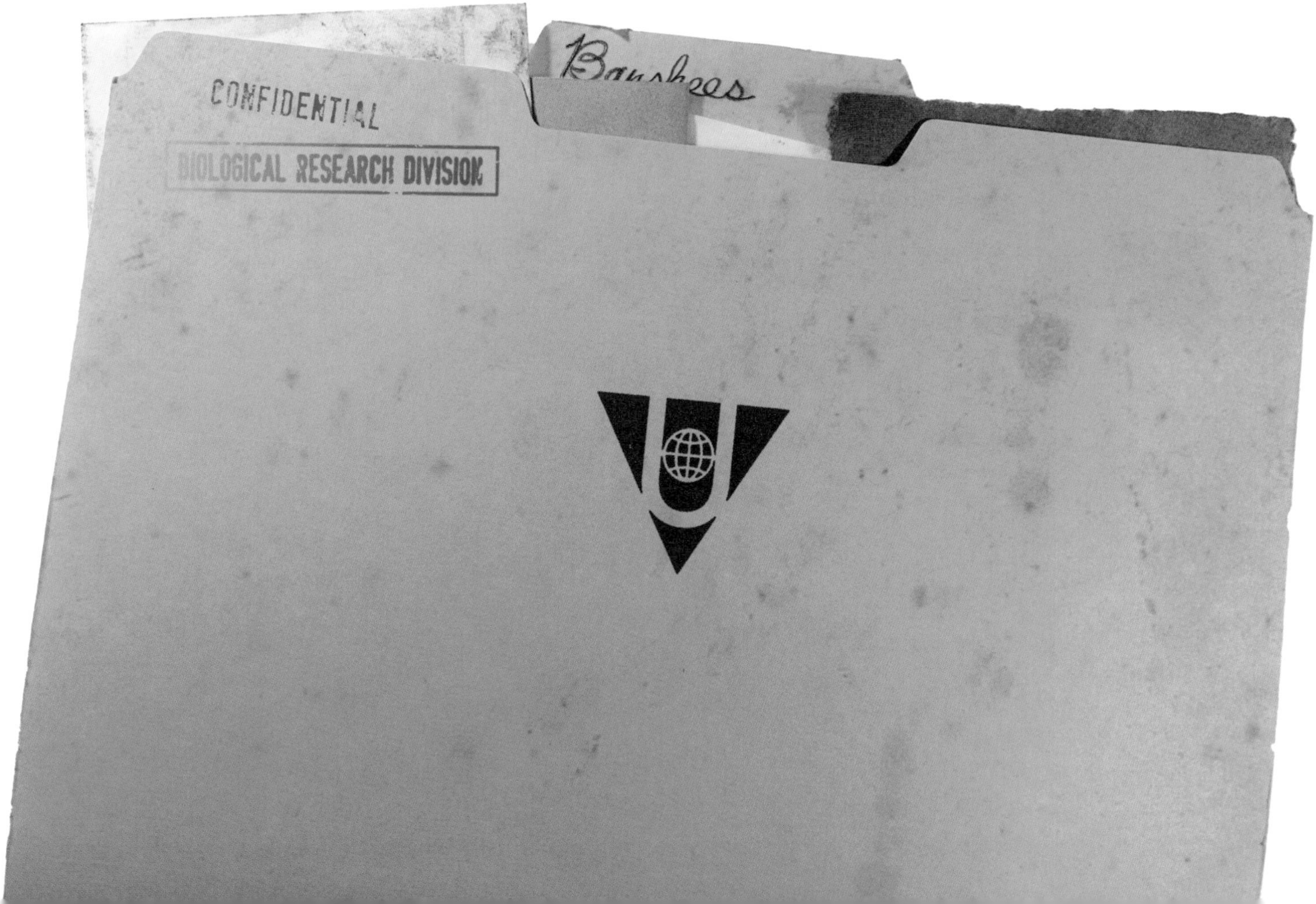
Banshees
CONFIDENTIAL
BIOLOGICAL RESEARCH DIVISION

Simurgh

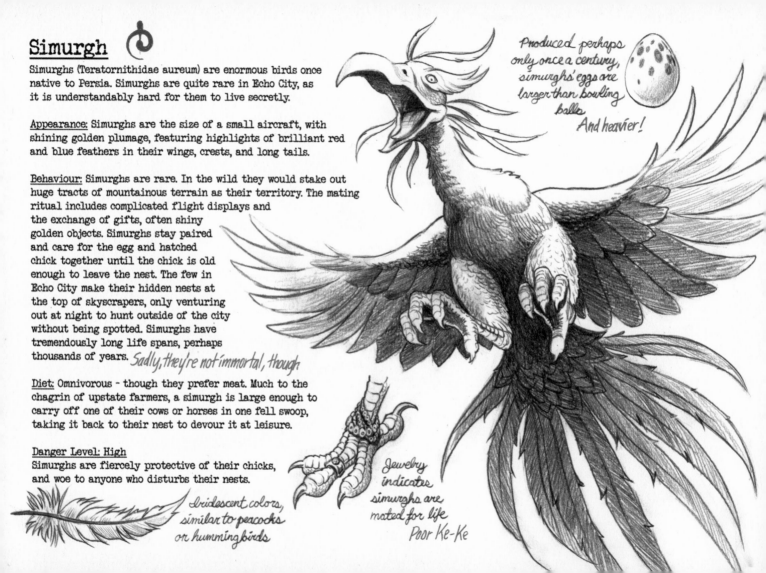

Simurghs (Teratornithidae aureum) are enormous birds once native to Persia. Simurghs are quite rare in Echo City, as it is understandably hard for them to live secretly.

Appearance: Simurghs are the size of a small aircraft, with shining golden plumage, featuring highlights of brilliant red and blue feathers in their wings, crests, and long tails.

Behaviour: Simurghs are rare. In the wild they would stake out huge tracts of mountainous terrain as their territory. The mating ritual includes complicated flight displays and the exchange of gifts, often shiny golden objects. Simurghs stay paired and care for the egg and hatched chick together until the chick is old enough to leave the nest. The few in Echo City make their hidden nests at the top of skyscrapers, only venturing out at night to hunt outside of the city without being spotted. Simurghs have tremendously long life spans, perhaps thousands of years. *Sadly, they're not immortal, though.*

Diet: Omnivorous - though they prefer meat. Much to the chagrin of upstate farmers, a simurgh is large enough to carry off one of their cows or horses in one fell swoop, taking it back to their nest to devour it at leisure.

Danger Level: High
Simurghs are fiercely protective of their chicks, and woe to anyone who disturbs their nests.

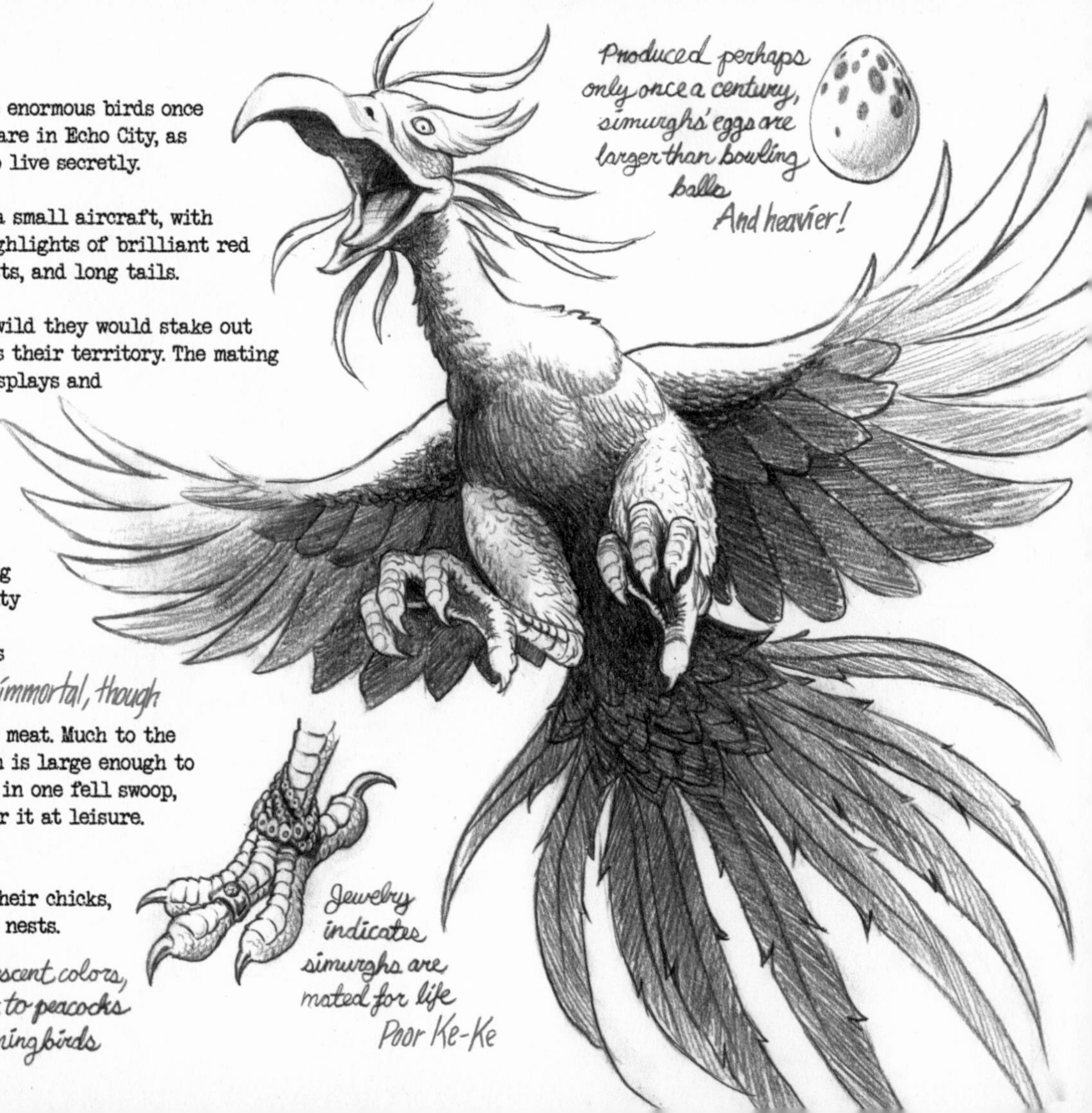
Produced perhaps only once a century, simurghs' eggs are larger than bowling balls
And heavier!
Jewelry indicates simurghs are mated for life
Poor Ke-Ke

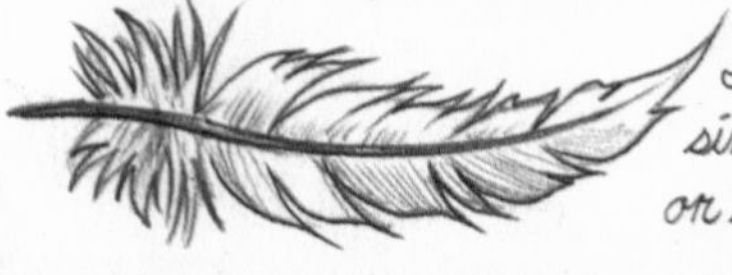
Iridescent colors, similar to peacocks or hummingbirds

Kappa

B

Kappa (Chelonia pilosus) are a semiaquatic, turtle-like monster once native to Japan.

Appearance: On land, kappa resemble bipedal turtles, with a mane of shaggy hair. They are green and scaly, and their dark green shells are smooth when young, but grow encrusted and craggy with age. They stand from 3 - 5 feet tall and weigh from 100 - 175 lbs.

Behaviour: Unlike turtles, kappa are quick and athletic. Young kappa are trained in a peculiar form of martial arts and seem to enjoy sparring with each other. Kappa live near isolated freshwater lakes and ponds.

Diet: Kappa are mostly vegetarian and consume large quantities of aquatic plant life. They enjoy terrestrial plant life as well - gourds, aubergines, and especially cucumbers are prized by kappa. A few cucumbers make a good bribe when dealing with them.

Not anymore! Try some avocados instead.

Danger Level: Guarded
Kappa can be dangerous if encountered alone, especially near the water. They are very strong for their size, and skilled at grappling.

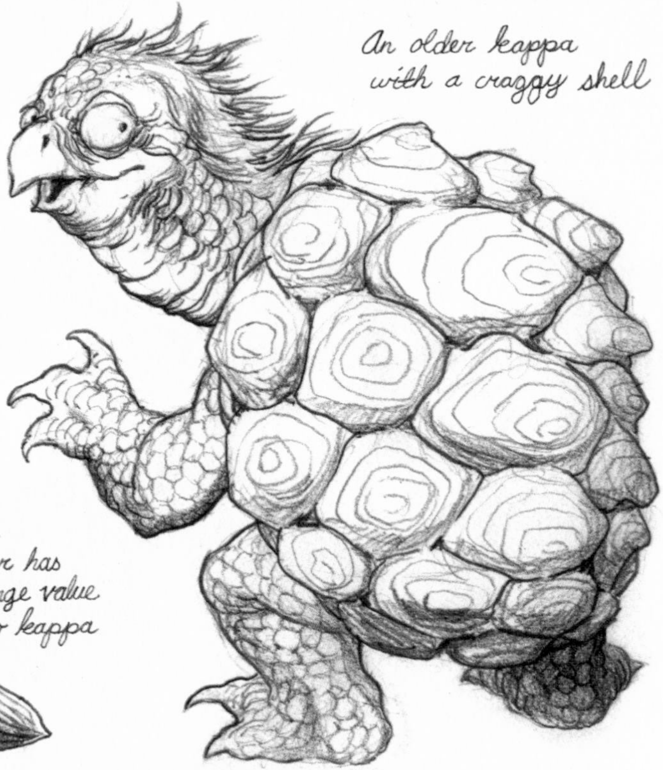

An older kappa with a craggy shell

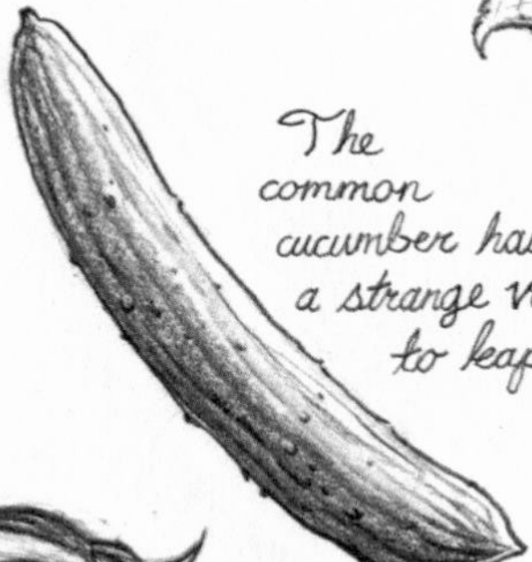

The common cucumber has a strange value to kappa

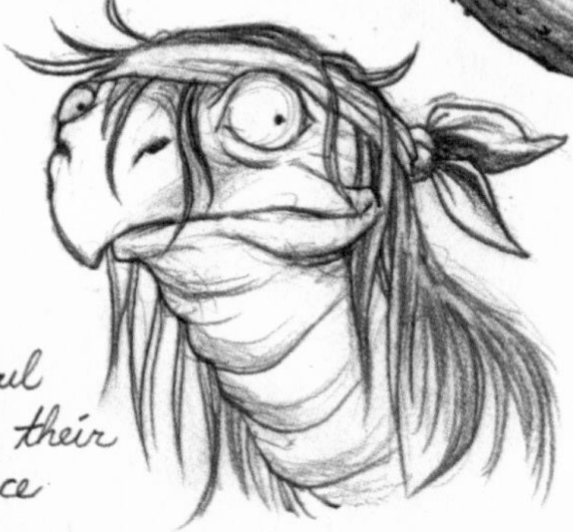

Young kappa sometimes wear colorful headbands to hold their manes in place

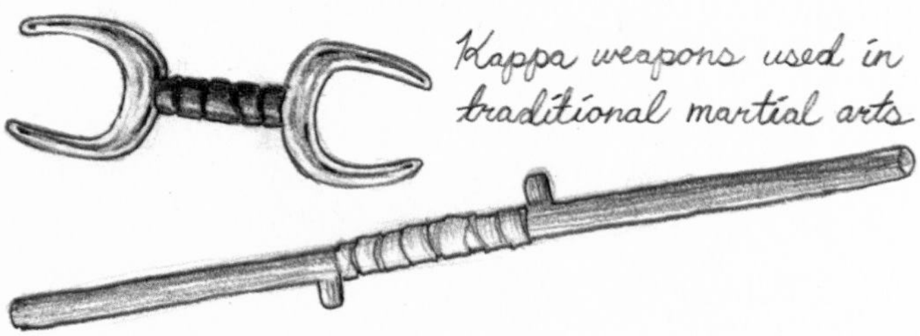

Kappa weapons used in traditional martial arts

Banshees

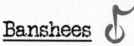

Banshees (Clamosus fluens), famed for their keening wail, are a very moist type of monster, once native to Ireland.

Appearance: Roughly human-sized and bipedal, but their body exudes long sticky strands of protective mucus in shades from yellowish green to greenish blue.

Behaviour: Banshees are famed for their singing, and their intergroup communication is done in long ululating cries that are hard for non-banshees to understand or even endure. Unlike the myths, their keening doesn't seem to portend death (but does often provoke headaches). Banshees congregate in small groups, preferring isolated, often subterranean areas where their singing can go unnoticed. Banshees organize their society by singing skill, with particular emphasis placed on volume.

Diet: Omnivorous, banshees generally subsist on snails, worms, and other subterranean insects.

Danger Level: Guarded
Banshees generally flee danger, but their piercing shriek can stun a human into unconsciousness or even rupture eardrums.

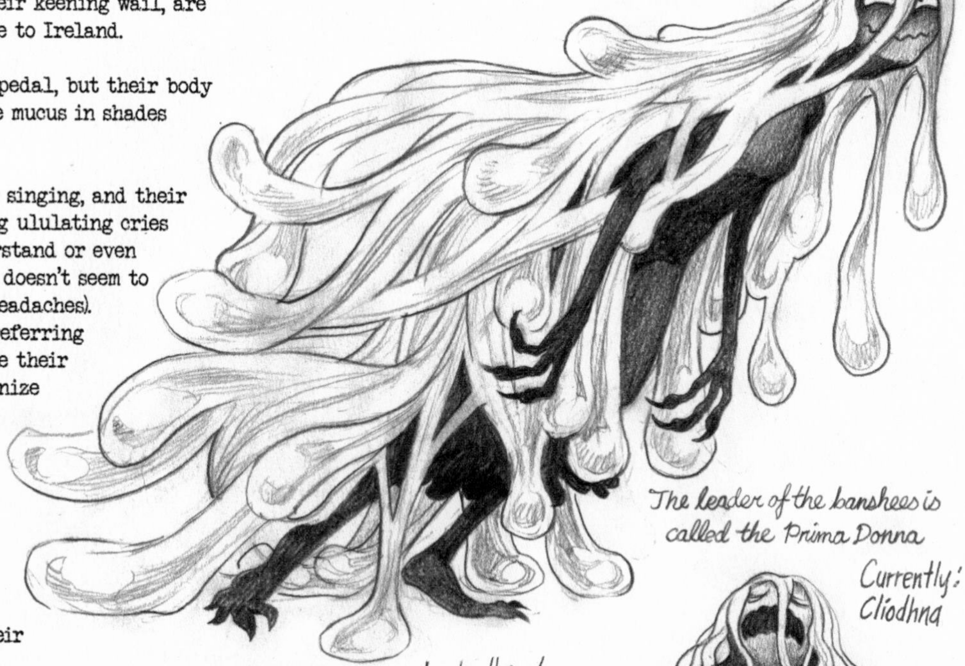
Slime probably evolved as a method to escape predators but now seems mainly ornamental
Banshees have no proper ears, instead "hearing" by picking up vibrations in their tendrils
Lucky them!

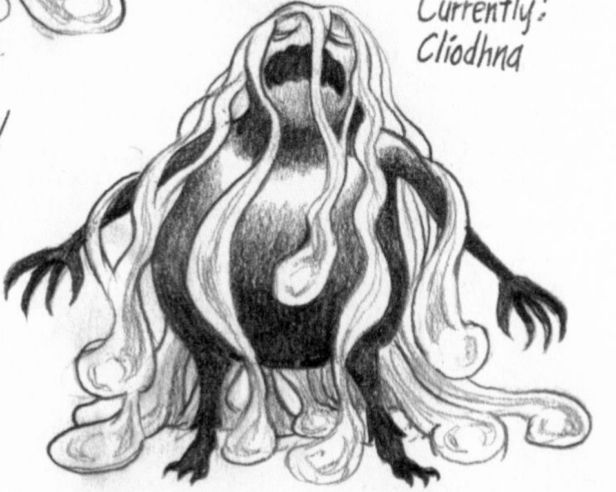
The leader of the banshees is called the Prima Donna
Currently: Clíodhna

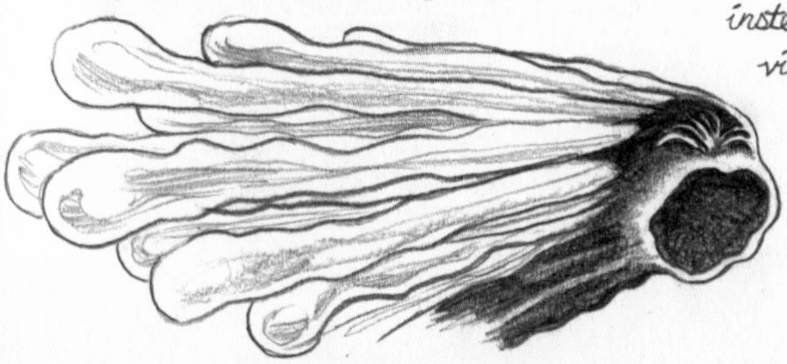

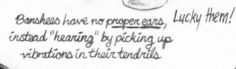

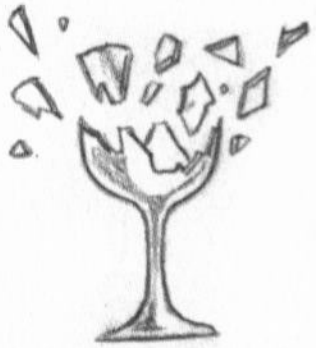
Banshees can easily shatter glass with their sonic force

Giant Spiders ✳

Giant spiders (Araneae giganteus) resemble the eight-legged garden variety spider in everything but size and intelligence.

<u>Appearance:</u> Giant spiders can range from about cow-sized to larger than an elephant, and come in a variety of colorations and patterns as varied as normal spiders. Some are covered with bristly fur. Female spiders both outweigh and vastly outnumber males.

<u>Behaviour:</u> Giant spiders are social, and several families will group together in a colony and cooperate to capture prey and share food. But unlike their smaller cousins, who produce hundreds of young (of whom only a few might survive to adulthood), giant spiders tend to produce only one offspring at a time and carefully nurture their hatchling. The head of Echo City's giant spider clan is called the Webmaster.

<u>Diet:</u> Giant spiders are predatory web-weavers and capture small animals such as rats, squirrels, raccoons, and the occasional unlucky dog or cat.

<u>Danger Level: High</u>
Giant spiders aggressively protect their webs and young, and their venom is extremely potent - a bite can kill within minutes.

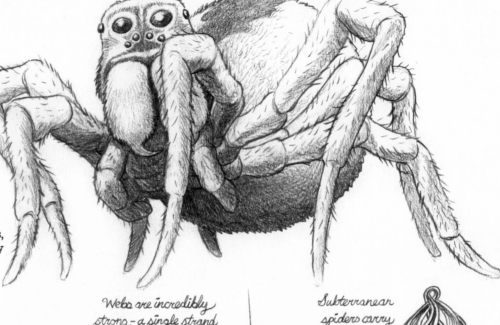

Webs are incredibly strong - a single strand of silk could easily suspend a city bus

Venom begins paralysing prey almost instantly. Only a rapid dose of antivenom can save the victim

Many spiders carry some, just in case

Subterranean spiders carry lamps for illumination, and they are passed down as heirlooms

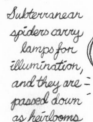

While their eyes come in many patterns, all giant spiders have tremendously good sight for hunting

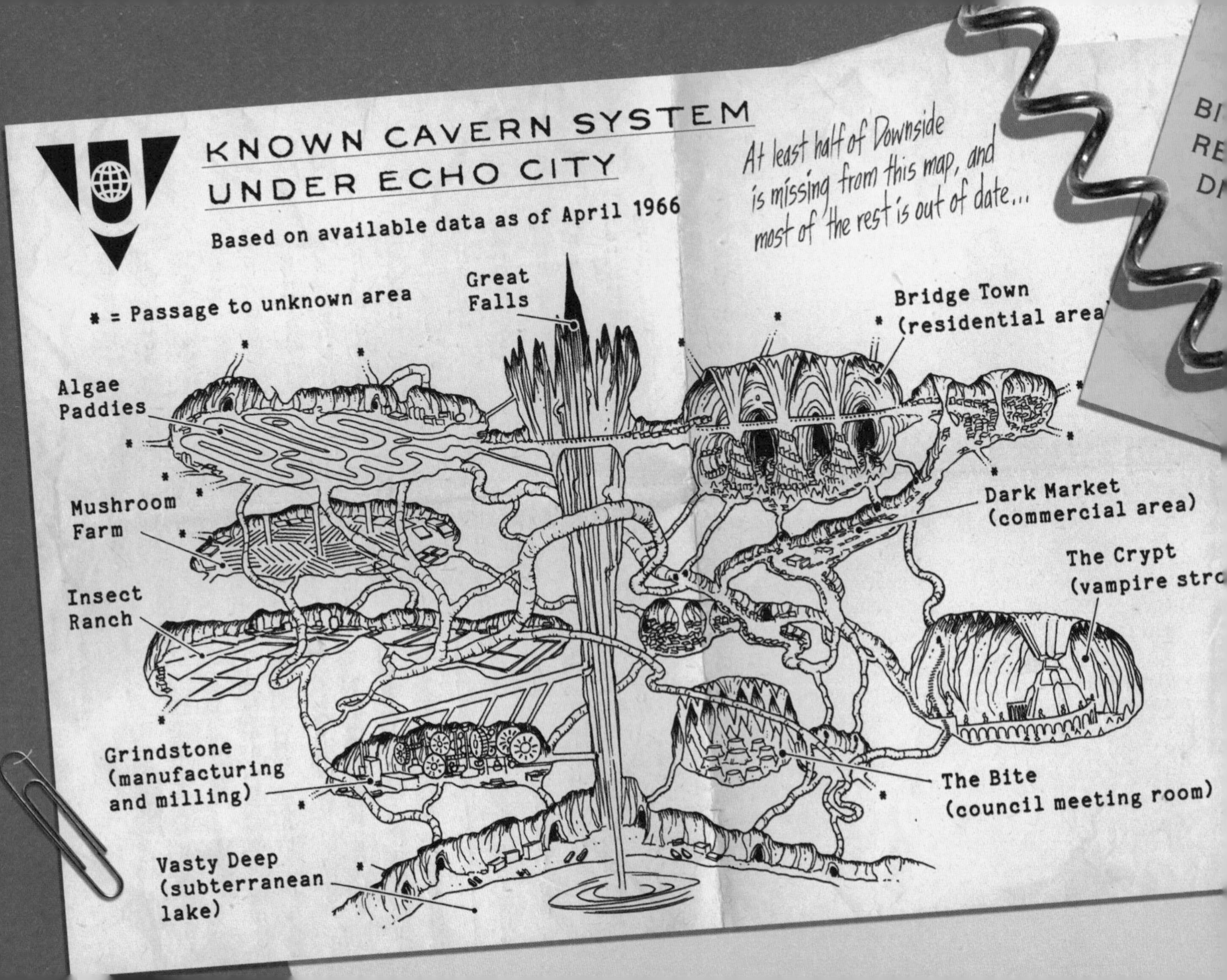

KNOWN CAVERN SYSTEM
UNDER ECHO CITY
Based on available data as of April 1966
At least half of Downside is missing from this map, and most of the rest is out of date...
* = Passage to unknown area
Great Falls
Bridge Town (residential area
Algae Paddies
Mushroom Farm
Dark Market (commercial area)
The Crypt (vampire str
Insect Ranch
Grindstone (manufacturing and milling)
The Bite (council meeting room)
Vasty Deep (subterranean lake)

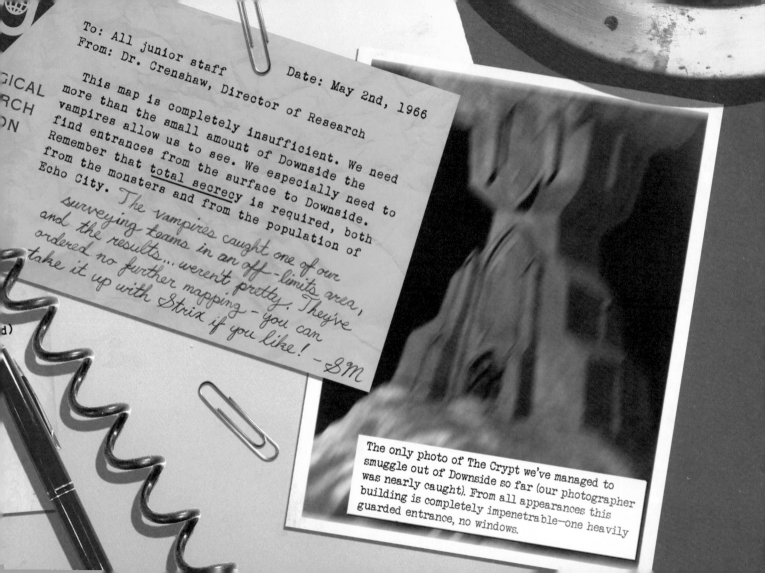

To: All junior staff   Date: May 2nd, 1966
From: Dr. Crenshaw, Director of Research

    This map is completely insufficient. We need more than the small amount of Downside the vampires allow us to see. We especially need to find entrances from the surface to Downside. Remember that total secrecy is required, both from the monsters and from the population of Echo City.

The vampires caught one of our surveying teams in an off-limits area, and the results...weren't pretty. They've ordered no further mapping — you can take it up with Strix if you like! — SM

The only photo of The Crypt we've managed to smuggle out of Downside so far (our photographer was nearly caught). From all appearances this building is completely impenetrable—one heavily guarded entrance, no windows.

As always, immeasurable thanks to the love of my life, Eleanor, who co-created Margo and is always my first reader. And thanks to both her and Sophia Foster-Dimino for jumping in and flatting nearly half of the book's colors when the deadlines started to pinch.

Thanks to my new little guy, Danny (whenever you're old enough to read this), and to Eleanor's parents, Ann and Ed Davis, who have put all three of us up for the last year, and in whose backyard I drew most of the last chapter of this book. Thanks to the patrons whose support allows me to keep making these things. Thanks to everyone at First Second, who always do such a good job.

And thank you to my late mom, Lorene Weing. She played D&D with me when no other kids were interested, helped me catalog my comic book collection, encouraged me to enter my pictures in the art fair. Her love and unfailing encouragement made me the person I am today.

DREW WEING makes comics for print and online, among which are the nautical graphic novel *Set to Sea*, the infinite canvas webcomic *Pup*, and the early reader comic *Flop to the Top* (which he co-authored with his wife, cartoonist Eleanor Davis). Drew, Eleanor, their kid Danny, and a fluctuating number of cats all live in a quantum state somewhere in between Athens, Georgia, and Tucson, Arizona.

The artist and family at the start of year two of the pandemic quarantine

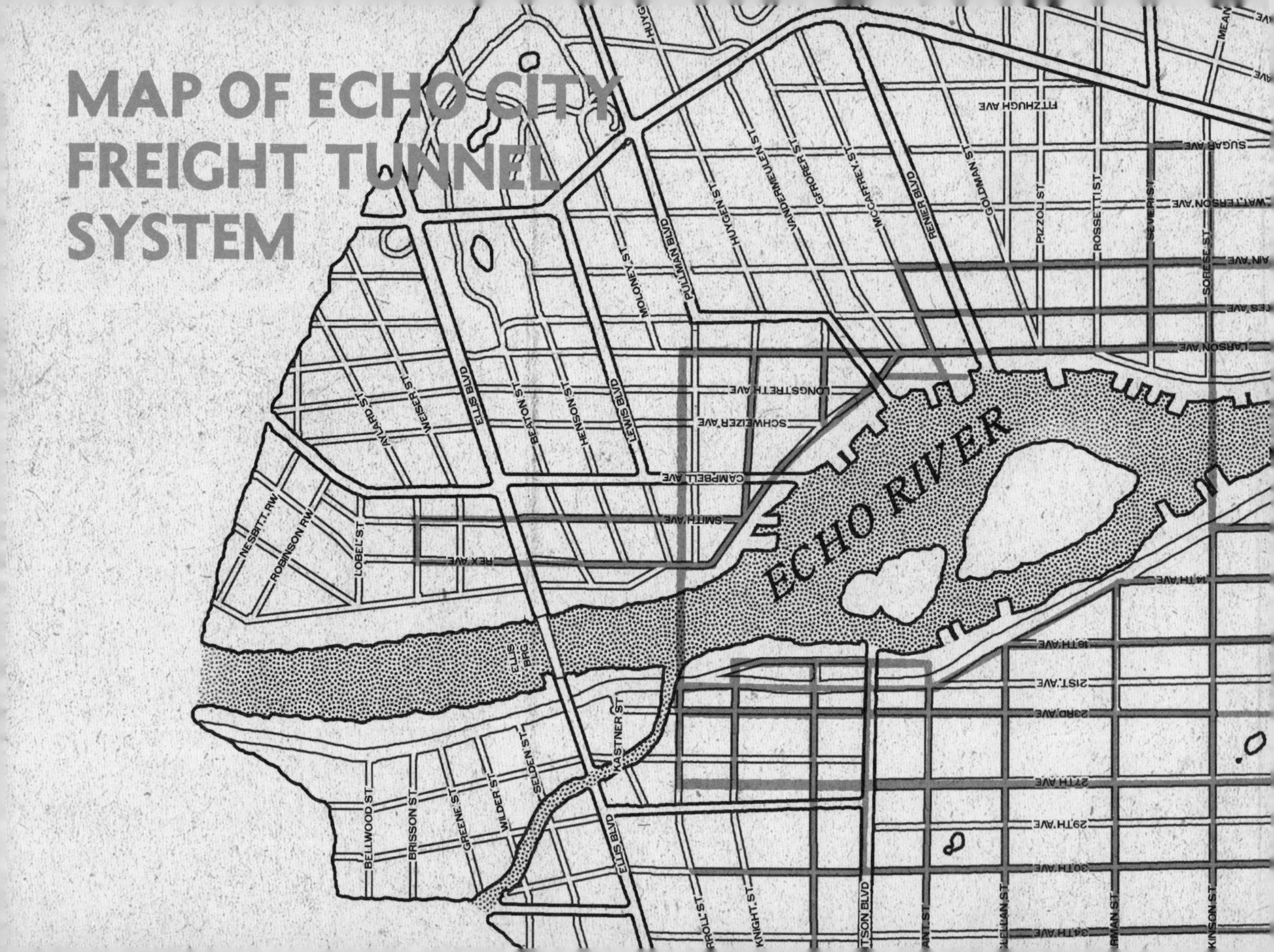

MAP OF ECHO CITY FREIGHT TUNNEL SYSTEM
FITZHUGH AVE
SUGAR AVE
WATTERSON AVE
LARSON AVE
LONGSTRETH AVE
SCHWEIZER AVE
CAMPBELL AVE
SMITH AVE
REX AVE
14TH AVE
18TH AVE
21ST AVE
23RD AVE
27TH AVE
29TH AVE
30TH AVE
34TH AVE
HUYGEN ST
VANDERMEULEN ST
GFRORER ST
MCCAFFREY ST
RENIER BLVD
GOLDMAN ST
PIZZOLI ST
ROSSETTI ST
SEVIERI ST
SORESE ST
PULLMAN BLVD
MOLONEY ST
LEWIS BLVD
HENSON ST
BEATON ST
ELLIS BLVD
WEISER ST
AYLARD ST
LOBEL ST
ROBINSON RW
NESBITT RW
ELLIS BRG
ECHO RIVER
KASTNER ST
SELDEN ST
WILDER ST
GREENE ST
BRISSON ST
BELLWOOD ST
ELLIS BLVD
KNIGHT ST